THE PRINCESS AND
THE BARBARIAN

"It would seem you wish to be a warrior. Fight me then, Viking, instead of freezing my brother in the sea. If you win, your people go free. If I win . . ." He shrugged, and his hair glinted fire in the sun.

Laughter rippled through the Scots. No man could best the Sinclair, so what could a woman do? They smiled and smirked at each other. The Viking princess would be properly chastised by the Sinclair.

Iona hefted the heavy sword of the enemy. It was too difficult for her to handle, but she couldn't give him the advantage of knowing that. And the weapon's weight wouldn't impede her if she could get close enough . . .

"Agreed," she said. "I'll pick up your gauntlet, Scot. 'Tis my right to choose the time and the weapons." She paused and stared at the giant, who was as comely as the devil. Then she smiled as the thrill of the challenge raced through her. "I choose now!" she suddenly shouted. "And oar running!"

11TH CENTURY ENGLAND

Atlantic

Ocean

ORKNEY
ISLANDS

North

Sea

SCOTLAND

NORTHUMBRIA

IRELAND

Irish
Sea

MERCIA

EAST

ANGLIA

WESSEX

PRINCESS
⤬ OF THE ⤬
VEIL

HELEN
MITTERMEYER

BANTAM

NEW YORK TORONTO LONDON SYDNEY AUCKLAND

This edition contains the complete text
of the original hardcover edition.
NOT ONE WORD HAS BEEN OMITTED.

PRINCESS OF THE VEIL
A Bantam Fanfare Book

PUBLISHING HISTORY
Doubleday Loveswept edition published July 1992
Bantam paperback edition / February 1993

ISBN 0-553-29581-0

Published simultaneously in the United States and Canada

Bantam Books are published by Bantam Books, a division of Bantam
Doubleday Dell Publishing Group, Inc. Its trademark, consisting of the words
"Bantam Books" and the portrayal of a rooster, is Registered in U.S. Patent
and Trademark Office and in other countries. Marca Registrada. Bantam
Books, 666 Fifth Avenue, New York, New York 10103.

PRINTED IN THE UNITED STATES OF AMERICA

OPM   0 9 8 7 6 5 4 3 2 1

I dedicate this book to my forebears, the red-haired Vikings who crossed the seas to Scotland; a much maligned and misunderstood people. If I cannot set the record straight, perhaps I can bend it in the right direction.

I also dedicate this to my children and husband. I need their support.

To Ann, who read the manuscript and said push on.

Also to Richard Loomis, Ph.D., Professor of Literature, who piqued my interest with the Viking sagas and tales. My profound gratitude for the introduction to my predecessors.

To Kay Brion, a friend through it all, who wouldn't let me give up. All my love, Kay.

And to Mom and Dad. I miss you still. You started it all, so this is for you.

∾ INTRODUCTION ∾

Books need no explanation. They live or die on their inborn strength and determination. They're alive, and they can fight and do well, as I hope *Princess* will do.

But I'd like to tell you, my friends and readers, how this book was born. I found out I was descended from the Vikings who roamed the busy sea lanes from Norway to Norwich. When tracing my ancestry recently, I discovered something interesting—feminism isn't new. The struggle for women's rights has been going for a long time. And we've had some winners, not just in our time, but in earlier times as well. Women such as Boudicca, Cleopatra, and Queen Elizabeth I were fighters and winners in a man's world. They did things—righted wrongs; wrote books, as did Christine de Pisan; and waged great sea battles, like Grace O'Malley.

That knowledge whetted my appetite to write about a free-swinging, tough but lovable lady from a long-ago age. *Princess* was born, and I liked its heroine, Iona, more every day I wrote about her. I hope you'll share my joy in the princess of Icelandia who thought she was every bit as good as anyone else.

My best to you, loyal friends and readers.

—*Helen Monteith Mittermeyer*

∽ PROLOGUE ∽

Beyond Britannia, where the endless ocean opens, lies Orkney.

—Orosius

1048—THE ORKNEY ISLANDS, NORTH OF SCOTLAND

Why would the sun go dark on a bright day? Could it be the goblins and trolls of ancient lore? And why not? The Orkney Islands were Viking land. Or mayhap 'twas an omen that the sun went black for a moment.

Asdis Iona, called Iona, daughter of Sigurd and Margaret, royals of Icelandia, didn't know, but she wasn't afraid. She was a Viking. She was ten years old and well able to hunt alone. Though some girls weren't comfortable with weapons, she'd been well taught by her father and Rolf, her protector. But now . . . ? Despite herself, she shivered as though an ogre had risen from the earth to confront her. Nay! she told herself. 'Twas foolish.

Her practiced gaze studied the sky. Often it was as stormy as the sea, the clouds like roiling waves. Now it was a solid blue, with only wisps of white swirling high over the dull argent caldron called the Pentland Sea.

The patch of cloud that had masked the sun for that long moment had moved away as quickly as it had come. There was naught to fear. She wasn't that far from the stone castle where her family was housed. Stone! Everything was built of stone on the dark, forbidding Orkney Islands. In Icelandia they used much stone as well, but it was friendlier somehow. The days there caught more sunshine, except for the long winter ones. If truth be told, this island called Stroma was not unlike Icelandia, but Reykjanes was her home. And yet, as much as she missed Icelandia and wanted to return, she felt a kinship to the isles, as though a part of her were rooted in the rocky ground and the wild, unruly sea. She could not explain it, except that her mother had been born on a similar island named Iona, south of the Pentland Sea.

The sea was far below the cliffs where she hunted, but its sound roared upward like battle cries. The water crashed in froths of white only to scuttle back again into the gray depths, boil itself into strength, and once more hurl its might against the rocky bastions. Nothing could breast those protective walls. The Vikings had thrust back more than one enemy with the help of those cliffs.

The thunder of the waves could drown out any other sound, yet despite the booming cacophony, it was a brooding, lonely place, with gorse and sea grass tumbling among the dark rocks. Terns suddenly took flight from their rookeries, their screeches high and piercing above the noise of the sea. Their abrupt movement startled the hare Iona had been stalking, and it scurried away through the gorse and heather. She looked around to find what had disturbed the birds.

A man stood but ten feet away. Her uncle, Erwic Skene of Iona, armed for hunting. She glared at him. His sudden appearance from behind a tree was the reason the birds had taken flight, scaring away the hare. And game was scarce on the island. " 'Twas ill timed, uncle," she said, speaking in his Gaelic tongue, as her mother had taught her. "I almost had him."

"Aye. I've seen your skill, niece," he replied. "More than once you've filled your game bag."

She was about to say she'd even caught more than he a time or two, but something held her silent. She watched him closely and assessed her position. With the cliff at her back, she was at a disadvantage. She moved to change that. He moved with her.

He removed the dirk from his belt, and an unnatural silence enveloped Iona. The crashing sound of the sea seemed muffled; the screeching terns had vanished. Skene stepped toward her.

"This is a dangerous place, niece. If one could survive a fall from the cliffs, the boiling sea would crush and drown one before help came."

"I am surefooted," she said, her gaze fixed on him.

"And you rarely miss with your bow." He sidled nearer, angling toward her. "Your father, the accursed Sigurd, taught you well, didn't he? My sister brags of your aptness in shooting, wrestling, and oar running, though these are men's skills." Skene looked around. "Where is the giant who guards you?"

"Rolf? He's with my father, probably searching for wood." Wood was scarce in Icelandia and getting so on the Orkney Islands. Had her uncle just called her father accursed? Iona's hands tightened on her bow.

"So you're alone." Skene laughed. "Your mother taught you all her skills. And the priests instructed you in the ancient books and ways."

He laughed again, the harsh sound sharpening her wariness.

"This conversation is not to my liking, uncle." She notched an arrow in her bow.

"And Sigurd teaches you the Icelandic Law," he went on, sneering. "Forsooth, you're a twelfth-blessed creature."

"What is that to you? Leave me." The strong winds of Stroma drowned her shouted words.

"Aye. My intention is to leave this day and return to

Iona. But I'll not let you, with your tainted blood, grow to womanhood, lest you try to lay claim to our clan one day. Your clever father taught you the ways of court in order to rob us."

" 'Tis falsehood you speak!"

"Nay. Not all my father's words that you are kin will sway my vow to expunge the hated blood from our clan."

Iona looked over her shoulder at the rocky lip of the cliff. Where was her father? Had he left the island? But it didn't matter if he were near or far. Unless he could see her, he would not hear her cry out. Her uncle meant to harm her, and there were none to help her.

The roar of the sea and the constant calling of the terns had risen, whirling through the roar of the wind. No cry of hers would be heard. She glanced right and left. There was little room to move, but she might have the chance to pull off one shot. Her arrow would have to be true. Her eyes touched on the dirk in her uncle's hand. Was he expert with it?

"I'm past time," she said. "My mother will have sent her handmaiden to fetch me."

"Your mother." Skene spat. "She betrayed our clan by marrying a Viking dog. She's no Skene, no kin of mine."

His face twisted with rage, his eyes narrowing on her. A dot of spittle appeared at the corner of his mouth. The dirk spun in his hand. Iona hated him at that moment, and fury shook through her. "You speak of my mother as though she were less than you. 'Tis you who are beneath her. My mother is a queen of Icelandia, daughter-in-law of the great Thorfinn, and you are on Norse land. 'Tis not wise to forget that."

She stiffened when he squealed in anger, sounding like a wounded falcon. He thrust his one free hand heavenward, as though he cursed her and all her blood.

"Viking slut!" he shouted. "All these islands should be part of Scotland. 'Tis what I am. A Scot. Soon there'll be just Scot, not Ionian, Hibernian, Northumbrian. And all this will be ours, as it should be."

"No!" Iona shouted, anger blinding her to her peril.

"Return to Scotland if you are a Scot. This is Norse land. The Orkney Islands belong to us."

" 'Twould be better," he said, his voice eerily quiet, "if you had not been born, devil child. And I shall tear the woman from you before I send you to hell."

He swiftly cocked his arm to throw his dirk, but Iona aimed her bow and shot first. She was too hasty, though, and missed. She whirled and began running along the cliff edge.

With a hellish war cry Skene sprinted after her, the dirk raised. She angled downward toward the prickly scrub that could offer protection, her soft elk boots pounding over the rough ground. If she could get to the cliff path—

A rough hand caught her hair and jerked her back. The knife glinted in the sunlight, hovering above her face, then disappeared as his hand swept downward. He sliced her tunic, shoving it aside, then forced her legs apart. She struggled, cursing him, then screamed at the sudden pain as he thrust his hand upward inside her. Then he slashed the dirk across her thighs.

"Now you're no maid for any man, slut." His voice was a venomous whisper in her ear. "Not in this world or the next. But before your soul is sped, your face will match it."

The knife flashed across her eyes, then fire spread across her face. She choked on her cry of pain as he slammed her down on the ground. Blood was everywhere. She knew she would die.

Then, through the mist of her agony and fear, she heard shouts. A Viking war cry. Her uncle released her and ran, his triumphant laughter trailing behind him as darkness swirled around her.

Other arms lifted her, then the blackness took her completely.

"She's in deep darkness now from your powders, milady," the handmaiden said, touching Iona's face. "You need to draw this terrible gash together at once, and mend the bone as well. Then you can sew her legs." The handmaiden washed the deep cuts on Iona's thighs, which still oozed blood.

Margaret stared down at her only child. "I will curse my brother all my days for this attack on my daughter. Get me my other things. 'Tis best if this is done quickly. You must get a messenger to my husband too. As soon as the winds are right we sail for Icelandia. I will not stay in the Orkneys any longer, so close to Scotland. 'Twas there my satanic brother was spawned. I close my eyes to it forever."

"Very well, milady." The handmaiden paused when Iona stirred. "You haven't much time."

Margaret held her child, rocking her, soothing her, even as she cursed her own family. She must complete the sewing on Iona's face before she opened her eyes. Her hand must be steady so that the stitches would be fine.

She cleaned the gash that curved up the left side of her child's face from chin to brow. Then, taking a small leather bag from the bigger one at her waist, she sprinkled some powders on the wound. They would stop the pain from reaching into her daughter's sleep.

"Damn my brother's soul," she muttered. "I trust Sigurd will find the hound of hell and slay him. We shall return to our home in Reykjanes where we're safe, my darling child. One day, if Wotan is good, your scar will be gone. And they dare to call the Vikings barbarians."

Her bone needle moved smoothly, slowly, surely, closing the wound. When she finished she dabbed at the blood, then dusted the puckering redness once more with another medicament. Finally, she mixed a powder in water and held it to Iona's mouth. It would deepen her sleep and begin the healing.

"You will be beautiful, my child. I'll see to it. And you will be Viking, not accursed Ionan." Margaret looked up to the heavens. "Dear God, protect this child from the hated Scots who tried to maim her, she, who is a princess of Orkney and Icelandia."

Deep, deep in her sleep, Iona began to fear, a fear that would curdle her love and keep the wounds in her soul from healing.

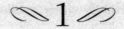

Seize the day, put no trust in the morrow!
—Horace

SPRING, 1058—SINCLAIR LAND ON THE NORTH
COAST OF SCOTLAND, ACROSS THE PENTLAND SEA
FROM THE ORKNEYS

The shadowy figures, cloaked in dark linsey-woolsey from
head to toe, met just past midnight, in the eerie light of the
cloud-covered moon. They whispered, only the neighing of
a nervous horse and the soughing wind making a sound.

"It will take time to do it your way," one whispered
angrily to the other.

"My way is sure," the second said. "Magnus Sinclair
will be gone, and the way will be clear to take the land.
And he will be known as a renegade."

"'Struth, I like it not. This once I will wait, but if
nothing is—"

"Fear not, there are others who wish him dead. They
will be at our side and will testify for us."

The first speaker turned away abruptly, then whirled

back just as fast. "See to it. For if it does not work I shall take a hand."

The moonlight flashed on the second man's face, briefly revealing a hard, cruel smile. Then the men parted, and the only sound was of horses galloping away, one heading south, the other to the north.

The black, shadowy enemy, swollen with hate, had come to kill.

Magnus's blood turned cold when he saw the giant and the enormous sword he wielded. He'd battle him again, and this time he'd finish the enemy. Magnus thrashed around on his bed, fighting the skins covering him as though they were the black hands of his nocturnal nemesis. Still in the threatening grip of his recurring nightmare, he rolled off the heavy bed, landing on his feet, sword in hand. Rocking, he inhaled shuddering breaths, trying to calm himself.

Damn the night vision. Would it never leave him? Sweat bathed his body and he shook like a boy, his hand locked around his weapon. Swiping at the moistness on his face, he ground his teeth, fighting the weakening of his knees, the trembling of his body. It was always thus after the dream.

After a time, his thundering heartbeat slowed, the shivering ceased. He shook himself to clear his thinking, then, his sword still gripped in his hand, he sank down on the bed. The hemp supports squeaked in protest. He was so lost in his memories, he didn't hear the swish of a garment disturbing the rushes on the stone floor.

" 'Tis the dark night visions you've had again, Magnus." The voice came out of the blackness of the room, the diminishing fire not strong enough to light the corners or the man walking toward him.

Magnus didn't need a torch, though, to tell him that Old Terrill had come to him. His guards would've let few others in. Nor was he surprised at Terrill's appearance. His mentor always seemed to know when something was awry, and he moved like a cat though his years were many.

"Yes," Magnus answered him, "the night vision again. What does it mean, Terrill? You read the stones and sand writing. Tell me."

" 'Tis not I who will explain this to you, my son. It is beyond my ken, I fear."

Terrill studied Magnus's face, which he knew almost as well as his own. The leader of the Sinclairs was a man of great strength and agility who feared nothing. His very size had struck fear into the hearts of many men.

Terrill sighed. The Sinclair would need all his intrepidity, all his strength of arm and purpose, for the days ahead. He'd seen fearsome quiverings in the runes when he'd questioned the future of the Sinclair. A bright white light with a green center could save him, but Terrill didn't know what the white light was, or how it could be procured for the Sinclair.

"I've had this vision for years," Magnus said, staring at the fire. "Since I was in Bretagne with my family, since the night my parents were murdered. 'Tis a man in the vision, but I cannot see his face. There's no speech between us, just his blackness that grows larger with each step toward me. I know he's going to kill me, and then I wake up."

He shook his head, more angry than frightened. "But I don't need the vision to tell me who wants to slay me, as he most foully killed my father and mother when I was sixteen. It was Urdric Kildeer, black-hearted baron of Northumbria. I feel it in my soul."

"You've hated the baron these many years, but you cannot find any with proof to vouch for your feelings, or who would bring you strong support to lay before King Malcolm."

"I will. And Kildeer will not live a day when I do. He's always wanted Sinclair land as his own, and his liege, Siward, publicly promised it to him when we were in Bretagne. All know how Kildeer hated my father from the moment he received permission from Macbeth to seek the north of Scotland as his own. Kildeer covets this land."

Magnus shook his head. Northumbria, that slash of
land along the North Sea, south of Scotland and north of
York and Mercia, seemed to spawn only dissidents, angry
men who always wanted more. From the moment of set-
tling on his own land, he had fought nearly daily to keep
his legacy. And if it wasn't Northumbrians he battled, it
was the Danes from Mercia, the Norsemen from Norway,
or any manner of renegade set on bounty and booty. Peace
had never been a part of Magnus Sinclair's life.

"Kildeer may covet your land," Terrill said, "but it belonged to your mother by blood, and when her father peti-
tioned to make it his holding, he followed all the rules of
our king's covenant."

The old priest sighed and touched a red-hot faggot to
the candle set inside a lamp fashioned of Egyptian glass
beads. The lamp had come from the Gallic coast with the
St. Clair family. They'd been driven out of Normandy in a
fierce battle and had lost most of their possessions. The
precious glass candle holder had been saved and taken to
Bretagne, where they'd lived until Magnus's parents' death.
Magnus had then led his clan back to the north land to
claim it for Sinclairs. The lamp had accompanied him.

"Your family," Terrill said, "has suffered much. Your
father and mother should've lived out their lives happily
on this land. But they were betrayed and set upon by renegades who forced them back to Bretagne—"

"And those armies were Northumbrian too."

Old Terrill nodded. " 'Tis true, their insignia was seen.
But you've reclaimed the land belonging to your mother's
forebears. Now it belongs to Sinclairs—"

"As it should," Magnus interrupted harshly.

"Yes, my son. But you must let go of your anger, or the
visions will not cease. I cannot see into the clouds of your
mind, my lord, but I do know you must be careful. There's
great danger all around you. I have seen it in the runes. I
feel the black shadow of your night visions could be your
nemesis in the future. If it is a man."

Magnus shook his head, tossing his thick mane of

chestnut hair, and laughed. " 'Twould be magic if there was a lass so big or menacing."

"Do not tempt the Fates by laughing at them," Terrill said sternly. "Death has a thousand faces and forms."

"Death? Truly, I've met it more than once. I will again . . . and it might not be my choice." Though he was naked, Magnus moved his shoulders as though a heavy mantle draped them.

"You're thinking of our good king Malcolm. 'Twould be simpler had the ambition not been greater than the man," Terrill said dryly. " 'Tis said he mounts a campaign against Northumbria when clan loyalty to him is shaky at best."

Magnus gave a hard laugh. "You don't fully trust our precious royal. It is true Malcolm is sometimes foolhardy, but uniting the clans is a good thing. Since he killed Macbeth he's been determined to unite Scotland, make it a powerful kingdom, not one of divisiveness and infighting. I do not fault the concept, but I do question his methods from time to time."

Magnus stood and strode up and down his large chamber, the firelight making his naked body gleam ruby and bronze. "But you needn't concern yourself that the clan is not first with me. Our people have fought many brave battles to reach the proud status of being members of Clan Sinclair. They've a right to the name and the land, and would protect both to the death."

"Malcolm knows you are the most powerful lord in the north," Terrill said.

" 'Tis true, old man. But he doesn't know if I will follow where he leads. I'm still pondering that." He drummed his hand on the back of a mammoth oaken chair, then stalked to the bed. "Malcolm wants Northumbria. It would make for a stronger Scotland. I too have a stake in Northumbria."

Terrill, who was not above reverting to the old pagan ways when it suited him, rolled the runes through his fingers. "The ruthless Kildeer would better himself in large measure by wresting Sinclair lands for Northumbria's new king, Tostig, and himself."

Magnus smiled grimly. "He hated my father when he claimed this land as his right through marriage to my mother. Now Malcolm supports my claim, and it must gall Kildeer."

"And Malcolm would remind you that he has supported you in your claim," Terrill said softly.

"So he would. But the king can't deny it was my people who fought long and hard for this. Malcolm has my loyalty, but not before my clan." Magnus shrugged. " 'Twould serve me no purpose if I weaken myself by supporting him. I will not leave my back unguarded to an attack from the Vikings."

Old Terrill studied his protégé. Magnus was a great warrior. The scars lacing his body proved that. But not just his frame was strong. His mind and spirit were as well. Like many natural leaders, he was intelligent and commanded respect and loyalty. But there was a wildness in him, a barely restrained anger. If it were unleashed . . . Terrill shook his head.

"You are making our people strong again, Magnus," he said. "Babies are being born. Food is ample and the stores are growing. There is wood to build homes. Your people would follow you to the death."

Magnus nodded grimly. "They would follow me to the doors of Hades, but I'll not take them there unless 'tis to protect Sinclairs and Sinclair land. I'll pick and choose my own battles, king or no. Before I loose my clan to Malcolm's battle, I'll make sure the clan is strong enough to withstand any assault. And I'll choose a good leader to follow me, if I fall in battle. But first and foremost, we will protect what's ours." He looked up at Terrill. "Death does not intimidate me or my people."

"That I know, Magnus. But you tempt the Fates with such words. Their power is too strong. To do battle is to gain glory, we know that. But the safety of the clan *in perpetuity* is vital."

Irritation drew Magnus's dark eyebrows together. "I must answer all challenges to the safety of the clan now, old man."

Terrill shook his head. "You're thinking like a warrior, Magnus, not like the leader of your clan. 'Tis better to be as eager to live for the clan in order to lead it as you are to die for it in battle. You do not have a successor, nor is there another Sinclair that could command the loyalty you do. Not even your brother." Terrill held up a hand as Magnus opened his mouth to retort. "Yes, there are choices, but it would be better if you fathered a son, rather than hand the leadership of the clan over to another. And 'twould strengthen the clan like naught else," he added slyly. "Surely such a happening would encourage other men to provide more sons before they die in battle."

Magnus frowned. " 'Tis fool's talk. I'll not hang back in battle to save my own skin, old man. I'm a warrior, the leader of the Sinclairs." He stabbed the air with an angry hand. "And if I should die, my brother Kenneth will lead our people, with our good uncle Cormac at his side, just as he is at mine."

Terrill spread his hands in a placating gesture. "Kenneth is a loyal Sinclair, and your uncle Cormac is heart and soul for the clan. There's no doubt of that. But you're the Sinclair. Even as a child you were a warrior. Now you are a leader, back in the north with your people on the land that belongs to them. You must keep those lands for those that follow. 'Tis your duty to protect that trust, over all else."

"I will," Magnus said, though he watched his mentor warily. Why all this talk in the middle of the night? What was Old Terrill leading up to? More and more it was clear that it was not the night vision that had brought the old man to his bedchamber.

"You can't protect the clan if you're dead," Terrill said. "Land can be parceled off by those who don't love the clan as you do. The Vikings can conquer it."

Magnus smacked a bedpost with the flat of his hand, making the bed shake. "I will not allow them to take any Sinclair land." He stood and began pacing again, gesturing angrily and cursing when he stubbed his toe against a chair.

"I have heard," Terrill went on, "that the Vikings will

not give up those islands in the Orkneys that you say belong to us, Magnus. I am told that even now, they send more warriors from Icelandia and Scandia. They are proud and fierce, just as the Sinclairs are." The old man watched as Magnus halted his pacing and scowled. Magnus was unafraid of a fight, and he'd go to great lengths to protect what was his. Terrill knew he could not change what Magnus was, but he did not want that blood spread on a battlefield before there were children of it. He only hoped he knew the right words to convince Magnus of the rightness of his plan.

"Those islands belong to the Sinclairs through my mother," Magnus said. "I'll not give them up." He thought of the raw, rough land to the north, across the wild water that separated it from Scotland. The people there knew him, for he often brought them much needed food and supplies to supplement their hard and meager living. Some of them were Icelandic, but he'd found them to be like good, hardworking Scots. They were loyal to him, but if a Viking force should come . . . "We'll fight any Viking attempt to take our lands."

Terrill looked up and murmured a prayer to the Christian God to watch over the Sinclairs, then touched the sacred runes to insure it. Returning his gaze to Magnus, he sought the words that would blunt the younger man's warrior instincts.

"Magnus, many of your men still suffer wounds from the war to regain our land, and from the bloody skirmishes with the renegades and outlaws."

"I know that, old one," Magnus said testily.

"The Vikings are coming," Terrill went on in a calm voice. "It's been written in the sand and in the runes. A war with them would take the young men, weaken the clan, leaving too few to protect it. You must find another way, rather than fighting, to bolster the clan."

Terrill held his breath as Magnus swung away from him, cursing. It wasn't wise to give orders to the Sinclair.

"And what would you have me do?" Magnus asked,

rounding on him again. "Run like a dog with my tail between my legs? No! Not if all the devils in hell attack us."

" 'Tis simpler than that, Magnus. My plan would keep your honor and that of the clan intact." Terrill hesitated, then asked, "Surely 'twould be more politic to marry one of the Viking women and secure your rights that way?"

"Marriage?" Magnus roared. "To a Viking?"

Terrill rushed on, sensing Magnus was about to toss him out of the chamber. "The great Sigurd, son of Thorfinn, has a daughter. She's a Viking, but she comes of good Scot stock as well. Her mother was Margaret of the Skenes, born on the island of Iona. As granddaughter of the great Thorfinn and only issue of his son, she has inherited much wealth from her parents and grandfather." Terrill put one finger to his lips thoughtfully. "And there is great wealth among the Skenes as well. Mayhap some of this belongs to her too. And she is unmarried at present. No doubt she's a widow, though that was not told to me."

"I have wealth enough," Magnus said. He put his bare foot into the grate and toed another log into the flames, not feeling the sting of burning. "So this is why you pay me this nocturnal visit, Terrill. 'Twasn't my vision that called you."

Terrill remained silent. Spikes of firelight outlined Magnus's features, giving them a harshness, even a demonic cast. The leader of the Sinclairs hadn't liked his proposal. Terrill put his hands in the sleeves of his chasuble and waited.

"I'd probably," Magnus said at last, "have to down gallons of the heavy brew made by the friars to marry a Viking woman. I've seen a few, and they were as tough and coarse as the men."

Still staring into the fire, he thought of the beauteous Lady Elizabeth of Asquith, who warmed his bed from time to time. Her hot and lusty ways suited his, and he always responded readily to the liquid welcome of her black eyes and the wet heat between her thighs. Though he had no intention of taking her to wife—he wanted no such encumbrance, and if he did, he would marry to a higher station than she—he needed the passion between them. To give up Elizabeth and then marry a prune of a Viking woman with hair under her nose? Christ!

As Magnus's thoughts spun, Terrill studied the younger man. Many called him handsome, and indeed, at the age of twenty-seven, he'd known more than his share of women. His sky-blue eyes, ringed with a deeper blue, were clear and purposeful. He was taller than all the other Sinclairs, a clan of tall men, and his body was well muscled and sinewed. He was a dangerous opponent with the lance and bow and arrow, and he'd even mastered the Genoese and Venetian style of swordplay, and the Greek way of tossing a man. Magnus loved challenge, and if Terrill sometimes thought him too reckless, he knew Magnus was the best and greatest leader the Sinclairs would have for years to come.

His life had been difficult. From his early childhood his family had been on the run, from Normandy, to Rome, to Genoa, to Bretagne, then, after the murder of his parents, on the attack to Scotland to wrest their God-given legacy from the Norsemen and outlaws.

All along the way Magnus had learned, until he was as finely honed and tempered as the mammoth sword he carried. Terrill knew all the scars on that muscular body. The cleft in Magnus's chin defined his diabolical temper, though it took much to raise it. He didn't have his father's black hair, though his skin darkened quickly in the sun. His hair was like his mother's, a thick chestnut laced with auburn. Terrill didn't doubt that he could please any Viking woman he chose.

The old man waited quietly, his fingers worrying the flesh of his forearms encased in the linen garment. He was glad of the warm fire. Though naked, Magnus seemed impervious to the drafts in the tower suite of Sinclair Castle.

At last, the younger man nodded slowly. "You're right, Terrill. Marriage might be better than war. Where do I find this daughter of Sigurd?"

Marriage wouldn't mean he had to forsake Elizabeth, Magnus had told himself. He would simply be discreet. At

Malcolm's court, all the courtiers had courtesans, married or unmarried.

"The runes have told me she comes to you, my lord," Terrill said. He did not add that the runes also foretold of danger arriving with the Viking woman. He hadn't been able to understand from whence the danger came, but he knew the woman herself was not a threat to Magnus.

Magnus turned to Terrill, smiling. "Do not the priests and monks of the abbey curse you for your heathen ways of reading the dreams, the stones, and the sand writing, you a consecrated priest?"

Terrill shrugged. "Mayhap they do. But I cannot read your dream. I will leave that, and the colicky thoughts of the abbot, to God."

Magnus's smile faded at the mention of his dream, and he turned the conversation back to the Viking woman. "What do you know of this granddaughter of Thorfinn, daughter of Sigurd?" When he saw Terrill hesitate, he closed his eyes as though in pain. "Tell me."

" 'Tis not what you think," Terrill said hurriedly. "I do not know how she looks. But I do know she is a woman of letters."

"What?" Magnus's eyes snapped open as he pictured the nuns he'd met in Bretagne, who lived behind walls and veils.

Terrill nodded. "She has been tutored by the monks that went from Kirkwall to Icelandia. She reads and writes the Latin of the scholars plus her own language, and the Frankish and Roman."

Magnus sighed. A learned woman. A nun. More than a prune, she was probably a hag. "Go on."

"She has spoken before the Althing, and she has mediated in disputes."

"What? How old is she?" Magnus envisioned a bent-over crone. Would he have to do that for the clan? But he could not imagine a woman such as Elizabeth speaking before the Althing, the open-air assembly that was held for a fortnight every summer at Thingvellir in Icelandia. Magnus was always careful to find out what he could about his enemies, and he'd discovered that the Vikings were much more than the barbarians most thought them to be. Not in all of Scotland was there such an old and venerable court. Any person, man or woman, could right a wrong against himself or his family, and each had the right to prosecute an accused murderer, if the victim was family. Most Vikings did not speak before the Althing, though. They had surrogates who did. And this princess was one of those?

" 'Tis true she has twenty-three summers, lord," Terrill said. "But that is not always past birthing."

"Almost." Magnus shook his head. "Why is she not married?"

"Mayhap she is still a grieving widow. All I have heard is that she does not choose to be a wife . . . at this time."

"Damn!" A widow who hated marriage? He envisioned the women of Lesbos, whom the great poet Sappho had gathered round her eons ago. Could this Viking princess be a woman who loved women? "No!" he shouted. "Not even for the clan!" Glaring at his mentor, he pointed to the door.

Old Terrill left quietly.

Magnus did not go back to sleep. He quickly dressed in the usual garb of the Sinclair men—leather brecks that covered his hips and thighs, a fine linsey-woolsey shirt, and, swathed around his waist, the fifteen yards of fabric that made up his kilt. The pattern was a red crossed with green and blue, striped through with white. Since the night was cold, he also pulled on woolen socks knitted in the same pattern, then threw a length of tartan over one shoulder to use as a cape.

He left the relative warmth of his castle and rode out past the village to a nearby hill. Near the lodge where he met Elizabeth, he lit a fire. The fire was a signal to each other, and not once had she failed to appear. The lodge was not much bigger than a crofter's hut, but it was tight and leak proof, warm and shut away from avid eyes.

Within the hour Elizabeth arrived. They did not speak. Minutes later there was nothing between them, and their hot bodies pressed together. Magnus buried himself in the warmth between her legs, and as always she brought forgetfulness as they tumbled to climax.

Magnus lay still for only a few moments as Elizabeth panted softly beneath him. Then he thrust himself off her and began to dress.

"Magnus, why do you hurry away from me? Did I not satisfy you, milord?" Sitting up, Elizabeth swept back her lustrous dark hair with one hand, deliberately displaying her bare breasts. She smiled as he stared.

Magnus, though, saw the irritation behind her smile, and he grinned. "Dawn is but an hour away, and I must meet with my men for training." He buckled his short sword to his belt, appreciative of the picture she made, nude upon the pallet. "You may sleep the day away, my beauty."

She pouted. "Magnus, have I not shown you my love? Would I not make a fitting consort for the Sinclair? My father would have me wed MacDonnell of Kilford, yet if you but said the word, that would be forgotten."

"You're lovely, and so is our lovemaking, but I fear I would not hold your attention for long, my beauty. Many seek your hand, Elizabeth."

Her smile was genuine this time. "True. But if you asked, I'd save myself for you, Magnus."

He only laughed and quickly kissed her, then left. Elizabeth's smile instantly changed to a frown, and she pounded her fist on the bed.

"Damn you, Sinclair. I vow I'll be your wife e'er you know it's done, and all the clans will call you blessed for my consort."

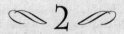

2

Then the father held out the golden scales, and in them he placed two fates of dread death.

—Homer

The Viking ship plowed through the wind-tossed waves, the north wind driving her on toward the Orkney Islands. Sitting beneath sheltering skins in the ship's stern, Asdis Iona, princess of Icelandia, gazed back over the water toward where her home lay far to the north and west. She would never see it again.

Her family was all gone; her grandfather, the great Thorfinn, had died the previous year, and her parents had both died that winter, within weeks of each other. Though she missed them all with a pain she feared would never ease, their deaths had freed her to seek at last her destiny. With the blessing of Haakon, king of Norway, she was traveling to Eyin Helga, a Viking island in the Orkneys. There, with the help of her cousin Spes and her handmaiden Marta, she would establish a sanctuary for women and children, a place where they would be protected and could learn if they wished.

Protected . . . Iona lifted a hand and touched the

silken fabric from Cathay that covered the left side of her face. It draped over her chin and neck, leaving her right cheek and mouth bare. A new world awaited her on Eyin Helga, the island her people considered holy. Once there, perhaps she could conquer the fear that had lived within her since her last visit to the islands. None knew of the fear, not her parents nor her grandfather, for she'd kept it locked in her heart.

But that fear, she knew, had ruled her life. She had refused to marry, despite the many offers she'd received. Often she longed for a home of her own and the shelter and love of a husband and children, but she'd chosen her path years ago. When she was thirteen, she'd traveled to the great continent with her father and grandfather, and they had visited a Benedictine abbey near the city of Florence. Loving the serenity, beauty, and sanctuary of the abbey, with its daughter houses for women, Iona had vowed to build the same for Viking women. Now her lot was cast. There was no turning back. Only God knew what the future held.

She shivered, not just with the cold, as she huddled under her elkskin cloak. For a black moment she wondered at the rightness of her journey. Perhaps it was foolhardy to travel so close to Scotland, home of the barbarian Scots. Her uncle Skene still lived among them. She carried the scars of his heinous deed on her body, though they had faded. But the scar in her heart was hers alone: She'd not shared the pain with anyone. Iona shook her head to clear it of such thoughts and glanced over her shoulder. Even if it had been her choice, she could never marry. Under all laws she was unclean, though none knew of it. The deep cuts her uncle had made on her thighs had hidden the fact that he had robbed her of her womanhood with his vicious hand.

The fire pot beneath the sheltering skins gave off some heat, warming her and Spes and Marta, who were trying to sleep. They had to be sparing with the wood to feed it, though. For Icelandians, wood was a treasure. They would replenish their supply when they reached the Orkneys, but even that source of wood was diminishing. Seamen had to travel farther and farther from Icelandia to find precious wood. Scotland had a good supply of wood, but the warlike Scots did not give up their trees easily.

Iona inhaled deeply of the cold, salt-scented air. Though the storm the previous night had thrown them off course, perhaps the strong currents would carry them to the inland seas, away from Scotland. She rose and stepped out of the enclosure to the wooden rail. Lifting her face to the cold North Sea spray, she smiled as the sun warmed her.

"It feels good, does it not, milady?"

Iona turned her head and nodded at her captain. Einar was a big, handsome man. His head and face were covered with red hair, and when he shook his head, his beard and hair glittered fiercely. He was an honored warrior, who'd brought back many spoils from the east and south. Fearless and loyal, he had been placed by her father as chief captain of their fleet.

"Yes, it does feel good," she answered. "Einar, you've told me how dangerous these waters can be, and I'm anxious to see the caldrons you spoke of."

Einar frowned. " 'Twould be best if we didn't, but the wind last night was too strong for us, I fear." He shrugged. "It has been clear so far. Perhaps we're not too far south."

Iona nodded. "The waters are wilder here than near our Icelandia, I think."

"In some places, yes." He pointed to the cliffs rising in the mist. "But the opposing currents we'll face close to land will be the most dangerous. We must be wary, ere we're drawn into the rocky cliffs. They've been known to swallow ships."

Iona nodded. She'd heard all the sea stories. She glanced at the oarsmen. "They seem not to feel the icy spray of the sea." Waves crashed against the boat and over the bow, but the oarsmen stood stoically at their posts.

Einar smiled. "They're used to it, milady."

Iona looked upward at the sail that bellied out full with the strong north wind. They'd had a good wind most of the way, and rarely had to depend on the oarsmen.

With Iona's attention elsewhere, Einar took the chance to stare at her. The princess was loved by the people, as her mother and father had been. It saddened him, as it did many of the Icelandic people, that she covered one side of her face. Most of them knew that the holy women and the good Lady Margaret, Iona's mother, had healed her wounds so completely, only the faintest of scars remained. Einar thought her beautiful. If only she hadn't made a covenant to start a place of sanctuary, she could have had any husband she chose. And he would've been first in line.

"We've made good time, milady," he said, forcing his thoughts away from what would never be. "Mayhap today we'll see land."

He turned and called instructions to his men. Despite his words, he couldn't rid himself of the unsettling feeling he'd had since they'd been blown off course the previous night. Usually he shrugged off omens, but this . . .

His eyes narrowed on the horizon. "We'll be coming in more south than I wanted to be."

Trepidation ran over Iona. "Do you mean we're past the waterway to Eyin Helga?" They would be closer to Scotland and Erwic Skene!

Einar nodded. "The wind is in our favor now, though. As we come closer to land it's dying, and we'll soon be able to change course and go north again."

"Good." She didn't even want to see the land of her mother's family, the Skenes, despoilers of children.

"You have not seen the sacred island since childhood, have you, milady?"

"No." Eyin Helga was a barren, cliff-faced isle surrounded by strong currents and rough waters, with scant places for safe mooring. It had been deeded to her by her grandfather, and she would soon call it home.

"The cliffs are still filled with birds, milady," Einar said, "and their loud cries can burst the ears." He smiled when she did. Ah, 'twas sad to lose the princess to such a lonely isle, though the ancients did say it was blessed.

Einar's smile quickly faded. If only the strong winds hadn't blown them so far south. 'Twouldn't be good to run afoul of the barbarian Scots with the princess on board. His scowl deepened. It had been a Scot who'd scarred her.

Misinterpreting his frown, Iona touched his arm. "Spes and I will not be lonely, dear friend, even after you return to Icelandia. Others will come soon to stay with us. And you, I hope, will return from time to time."

"I will, milady, but I would be happier had you stayed in Reykjanes where you would be safe."

"I shall be safe on the isle. No Scot will bother us there. It's too out of the way for them. Nor can the waters be sailed by any except Vikings."

Einar smiled at her pride in her boatmen. But still a foreboding filled him. He would not feel at ease until they reached Eyin Helga.

Iona smiled at her frowning friend. He shouldn't worry, she thought. After all, it was her destiny to come here. The holy women of Icelandia had predicted a voyage for her back to the Orkney Islands, that she would find her destiny there. At twenty-three years of age, past marrying and childbearing, she knew this was right for her, the solitary life she'd chosen.

When she was younger, she'd indulged in girlish dreams of love and marriage. Yet fearsome dreams would visit her at night, and she'd wake up crying. She hadn't been able to bear telling her mother that it was her uncle's assault that made her shudder at the intimacy of marriage. Her mother would've gone mad with anguish, and her father might have mounted an assault against the Skenes. She would not have the blood of her people shed for such a cause.

Yet over the years her secret had grown to gigantic size, until she'd come to believe that no man must ever get close enough to her again to scar her. Eyin Helga would be her haven and refuge. 'Twas far enough from Scotland, yet not too far from the waterways the Viking ships traveled from Iceland and Norway. She would not be isolated from her people, and she would be satisfied in helping others.

She shook off her reverie when she saw Einar stiffen beside her. "Is something wrong?"

" 'Tis nothing," he said, though his frown had deepened. "We will soon enter the waters that the Scots sail, milady. I will feel easier once we've turned more north." Einar tried to smile. "And the Pentland Sea is dangerous with its boiling water, and takes skillful sailing . . ." His voice trailed off, and the taciturn man fell silent, looking out over the sea.

Iona bit her lip, swallowing her impatience at his stolidity. "But you've sailed these waters many times and know them. What bothers you, Einar?"

He hesitated, then said, "A man called Magnus Sinclair. It's said he's banded together the St. Clairs and the Dugalds—his father's and mother's families—who are in turn linked with the Monteiths, Grahams, and Stewarts. He has trained the men of his own family into a large and well-armed fighting force, and has now begun to train the others. He claims that islands in the Orkneys are deeded to him by blood. And some of those are our islands."

Anger rose like a flood within Iona. It was the Skenes all over again, she raged silently, thinking they were better, wanting what wasn't theirs. Her uncle had savagely attacked her for that reason, and now this Sinclair was trying to rob the Vikings of their lands.

"Then he must be disabused of his foolhardy notions," she said fiercely. "Our people have claimed and used the islands for hundreds of years. The inland waterways have always sheltered our ships and the king of Norway concedes our claim. How can these upstart renegades question it?"

" 'Tis true what you say, milady. The Orkneys' waterways have been our busy and safe passages since long before my grandfather's time." He shrugged. "But these Scots are not so easy to convince."

Iona shifted restlessly, gathering her cloak about her. "I've heard tell about the formation of these large extended families, which the Scots call clans. But most of them gather in Scotland, and so it must be with this Clan Sinclair. They must get off our lands. The islands belonged to my grandfather, and from him to me. 'Tis Viking land.

"If there is trouble," she added, "we will consult Britannia's king, or the Northumbrian. Perhaps we could deed him an island in the passage in exchange for his harrying these troublesome Scots for us."

Einar nodded. "But that Northumbrian king, Tostig, does not trust us any more than he trusts the one called Malcolm, who is king to the Scots."

"If we promise him a piece of our lands, mayhap we can count on his biting at the heels of the blustering Scots."

Einar smiled. The princess had a Viking mind.

"Land!" the lookout suddenly shouted. Close following came another sharp call. "Ship!"

Iona leaped to the railing, casting off her cloak. She wore a heavy woolen bliaut, and her hands were only lightly covered by fine wool gloves. Neither gave her much protection, but she did not feel the harsh wind or spray as wild, angry blood pumped through her. Were they Scots? She shaded her eyes with one hand, then glanced at Einar. He nodded. They were Scots! They would attack.

Whirling, Iona ducked under the sheltering skins and lifted her leather shield. It was lighter than what the men wore, and she slipped it on like an apron. Pulling her sword from the leather scabbard, she turned to leave, when a voice stopped her.

"No!" her cousin cried, her voice reedy with fear. "You are a princess, Asdis Iona. You cannot fight."

Iona turned to the younger woman. Her face was white, her bright brown hair whipping around her head. Their handmaiden, Marta, crouched behind her. "I must, Spes," Iona said. "I will stand with my people as I've been trained to do. 'Twas my parents' wish that I be ready to live and die as a Viking, and so I will. Stay where you are, cousin. You know what to do if they board us."

Iona looked away as Spes clutched a knife to her breast. It was a sin to take one's life, but it was a greater sin for a woman to be taken by the rampaging Scots, Northumbrians, or Britons. Slavery and violation were anathema to a Viking. Better to die sword in hand. And she, Asdis Iona, had been taught how to fight and defend herself. She started toward the raised portion of the deck, in the center of the ship, when a man stepped in front of her.

"Highness, you will stay behind me," Glam Asnarson told her.

Iona stared up at the huge man. He was her protector, as had been his older cousin Rolf before him. She nodded, then followed him to where Einar stood, sword in hand and ready to battle.

They had just reached the captain when a strong male voice called across the water, commanding them in Gaelic to give way.

"You give way, Scot," Einar shouted back in the same tongue. Though the barbarian Scots didn't speak Icelandic, the Vikings knew their speech and used it.

"Einar," Iona said, struggling to control the shock shuddering through her, "their ship is almost the size of ours." Could it be Skene? she wondered. Did he know she was returning to the Orkneys? Would he try again to kill her? If he did, this time she'd fight him and win. Perspiration pearled her body. No, no, she wouldn't think of him. This was not Skene land. The island of Iona was on the other side of Scotland.

"I see that, milady," Einar answered, then turned to roar instructions. The Vikings scattered quickly to their battle stations, the oarsmen arming themselves without releasing their oars. If the wind died even a little they would bend their backs to the rowing, angling the ship north and trying to outdistance their pursuers.

Einar moved to the rail, his gaze flicking constantly from his ship to the enemy's, attempting to gauge distance and the chances of avoiding conflict.

Glam held his sword loosely in his right hand as he spun his throwing dirk in his left.

Iona too readied herself.

If it was the will of God and Wotan, she'd die like a Viking with her sword in her hand. But not even that vow nor all her adjurations to herself excised the lump of fear that stopped her breathing.

Einar looked back at her, his features taut. He ran a

practiced eye over his men, then stalked to the prow to direct the attack.

Iona blinked as perspiration ran into her eyes. The North Sea wind was icy, but heat trembled through her. Her fingers tightened around the hilt of her sword.

The Scots had come around and were closing fast, so that they'd strike bow to bow with the large Viking craft. Iona's heart squeezed in anguish for her people. Because of the many dangers inherent in the crossing from Icelandia to the Orkney Islands, she had a full complement of fearless Viking warriors. She prayed for victory even as her soul wept for those who could suffer injury or worse. She and some of her Vikings might not live out the day. She did not fear death for herself. Her Christian God and Wotan, the ancient god of the Vikings, would be waiting to greet her. But she did not want her people harmed, and it tore at her heart to think of them being sacrificed to Scots.

The Scot craft was almost on them, near enough that Iona could make out the features of its men.

The Scots were enormous! From her mother's words she had always pictured them short, squat, and painted blue. Not so. Their leader, a blond giant of a man, was laughing and calling to his men to close with the foe. Then Iona saw why.

"Einar!" she shouted.

"I see, milady," he called back. "Vikings! Row!"

Grim-faced, the oarsmen bent to their task. They needed all speed to escape their enemy now, for it wasn't a single Scottish ship on the attack, but three. The other two were circling in, forming a phalanx. Seeing the deadly flank attack closing swiftly, Iona knew her people would be slaughtered, and all because she had wanted to seek her destiny in Orkney. She prayed fervently, then the first boat grazed their prow.

The blond giant yelled some bloodcurdling Gaelic war cry. It was answered by a deep-throated Viking one, and the battle was joined. Grappling lines were tossed across the rocking ships, and harsh yells mingled with shrieks of pain as swords found their mark.

Standing with her back to Glam, Iona fearlessly met an attacker, a hairy bull of a Scot with a leather patch over one eye.

"Put up your sword, lassie," he shouted at her, his sword poised to strike, "and I'll let you live. 'Tis not proper for ye."

"Look to yourself, Scot. This Viking gives no ground."

He was stunned to hear her answer in his own tongue, and she took advantage of that moment of surprise. As his sword began its downward swing, she easily stepped aside and smote him on the side of his head with the bronze hilt of her sword. His hoarse grunt of pain as he went down satisfied her that he wouldn't waken for a time. As she whirled to engage another, though, a hard arm grasped her around the waist, pinning her sword arm to her side. Struggling, she tried to free herself.

"Easy, lass," a voice said in her ear. "I have you."

Twisting her head around, she saw it was the blond giant who held her, squeezing the breath from her.

"Vikings!" he shouted above the warriors' yells and the wounded's groans. "Hear me. Fight on and I'll cut her throat and toss her into the sea. Give way and she lives."

"Fight on, fight on," Iona called, then gasped when a hand clamped over her mouth and nose, cutting off all air. Light flashed behind her eyes as the agony increased. She barely heard the lessening of sound around her, but knew the Vikings were stopping their fighting. She tried to shake her head to urge them on, but the hand tightened and she could feel a blackness overcoming her. She thought she heard Spes scream, but she wasn't sure.

"Stop!" Spes struggled from her hiding place. "You're killing her. Release our princess or we'll die with her."

The blond Scot studied the brown-haired spitfire who'd dared to order him, then looked again at his captive. She wasn't as young as the other woman, he saw as he loosened his grip, but she was amazingly beautiful. He'd never seen hair such as hers, the color of winter frost with the sun on it. Her eyes were like the angry North Sea on a winter's day, icy green and shimmering. A faint but intriguing line ran down the left side of her face. He removed his hand completely from her mouth, but kept his arm around her waist.

"I am Kenneth," he said, "brother to the great Sinclair."

He pulled the woman back against his side so that he could look into her face. "Aye, lass, you're not so ugly that you might not do well for me."

Iona gasped air into her tortured lungs. "Never, pig swill," she said hoarsely, answering in Gaelic. She lifted her free hand to touch her bruised mouth and realized her veil had slipped. Dropping her head, she fumbled for the thin cloth, anxious to cover her face again.

Kenneth was more taken aback by what she'd called him than by her command of Gaelic. Looking around, he saw the Viking men were averting their eyes from her. Was she a witch? He tightened his hold on her. "Scotswomen wouldn't talk to a man in such a way."

"No Viking woman would call you a man," Iona countered, her head still down.

Kenneth bared his teeth in frustration at her defiance and the encouraging utterances of the Vikings. That they revered the sharp-tongued beauty was a surety, and he knew they only waited for an opening to resume the fight. 'Twas good that Tiam's and Hethrow's ships hovered near.

He frowned down at his captive anew. 'Twas a wildcat he held, ready to rip and tear with tooth and claw. Weren't Viking women human? He debated teaching her a lesson in proper respect, then decided not to. After all, her Vikings had given way. The Sinclair clan had a new ship, and a stout one at that. He waved his sword.

"To shore," he called to his men. "The Sinclair will be waiting." He gestured to the other two Scottish vessels that the Viking ship be towed into the harbor, where a small gathering of warriors waited with Magnus.

Iona forced herself to stand passively in the Scotman's grip as their ship neared land. They almost reached the narrow, stony strand when another giant, standing on shore, stepped forward, away from the other men. His hair glinted bronze in the sun as he cupped his hands around his mouth and shouted something. The grip around Iona lessened as her captor turned to answer, his one foot propped on the railing, the other on a pile of skins protecting some Viking stores.

'Twas a precious second in eternity, but it was all Iona needed. Like lightning she struck out with her foot, catching the Scotsman at the back of the knee. Yelling and cursing, he fought to stay upright. Iona kicked again with all her might.

The Scotsmen stared, open-mouthed, as their leader, his arms flailing, fell backward into the sea. Iona didn't even glance at the submerged man. Instead she bent, grabbed his sword, and jumped out onto an oar just above where the giant was surfacing. She grasped the sword in both hands and pointed it downward, the tip wavering just inches from Kenneth's head. Then she looked up at the bronze-haired man on the strand.

" 'Tis my people's safety I would have," she called to him. "Swear by God that you'll grant this or I'll drive this sword through his skull."

Time stood still. Not even the terns cried above them. No one moved. Iona's words echoed and re-echoed like a clarion call.

After an endless moment, the bronze-haired man moved. Sword in hand, he strode into the water, then leaped up onto the Viking boat. Iona stood motionless, watching as he walked toward her along the oars.

"Mark me!" she called when he was three oars away. " 'Twill be done as I said, Scot."

"I am Sinclair," he said, and stepped onto the next oar. "Give way or die. You might kill Kenneth, but all of you will die, my lady Viking. What then?"

"Scots might kill us anyway. You're a treacherous lot," she said coolly.

He stepped onto the oar beside hers and smiled thinly. "It would seem you wish to be a warrior. Fight me then, Viking, instead of freezing my brother in the sea. If you win, your people go free. If I win . . ." He shrugged, and his hair glinted fire in the sun.

Laughter rippled through the Scots. No man could best the Sinclair, so what could a woman do? They smiled and smirked at each other. The Viking princess would be properly chastised by the Sinclair.

Iona hefted the heavy sword of the enemy. It was too difficult for her to handle, but she couldn't give him the advantage of knowing that. And the weapon's weight wouldn't impede her if she could get close enough . . .

"Agreed," she said. "I'll pick up your gauntlet, Scot. 'Tis my right to choose the time and the weapons." She paused and stared at the giant, who was as comely as the devil. Then she smiled as the thrill of the challenge raced through her. "I choose now!" she suddenly shouted. "And oar running!"

3

The heart of woman is deeper than the deepest sea in the world.

—Breton proverb from the Ile de Batz

Before the Scot could move, Iona jumped up into the air and landed hard on the oar where she'd been standing. Instantly, her feet began a running cadence that would keep the heavy oar straight and spinning. The object of oar running was to spin the oars until one person overbalanced and fell.

The Scot hesitated only a moment before he too jumped on his oar and began running. Iona watched him critically as she recalled every lesson she'd ever learned.

Long ago the perils and tricks of the sport had been drilled into her. A slap from the oars could break a limb or crack her skull; a misstep could send her crashing down on a spinning oar, maiming or killing her. She forced away those thoughts and concentrated on her other lessons—the speed needed to keep the oar parallel with the water, what would make it rise or fall, the best balance for using a weapon, when to strike, to feint, to back off. More times than she could count she'd been dumped in the frigid waters of BorgarFjord. But she'd struggled on until she'd mastered the skill, until she'd been able to stay on longer than some of the best Vikings, managing even to dunk them a time or two.

The Viking oarsmen had hooted and released their oars when Iona began running. Ignoring the Scots, who trained their weapons on them as soon as they moved, they flung themselves away from the two dangerously bobbing oars. Calling out their encouragement, they beat their hands against their leather-covered thighs, keeping time with the running Iona and Scot.

It took Iona only minutes to realize that her opponent had run the oars more than once. He was good, but not as good as she. He had strength, determination, and agility on his side, while she had the edge of her well-honed skill.

He often tried to reach her with the flat of his sword. She stayed just far enough away and speeded up, so that he'd have to do the same in order to prevent a collision of oars. If hers spun faster it would be atop his, giving her the advantage.

It was impossible for her to do much damage with the unwieldly sword she held. It did help her balance, though, so she used it that way rather than wasting energy using it as a weapon. Her heart was pounding already from exertion, her lungs screamed for air. But exhilaration poured through her too. She needed to win. She must. Every sense was tuned to her opponent. She noted that her tiniest increase in speed cost him precious moments of concentration. But she also noticed that while she was gasping for air and sweat was pouring down her face, he was hardly breathing hard at all. Damn him.

Magnus watched the Viking woman closely. She was damned good, and he hadn't expected that. Hell, he hadn't expected her to take up his challenge. She was a woman, outnumbered, her people's weapons down. But what a warrior she was. She looked as fragile as the silk that had been swathed around her head and now flew like a banner behind her. She was a beauty too. Silver and gold sparked her hair and skin, and her eyes were like the green leaves of summer, or like—

Damn! Her beauty had distracted him, and she'd almost toppled him. She was able to control her oar well. Ah! He could reach her. He tapped her backside with the flat of his sword, thinking to take her down, but she danced out of his way, her movements as sprightly as a nymph's. He'd get her, though. And maybe he'd keep her.

Iona saw the sudden dangerous glitter in his eyes and swore. The Scot might not intend to kill her, but he did intend to win. She had to do something soon, or he'd have her. There was one maneuver, perhaps unknown to him, that her father had called mortally perilous. Calling on the Holy Virgin, Christ, and Wotan, she made her decision.

She stared down at the whirling oar, counting every other beat. It had to be just right, or she'd break her leg.

"Wotan!" she shouted, and the age-old war cry was answered by her Vikings. Then she leapt high and came down hard on her opponent's oar. The landing jarred every tooth in her head, rattling through her like a blow. The instant her feet hit, she began running backward, the motion sending every muscle in her body screeching in pain and protest and wrenching a curse from her.

Could she hold on? Only if she'd caught him off guard enough, so that he couldn't bring his superior strength into play. Surprise flashed across his face, and she bore down with all her strength, spinning the oar as hard as she could.

The oar quivered, warning that the Scot was off balance. Pain spasmed in her back and neck as the Vikings roared behind her. They saw her advantage and sensed what she intended to do with it.

Iona increased her speed as she moved closer to him. Hefting the heavy sword, she swung it slowly, catching him on the arm. At the same moment, she jumped up and down, reversing once more, the action slamming through her head and body. The quick change sent the heavy oar splashing downward. She dug in, curling her toes around the wood. The Scot comprehended the ploy and fought for purchase, but he lost it.

Incredulity, fury, and stupefaction chased across his face as his sword flew from his hand. Then he spun in the air and fell backward into the sea.

The Scots cried out in anguish, and several men leapt up to grab his sword before it could follow him.

The Sinclair surfaced, and Iona easily saw both the anger and the vengeance in his eyes. "You win, Viking," he shouted up to her. "Your people shall be free. But you are my prisoner."

The Vikings roared in protest, and looked ready to rush the Scots, but Iona stopped them.

"Wait!" she called. She glared down at him as she tried to remember what she'd said. She'd told him she wanted her people freed. He'd said he would, but he hadn't included her in that. Cur of a Scot. But she would not go back on the agreement, and she nodded to him.

The Vikings roared their disapproval. The Scots hoisted their weapons, but their sodden leader ordered them back.

"We will stay with our princess," Einar said from where he lay on the deck, wounded.

Iona leapt off the oars, her shoulders and back aching. She dropped down on her knees next to her wounded captain, quite sure she'd never be able to stand again. "Listen to me, my good Einar. I order you away from here with your ship and our people. Go to the island. I'm not afraid."

It was a lie. She was terrified. All the tales she'd heard of Scottish cruelty and savagery screamed in her head. The thought of being alone with such a man as the Sinclair had her body shuddering. The specter of her uncle faded before this man's threat. This time she would die.

"You must go," she told Einar again. "I order you. 'Tis the only way our people can be freed."

He shook his head, closing his eyes. "No."

She sensed the presence of the Sinclair before she turned to look at him. He stood over her with his brother. Both men had skins wrapped around them, but she could see their sodden garments were freezing to them.

"You gave your word," she said to the Sinclair. "I ask

you to let me tend to my people's wounds so that they may leave."

Magnus gazed down at her. What an unusual mark on her face, he mused. If it was a scar, it was a lovely one and only enhanced her milky skin. It was as though the scar outlined her cheek to draw attention to its beauty. What would it be like to taste that unusual mark, to suckle its length? She was an exquisite creature, with a tall, strong, and curving form. She reminded him of the heather that grew on the cliffs overlooking the sea. At the center of the hardy flowers was a hint of flame. That same creamy orange blushed the cheeks of his Viking adversary, entrancing him.

"They call you a princess," he said abruptly. "Who are you?"

She barely looked up from examining her captain's wound. "I am Princess Asdis Iona, daughter of Sigurd and Margaret, granddaughter of Thorfinn. Now I must get my people cared for. I will need fire. Can one be lighted on the strand?"

When he did not answer, she glanced impatiently at him. Was this leader of the Sinclairs slow? Why did he look at her so strangely? Didn't the Scots minister to their wounded?

He threw back his head and laughed, startling her. "Kenneth, get the ship moored. Bring our wounded first. Then have the men gather wood for milady."

Iona glared at him. Why was he laughing at her? As the ship was towed to shore, she turned away and ran a practiced eye over the wounded. It hurt her to see the number of men who were gone, some still floating in the sea. The ship landed with a bump, and she gestured to the well ones to aid the others.

Spes appeared at her side. " 'Tis true they aren't as ugly as I thought they'd be," she whispered. "The blond leader is almost comely. And that Sinclair is a devilish giant." Spes glanced at Iona, who grimaced. "Well, 'tis better than I thought 'twould be. They don't have horns coming out of their heads."

"Never mind them," Iona said sternly. "Bring Marta. We have work to do."

Still, she could not dismiss her cousin's words. The Sinclair was big, and his features weren't coarse, nor were his arms hanging below his knees as she'd pictured the Scots. She glanced at him as she disembarked. Some might even call him handsome . . .

She pushed the unwelcome thoughts away. She was in Scotland, land of her uncle, and she must keep her wits about her, not be distracted by an overbearing man. Skene might never know she was there, and if he did discover her whereabouts, she would be beyond his power.

On the strand Glam took charge of the fire, feeding the flames until they reached the white heat that Iona would need. Four other Vikings erected a skin shelter nearby to protect both Iona and the wounded. Not far away Marta worked hurriedly, preparing the injured men. She would not look at the barbarian Scots. Helping to carry Iona's herbs and powders, Spes followed after her cousin as they assessed the severity of the different injuries. Unlike Marta, Spes looked around eagerly, curious about these fearsome people.

After ordering Einar brought to her first, Iona joined Glam at the fire. She pulled several thin iron pokers from their pouches and laid them over the white-hot wood. She carried the pokers with her wherever she went. With them she could burn torn flesh and keep it from putrifying. Sacred fire could do that, her mother had told her, though Margaret did not know why.

Einar protested at being tended to first, but the Vikings ignored him. At Spes's direction he was laid on a roughly fashioned cot, a plank of wood that rested on two flat rocks. The working table was rough, but it was almost level, and it was high enough so that Iona could reach her patients without tiresome bending. As she began to work on Einar's leg, Spes and Marta oversaw the other wounded men, ordering able Vikings to carry the more seriously injured ones closer to the shelter. Other Vikings built fires, until the wounded were in a circle of heat.

On the other side of the strand, Magnus and Kenneth watched the Vikings.

"What do they mean by building those crafts?" Kenneth asked, pointing toward the sea. "They're not seaworthy, but they put their dead in them. Do they mean to bury them in boats?"

"No. 'Tis my understanding they still handle dead seamen in the old way. They'll be set adrift in the burning crafts, their ashes left to float on the water until they reach a Holy Sea."

"Barbarians."

"That's what they call us," Magnus said dryly, his gaze moving to Iona. She had completely ignored him since they'd left the Viking ship. He wasn't used to that.

Magnus watched her for a time, then moved with Kenneth to the relative shelter of some rocks, where the wind was not quite as strong. There by a fire he and his brother rubbed circulation back into their limbs with soft squares of linen. These and dry clothes had been brought by several clanswomen, whom Magnus had sent for.

When he was clothed again, Kenneth shifted so that he could see Iona. "Magnus, do you notice how she mixes powders over the fire? A witch, do you think? She could be with that hair. I've never seen the like. 'Tis a shame she covers it and her face."

Magnus moved next to his brother and again stared across the strand at the Viking princess. She was all but swathed in cloths once more. Only her hands and arms were free, and he noticed that she tended to the wounded with great surety. Even the women of his own clan watched the princess as they worked among the wounded Scots.

Curious, Magnus walked across the strand toward the Viking enclosure. He'd seen such healing ways with powders before, when he'd been in Rome. Had the Viking woman traveled so far? 'Twas not likely. Then how did she know such things? He frowned at her, then turned to study his own people.

"What troubles you, Magnus?" Kenneth asked, walking up beside him.

"Why aren't the Viking wounded groaning and screaming as ours do? Perhaps she is a witch, brother."

His gaze swept over the injured Vikings. Most lay at peace, eyes closed and unmoving, not writhing in pain as his men were doing. He glanced at her again, watching as she bound a wound on a man's chest. How would it feel to have those long fingers sweeping across his flesh? His lower body hardened at the thought, angering him. He whirled away to speak encouragingly to his own wounded men, yet often his gaze was drawn back to the Viking princess.

She'd said her name was Asdis Iona, though he'd heard the younger woman call her Iona. She was the Viking princess Old Terrill had said was coming to him. Now she was here, and she was no hag. She was tall, and strong, and quite beautiful. Her long, thick plait of white-blond hair hung almost to her ankles, shining and glistening like silver. It had been wound around her head, but had loosened during the oar running. She had not bothered to twist it back up. Her face was exquisite, as if it had been carved by a master sculptor. And there was that intriguing mark . . .

Her hands moved surely and quickly. Her curvaceous body swayed rhythmically as she worked, sending hot shafts of desire through him once more. What would she say when he told her they would marry? For he'd decided to do just that. He had to marry her for the clan—and he knew he'd enjoy having her in his bed.

"Why do you smile when you look at her, Magnus?" Kenneth asked. "She beat you roundly."

"So she did," Magnus murmured. He waited in vain for the rush of anger. No woman had ever beaten him in any way, especially one who had such a fragile look. But her legs must be uncommonly strong to have balanced on the oars. What would it be like to have those legs around his middle as her body took him inside her? Fire flared within him, as white hot as the actual fire beside him. Marriage. For the clan, of course. His smile widened.

"I thought you'd be angry with the Viking wench," Kenneth said, obviously confused.

"I'm not," Magnus said, and started toward the shelter where she worked. Every movement she made was graceful and sure as she examined and worked on the bloodied bodies. She was calm, not squeamish. He saw how the wounded smiled when she talked to them, and noticed again how quiet it was with her people, how chaotic it was with the Sinclair wounded.

As he neared the shelter he was aware of the hard-eyed Viking stares that followed him. More than one man moved closer to where their princess tended the wounded. Magnus walked around the watchful Vikings until he was standing behind her as she finished sewing a man's arm with a long bone needle.

Iona sprinkled more white powder on the stitched wound, then leaned back, sighing. She bumped into someone and glanced over her shoulder. It was Magnus Sinclair, monstrous big, with a strange glitter in his eyes. She fought down the shiver of dread she felt whenever she considered facing Scots again. And this one was particularly treacherous. His face, his unusual blue eyes, his wicked smile, had appeared to her more than once while she tended her people, even though she hadn't looked his way.

"The warrior didn't move while you stitched him, milady," he said.

She nodded, too tired to talk. And the way this Scot made her feel, she wasn't sure her voice would work.

Einar, lying on the ground wrapped in skins, opened his eyes when he heard Magnus. " 'Tis her way. She's been taught since childhood in healing and the law. The healing skills came from her mother, our lady Margaret."

"And the great Galen instructed some of the friars who accompanied Columba when he went forth," Magnus murmured, and smiled when Iona looked at him in surprise. "Knowledge has made its way here, Princess."

Iona said nothing. She leaned over Einar and gave him a small drink. "He needs rest," she said to Spes, then looked around. There was only one more.

The same could not be said for the Scots. All the time she'd worked she'd tried to close from her mind the screams of agony from the Scots' wounded. Still they had penetrated, tearing at her heart. She could have helped them, but her duty was to Vikings first. If only they knew the curatives, the blessed oblivion that could come from the right herbs and roots. Perhaps when she finished with this last Viking she would help the Scots.

Magnus watched as she briefly closed her eyes in obvious weariness, then determinedly set to work. The man's injuries were minor, so Magnus turned his attention to Einar. The man seemed asleep, and Magnus stared at the captain's leg. A long gash had been sewn shut, and strips of wood were fixed to the leg by strips of cloth. He could've sworn the leg had been smashed by a broadsword. Surely she couldn't have knitted it up! But the man wasn't dying, nor was he writhing in pain.

The princess finished with the last man and patted his arm, which she'd wrapped in clean linen. The man smiled and thanked her. As he left, Magnus stepped in front of her.

"I want you to look at my people, Asdis Iona, Princess of Icelandia," he said.

Iona stared at him in surprise for a moment, then quickly saw the advantage he'd given her. She opened her mouth to wrest a promise from him that she would be freed with her Vikings. Then a terrible scream rent the air, chilling her blood. She knew instantly what it was.

"Stop them!" she said to Magnus. " 'Tis his limb they would remove. I can tell. Stop them now, and I'll help your people." The man's screams rose higher. "For God's sake, stop them!"

Magnus's bellow stopped all sound and motion. Iona grabbed his arm without thinking, not noticing when the nearby Scots looked stunned.

"Get the man here at once," she said. "And carry him gently. Spes and Marta will tell you how to line up the other wounded. Hurry, man. As it is I might not be able to save him, but if I'm quick, and with God's help, I can do something. Glam, go at once and get my other medicines and instruments." She pushed at Magnus. "Hurry along, there's little time to waste."

Goggle-eyed Scots watched the Viking woman shove their chieftain, and were dumbfounded that he actually obeyed her orders. They gaped until he turned a dark glare on them, then they scattered to do his bidding.

The man with the horribly torn leg was brought to Iona. He was senseless and pasty white, and dark blood oozed from the terrible gash. Iona studied him. He had a patch over his left eye as her first adversary had! Was it the same man? No matter. Leaning over him, she pressed her face and hands to his chest, listening to his breathing. Then with one finger she gently lifted his eyelids. She shook her head.

"The pain has filled his brain," she murmured, more to herself than Magnus. " 'Twill fight all the healing that the body wants to do. I do not know if I can save him."

Magnus didn't answer, but watched impassively, not revealing his inner turmoil by so much as a flicker of his eyelid. It puzzled and yet strangely excited him to see her hands run over Dugald's body. He wanted that touch on him, and that inexplicable, potent desire angered him.

"She has wondrous healing hands, does she not, Magnus?" Kenneth whispered.

"Aye," Magnus answered shortly, and shifted so that his back was to his brother. He didn't like how he felt, and he didn't want his brother to have a hint of it.

Iona took a ladle of water from Spes and mixed some brown powders in it. "I will need help with this. What is his name?"

"Dugald," Magnus said.

"Dugald!" she shouted into his ear several times. When she saw a flicker of movement, she tried to pry his lower jaw down. Glam reached around her and forcibly opened Dugald's locked jaws. She poured down the liquid at once.

Magnus stepped to Glam's side and held Dugald's head as the man choked and tried to spit out the liquid, but he was too weak and most of it went down his throat.

Iona waited, her hand on the man's wrist, checking the uneven throb of his blood. At last the spasms began to dissipate, and the man slipped into a deep, relaxed sleep.

"Spes," she said, handing her cousin a bag of herbs. "Grind these and put them on the leg, quickly."

Spes did as instructed, and instantly a burning smell arose. The Scots muttered among themselves as the leg began to smoke, but Iona didn't even look up. Over and over she cleaned the wound, slowly moving back the torn flesh until she found what she'd feared she would—bits of bone. Painstakingly she cleaned the injured leg, removing the tiniest bone fragments. Clean, clean. How often had her mother stressed the importance of this?

When she was finally satisfied, she looked up at Glam and nodded. "I'm ready," she said to him. "You must hold him tightly. When I say to pull, you must do so slowly and steadily. It will not be easy."

"Yes, milady," Glam said.

Magnus saw what she was going to do and went to Dugald's shoulders. "I'll help," he said. "I saw this done when I was in Genoa."

Iona glanced at him and nodded. Turning away, she thoroughly washed her hands. They were shaking, and for a moment she was tempted to take some of her own calming powder. But it might cloud her mind and make her clumsy. At last she turned back to the sleeping man. Taking a deep breath, she put her fingers into the open wound and searched slowly and carefully until she found the ends of the bone.

"Now," she said.

Glam firmly grasped the man's foot and ankle and pulled, while Magnus held his shoulders. Even in his deep sleep Dugald groaned as the pain penetrated. Quickly Iona pushed the two bone ends together, pressing tightly.

"It's set," she said.

Slowly Glam and Magnus let go, and the bone fused tight under her hands. She washed her hands again, then took her bone needle and thread. Carefully, folding the flesh around the bone, she sewed the wound closed. When that was done she laid thin strips of wood up and down and around his leg, then with Glam's help wrapped clean linen around the strips until all the wood was tightly covered and the man's leg looked twice the size of his other one. Leaning back, she smiled weakly at Glam as she massaged her neck, trying to ease its cramping.

"I want a fire in here," she said. "He must be kept warm and not moved. I will stay with him after the others are tended."

A small young woman approached her tentatively, one hand outstretched. "I will stay with him, milady. Will he live?"

Iona saw the woman's fear, but she would not lie to ease it. "I know not. He's very strong. You must pray."

"I will, milady, thank you. I'll tend him carefully if you wish to look at the others. I'm his sister, Mavis." The woman swiped at the tears on her face.

Iona touched her arm. "See that he stays still. Perhaps if all is well, he can be moved tomorrow."

"Thank you, milady." The woman turned to her brother, tucking more skins around him and gesturing to another woman to bring a fire pot into the shelter.

Iona was too tired even to speak, but she nonetheless looked at the other wounded Scots. Some she tended, but most of the injuries were minor and could be handled by Glam, Spes, and Marta, with the Scotswomen helping. At last she returned to the shelter where Dugald lay. She was surprised to see that Magnus was still there.

"Will the waters rise and cover this place?" she asked, looking at the sea.

"Not here. It stays dry even in flooding season." Magnus glanced at her and saw how she swayed with fatigue. Instinctively, he longed to sweep her up into his arms, but he didn't move. He sensed she'd be distressed, and so would her Vikings. There'd been enough war for one day. "Mavis is grateful for what you've done," he added. "And I thank you."

She looked at Mavis, who hovered over her brother a

few feet away. "I really don't know if he'll live. Sometimes the blow to the body goes to the very innards and congeals the blood. It can be enough to cause death. I have seen it happen with lesser wounds. We'll see how he does through the night. I will remain with him."

"There's no need for you to stay here," Magnus said. "Mavis and others will watch Dugald. My home is warm. You can rest there." And he had no intention of letting her leave once she was inside his home. She could rail and scream the castle down, but for the good of the Sinclair clan, this princess of Icelandia would marry him.

She was shaking her head, though. "I'll stay here. I must keep watch over him." She glanced back, seeing how the Scotswomen eyed Glam, Marta, and Spes as they tended to the wounded. "They're good at this. Your people need not worry."

"I think they want to learn," Magnus said.

She looked back at him in surprise. "I never thought I'd hear a Scot admit to needing to know anything."

He threw back his head with a shout of laughter. She'd just insulted him, this brave Viking woman.

Iona tried not to smile, but she couldn't stop herself. The barbarian Sinclair was a strange man. He'd not gone for his sword when she'd smote him with her words, and she didn't have to ask if he'd understood. Whatever else the Sinclair was, he wasn't stupid. As his laughter faded, he looked down at her, his gaze eerily intent, and she felt a strange melting sensation in her lower body. She'd never experienced such a hot, liquid feeling. She must be more tired than she thought, she told herself, and turned away. It would be far safer to tend to the wounded than to remain with the Sinclair.

Finally the last dead Viking was set adrift in his flaming boat, and the last of the Scots' dead were carried up the winding cliff path to Sinclair Castle. The wounded Scots who could be moved followed them.

Magnus joined Iona when she returned to look at Dugald. As she took Dugald's hand to feel his pulse, her knees buckled. Instantly, Magnus lifted her into his arms. When she would've protested, he silenced her by shaking his head. "You can't even stand. You're exhausted, milady."

Iona stared at him in shock and consternation. Didn't the man know how unseemly it was to hold her like this, her feet off the ground? The Scots had no understanding of what was right. She didn't have to turn her head to know that her people were watching . . . waiting. She had only to cry out in protest and there'd be another attack.

"Put me down," she said through her teeth, trying to keep a smile on her face.

"No," Magnus whispered. She was light as a feather, and her body excited him as no one's ever had. Her lips were like frosty petals, even pinched closed as they were. They had the beckoning fullness of luscious spring berries. He wanted to kiss her.

"Sir!" she exclaimed, stiffening as his head lowered toward hers. "Did you not say we are your guests?"

"No, I did not. I said you are my prisoner." Her wonderfully firm buttocks were pressing against his arm, and he couldn't help envisioning her spread upon his bed with his body as her only cover.

His desire must have shown in his eyes, for hers widened with alarm. "My lord Sinclair!" She wriggled, trying to free herself. "You go beyond the bounds, sirrah."

Her movements only further fueled his arousal, and he suppressed a groan even as he tightened his arms around her.

"Since you're a Viking," he said, "and used to the roughest of men, how can you accuse me of—"

"My Vikings are gentlemen," she interrupted angrily. "I'll not listen to you malign my good people. Now release me."

He did, but only because he noticed the giant Glam approaching. He didn't fear to fight the man, but he wouldn't let his people fight again that day. He let the princess slide down his body. "Since you insist on staying here, I'll have my people make you a tighter shelter and get you a more comfortable bed."

"I'm fine," Iona said faintly, though she wasn't. She was hot and dizzy, and she saw two of Glam. His mouth moved, but she didn't hear what he said.

Sensing a possible confrontation, Kenneth moved up to his brother's side. His smile was relaxed, but he kept a wary eye on the Viking giant. " 'Tis a wondrous job of healing she's done, Magnus. As good as I've seen." He lifted his sword a bare inch from its scabbard, then let it drop back in place again.

Glam caught the movement, but he kept his gaze fixed on Iona.

"Of course," she said tartly. She too felt the tension, and blamed the boorish Sinclair for causing it. We are a people who understand healing," she added, then nodded toward the two Scotsmen. "Good day to you, Lord Sinclair. I'll just gather my things and—"

"Milady," Kenneth interrupted.

"We were not properly introduced. I am Kenneth, brother to Magnus, leader of the Sinclairs, at your service." He swept her a gracious bow. "And I shall gladly gather all your medicines and bring them to you."

"I will be staying here with the wounded who cannot be moved," she said, glad it was Kenneth who spoke to her. She could look in his eyes without getting that annoying fluttery feeling in her middle. Though she refused even to glance at Magnus, she sensed his gaze on her. That was enough to set her body to trembling. She hated the weak feeling he caused in her, the barbarian.

"You dealt well on the oars, milady," Kenneth said smoothly.

"Thank you."

Magnus gave his brother a dark look, and Kenneth wisely moved a step away. He'd felt Magnus's iron fists more than once, yet he couldn't resist pulling his brother's tail. "And how is it that you come here, milady?"

"We are headed to the Orkney Islands to our land there," Iona answered.

Kenneth pursed his lips as though to whistle, though he made no sound. "Most of the islands across the waters are ours, milady." He swept his arm northward.

Iona lifted her chin and gazed at the two Sinclairs. "Where I go, the islands belong to me."

∽ 4 ∾

My soul thirsteth for thee, my flesh longeth for thee in a dry and thirsty land, where no water is.

—Psalms 63:1

Magnus couldn't take his eyes off her. She'd fallen asleep as soon as she'd sat down next to Dugald's cot, her body sagging into a twisted position that would've been painful had her slumber not been so deep.

One hand lay across Dugald's middle. Sometimes her fingers twitched over him, sometimes they clenched, but always they touched.

Magnus's own fingers imitated hers and curled into a fist. Anger pitted his innards and he cursed himself for it, but still sensual questions rose like black clouds and taunted him. How would it feel to have those fingers feathering over his chest . . . and lower? How would it feel to loosen that magnificent hair from its braid and drape it over his body? How would it feel . . .

His nipples puckered and stiffened, his loins grew taut in response to the images that filled his mind like smoke, smothering reason. Damn! She'd ministered to Dugald and several other of his men, saving some who might have been lost to Clan Sinclair. He should feel grateful toward her, but instead he felt unreasoning anger.

Gray twilight was darkening to night. Stars flickered as the sky turned to black velvet, no wisp of cloud to mar its fine surface. The north wind had abated somewhat, but there was still a bite to the strong breeze. 'Twas a night to be wrapped in a plaid in one's own bed, or by a roaring fire if out in the weather.

Magnus stepped closer, then leaned forward to touch Iona's bare hand. He cursed softly. She was frozen. The fire pot near the cot gave Dugald most of the heat. Iona relied on the elk skins wrapped around her. Though they were warm, they had partially slid off her body.

He swept his heavy plaid off his shoulders and swathed it around her, then lifted her into his arms. She made not a sound or movement, and her head lolled easily onto his shoulder.

"You'll soon be warm, milady," he whispered. As he started to move away, even his sharp ears didn't catch the faint sound at his side. But he did hear Glam's voice.

"The princess wouldn't like being far from the ones needing tending," the Viking said from the dark area just outside the shelter.

Magnus swung around and stared at the big man, who moved like a wraith in the dark. "Aye, but she's very cold. It could make her ill."

"I could see to her." In the faint light of the stars and quarter moon, Glam could see the Scots' leader's face. Temper had tightened his rough features. The Sinclair hadn't liked his words. That didn't weigh heavily with Glam.

"I'll not take her far," Magnus answered in the same level tone. There weren't many men who could look Magnus in the eye, but Glam was his height, and broader. And Magnus had recognized the challenge in the man's bland tones. But he did not care what the princess's watchdog thought. He wouldn't give her up.

"I'll not see you live a day, Scot," Glam said, "if you try to give her pain."

"You will do what you must, as I will, Viking." He was set on what he had to do. It had been written in the sands. Old Terrill had said he should marry to protect the clan from an attack by the Vikings. 'Twas better than war, and marriage to Asdis Iona wouldn't be the crucifixion he'd envisioned.

Glam didn't break eye contact for long minutes. Then he nodded slowly. "But be warned. If she is blemished, not sailing beyond the Poison Sea will hide you from me. One other sought to kill her, and though he is not dead, he will die. So will you if aught but good comes to her."

Magnus was intrigued by the words, not frightened by the implied threat. "Then, 'tis a scar on her face?"

Glam frowned. "Yes."

"It must have been a mere scratch to have healed so well," Magnus murmured, gazing at her lovely veiled face. He wanted to know more, especially since the Viking looked so ferocious all at once. Why would such an intriguing mark cause such fury?

" 'Twas no mere scratch," Glam said. "It sliced the flesh and cracked the bone. Her skin was torn fearfully, and she could've lost her face or died if not for our good queen Margaret and her healing powers. Our princess still covers her face, though her mother and the holy women took most of the mark away." As though so many words had tired his mouth, Glam clamped it shut, scowling.

"Perhaps I will find who marked her," Magnus said softly, shifting the princess closer to his body. Anger filled him that a Viking swine would act so. "And when was this done to her?"

"She'd had but ten summers."

"And the name of the Satan's paw who did this?"

Glam's lips peeled back, baring his teeth.

"A Scot," he said bitingly, and turned his gaze to the cliff that climbed to Sinclair land.

Magnus stiffened. "What?" He followed the Viking's gaze. "No Sinclair attacked her."

"A Scot is a Scot," Glam said succinctly.

Magnus smiled tightly and nodded. "I think we understand each other. Do you believe I do not intend to harm your princess?"

"If 'twere otherwise, you'd have been dispatched with the other dead Scots."

Magnus eyed the Viking long and hard. "I'll bed her down in a warm place, then I shall watch the wounded in her stead."

Glam shook his head. "There are Vikings enough to answer any call."

Magnus peered into the darkness but saw no one. The warriors from Icelandia were as canny at hiding as were his own men who stood watch. "Fine." He started to turn away, but Glam stopped him.

"I would tell you one more thing. Our good queen Margaret was a Scot, but naught will save you if you do not honor our princess. Queen Margaret hated her people. Our princess does not hate . . . and she hides her fears. She is blessed among us, Scot. Remember that."

Magnus nodded sharply, then walked away to the protected shelter he'd had erected for Iona. Inside, he was strangely reluctant to lower her onto the bed of skins. He wanted her in his own bed, holding her, feeling her hotness surrounding his eager member, which even now throbbed at the thought. She made him hard and wanting. For the first time in his memory, he had to fight to keep the desire in check. Control had been honed sharp in him. He was a leader, always contained. Iona and her beauty threatened that.

The wind was picking up again. He could smell snow, though the spring planting had begun. After laying her on the thick layer of skins, he covered her plaid-swathed body with other skins, then moved back, staring down at her. It was good to know the Sinclair plaid warmed her. Soon she'd have one of her own. He smiled at the notion.

He was about to leave when he thought he saw her shudder. Turning back, he watched her closely. There! She did it again. Without thinking, he knelt down next to her, pushing back the outer skins and unwrapping the plaid. Sliding beneath both, he curved his body against her curved back and settled her close to him. Putting his arms around her, he tightened the plaid around both of them.

He felt a rightness, a peace hitherto unknown to him, in just holding her. He didn't want to dwell on that. Instead, he wondered what she would say when she woke. Laughter rumbled in his chest, but he didn't let a sound escape his lips. He was still, content, warm. For a moment he thought he could sleep.

His eyes closed, then sprang open. The beat of her heart reverberated through her body, through the plaid, and into him. Blood thundered through him and excitement made his being tingle, yet he was calm, serene. The sea breeze whistled behind him, biting at any exposed area, yet he felt only heat . . . and contentment.

Magnus frowned. It was not for the leader of the Sinclairs to feel so. He inhaled her subtle fragrance. She was just another woman, and she would learn to know him as master. It was the duty of women. Tomorrow he'd deal with his own foolishness. Tonight he was too filled with well-being. What was one night without sleep? He closed his eyes and tightened his hold on the beautiful Viking.

Glam saw the way the Scot held her, and he moved so that he blocked the view of any who might dare to look. It wouldn't be easy to kill the Sinclair, but he knew he could do it. He didn't know when, though. For now the princess was warm and safe.

Looking around, Glam sniffed the air, his sharp eyes piercing the darkness. Yes, it was safe . . . for the moment. He could kill the Scot on the morrow, or later. He'd made a covenant to get the princess to Eyin Helga. He would do that, and kill anyone who got in his way. Leaning back against a rock, his thick skins keeping out the cold, Glam slept as he often did, standing up with sword in hand.

•   •   •

All the frosty night the moon and stars lit the coldness, the roar of the North Sea a fitting accompaniment to the icy black velvet. Those who stood watch shivered and pulled their wraps tighter. The air seemed sharp enough to slice the skin.

Morning came with a blast of sun and rising wind. Iona blinked at the slash of light across her eyes, then snuggled deeper into her skins. She was so warm. Perhaps the fire pot was too close, but she was too content and comfortable to do something about it. What was it that nagged at her brain, though? She had to do something. The ship? No! The battle with the Scots. The wounded. The horribly hurt Scot. She struggled to rise, but the skins that should have slipped off her were constricting her, holding her back. She couldn't even free her arms!

"Wait," a man said from behind her. "There's no need to rush. Everything is fine. All your wounded have been seen to, milady."

Iona was stunned as shame poured over her. What had happened in the night? She couldn't turn her head, but she knew whose breath she felt on her cheek. Magnus Sinclair's! His body was the warmth at her back, so close she could feel the pulsing of blood in him. Or was that her own? She gazed down at herself. She was wrapped in the Scot's blanket, and his arms imprisoned her!

"Release me," she said, her lips frozen, not from cold, but from horror. "Have you no decency?" She'd slept with the Scot through the night! Her people would be shamed. She was shamed.

"We didn't descend to indecency, milady . . . as yet."

The laughter in his voice goaded her. Again she struggled to free herself, but again to no avail. "I wish to rise," she said through her teeth.

"Don't fret yourself, milady. You're still fully clothed."

Magnus was beginning to lose his good humor. Despite the agony of wanting Iona, despite the erotic visions that had filled his head all night long, he'd never slept better. He'd awakened content with the feel of her in his arms. She, however, looked revolted at having slept with

him. That hadn't happened with other women. Surely, at
her age, she was used to the feel of a man at her back. How
long had she been a widow? So long, perhaps, that she'd
forgotten what it felt like to have a man in her bed? Or
maybe her husband had not been a cherishing lover. Perhaps he'd been a pig who didn't understand the many ways
of loving. He knew them all, and he would teach her.
Thinking that made his body harden once more, but he
didn't loosen his hold. Embracing her was a special heat,
unlike any he'd ever known. Marriage to this princess
might be a duty, but it would not be a painful one. He was
actually eager for the night when he could bed her properly, in all the ways that would excite her, that would make
her cry out for him, not turn from him.

"Do you hear me?" she whispered fiercely. "I cannot
remain like this. It's shameful. It's degrading. It could damage my sacred vow. Untie me from this awful blanket."

"You're in my plaid, Princess," he said curtly. Her demanding tone had quickly dampened his ardor. "It's kept
you warm the night through. In our land, when a woman is
wrapped in a man's plaid it can mean she belongs to him."

His words either angered or frightened her, for she re-
doubled her efforts to free herself. In her struggle, she
pressed her hips back against him, and he groaned as flames
of arousal blazed in him. He throbbed to have her, to be
inside her, to hold her and to have her hold him.

She stilled abruptly. "I heard that groan. What is
wrong with you? Are you in pain?"

"A type of pain, yes. I'm sure you understand it, milady." He pulled her to him so that she could feel his need.

"Ow! You're squeezing me. Stop that." She strained to
turn her head so she could glare at him. "Have you no
shame? My people will be dishonored by this."

"Have no fear, milady," he said smoothly, though her
horrified reaction to him was sparking his temper once
again. Damned Viking! Didn't she know that in marrying a
Scot she could better herself? He laughed silently at what
her answer would be to that.

"What do you mean?"

"I have naught in mind to shame you, milady. I will talk to my priests. If they say this is shameful behavior, I give you my word that your honor shall not be impugned. The right thing will be done."

He smiled as her eyes widened. They were wonderfully expressive sea-green eyes that he could drown in. First he'd marry the wench to secure the safety of the clan, then he would teach her the ways of loving. Soon she'd settle into being his lady, a Sinclair. It would be an honor for her, and she'd come to know how fortunate she was. Magnus chose to ignore the little voice in his brain that insisted it might not be that easy. Nonsense! He'd found a perfect way to push ahead the marriage.

In the eyes of his priests, she would be compromised by being in his bed. Though he often disagreed with the priests' rigid dicta and ignored those who tried to order him, he would find them useful now. And he wouldn't have to worry that the priests wouldn't hear about it. The clan carried gossip and news faster and farther than the wind. He frowned for a moment, pondering the lewd comments some might make about Iona, but then consoled himself that all slander would stop once everyone knew she'd be his wife.

He grinned. All women were boring at times, even Elizabeth, but he was sure Iona would be more diverting for longer. When he tired of her, he'd find another to warm his bed. For now though, she intrigued him.

"Why do you smile so?" Iona asked warily. Her neck was beginning to ache from turning her head to look at him. And her face felt on fire with embarrassment at the way his hard body was pressed against her. She knew full well what quivered with aroused life at her backside. She forced her thoughts away from the shameful excitement stirring within her and concentrated on what he'd just said.

"What did you mean," she asked, "that you'll talk to your priests? What 'right thing' will be done?"

Amusement and a strange light, that both intrigued and frightened her, shone in his eyes. Understanding jolted through her, and she struggled anew to free herself.

"Unhand me," she said through her teeth. "I don't want priests knowing you were in my bed. Or anyone else." Intent on breaking free of his embrace, she didn't notice anyone's approach until she heard her cousin's voice.

"Iona? Are you all right?" Spes asked faintly in Icelandic.

Iona threw Magnus one more glare, then faced Spes. She tried to keep her voice and expression calm, even as she renewed her battle to get free.

"Spes, go at once and see to the wounded. I'll be right along."

Seeing Marta standing behind Spes, Iona nodded for the handmaiden to leave also. Marta simply stared at her for a moment, then tapped her cheek. Instantly Iona felt for her veil. Her face was uncovered. Gasping, she scrambled for her veil, pulling and tugging until she could get a swath of it over the left side of her face. "Go, Spes," she said hoarsely. "You and Marta must check the wounded."

"I won't leave you," Spes whispered, and Iona saw her cousin slip her knife from its sheath.

Before she could speak, Magnus's brother appeared beside Spes and swiftly removed the weapon from her hand. He grinned down at Magnus. "Everything is well with you, brother?"

Iona closed her eyes, angry enough to scream. Did everyone know she was in the shelter with Sinclair?

"I'm sure it could be better," Magnus drawled, staring meaningfully at his brother. Kenneth grabbed Spes's arm and pulled her away from the shelter, ignoring her protests. Marta followed, shaking her head and muttering about barbarian Scots.

Magnus grinned at Marta's parting remark, then grimaced when Iona pinched his hand hard. She wasn't just irritated now. She was bloody furious. He hadn't meant to remain in bed with her past dawn. Ordinarily, he would have been up before most others, but Iona had been so warm, her body so enticing.

"There's no need for you to congest yourself with angry bile," he said. "The bile will back up into you and you'll have a liver complaint, milady. Nothing happened last night. Your giant was never far from you."

"Glam saw you take me to bed?" Iona asked, stunned. Why wasn't Sinclair spitted through the middle with Glam's giant sword? "Have you invited everyone to see this —this disgrace?"

"Milady, I kept you warm. I assure you that when we bed—oof."

He grabbed his private parts as she brought her leg up and kicked him in the groin. The instant he released her, she rolled out of the plaid and to her feet. She fastened her veil securely, then turned to him. Magnus lay supine, one hand still between his legs as though to guard his private parts. "You, sir, have no honor. I ask that you release my people at once."

"There won't always be interruptions, milady," he whispered.

She stiffened in anger at his implication, but before she could speak, he went on. "I would caution you against striking me again as you just did. I assume you want us to beget children. It wouldn't do to impede that."

Her face flushed red, and she clenched her fists. "How dare—"

"You may use that large bend of rocks as your privy," he interrupted, pointing to a cluster of boulders near the sea. "None will disturb you." Rising, he began to strip off his clothes. At her raised eyebrows, he smiled. "I'll swim in the sea to bathe, milady. Join me?"

Iona turned away and strode swiftly to the rocks he'd indicated. After relieving herself, she explored further until she found a stretch of empty beach. Sheltering from the cold wind behind a giant rock, she removed her bliaut. She laved her arms, hands, and face, shivering at the coldness of the sea.

Magnus quickly finished his own bathing, then dried and dressed again in his kilt and soft shirt. Slinging his plaid over his shoulder, he went in search of the princess. He had no intention of leaving her alone for long. She had too sharp a mind and could too easily plot to escape. He rounded the cluster of rocks, but she wasn't there. Shock held him immobile for a moment, then he was off running.

He leaped from rock to rock, certain that Scots and Vikings alike must be watching him. At last he saw her, kneeling alone in the sand, running a bone comb through her hair. The long locks rippled around her face, their luster rivaling the moon.

She had not heard him approach, and he stood motionless for a moment, captivated by her beauty. Then he stepped forward. "Didn't you know I would have had hot water fetched for you?"

She didn't turn at the sound of his voice. "And would you have given me as much privacy as I have now?" she asked.

He did not answer as she rose and stood with her back to him, clothed only in a fine linen undergarment. It hugged her body, outlining her supple, strong legs and slender, curving form. She made his blood boil with need, and he vowed he would make her feel the same way about him. With regret, he watched as she pulled her bliaut on, then faced him. He saw instantly that she was angry, again. What a termagant she was, he mused, constantly flaming up like dry faggots in a fire pot. She gave him one fiery glance, then strode back toward the encampment. Smothering a grin, Magnus followed her. Oh, she was a beauty. And she was his for the taking.

"There you are, Magnus," Kenneth said as Magnus entered the encampment. "Come see the spectacle of the Viking princess ordering our men." Kenneth laughed, then was puzzled when he didn't see an answering gleam in Magnus's eyes.

"Are our men respectful?" Magnus asked instead.

"Of course," Kenneth said slowly. "But would it matter? She's a Viking."

"It matters," Magnus said shortly. He strode past his brother and eyed the activity on the strand. The temporary shelters had all been struck, and already a line of men, women, and the wounded who were able to walk was winding up the cliff path to Sinclair Castle. In the midst of the commotion was Iona, calmly seeing to the care of the most seriously injured. He strode to her side. "Milady, you will ride with me."

She stiffened at his imperious tone, then turned slowly to face him. "I will not ride when my warriors are injured, Sinclair. I will walk with the wounded."

Magnus did not show by even the blink of an eye that she'd stunned him with her audacity. He liked women with spirit, but he disliked anyone gainsaying him, especially in front of his people.

The chattering and calling of Scots and Vikings, even the cry of the wind and the crashing of the waves, diminished to almost silence. Still as statues, everyone stared at the man and woman, who faced each other like warriors.

Old Terrill, who'd come down to the strand at dawn to help with the wounded, stood nearest. He shut his eyes, calling upon God to temper Magnus's hot blood. 'Twould have been easier if the princess were more biddable, but perhaps the Sinclair needed a woman of such fire.

"She's a beauty, is she not?" he murmured to Kenneth.

"Aye, she is, old one. But she's testy as a wild boar as well, and has fey ideas for a woman." Kenneth smiled reluctantly. "Yet she also has the courage of a man behind that beauty. She's outnumbered, outmanned, and yet she stands up to Magnus like a queen."

"Perhaps because she is a queen," Terrill said quietly.

Kenneth shook his head. "No matter. Magnus will have her clapped in irons in our dungeon."

"I do not think that's where he means to keep her," Terrill murmured.

"What did you say?" Kenneth asked, but Old Terrill had already moved away, heading toward Magnus and Iona.

The two had not moved, but stood glowering at each other, silently daring the other to relent first. Terrill smiled. Yes, the Viking princess was a fitting consort for the Sinclair. He stopped a bare foot away. Neither noticed him.

"I've come," he said, speaking to the air between them, "to see if Dugald could be moved to the castle, or even to his home. It's sinfully cold for the unwell, I'm thinking."

Iona heard the words through a red cloud of anger. She was still seething from the pompous Sinclair daring to order her. Then the import of what the old man had said penetrated her ire. She whirled to face him. "Dugald? I cannot say. I have not seen him yet." Guilt assailed her. She'd been jousting words with Sinclair and not tending her patients.

"Of course," the elderly priest said, "I'm sure whatever you're discussing is far more important than seeing to the poor man, but—"

"It isn't," Iona snapped. She twitched at the veil that swathed the left side of her face, then glared at Magnus. "I will see to Dugald at once."

"Good of you, milady," Terrill said, then turned to Magnus as Iona stalked away. "Perhaps you need a firmer hand with the woman."

Magnus scowled. "And perhaps you interfere too much." He glanced at Terrill. "She has a temper."

"So do you." Terrill hid a smile as Magnus's expression slipped from anger to acceptance to humor laced with ire. The old man sighed with satisfaction. Too long had the Sinclair gone without true hotness in his innards. In just one day he'd been caught in more webs of feeling than he'd known in his lifetime. The cold, calculating, ruthless leader of the Sinclairs had been knocked off his feet. 'Twas more than time for that to happen. The runes and the sand writing had been right, as always. Asdis Iona would make the Sinclair's blood run hot, and he'd come alive. Now he would be more than the leader of the Sinclairs. He'd be a man who would know joy and would revel in it, and as such would give joy to his people.

"I have heard from many this morning," Terrill went on, "that you've compromised the princess. 'Twill be war if you do not wed her."

Magnus sent him a baleful glance. "Do not prate to me, old man, that this was not your plan."

Terrill shrugged. "There are easier ways to do things than those you choose, Magnus."

Magnus only scowled again, then strode off to see to his horse, which had been brought down from the castle stables that morning.

Old Terrill put his hands into the sleeves of his woolen chasuble, hunching his shoulders against the wind. He watched as the princess tended Dugald, then moved among the others, smiling and nodding, reassuring. 'Twould seem that the miracles attributed to Asdis Iona of Icelandia by some of the Sinclair women were not exaggerated. Moving slowly, he crossed to her side.

She looked at him. "Father?"

" 'Twould be an honor to help you, milady, if you have need of my assistance."

"I thank you, Father." What was he thinking? Iona worried. If he knew how she had spent the night, surely he'd berate her. Certainly any of the friars who had taught her would. "There are many hands today, God be praised."

"Amen," he said.

Disconcerted by his serene gaze, she asked, "Are you kin to the man called Dugald that you single him out?" Any conversation about an injured warrior would be welcome.

"We are all Sinclairs, milady. And I am friend to both him and his sister, Mavis. I hear you've wrought great miracles, milady."

"I've had great help, from God and man." She shot a look at Dugald, a small crease between her eyes. "I think he can be carried up the cliff today. 'Twould be best if he were taken by strong, surefooted men who won't jostle or drop him."

"I'll see to it," Magnus said shortly, coming up behind her.

Iona steeled herself. His voice had all but made her leap out of her skin. She didn't face the lord of the Sinclairs, but moved on to another of the wounded.

Terrill watched as Magnus ground his teeth, yet managed to hold his temper. Magnus shouted out orders for men to carry Dugald, and finally the last of the Scot and Viking wounded were heading for the cliff path.

Old Terrill breathed a sigh of relief. Once all the Vikings were up at the castle, Princess Iona among them . . . He smiled, tucked his hands inside his sleeves, and walked toward the cliff path. The North Sea was biting into his bones. He longed for the warmth of his rooms so that he might contemplate the future. The Fates had brought the princess. Now Magnus must keep her. He hurried on, thinking of hot scones with gooseberry jam and warm ale.

Cormac had been hurrying, pushing his horse hard. He had many things to discuss with his nephew Magnus, many directives to relate from their king, Malcolm. And all he had to disclose to the head of the Sinclair family was not pleasing.

As he rounded the cliff head near Sinclair Castle, he saw a figure standing on the cliff's edge, her linsey-woolsey cloak lashed to her body by the wind. He paused, frowning, then dismounted.

As though she'd heard some sound over the crashing of the sea and the pounding wind, the woman swung around, startled. Recognizing him, she relaxed and smiled, nodding her head in greeting.

Cormac recognized her too. She was Elizabeth of Asquith, daughter of Tarquin Asquith, a neighbor and ally to the west. Though he liked Elizabeth—and certainly admired her beauty—he studied her warily as he approached. She could be as volatile as ancient Greek fire if she chose, and although she smiled, he sensed a stiffness about her, as though she held smoldering thoughts in check. It was best to tread softly with the leman of Magnus Sinclair.

"Why do you stand so in the cold wind, good lady Elizabeth?" he asked. I would be seeking my own fireside myself, had I not messages for the Sinclair."

Elizabeth, who'd again looked seaward, spun around once more, grim-faced. "Greetings, Cormac. I too sought the heat, until my woman told me of interesting happenings on the strand." She spun seaward again and pointed down. "I wouldn't worry over your messages, good Cormac. Magnus is on the strand with the Vikings and—"

"Vikings! Say not they are among us!" He brushed past her, drawing his sword as he looked over the cliff. He could clearly discern the Viking warriors striding among men and women in the Sinclair plaid. Although he saw no weapons, no sign of impending battle, the sight of the huge Viking ship with its dragon-headed prow sent chills through him. "Christ's blood!" he muttered through his teeth. "What can Magnus be thinking of?" He swept his left arm in an arc, as though with one stroke he'd annihilate the invidious vision below him.

"Stay your hand, good Cormac. The battle is over. Kenneth and two other ships brought the Viking to heel yesterday. And 'twould seem the prize is the princess of Icelandia, so my woman tells me. 'Tis she who tended the wounded."

"She'd kill them, given a chance, I'll vow."

Elizabeth tossed back her head. "So says my father. I tell you she brings evil. I have heard she did things to Dugald's leg that smacked of witchcraft, when it should've been removed. I pray it doesn't putrify." Elizabeth moved closer to him and pointed down to the strand. "See, even now, Magnus is at her side."

Cormac narrowed his eyes and stared at the woman beside Magnus, then he sheathed his sword. "She's comely, this princess?"

Elizabeth shook her head. "She cannot be. 'Tis said she's scarred down one side of her face."

Cormac smiled. "Then you've naught to fear, Lady Elizabeth. Your beauty is sung far and wide."

She smiled at the compliment, but the smile was soon overtaken by a frown. "It would have been better had she not come to our shores, or that her Viking renegades had been sped to hell. To be sure the woman has prevailed on Magnus to spare her wretched countrymen. They're dangerous and a threat to our shores."

Cormac's expression turned grim as well. "I can but agree with you. I shall talk to my nephew, but if I know Magnus, he will not let them off lightly. No doubt he already has a plan to destroy them."

Elizabeth turned to him, her expression troubled, even fearful. "How can you say so, good Cormac?" She waved her arm at the gathering on the beach. "Does this not make your blood run cold?"

"I fear this not, Elizabeth. You forget that Magnus's parents were killed by Northumbrians, and that Vikings were with them. Magnus will not forget that."

"Well . . . perhaps you're right. But what precautions have been taken? Can we know for sure that there's but one ship?"

Cormac grinned. "You think like a man, fair Elizabeth."

Her lips twitched. "My father says as much."

"I'll speak to Magnus about posting more guards."

" 'Tis wise. I'll not rest well until they've left our shores . . . or been dispatched."

Cormac nodded. "Come. It grows chill."

He helped her mount her palfrey, then they cantered away, sea terns swooping and crying above them, the roar of the ocean growing muffled as they circled away from the cliff.

As the people melted away from the strand, so did much of the noise, until there was only the sounds of the sea and the whirling, screeching terns. Gray clouds puffed and scudded across the ever tossing waves.

Iona finished rebandaging a shoulder wound that had started to bleed again, then stood. She stretched, trying to work out the kink in her lower back. It must be from the awkward position in which she'd slept— Blood ran up into her face. Slept with the Sinclair! He'd touched her. His arms had been around her. Shame and a peculiar hotness flooded her at the memory. Shaking her head, she tried to blot out the vision.

Looking around, she saw Glam and started toward him. Before she reached him, Magnus shouted to him, directing him toward the sling that held Einar. When Glam glanced at her, she hesitated, then nodded. It was better for Einar to have Glam with him. Seeing that no one else needed tending, she started toward the cliff path herself.

"Wait, milady," Magnus called to her. "You'll come with me."

"Thick-headed Scot," she muttered, then turned toward him. "I already told you that I will walk with the wounded."

She would have said more, but Magnus abruptly whistled. A moment later a mammoth black stallion pranced across the sand toward Magnus, snorting and tossing his head.

"Beautiful," she murmured despite herself. Built along destrier lines, he was much sleeker and faster-looking than the more stolid, steady warrior horses. He gamboled like a colt, with a glint of Hades and playfulness in his eyes. "His nose is Arabian," she said, walking toward the animal, "and his wide eyes, but I've never seen his hue among such horses."

"You know horses, milady?" Magnus asked. He was proud of Perseus. When he'd visited the Holy Land several years earlier, he'd brought back his grandfather for stud. The line was strong.

"I have some knowledge of them," she said, "and I've seen the Arabian stock at other times. When I was younger I traveled to Genoa, Rome, and Venice, and twice to Byzantium. 'Twas there I saw the horses." Inclining her head in the smallest curtsy, she walked away, back toward the cliff path. Behind her, she heard Magnus mounting.

" 'Twould seem"—his voice grew louder as his stallion trotted up to her—"you misunderstood me, Princess." He leaned down and scooped her up and across his saddle.

"Will you never stop this unseemly conduct?" Her arms were pinioned to her sides, and she was aware that once again, Vikings and Scots alike had paused in what they were doing to watch. Hot blood cascaded through her as

she felt Magnus's breath ruffle her hair. "You disgrace yourself and me in doing this."

"I think not." It was all Magnus could do not to tip her
face up and kiss her. Her firm backside was pressed to his
thighs, and his manhood strained against his clothing, eager for her.

Higher up on the cliff path the Scots watched. Some
smiled but many frowned. Vikings were dangerous guests.

The ride up the cliff should have been a quick, enjoyable trip. But it swiftly turned to torture for Magnus. With
the slow caravans of wounded all around them, he had to
hold his stallion to a sedate walk, a pace the high-spirited
horse objected to. And then the princess, instead of sitting
quiet and still as a lady should, continually turned in the
saddle, checking the wounded they passed and calling out
advice. With each movement, her hip or thigh pressed
against his already aching loins, until he feared he'd lose all
sense of rightness and tumble her to the ground right there.

He was relieved when they reached the top of the cliff,
then groaned silently as he saw Old Terrill heading toward
them.

"It was good to get Dugald and the others up the cliff
this day," Terrill said, walking alongside Perseus. "They say
a great storm sweeps down from the north this eve."

Magnus glared down at him, annoyed at the interrup-
tion. He had a book's worth of words to exchange with the
haughty princess from Icelandia. "Who says the weather's
worsening, old man?"

Iona gasped. "You'd use such a tone to a holy man?"
she asked, frowning at Magnus. She bowed awkwardly to
Terrill. "All is well, Father, have no fear."

"Thank you, child," Terrill said solemnly.

"Sit still." Magnus ground the words out from between
clenched teeth. His body had hardened painfully when
she'd moved against him.

Iona shot him a sour look, then smiled down at the old
priest. She noticed that his cassock was darned in more

than one spot. Magnus was no doubt penurious with his retainers, the barbarian. Scanning the sky, she saw that indeed, clouds were billowing to the north.

"I hope your castle is high and dry, Sinclair. It would not do for my patients to be subject to the raw elements." She beckoned to her cousin. "Spes! Come. We must see to all the wounded, make sure everyone is sheltered. Glam!" She waved to her protector, heading back down the path to the beach.

"Christ! Be still," Magnus muttered. He closed his eyes, desperately trying to control his urges. Her damned buttocks were caressing his thighs and driving him mad as she swung this way and that, giving her infernal orders. Was this how she killed her husband, by setting fire to his loins every hour of every day?

His eyes suddenly popped open as she hit his arm.

"Put me down! I'll walk the rest of the way."

"I'll take you," he said hoarsely and spurred his horse on to the castle.

"No milk-and-water miss, is she, Kenneth?" Old Terrill said as the horse and riders disappeared around a turn.

"Milk and water?" Kenneth muttered. "Christ's cross, she's more vinegar and piss, I'm thinking."

Terrill nodded. "Exactly."

Magnus was growing more irked every second, as much from the princess's tart tongue as from her body bumping against his as they cantered through a small glen on the road to the castle.

Even his Scots were taken with her. Those who passed them, returning to the beach to complete their chores, glanced at him respectfully, but smiled at her. Magnus realized she didn't know the honor they bestowed on her by smiling, but he guessed she knew how they felt about her saving their comrades. And when she'd taken charge of the evacuation of her patients up the cliff, both Scot and Viking had moved to do her bidding. They cleared the glen and rounded another turn, and there stood Sinclair Castle, poised on a promontory over the sea. Carved almost out of the cliff itself on three sides, with walls fitted to the natural rocks, it was nearly impregnable. No marauders could scale those sheer faces.

As many of the castles in Bretagne were constructed, there was one high tower on the seaward side, then as the ground graded downward there were two more, which formed the security enclosure for the people. Only Magnus and his family slept in the castle itself, but many homes and shops were within its outer walls, so that the people could be self-sustaining for long sieges if necessary.

Magnus let the destrier fall to a walk while he waited for her to comment on his castle. It was one of the largest in Scotland, well built and solid, and overlooked the hilly countryside. Its highest tower could be seen for many miles. She didn't even glance at it, though.

When they passed through the high wooden gates, however, Iona was amazed. A veritable town was hidden inside, with shops of all description and several well-kept domiciles. She hadn't expected such space, yet it seemed as though every inch was covered by people hurrying thither and yon, all clad in the Sinclair tartan. The castle itself was tall and turreted, its brooding stone walls frowning down on the hillocks and crofts of Scotland.

"Let me down," she said. "I must to see to the wounded." A fluttering sensation assaulted her when he dismounted and lifted her to the ground, holding her to his body for a moment. It must have been caused by fatigue, she thought.

Magnus watched her go, standing next to his horse. Minutes passed, and he didn't move until his brother walked up to him, Old Terrill at his side.

"She gets the job done, doesn't she, Magnus?" Terrill said, shivering slightly in the still strong wind.

"She's bloody-minded when it comes to getting her way," Magnus muttered. Terrill raised his eyebrows. "And you're no such thing."

Magnus whirled on him. "Of course I am. I'm meant to be."

"Ah, yes, it comes from being a leader . . . or a princess."

"Old man—" Magnus's hands flexed into fists.

"She's wondrous caring," Terrill went on serenely, "and filled with love, is she not?"

"She's a termagant and a tyrant," Magnus said, his gaze going back to her. She was some distance away, but he could discern the sway of her hips as she walked alongside a litter, directing where the wounded man should go. Her body was slender, pliable, soft, and strong, and he ached to see again that white skin beneath her bliaut.

"I imagine," he heard Terrill murmur, "many men would seek to be in the company of such a . . . kind woman and would want to teach her certain . . . skills."

Magnus spun around, glaring at his mentor as a curse shot out from between his tight lips. "What?" He could picture her laughing, drinking wine, her graceful hands gesturing as princes of many realms courted her. Damn! She was a temptress.

"It was but a musing," Terrill said. "After all, she's a princess. No doubt she had an array of . . . tutors in every aspect of her life. Don't you agree?"

"You're trying to goad me, old man. I don't like it." Magnus's hands clenched again as his gaze flew back to the Viking princess.

"Well, then, I shall leave you to your thoughts, not wishing to fire your temper. And I shall see to all arrangements." Old Terrill turned away.

"Wait!" Magnus called. "What do you see to?"

"Whatever you would wish, my lord," Terrill answered over his shoulder. "Are you not the leader of all the Sinclairs, and am I not a Sinclair?"

Terrill faced forward again, not wanting Magnus to see his smile. He would have to call upon his old enemy, the abbot, in the next day or so. The abbot may not know otherwise that the Sinclair had held the princess in his arms throughout the night. Terrill's smile broadened as he pictured the abbot's scathing reaction to that news. This time he'd listen to his superior's vitriolic ravings. How much more bitter the abbot would be if he knew he was falling in with Terrill's plans, for the old priest knew the abbot would demand the nuptial blessing on the sinful night. Old Terrill chuckled out loud.

"What are you devising, old man?" Magnus roared after him. "Your clever tongue won't beguile me. I know your machinations full well."

Everyone in the courtyard turned to stare at him, including Iona. Her expression was haughty, and he ignored the others as he glared back at her, his ire fueled afresh. Then she turned away from him and spoke to one of his servants. How dare she! he fumed. No woman or man had treated him in such a way since he'd become clan leader.

Spitting frustration he looked around for Terrill, but the old man moved fast. He was already at the small side gate to the courtyard. That made him uneasy, as did their conversation. What was the old man not telling him?

Something was in the wind, but it didn't matter. Nothing would be done without his permission. He was the leader of the Sinclairs.

He strode into the castle. Momentarily blinded by the dimness inside, he didn't see the man standing before the great hall until he walked into him.

"You're deep in thought, nephew," his uncle Cormac said, laughing. He steadied Magnus by gripping his upper arm, then embraced him.

"Sorry, Cormac." Magnus shook his head at his father's younger brother. "Vikings."

"Come, Uncle," he went on before Cormac could speak. "Have an ale with me, and I'll tell you what happened before I visit with the widows." He clapped his hand on his uncle's shoulder as he led him over to the trencher table, which was angled toward the fire on this crisp day. He was happy to see Cormac, who was always willing to tell him stories about his father and mother. He and his brother were devoted to their uncle, the only relative left to them.

"And tell me all," Cormac said. "I like it not that they're on our land."

"Nor I," Magnus said, his thoughts fixed upon the woman outside who succored the wounded.

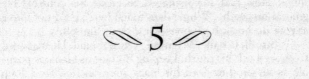

5

*I both love and do not love, and am mad and am not
mad.*

—Anacreon

"What?" Magnus shouted. "How? When?" He couldn't
believe his ears. He'd only been gone from his castle one
day. Even so, since the princess Iona's arrival three days
past, there'd been naught but chaos. Now she'd had the
audacity to convene a court without consulting him. Damn
her! Courts were convened by rulers when a wrong needed
to be righted or laws had to be set down. It was not done
by barbaric foreigners!

"Yesterday, Magnus," Kenneth answered, "after the last
of our wounded was safely settled in his own home." Kenneth watched his brother with both concern and amusement. The Viking princess was certainly stirring up a
caldron of troubles. It could be painful for all Sinclairs if
Magnus got his ire up . . . but it was good to see Magnus
hot again, burning with fury instead of freezing with it.

"It would be a shame to break her neck now," Kenneth
went on as he and Terrill followed Magnus into the great
hall. "And it would cause war. Malcolm would be angered

if his plan to mount a campaign against Northumbria was thwarted."

"Who would break her neck?" Magnus asked. He was harried on every side. It took concentration and great fortitude to run a clan the size of his, but he'd enjoyed the challenge . . . until Princess Asdis Iona landed on his shore. How had she managed to erode his control? He ground his teeth. "Who'd dare touch her?" He'd not allow anyone to break her bones. He'd do it himself.

" 'Struth, not me, Magnus," Kenneth said. He managed to choke back his mirth, keeping his face as blank as possible as his brother fixed his black stare on him for a long moment. Magnus was angry enough to bite through his sword.

Magnus shifted his attention to Terrill. "Did you know about this?" The old man nodded. "And that's what you meant when you made that remark about arranging things?"

Terrill pursed his lips. It would be quite wonderful, he mused, if the leader of the Sinclairs had less clarity of mind, that he might forget a detail now and again. It hadn't happened yet, though. Terrill sighed. "To tell the truth, milord, I'd all but forgotten her abilities in the law."

"Well? How did this come about?" He slammed his fist down on the oaken table. "One of you must know." The hall's great domed ceiling, with its blackened beams, echoed back Magnus's imperious tones. The room was large enough to accommodate a hundred people easily, and many more if they were crammed in. Tall lancets let in a small amount of light, but most of the illumination was from torches set high on the wooden wall beams. The three fireplaces, one at each end and the third on the long outside wall, heated the room. On freezing days the wide doors at the top of the two steps that led into the room from the entry hall could be closed. But in Magnus's time they never had been. He found his castle comfortable and liked it as open as it could be.

Kenneth had been waiting for him when he'd arrived from his journey. He'd heard the laughter in his brother's voice as he told him of Iona's fresh caldron of trouble, though Kenneth had tried to hide it. Slumped in his chair, he glared at the two people he trusted most in the world, along with Dugald and his uncle. Lucky Cormac, he thought. He'd left the day before, beginning the three days' hard ride back to Malcolm's court. Better that turmoil than the chaos in Sinclair Castle.

"I don't know how she found the priest and contacted the abbot," Terrill finally said. "I would guess she had her protector summon them. No one would refuse the Viking. He's a big man, if you recall." Terrill had been impressed the day before when he'd gone to the abbey himself, only to have the abbot tell him that he would be at Sinclair Castle the next day for the convening of court. Terrill had struggled to hide his glee, resorting to scowling to tamp it down. That had seemed to please the abbot, who'd informed him that nothing would keep him or his friars from the court. No doubt the abbot thought to exacerbate the temper of the older man, who'd defied him innumerable times. But Terrill had laughed himself silly all the way back to the castle.

"I remember the Viking," Magnus said impatiently. "Get on with it."

Terrill shrugged. "I imagine they feared not to let him into the abbey. A very imposing warrior—"

"We've covered that," Magnus growled, leaning forward in his chair.

"Ah, yes, so we did. Well, perhaps he used your name to gain entry, Magnus. That would've worked." Old Terrill coughed as the younger man's features contorted with rage. "It matters only that she has convened a court for this day, Magnus." He paused. "The criers have gone forth."

"Without my permission?" Magnus's bellow stopped all action in the great room, and many servants scurried from it, eager to be away from the angry wind brewing.

"It's not necessary," Terrill said in a calming voice, "to ask permission to send out criers. In our clan anyone with a grievance can—"

"I know the law," Magnus interrupted. "But tell me exactly why she convened the court."

"I fear there will be discussion as to the ethics of your conduct on the strand with Princess Asdis Iona. Of course, there might be other points meriting attention—"

"My conduct!" Magnus's words flew around the cavernous chamber like thunderbolts, sending the last servants scattering.

Terrill and Kenneth straightened in their chairs, all amusement gone. For a long minute the only sound in the room was the crackling fire. When a giant log fell in the grate, both men jumped.

Kenneth cleared his throat. "The Vikings saw you lying with the princess, Magnus. As did our Scots."

"It might not be a bad thing, Magnus," Terrill added. "Convening the court to address this matter might stave off a scandal, or worse. You did say that Malcolm—"

"Yes, yes, I know all about Malcolm," Magnus said tightly. The king would be furious if anything upset his plans for the Northumbrian campaign. "Get on with your tale, old man."

Old Terrill wondered when he'd last seen the lord of the Sinclairs so vexed. It was no small miracle that this battle-scarred warrior, described by many as having the North Sea for blood, kept losing his temper time after time. It could give a man profound delight and a deep faith in his Maker.

"Well," Terrill continued, " 'tis true it was not my idea that Princess Iona question the priests. That was her own. She seems to feel she has a right to present her case against marrying you."

Terrill paused as Kenneth made a strangled sound in his throat. Magnus looked as if he'd swallowed an unripe persimmon. His features took on a satanic cast, and when he spoke, his voice was hoarse with disbelief.

"She is presenting a case why she should not be married to me?"

"She is," Terrill whispered.

Magnus drummed his fingers faster and harder on the

heavy trencher table, his face mottled, his eyes as piercing as damascene steel.

Terrill kept his gaze on a point just past his laird's shoulder. "Not that she doesn't have the right to defend herself against charges."

"What charges? Who made them?" Though he asked, Magnus didn't need answers to those questions. He didn't like to admit that he felt guilty for his part in it, for he'd foreseen that the princess might suffer from wagging tongues.

Terrill coughed into his hand. "You were bedded down with milady three nights ago, Magnus. Many saw this. I knew it would reach priestly ears, so I arranged to talk to them." He coughed again. "I had not heard that the princess would do so as well, of course."

"Of course," Magnus said dryly, but he wasn't fooled. Old Terrill had avoided contact with the abbot and his friars at every turn since their return to Scotland. The antipathy was mutual. He'd only go to the abbey if he had no other choice. "Go on."

"Ahem, yes. Where was I?"

"In dire straits," Kenneth muttered.

"Ah, yes. She sent word to me that she'd convened court and that it would be here in the great room." He smiled. "She added that even the Scots must have some laws."

Kenneth smothered his laughter when his brother glowered at him.

"When is this . . . court upon us?" Magnus asked.

Terrill kept his gaze away from Magnus's face. "They arrive as we speak. They will be waiting in the courtyard."

"Sweet blood of Christ!" Magnus smacked the tabletop so hard, tankards and trenchers slid haphazardly.

Old Terrill winced and rolled his runes in his hands, which he'd hidden in the sleeves of his cassock.

Kenneth jumped to his feet. "I'll bring the priests to you, Magnus."

As Kenneth strode from the hall, Magnus leaned back in his chair on the raised dais, staring broodingly at the door. What in hell had happened to the relative peace of Sinclair Castle? Princess Asdis Iona of Icelandia had happened! Wars were simpler.

As he thought her name, she appeared atop the two steps leading down to the great hall, a vision of moonlight and silvery gold.

Old Terrill gasped when he saw her. The runes had spoken of a great white light with a green center that would aid the Sinclair. And that light was the princess, with her brilliant silver hair and vivid green eyes. The old man crossed himself and thanked God.

Magnus could only stare. For a moment he wondered if he'd conjured her up, for the annoying Viking wench had been much on his mind. He found himself on his feet, though he didn't remember rising. She was real, though, fire and ice in flame-colored linen. Her bliaut had insets of saffron-and-cream silk defined with clusters of jewels. Her wonderful snow-sun bright hair was braided and threaded through with ropes of gold, then wound atop her head. Encircling it was a jeweled coronet of her station. From it swathed a gold gauze veil that masked the left side of her face. A gold and bejeweled belt sat loose and low upon her hips, and a gem-encrusted dirk hung from it. Her slippers were scarlet leather, and when she descended the two steps, her finely woven gown flowed out and then settled around her body, delineating every curve.

Magnus smiled to himself. The Icelandic princess was not above seeking an advantage. With her hair piled high she was imposing—and taller than the abbot and most of his friars. His gaze roved over her slowly. She was a goddess. It amused him that she thought her scar marred her beautiful skin. Her veil only added to her beauteous witchery. How could she not know how lovely she was? Had she been married to a clod who never told her so? She was magnificent. Magnus didn't move. He didn't think he could.

He barely noticed the tight-lipped abbot and his friars who followed in her wake. His own priest, Monteith, walked with them. He looked harried, his fading red hair standing in tufts around his cherubic features. Monteith stared at Magnus, then looked away.

Magnus bowed to the princess. She bowed in return. He took a deep breath and nodded to Terrill, who crossed the floor to stand with the other priests. Then Magnus looked back at Iona. "Milady, if you would join me up—"

"No, thank you, milord. I'll stand here, since I will be representing myself in this." Iona noted that the Sinclair's features tightened and his wonderful sky-blue eyes glittered threateningly. If he'd been a Viking he might have been called Thor, after the ancient god of thunder. But he was no god, and it was foolish of her to think of him as such. Still, the image didn't vanish. It stuck like a nettle and was twice as annoying. She lifted her chin and inhaled deeply.

Magnus resumed his seat. "Abbot Thomas, you and your friars may sit or stand."

"We will stand, milord," the abbot said stiffly. His narrow gaze slid to Old Terrill, then on to Father Monteith. "This is a Church matter, milord. Since I represent—"

"Terrill is a Sinclair and a holy man," Magnus said, "and Father Monteith is confessor to me and my family. As such their presence is essential to these proceedings." Magnus smiled thinly when the abbot's nostrils flared.

"I do not cavil with the presence of your chaplain, milord, but—"

"Father Terrill is a priest as well," Magnus interrupted again. "And you are here to give an opinion about the matter in question. You don't dictate family or court policy to Sinclairs."

The abbot bowed and was silent.

Magnus watched as his clansmen slowly filled the room, several Vikings among them. None were armed, as was the law. Not that the Vikings had been given back their weapons. That wouldn't happen until they debarked for Iceland. When the flow of men ceased, Magnus looked at Iona. "Begin."

"Milord Sinclair, it is my intention to leave your lands and sail to the island belonging to my people called Eyin Helga. It is a place sacred to my people and inhabited by

Viking shepherds. There I will start a sanctuary for women and—"

"That you cannot do," Abbot Thomas interrupted ponderously. "Your life has turned away from the Church; therefore you cannot start a nunnery—"

"I never used the word *nunnery*," Iona interrupted in turn.

Tight-lipped, Abbot Thomas looked at Magnus, then clasped his hands and gazed heavenward. "The laws of the Church have been broken. A marriage must take place at once, unless you wish to have your soul at risk. Certainly your reputation is in ruins. You have been compromised, milady."

"I find your words unduly harsh, Abbot Thomas," Magnus said softly. A thunderous quiet fell in the great hall. If he'd cursed or shouted, he could not have gained everyone's attention more quickly. Magnus looked at Old Terrill and nodded.

Iona coughed meaningfully. Magnus glanced at her. He knew it was still her place to speak, but he motioned her to stay silent and nodded again to Terrill.

"Milord Sinclair," the old priest began formally, "I don't often find myself in agreement with our illustrious abbot." Terrill bowed and smiled at the fuming churchman and his frozen-faced friars behind him. "But this time I must concur. I cannot conceive of anything that could give the Clan Sinclair a worse image than to have its famous and fearless leader . . ." Terrill faltered when he saw Magnus's raised eyebrows, the skeptical twist to his mouth.

"Go on," Magnus said abruptly, his gaze moving to Iona. She was bursting to speak, to state her case, to get away to the island she called Eyin Helga, but which the Scots called Eynhallow. It was a hell of a place to get to, even if the craft was handled by his most experienced sailors. More than one ship had foundered getting foodstuffs in and wool and fabrics out.

Why did she seek to immure herself there? Did she not see the peril she faced if she didn't wed him? She'd be branded a slut, a harlot. She needed the protection of his name. How could she not know that? Did she think her Viking royalty could protect her? Did she cast herself above him? She should be trembling in fear of him, yet there she stood, chin high, eyes on him, unafraid. 'Twould be better if she understood her place and adapted womanly ways. He almost smiled at the thought. That would take a miracle.

Terrill coughed as if to regain Magnus's attention, then continued. "The shame is greater to the princess, milord, than to Clan Sinclair. But 'twould be to our discredit as Sinclairs should it be said that a Sinclair would allow a dot of dishonor to touch a lady's name."

The unladylike snort from the lady in question had him pausing. Terrill noticed that Magnus had not taken his eyes from the princess for more than a second or two. When she made that sound, a muscle actually jumped in his cheek. Magnus could soon be caught in a rage. Terrill eyed him cautiously and went on. "Therefore, in the interests of the lady, Princess Asdis Iona of Icelandia, and aware of the danger of dishonor to the great Clan Sinclair, I agree that marriage vows must be exchanged between you, milord, and our honored guest, Princess Asdis Iona."

Once again there was an odd sound from the lady in question, but Terrill's quick glance caught something else. The princess's face had paled as though she faced some terror, as though she'd been given a death sentence. The old man frowned. What was amiss?

Iona gripped her hands together to fight the fear rising in her. Marriage! No. She would never wed. She'd been defiled, her honor sullied. No man must touch her. One man had dishonored her, and she'd give herself to no other. The shame wasn't hers, but if anyone knew of it, it would be laid at her door. In this accursed land where her uncle dwelt, she could be trapped like a grouse in a snare. No! No! No! No man would touch her again. She'd die first. The fear that had always been with her rose like bile in her throat and burst from her in one word. "No!"

Her husky outcry turned heads toward her. Iona was surprised herself. She'd never made such an outburst when a court was convened.

Still, she did not look away from Magnus Sinclair, though her insides quaked. "I would speak."

"Are you done, Father Terrill?" Magnus asked, his gaze fixed on Iona.

"I am."

Magnus rose and held up his hand, palm outward. "I would remind all who attend here that it's proper for churchmen and other advocates to speak at these convenings, and that what is demanded is adherence to the laws set out by just men who inhabit this land. Malcolm, as king, subscribes to this, as do I, Magnus of Sinclair. This I will see to, as leader of the Sinclairs. And as such I will render judgment."

He ignored the princess's gasp of outrage and looked about the hall, avoiding her fulminating stare. "We shall go on. You may speak, Father Monteith."

Iona seemed to swell with wrath. Had her sea-green eyes turned to lightning? he wondered. He smiled at her as he sat back down, knowing it would fuel her ire. It did. Reluctantly he turned his gaze to Father Monteith.

The priest cleared his throat, his sympathetic gaze touching the princess before he fixed on the laird of the Sinclairs. " 'Tis only of canon I will speak, milord." He coughed again and steepled his hands, as though he sent silent prayers into the blackened beams above their heads. "The Church is against the compromising of any lady. Ergo, I must be."

"But 'tis foolhardiness," Iona burst out again, "since I don't feel compromised." She drew a deep breath, fighting the urge to shout at the lord of the Sinclairs. She turned to Father Terrill. "Father, you must understand. 'Tis why I convened the court, to assure all of you I was not compromised. I wish nothing more than to speak of the law and justice. You see, nothing happened."

She stopped as her own words echoed back at her in the sudden silence, wishing she could unsay them. The disbelief, the horror, on the faces of the abbot and his friars made her realize how she must sound to them. Taking another deep breath, she began again. "Surely you can understand," she said, her hands outstretched. Why was she fumbling? So many times in court she'd been clear, cool. Why was she faltering now? "None of this can signify if I am on Eyin Helga. No one from this clan, or any other, will ever see me." For a dizzying moment she pictured that future. Never to set eyes on Magnus Sinclair again for all her days. Her heart squeezed painfully, her blood dropping sickeningly toward her feet. "I have made a covenant—"

"That covenant was broken when the commandments were," Abbot Thomas interjected.

"The commandments are intact!" Her angry riposte had the abbot glaring, and murmuring voices swelled through the packed great room.

"We'll carry this no further," Magnus said, standing once more. "Since 'tis the judgment of the clerics gathered here that such a compromise occurred—and they have the right to state their charges, as had the princess from Icelandia—it's my duty as leader of this land to weigh all arguments and make final judgment. This I do. I must and do concede to the law that a lady should be protected. Ergo, I concede to the arguments of clergy and, as such, must concur. The exchange of vows will take place." He rapped his fist on the table to signal the end of proceedings.

Groans and curses rose through the great hall, but one voice overrode them all.

"Are you out of your flaming mind?" Iona shouted, fear and anger strengthening her voice so that it carried to all clustered within and without the great hall of Sinclair Castle.

Abbot Thomas and his friars stared at the Viking princess as though she'd run mad. Kenneth's shocked laugh choked into a cough. Terrill patted Kenneth's back while struggling with his own mirth. Red-faced, Elizabeth of Asquith stormed through the assembly to the door.

"I have spoken!" the lord of Clan Sinclair roared back. His bellow cleared the great room like a giant besom.

Only Iona remained, hot with ire—and another emotion she didn't try to name. For an endless moment she and

Sinclair locked angry gazes. Then Iona lifted her chin haughtily, turned, and swept from the room.

That night Elizabeth lit the signal fire. She waited two hours for Magnus, anger like a fiery sword through her.

He strode into the hut at last, then paused when he saw her face. "It's not passion you seek, is it, but to berate me."

"Magnus, how could you? She's the enemy."

He nodded. "And how better to conquer than to disarm."

"But marriage? Surely you do not have to go that far."

"The Vikings build on Orkney. The people there are tied to them by blood. That's too close to Sinclair land to ignore."

"But what of me?"

He touched her cheek. He was a bit irked by her demands, but he was used to her high-handed ways. "In all the Sinclair holding and lands around it, I worry least about you, Elizabeth. You're strong and able, and I know you truly understand what I must do." He leaned down and bussed her quickly, then turned away, striding rapidly into the misty darkness.

Elizabeth stamped her foot and cursed roundly.

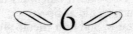

6

*Endure, my heart; you once endured something even
more dreadful.*

—Homer

"**Y**ou must accept the judgments of the clergy, Iona,"
Spes said, eyeing her cousin worriedly as they walked together through the outer courtyard, heading for the cottages beyond. "Our good priests at Kirkwall would agree
with them, as would our lawmakers."

"And I do not," Iona muttered. But she could already
feel that her cousin thought she had no choice. If she were
to marry Sinclair, though, she would be shamed. Even
more, she could lose her life. A husband could have his
wife killed if she did not come to him pure. Yet she didn't
think Magnus would resort to that. There were other pun-
ishments, like banishment.

Her brows knit together in a thoughtful frown as an
idea occurred to her. Ever since the court convening several days earlier, she'd despaired over her dreadful fate.
Now she saw a possible escape. If she married Sinclair,
would she not gain her objective, Eyin Helga, more easily?
Certainly without war, or more loss of Viking lives. It was a

dangerous wager, but she would have to take it. She was a Viking, she could turn this around to her advantage. For could a man deny his wife a gift on their marriage day? She would ask for Eyin Helga.

And if he banished her, she would then try to arrange that it be to Eyin Helga. Either way, she would be where she'd wanted to be, on the barren, windswept holy isle. Her frown deepened as a sudden loneliness touched her, then she forced herself to smile at Spes.

"You're my cousin and dear friend, and all I've done is rail at you since the convening of the court."

Spes shook her head. "You've not done so, cousin. I know you're overset by what has happened." She frowned. "Dugald's sister told me that her brother said the Sinclair was very surprised when you convened the court. It would seem that Scotswomen would not dare." She smiled. "They do not know our ways. But the Sinclair is a mighty man, and it is said that many fear him."

So, Iona thought, even Spes was using the clan leader's title of reverence. The Sinclair. His power was reaching into Viking ranks. She fought down her fear and uncertainty, trying to maintain her smile. She'd never felt so . . . so solitary. "And how is Dugald progressing?"

Spes frowned. "Quickly, though he is too feisty for his own good. Not even Marta can handle him at times, and she does it best."

"At least he is recovering," Iona said, then glanced closely at Spes. "And how is the brother to Magnus Sinclair?"

Spes reddened, her gaze sliding away from her cousin's. "He's a very stubborn man. Not that I see him much, of course. But he sometimes comes to Dugald's to inquire after his health."

"I see." Spes looked alight, and her facade of indifference was thin. Once more a heavy loneliness settled over Iona, and she felt a sudden need to be alone. Though there was but five years' difference between herself and her younger cousin, she felt like Spes's mother. She looked around. "Beyond the trees is Dugald and Mavis's lodge, is it not?" Spes nodded. " 'Twould be a kindness if you would check on Dugald's progress, since we're so close. I'll go to the other homes close by, then join you back at the castle later."

"If you're sure . . ." Spes began, but she couldn't mask her eagerness.

"I am."

Iona watched her cousin's quick passage through the glen. Often she'd heard Spes and Marta laughing together as they talked of the day's happenings. They seemed to have no fear of the Scots.

Another rush of loneliness had her shivering. Rubbing her arms briskly, she forced the black feelings away and strode toward a collection of cottages in the other direction.

She was greeted more openly each time she visited a cottage, and she was coming to like the Sinclair people. And, as always, when she began any treatments, her work absorbed her. Healing was an integral part of her being, and she considered the important follow-up care as necessary as the initial treatment.

By the time she'd visited four cottages, the afternoon was waning. Because it was such a beautiful day, she headed back toward the castle through the glen. Though it was farther than the upper path, it was prettier. Colorful bracken vied with the gorse underfoot. Overhead the new leaves on the oaks were set off against the dark green of the stately swaying fir trees. As Iona strolled along, she picked some of the early-blooming wildflowers.

When she heard the growl she stopped, not sure if she'd heard right or from what direction it had come. She swept her gaze around the area, and went rigid when she saw the red-eyed wolf, larger than any she'd ever seen. Looking for a tree to climb or a high place of any kind, she spied a thick branch on the ground. She snatched it up, balancing it in front of her. It was then she saw the leather binding the wolf's mouth. The animal was muzzled. Lowering the cudgel, she studied her adversary. Gray, matted fur covered its broad chest and shoulders. Despite his menacing stance, he looked as though he were starving. Marks on his head and shoulders indicated he'd been whipped.

"And who did this to you?" she whispered.

The gaunt creature cocked its head, as though surprised by her low voice, then it growled again.

" 'Tis naught to do with you, my fine missus," a rasping voice said from a stand of trees behind the wolf. A black, misshapen form separated itself from the darkened area, and his gap-toothed smile widened when she gasped. "Aye, I ain't no pretty piece, as you can see. Do it frighten you, my fine lady?"

"No," Iona said shakily, gripping the cudgel tighter. The man was humpbacked, and his face twisted to one side as though God had pushed his features off center. He was caked with dirt from head to toe and had two full game bags slung over one shoulder. "If that is your pathetic animal, I insist you feed it. If you do not, I'll take it from you."

"Oh, will you now, my fine lady? That's to be seen." He wiped his one hand on his greasy tartan—so dirty that its colors were indistinguishable from the dirt—and his dark eyes glittered with challenge. Cackling gleefully, he kicked the wolf out of the way, ignoring its wrathful growls. "We'll see if you can take my wolf, my fine lady. If you beat me with the sticks, I'll make you a gift of him. If you don't, you go on your sorry way and leave Geordie McInally alone."

"A bargain, is it?" Iona said, understanding the half-hearted compromise. No doubt his pouches were filled with poached game, and he wanted to be on his way quickly. "And are you a poacher on Sinclair land, Geordie McInally?"

The man growled, sounding eerily like his beast. "What I takes is for me own, and is naught to you, fine missus. Now, grab thee cudgel."

"A moment," Iona said calmly. "If I strike a bargain, I would make it clear how it would be. If I win, you'll care for Sinclair sheep properly, and if you poach Sinclair streams and grounds, you'll take only what you eat."

His dirty face contorted into a frown. "I care for me

sheep. And what I takes *is* only for eatin', ya foolish missus."

"And the next time you see me," she went on, "you be clean, or I'll have my men douse you in the sea." She shook her finger at him, deliberately baiting him.

He roared with anger and charged her.

Iona had banked on that. She'd have few chances with the burly McInally, since he outweighed her by many stone and he had a far longer reach. Catching his cudgel with her own, she dropped her hip and swung about, using her body as leverage. The force of her cudgel, now doubled, arced his out of his hand. As quick as a cat, he threw himself forward and was on it.

Iona brought hers down on his head, a glancing blow but enough to stun him. Then she kicked his cudgel away and put her foot on his neck as he lay spread-eagled on the ground. She kept her cudgel aimed at his head. "The wolf's mine."

"Aye." His voice was muffled with his face pushed into the dirt. "You're a tricky missus."

"You'll bathe when I see you next, and only poach for eating?"

"Aye."

"Good-bye to you, then, Geordie McInally."

Iona backed away to where a length of hemp was tied to the wolf's muzzle and looped around a tree. She gathered up the free end, quite sure that if the animal chose not to go, she wouldn't be able to pull him.

"Come," she said firmly, and yanked. The wolf growled and glanced at Geordie, who was now sitting up. Looking back at Iona, the big bony animal moved around her as though expecting a kick.

"Dinna' let your guard down, my fine lady," Geordie warned her. "He can claw you to death with those paws of his and be glad of it. I call him Devil. 'Twould be wise to use the cudgel on him each time you command him."

Iona glowered at the cackling Geordie and kept the cudgel between her and the animal. It had been a fool's bargain and Geordie knew it. But at least the wolf came with her as she urged it down the path.

"I'll not call you Devil," she said to it. "That would only invite the dark angel to your side. You shall be Thor. Though naming you is foolish since I don't know what I'll do with you." She decided at that moment not to tell anyone about the wolf. Neither Scot nor Viking would hesitate to kill such a beast. Hadn't he already suffered enough?

Iona was wondering where she could hide Thor, when she was startled by a woman's voice.

"You have a dangerous animal, milady." Mavis, Dugald's sister, stepped from a small copse of bracken and bush, her wary gaze on the wolf. "Forgive me if I frightened you. I know you didn't hear my approach, but I feared for your life until I saw you have a rope on the beast." Mavis kept her knife in her hand, however, looking puzzled. "What are you doing with the wolf? Shall I help you kill it?"

"No, no." Iona smiled. "He can have a chance at living. If I could just find a place to keep him until I see if he can be trusted."

Mavis shook her head. "He can't be trusted and he's sore dirty, milady." She bit her lip. "But I do know a place, near a pool of water that doesn't ice over. Not many know of it. My family had a shelter there where we kept our skins before tanning. Now we have a larger place nearer the lodge. Shall I show you, milady?"

That evening Iona was late for dinner. Since the food was usually cold by the time it reached the table, she didn't really care. She had managed to avoid the evening meal ever since the court convening, using her duties to the wounded as an excuse. That worked no longer, since Spes, Marta, and the many Scotswomen were doing a fine job. So this night, and no doubt many nights hence, she'd be eating with Sinclair, his clan, and her Vikings.

She had not intended to be late, but it had taken her

and Mavis quite some time to secure the wolf in the enclosure. The worst part had been removing the muzzle so that he could eat. Iona had been glad of Mavis's help, but she'd still sustained some deep scratches. Fortunately, the long sleeves of her azure-blue bliaut hid the marks.

Adjusting her veil down the left side of her face, she entered the great hall and saw that all were seated. But what caught her attention was the trenchers of food. Steam was rising from them. Amazing.

Before she could move forward, someone stepped in her way. She looked up, startled, her smile hesitant. "Good evening."

Would she ever get used to the comings and goings of these Scots? she wondered. It would seem no one needed an invitation to arrive, to stay, or to go. The doors were always open to any and all, and the only way to tell if the person was family was by the colorful tartan worn. It was more confusing than living on the busy sea lanes that connected Icelandia, Norway, and the Orkneys. So who was this woman who didn't wear the Sinclair tartan? She was stunningly beautiful. Her bliaut was exquisite and molded to her body, displaying her full breasts and curvaceous hips. Though she smiled, her eyes, dark as midnight, were fathomless, revealing no friendliness.

"Good evening to you, Princess of the Vikings," the woman said. "I am Elizabeth of Asquith. As a very close confidante of the Sinclair, I give you welcome."

Iona watched as the full-bosomed woman glanced lazily toward the dais where he sat. "How kind of you to greet me," she said tautly. She read the message in that look— Sinclair and this woman were "close confidants" in a very intimate way. She nodded to the woman and moved around her, intent on courteously greeting Sinclair before finding a place to sit.

Magnus had watched the exchange between the two women, and was intrigued by the myriad emotions chasing themselves across Iona's lovely face. The blood fluctuating there gave it a blush to rival the most beautiful roses in Mercia. He was glad she'd finally decided to join them for dinner. He would enjoy getting to know her better, ferreting out her secrets. He stood as she approached the dais.

Iona saw that he was watching her. They'd seen each other often since her arrival, but they hadn't talked since the court convening. She preferred it that way, except . . . there was always that hot, questing message in his gaze. Even now, across the mammoth room, it seemed to reach out to her and wrap around her.

When his stare scored her from head to foot, then settled on her mouth, a strong, strange need quivered through her. She stiffened her already taut back, facing him as though the great room was empty, as though no one existed but the two of them.

He was so large and imposing, bigger than all his clansmen, who were themselves large men. He even stood out among her own Vikings. Her heart fluttered foolishly when he slowly stood and bowed his head to her.

As he did so, conversations faded away and all gazes turned first to him, then to her. Though she'd often been the center of attention in Icelandia, she felt a difference at Sinclair Castle.

Proud, yet oddly uncertain, she tore her gaze away from Magnus and smiled fleetingly at the assembly. For long moments no one moved, no one spoke. Then everyone there—with the exception of Elizabeth of Asquith—rose and faced her, then bowed their heads. Since bowing and scraping were anathema to both Scot and Viking, that slight inclination of the head touched her deeply. She replied with a trembling smile and a deep curtsy that brought murmurs and smiles to the group.

Uncertain of her place, she glanced to where the Vikings were gathered. Even a white-faced Einar was there, though she could see the lines of strain around his mouth. She would have to order him back to his pallet. Lifting her chin, she glided forward, intending to join her Vikings. Magnus, though, moving with swift grace, intercepted her, taking her arm.

She looked up at him, startled. "Yes?"

"As befits your station, you will sit next to me, milady."

Magnus did not add that he didn't want her sitting with her Vikings so far away from him, and perhaps enjoying their company more. The unfamiliar jealousy was like a burr under his skin.

She hesitated. "But I thought to sit with my people. Perhaps your clan would prefer it too."

"You are my betrothed. My clan knows that . . . and accepts it."

Iona thought of Geordie McInally and smiled.

"That amuses you?" What went on inside that beautiful head? he wondered. That Iona was as intelligent as any man of his acquaintance, and yet she was also so womanly and lovely.

"I do not think all of your people are in accord on that," she said.

"Nonetheless," he said as he guided her toward the dais, "you belong seated next to me, milady."

"I belong with my people," she said tightly.

"I am your people," he said, and glanced down at her.

Iona stopped dead, preparing to blister his hide for his pompous remark. She saw the anticipatory gleam in his eyes, though, and forcibly bit back her words. "I see. Doesn't the Deity become chagrined at your ways, milord?"

Magnus chuckled. She was all but wrestling herself to calmness. Not many men had that discipline. He admired her, yet wondered why she needed such reserve about her, such a barrier. Who'd fashioned that cool containment in her? There was a hidden Iona that he wanted to know. More than once he'd seen her fear, then her courage, which had her raising her chin and facing . . . what?

They reached the dais, and he lifted her hand to his mouth. As he brushed his lips across her fingers, he felt her stiffen. A shadow darkened her eyes. Why had his touch tautened her, as though she needed to arm herself against an enemy? She had none of the sophistication he would expect from a royal woman of such an age. At Malcolm's court and the others, those of Tostig of Northumbria and Atholl of Mercia, most of the women had had countless lovers by the age of twenty-three. It would seem that Iona eschewed such pleasures. Her touch of naïveté pleased him. She wasn't virgin bride, but he was pleased she didn't dispense her favors readily.

"People are waiting to eat," she said in a strangled tone, as he continued to stare at her. "We should seat ourselves."

"Of course," he said, and guided her to the bench. He seated himself next to her, cursing silently. He'd been eyeing her like a besotted fool. He could imagine the comments he would have to endure from his brother on the morrow. "My people are grateful to your Marta for showing them how to use the hot springs to keep the food warm as it's brought to the table."

She relaxed visibly, and he was fascinated to watch her stiffness melt with her smile.

"In a pan of boiling water, you mean?" she asked. "Yes, it's how we do it in Icelandia. Otherwise, we would be eating cold meals all the time, as is your custom." She blushed, realizing her words could be taken as an insult.

He lightly touched her cheek, amused by the pinkness coloring it. "Our food is not pleasing when it cools and congeals," he said. Her discomfiture deepened, and he bit back a smile. He pictured a life of trying to find all the things that would put his wife off stride, that would spark her hot-blooded temper. He knew that Vikings were wild and merciless in battle, cold and unfeeling at the kill. He had not imagined a fiery nature, though, such as Iona possessed. He longed for the time when such fire would keep him warm at night.

Iona stared straight ahead when her food was placed in front of her, feeling she'd been an ungrateful guest. She fingered the fork at her place, forcing herself to remember the rules of hospitality. She might have come to Sinclair Castle as a prisoner—well-treated, but a prisoner nonetheless—yet she was now betrothed to its lord. She would do well to treat him with respect if she ever hoped to see Eyin Helga. She turned to Magnus. "I beg your pardon. I did not mean to trod upon your hospitality."

He grinned. "You have the temperament of a Scot,

milady." Immediately her expression grew stormy, and he frowned. "I meant it as a compliment."

"I am a Viking. I have the temperament of a Viking. None other."

Old Terrill's words about her mother being Scot came back to Magnus. It was clear she hated that, and he intended to know why. "Did you have a busy day among the sick ones?"

She looked up at him in surprise. "Yes. I did see to some of those who are recovering slowly."

"I only ask because you were late for dinner. I thought maybe someone was in duress."

She started, then bit her lip and nodded. Magnus frowned. She was lying. What had she been doing? Was she plotting to somehow keep their wedding from taking place? He had kept a strict count of the Vikings and their movements. Though he'd said all but Iona were free to go, he'd ordered his men to make certain no Viking ship set sail. It would be too easy for Iona to escape that way. He knew she knew of his order, but she had said nothing. What did she think she could do?

At dinner's end, Iona noted that none rose to leave. She was about to excuse herself when jugglers burst into the great hall, followed by musicians and jesters and acrobats. Surprised and diverted, she sat back in her chair, clapping and laughing at the bits of nonsense, applauding the beautiful music. She wasn't even aware of Magnus leaning closer, his arm touching hers. Nor did she notice that she reached out and grasped his arm when one of the acrobats threw the other into the air. He twisted and turned before landing safely.

" 'Tis in Venice that such entertainments are common," she said breathlessly. "I had not thought to see them here." She remembered too the dancing bears she'd seen, which had appalled her with their leather muzzles, their heartbreaking whimpers. "Once my father bought a bear that'd been mistreated," she confided to Magnus, "and we released it. I always hoped it'd found its home."

Magnus studied her, hiding his surprise. That she had

spoken to him in such a friendly fashion, revealing a piece of herself, was startling enough. But knowing that she could look upon the bloodiest wounds with utmost calm, yet be saddened by a mistreated animal, revealed depths it would take a lifetime to plumb.

He looked down at the small hand that clutched his sleeve and covered it with his own. She glanced up at him, eyes wide and strangely shadowed again, and tried to free herself. His hold tightened and he smiled at her.

Turbulent, unruly thoughts tumbled through Iona's mind. None of the light banter that she'd learned at the courts of Venice and Rome came to mind. It was as though Magnus's hot touch had seared every sensible thought she had. Rather than being able to pull back from him in affront, or tease him with flirtatious scolding, she was beset by a strange yearning to lean against him. To twine her fingers with his and let him kiss her hand again. A hot throbbing began deep inside her as she remembered the feel of his mouth on her skin. What would it feel like against her lips?

This unfamiliar yet potent need had her turning to him, tilting her head back. His own head lowered toward hers, his eyes darkening, compelling.

When his mouth was mere inches from hers, he spoke. "Remove your veil."

His voice was so low, she thought she'd misheard him. "I beg your pardon?"

He took hold of her veil and began to push it back. Like a flash her hand was there, staying his. "You're beautiful, Princess Asdis Iona of Icelandia. Don't hide it."

She swallowed over the dryness in her throat. The tentative desire she'd felt had been frozen by dreadful memories of another man's touch. "I've always worn it."

"Why?"

Stymied by the simple query, she could only stare at him for a moment. "I—I must," she said at last. "I would rather not speak of it."

He released her veil, only to grasp a twist of hair that hung below it. "Your hair should be shown, as should your face, milady. Its silver beauty shouldn't be bound in plaits all the time, nor should your beauteous face be covered."

Iona could not move. He had spoken simply, plainly, yet the force of those words shattered her. Tiny shots of flame were running over her skin, through it and inside her. She felt as though she were melting, even as the icy fear still lived inside her. The strange mix of feelings swirled through her. "I must be sick," she murmured.

He leaned over her and pressed his long-fingered hand to her middle. "Your insides are upset, milady?"

Unused to the intimacy of a man's touch, she gasped. "Milord! Think of where you are."

He frowned at her. "I'm in my own hall, being solicitous to my intended spouse. That seems normal."

"Your hand. Please," she hissed, her gaze flying about the room. She was mortified to see some interested and speculative glances being sent their way.

"Please what?" Magnus asked huskily. He was so close, she felt his warm breath on her cheek. "You've yet to say my name."

"Sinclair," she said, deliberately misunderstanding him.

Magnus's shout of laughter turned heads and focused even more eyes on them. "You know what I mean." When she smiled, revealing a dimple at the corner of her mouth, his own mouth went dry. His heart thudded painfully. She might have been a mature widowed woman, but at that moment she was a girl, an intriguing, enticing maid who made him lustful enough to want to sweep her into his arms and carry her to his chamber. Visions of what then could be accomplished danced in his brain.

"What are you thinking?" she asked him softly.

"About war. Between your people and mine."

She stared at him. "And that makes you smile?"

"I was thinking about what would happen if I carried you up that stairway and claimed my betrothal rights this night."

Iona couldn't tear her gaze from his. "You presume, sir," she said hoarsely. When she tried to push back the cumbersome bench, his hand stayed her. "You wished something else?"

"I wish you to smile into my eyes, milady," he said softly.

He was wooing her, seducing her with his strong, melodic voice! She felt out of control, a child facing an ogre.

"Is it so difficult, milady?"

"N-no." She shot to her feet. "I must . . . must do something for one of the ailing ones." Before he could take hold of her hand again, she was past him and off the dais, aware that many eyes followed her. But it was Magnus's that bore into her back.

Magnus watched her go, his hands flexing and unflexing. He had felt passion for a woman before, but never had that passion ruled his head. And never had a woman he wanted refused him. Now not only had Iona fled from him —in his own hall—but the furious pounding of his blood was urging him to chase after her and take her, proving to her and the world that she was his.

"Damn her," he muttered. What sort of sorceress was she?

"Does the Sinclair find the Viking appealing?" a woman asked.

He looked up to see Elizabeth at his side, her hand on his sleeve.

He laughed harshly and called for a skin of wine. "About as appealing as a boar on the charge."

Elizabeth laughed too, and pressed his thigh lightly.

Magnus grinned at her. This was the way a woman should be, not argumentative and warriorlike, as the Viking princess was. "You look uncommonly lovely tonight, Elizabeth."

"Thank you, milord."

Iona didn't stop until she'd reached the kitchen. Then she hurried out and through the postern gate, carrying a cloth bag heavy with meat.

She saw some of the guards eye her curiously, but they

did not speak. She assumed they'd been told to leave her alone unless she tried to get away. Magnus had anchored the Viking ship among his own. None could get to it.

She could see clearly in the light of the full moon, and had no trouble finding her way. When she approached the sagging lean-to that was the wolf's shelter, she heard the familiar growling. She stopped, put down the food, and pushed it toward him. Now he wore no muzzle and his teeth were knife sharp. He gulped down the sizable meal, then watched her as he moved to the water hole for a drink.

"Soon you'll understand that there'll be no more lashings, Thor," she said softly. "Then we'll deal with each other."

When Thor lifted his head and gazed at her, but didn't growl, she considered it a coup.

Tentatively she put out her hand. Fangs appeared, and he began growling again.

Taking a deep breath, Iona pulled back, letting her hand rest on her dirk. "Good boy."

Thor stared at her a moment longer, then lowered his head and drank.

When it was time for her to leave, she spoke gently to him, saying, "You stay here, and I'll be back." He watched her steadily as she walked away.

The animal was a focal point for her beyond her dealing with the ailing and infirm. Though healing gave her great satisfaction and a sense of well-being, she never quite tamped down the worry that crawled through her at being a "guest" of Magnus Sinclair. She did her best not to dwell upon the future, for it roused both bile in her throat and dreadful memories of her uncle.

Nor was she easily adjusting to the ways of the Scots. The Sinclairs were a free and easy people—and constantly around. She rarely had any privacy. And their laird was the biggest nuisance of all. She tried any and all arguments she could think of to convince him that it would be better all around for her to leave with her people. Though he listened attentively when she spoke, nothing changed. She was still his espoused and they would wed.

Usually after one of their talks, with its inevitable stalemate, she hurried to tend to a patient or to try taming her wolf, hoping to put Sinclair out of her mind. But nothing she did quelled his elusive presence. He seemed to be with her always, even when he was elsewhere, and she wondered if she were going mad.

Most evenings she spent some time with Thor. She would rub him with the chamois of a mountain goat, careful not to come too close to the sharp teeth or provoke a blow from his mighty paws, and hum a Viking tune that seemed to quiet the wolf and soothed herself.

One evening she spent a long hour with him, currying him, feeding him, talking and singing in a gentle, low tone. Afterward, she felt more relaxed, and could sense the animal did too. She was stunned when, as she stood to leave, he touched her hand with his nuzzle and wagged his tail.

She left feeling triumphant.

The intelligent animal watched her walk away, then sat down, clawed at its hemp leash with his back paw, and shook it off. Catching up to his lady took little effort. He was well fed and cared for. He'd stay with her. He took exception to other humans they passed, but usually when they spied him they wisely ran, so he wasn't interrupted as he trailed behind his lady.

Unaware of her shadow, Iona frowned as several Scots took one look at her and ran. She'd thought they were getting on fine. She was puzzled when they parted like the Red Sea as she entered the bailey. She was saddened when they scattered as she passed through to the inner courtyard. Hurt and more than a little confused, she entered the castle. She'd believed the Scots liked her, had even reached out to her. But now they hurried to escape her. And she didn't know why.

As she walked through the entryway, she saw Mavis at the entrance to the great hall. When the young woman let out a yelp and ran into the hall, Iona was more than a little perturbed.

Inside the hall Magnus looked up in surprise as Mavis raced toward him, yelling and pointing. An instant later he saw Iona standing at the top step of the hall, poised as though to enter. At her side was one of the largest wolves he'd ever seen, growling, showing fangs as long as his dirk.

Growling as deeply as the wolf, Magnus rose, gaining attention and quiet from the many people still in the hall. Nearly maddened with fear, he forced all expression from his voice. "Everyone be still," he commanded. "Princess Iona, I don't want you to be afraid. Just walk toward me slowly."

Iona heard the growling as she was about to answer Magnus. She looked down, and her hand flew to her mouth in surprise.

"Great Wotan!" she exclaimed.

"Don't move!" Magnus ordered. "Be still, Princess. Kenneth, can you strike from your position?"

Kenneth grimaced, shaking his head. "No. I'm too far away for a clean thrust."

"Strike at him? Don't you dare." Iona put her hand down and, soft rumbles still issuing from its throat, the wolf put his muzzle in it.

Magnus roared with alarm. His body tensed as he prepared to throw himself onto the animal. Viking and Scot alike shouted as the men moved to cut off any escape for the dangerous animal.

Taken aback, Iona raised her voice to be heard over the uproar. "Please, don't be upset. I had no intention of bringing him in here. He must've followed me." She caressed the enormous head. "Thor is a good boy. I must not have knotted his hemp properly, and when he worked himself loose, he came after me. You mustn't worry. He's quite obedient."

"Is he?" Magnus said, not heeding the content of her words as he assessed the situation. She was petting the damn beast as though it were a lapdog! "Stay still, milady. I'm coming for you."

She looked up, alarmed, her hand tightening protectively on the wolf. Sensing her upset, the wolf displayed his magnificent incisors, his growls turning loud and menacing. Gazing at the circle of men closing on her and her animal, Iona had a moment's terror. Would they not listen to a woman? But she'd been used to issuing orders and being obeyed since she was a child. Lifting her chin, she fought the quaking of her limbs and looked steadily at those who faced her.

"Stop!" Her loud command ceased all motion. Thor's growls sounded even more ominous in the silence. "Don't anyone touch him. He's mine and I'm keeping him."

"That's Geordie McInally's wolf, Magnus," Kenneth said. "I'm sure of it. 'Course, it looks better than it did. I could be mistaken."

"Then he's damned dangerous," Magnus muttered, edging closer.

"Stop this and listen to me," Iona said firmly. When Magnus paused and nodded reluctantly, she murmured a prayer of thanksgiving. "He is mine. As Princess Asdis Iona of Icelandia, I claim him as booty as is my right." She glared at Magnus's brother. "He *was* McInally's wolf," she added loftily. "Now he's mine. I won him fair and square, with cudgels."

"Cudgels?" Kenneth gawked at her. "Geordie's been known to kill men with his stick. He was born mean . . . and dirty."

"He's certainly dirty," she said. "But he didn't win this time. I did. Now this is my dog."

"That's not a dog, milady," Magnus said. "That's a wolf." He was still moving slowly toward her, watching the creature as closely as it watched him. She'd fought for the beast! Damn her. McInally could've rended her limb from limb. Fury and fear rivered through him.

"Milord Sinclair, I won this animal, and he's mine. I insist that you and all here desist from trying to harm him." She gazed from the Scots to her own people, then looked back at Magnus, feeling unaccountably shy. "He's quite well behaved, actually. I call him Thor."

There were rumbles of approval from the Vikings. The Scots remained impassive, but ready.

"God of thunder," Magnus said, stopping a short distance from her. If it were Geordie's beast, it would be half starved and half crazed, as Geordie was himself. How the hell had Iona managed to best McInally in cudgels? He smiled to himself. The same way she'd sent him into the sea on the oars. The princess had a host of secret accomplishments. And he would know them all, Magnus vowed, as he would soon know her body.

What more would he discover about the princess of Icelandia? Would he ever understand what intrigued him the most about her—her fear?

She'd evinced no fear when she'd faced him or his Scots. Even seeing McInally could make a Scotswoman swoon, yet she'd taken him on and bested him. But she knew fear. Terror had laced her anger when she'd denounced him for proclaiming that they would wed. And he'd discover why, he had no doubt of that.

"So be it, Princess," he said. "Introduce me to your new acquisition."

He scanned the room once. Swords and battle-axes were lowered and arrows were pointed toward the ground. There was a palpable release of tension. Magnus was pleased to see his Scots had been as ready to protect her as the unarmed Vikings.

When Iona descended the two steps into the great hall, Thor at her side, many moved back. She snapped her fingers and the wolf moved closer to her. "See how obedient he is," she said to Magnus. " 'Tis little I've needed to teach him." She smiled and stopped a few feet in front of him. Putting her hand down to the wolf, she told him to sit. Thor dropped his backside, but to his wary audience he still looked ready to attack.

Magnus took a step forward, holding out his hand. The wolf stood immediately, hackles rising on his back. "As I recall," Magnus said mildly, "he had a muzzle. McInally didn't trust the beast." He stared at the wolf in wonder. The damned creature knew he should run, escape, but he stayed glued to Iona's side. What power she had over man and beast.

Iona nodded. "Yes, he had a muzzle. If you'd seen him, Magnus, I know you would've been appalled."

Magnus felt awareness ripple among the spectators as she used his given name. His own insides squeezed in a warm acceptance. 'Twas only right that she should so address him . . . but in private, not publicly. Still, the Icelandic princess set her own standards, and never had he liked his name more.

Iona saw a tiny smile on his mouth and felt encouraged. "The poor creature was half starved and becoming demented from so much abuse. And so I told McInally. What is more, he'll bathe afore I see him again, and he'll be most careful of your stock, Magnus. 'Twas our bargain."

"You bargained with McInally?" Magnus repeated as several Scots snorted and laughed with disbelief.

"I did, and he agreed to it. So you see, all is well. I'll just keep Thor with me."

"In the castle?"

"Yes, I think so. It will keep things calmer."

"It will? How? I see Sinclairs and Vikings looking for an escape now, and ready to leap from the lancets if need be."

Iona laughed uncertainly. "You jest," she said, but when she gazed at the men, she saw he didn't. Though a few tried to smile at her, none took their gazes from the wolf for long. She turned back to Magnus. "I'll take him outside."

He smiled again, a smile different from any she'd received from him. It held an unaccustomed warmth that fired through her, and an intimacy that set her heart pounding, driving the blood to her head. She must not let him know he affected her. This heat was unseemly . . . unsettling. The man would madden her, surely. She stepped back one pace, instinctively putting out her hand when he followed.

Magnus gripped her hand, lifted it, and brushed his lips across it, ignoring the growled protests of Thor. He didn't even hear the stunned murmurs from the others in the hall, but he did read the shock on Iona's face. He caught her gaze and held it. "You and what is yours are welcome here, milady."

For a moment she only stared at him, then she smiled, a smile that lit the mysterious depths in her eyes and sent a rich heat and want suffusing him. What was this power she possessed? He wanted to be alone with her, and wished all his people and her Vikings to perdition. But they were there, watching, and he recalled himself to propriety. "I would ask only that you keep your wolf from eating the clan. Otherwise, I'm sure they'll take him in strong disfavor."

"I'll keep him under my eye, milord, whenever he is in the castle with me," she said chastely, then he caught a gleam of laughter in her eyes. "You'd better be careful, though, Sinclair. Mayhap Thor will challenge you on the oars."

Thunderous silence fell over the hall as stunned Scots stared at amazed Vikings. But Magnus only threw back his head and laughed, the sound echoing up into the cavernous room. Relieved sighs whooshed through the air, and many stared at the princess of Icelandia in awe.

"I'll be on my guard every moment," Magnus murmured, gleeful that she'd forgotten herself so far as to bring up a subject that good breeding and a good guest would've forsworn. She had breezily crossed the line of courtesy and pricked at the great consequence of Scotland's greatest warrior. She'd chided him, gamed with him, and he'd laughed!

Magnus thought her brash . . . beautiful . . . courageous. Dueling with words with her amused and titillated him. He liked her this way, full of laughter. At the moment she was a carefree girl, not the learned princess of Icelandia, widowed, childless, and warriorlike.

His gaze slid down to her flat middle between narrow hips. Had she never borne a babe for her husband? It was not uncommon to lose a bairn. Yet why had she not spoken of her spouse? Was she in mourning? At what age had she married? Fifteen or younger, probably. His gorge rose at the thought of another man bedding the very young princess. He wouldn't think of that. It didn't matter. She was his betrothed now. They would wed, and he'd let Kenneth produce an heir.

Magnus gestured slightly with one hand, the signal clear to the Scots. They melted from the great hall, giving the wolf a wide berth. The Vikings waited for a similar sign from their princess, then followed Glam and Einar out.

"Perchance we could try again," Magnus said when they were alone. "Is there another sport you'd deign to try with me, milady?" Hot blood rippled through him as he envisioned what he'd like to do with her . . . in his own bed, locked away from Viking and Sinclair and all the world. A speculative gleam flashed in her eye, and he braced himself.

Unaware that she was doing so, Iona moved closer to Magnus. "I would have a wager with you."

"In what contest?" he asked, his voice husky as his body responded instantly to her nearness. Of its own accord, his gaze wandered over her, clinging to the wonderful fullness of her breasts.

Iona's mind went blank as she stared into his blue eyes, which were filled with such fire, she was sure they would burn her. "Bows," she said faintly, the word forced up through her closed throat. He was so large he screened out the room, swallowed all the air, though a breeze drove through the lancets, billowing the heavy tapestries that outlined them.

"Bows and arrows?" He stared at her, not sure he'd heard right. Sinclair bowmen trained in Normandy and Bretagne, were known for their prowess. They were skilled too with the heavy Scottish broadsword. The thousand men Magnus could call to arms were considered as highly trained as any in the known world. Only the Vikings could match them with sword and cudgel, but the Scots were superior to all, even the Anglians, with the bow. Their warrior powers had turned many battles in their favor, and their leader was considered the strongest and best of all.

"Did you not know that my people excel at such?" he

asked, offering her a way out. He was more than a bit chagrined she had not heard of him.

She looked up at him challengingly. "How poor-spirited you are, milord, that you'd think a Viking would undermine you by choosing a contest in which you're not skilled. We're not so rag-mannered as to need advantage, milord. It shall be even odds. Does that suit you?"

He inclined his head, blood thundering through him. Her eyes were jewels, her skin precious alabaster, and wild roses colored her cheeks. "And the wager?"

Iona swallowed, her courage failing her for a moment. "That I go to Eyin Helga on my own, with my ship, and—" She faltered at the naked rage that leapt into his eyes.

"Our marriage will take place, Princess," he said, his voice rock hard. " 'Twill not be lost or won on a wager."

"You mishear me, milord." Her voice rose with anxiety. Thor nudged her, his growls turning threatening again, and she realized her tone had alarmed the beast. "No, Thor. Sit." She patted the animal, glad to look down at it while she tried to gather her thoughts. Taking deep breaths, she looked up at Magnus again. "My wager was for a measure of freedom to carry out my covenant, not to break the law that has been sanctioned." She glanced down, unable to hold his gaze. Once he knew her shame, he'd be glad to get rid of her, to Eyin Helga or to hell.

"The contest will take place. Tomorrow," he said abruptly, and strode from the room.

Iona looked after him, then down at the wolf. "He does not countenance either of us, Thor."

The wolf pushed his muzzle into her hand, and she patted him absentmindedly, her mind on the leader of the Sinclair clan.

The growls of the animal alerted her to the approach of someone from behind her. She turned.

"Excuse me, milady," a man said, stopping before her. "I hesitate to intrude on your solitude."

She studied the man, recognizing him from when she'd first arrived at the castle. "You're Cormac, uncle to Magnus

Sinclair." She smiled when he bowed from the waist, his hand over his heart.

"Cormac Sinclair at your service, milady. Though I was not at the convening, I heard of what passed and have been wanting to tell you that you deserve every honor for your conduct. I but arrived back here this evening, and would've come forward earlier, but I have a healthy respect for wolves."

She laughed softly.

Cormac shook his head. "My nephew should not have gone along with the abbot . . . a stuffy man at the best of times."

"As are many of his confreres," Iona said.

"I agree." His smile faded. "Milady, I would that you would count me as a friend. And I will talk to my nephew further about this coming nuptial." He hesitated. "I could see that you did not wish it."

Startled, Iona stared at him, disappointment and hope warring in her. "Can something be done? I thought it certain, with the blessing of Church and king."

He took her hand and bent over it, just touching his lips to the back of it. "We can but try."

"Thank you," Iona said, feeling warmed by his kindly smile.

7

God always pairs off like with like.
—Homer

It had turned into a circus! Iona fumed. And Magnus Sinclair, damn his hide, was responsible. Pausing at the top of the glen, she scanned the growing collection of people below her. She had a good horse under her, a fleet-footed gelding with a snub Arab muzzle, wide shoulders, and long, strong flanks. For a moment she contemplated making a run for it, but not even her mighty steed could swim the Pentland Sea to Eyin Helga.

Did he think her a jester who would be entertaining his Scots this day? Her determination to best him hardened in her.

The sun shone brightly. The strong breeze off the Pentland Sea swept the clouds away like a giant besom. The glen was wide and gently curved on both sides, its wide flatness bisected by a twisting rivulet and extending to a croft. The grass was coarse, but there was no bracken to catch man or horse. Stones were piled in conical cairns between stretches of stone fencing, ostensibly to regulate grazing, but also to deter attackers.

On the hillocks Vikings and Scots had gathered. The women had made pasties, rounds of flaky dough filled with succulent ground meat, taties, and herbs. Steam rising from the hole in the middle of each one wafted over the crowd, making more than one mouth water.

For drink, the bitter dark ales brewed by the Scots were passed from man to man in the sheepskin casks in which they'd been stored. The stronger brews, fruited and malt, made by the monks, had been brought in their copper-lined wooden kegs, hammered copper binding them top, middle, and bottom.

Iona cantered down into the glen, looking around wide-eyed. Many of those gathered wore the vivid red, green, and blue plaid of the Sinclairs. But other mixes of colors assaulted the eyes. There were blacks and reds, blacks and greens, yellows and blacks, yellows and white and red, and all other hues intersecting and crossing. Who were all these people? Iona wondered, reining in her horse. She sat motionless, searching for anyone she knew, then the sound of approaching hoofbeats had her turning. Magnus was cantering up to her on Perseus.

"Milady," he said formally, bowing to her.

"Milord." She nodded in return, then swept an arm, indicating the crowd. "Who are these people?" she asked in exasperation.

"They are of clans friendly to us who've come to see the prowess of the Icelandic princess."

"But how did they know to come? We've but settled this between us."

His lips parted in a smile. "Words travel faster than the birds here in the Highlands, lass."

Iona looked away in confusion. His casual form of address, when he'd previously always called her "milady," sounded as intimate as a touch. She was relieved when he gestured for her to precede him along the rock-strewn path, and she could hide her bafflement from him.

Magnus deliberately rode behind her, loving the sweet way her body swayed in rhythm with her horse. The gelding would be one of his gifts to her when they wed. And today he would solidify his plan. For all her skill, he was quite sure she couldn't outshoot him. But fair or foul he'd set his claim on her this day.

Father Monteith watched as the beautiful woman and handsome man rode together. People gave way before them, while others rushed forward to get a better look at the captivating Icelandic princess. An unusually mellow sea breeze wafted over all, carrying the light chatter and laughter of the people into the air to mix with the thud and clatter of horse and weapon. The cacophony was homey, festive. An abundance of Sinclair tartans fanned the air with a large scattering of other vivid plaids. The priest turned to the Viking at his side, forcing a smile. He wasn't certain how to behave with this giant called Glam. That he was devoted to his princess there was no doubt. The man was never far from her side and he rarely took his gaze off her.

"They make a royal pair, do they not, my son?" Father Monteith said heartily. "I think they will be happy."

Glam reluctantly turned his gaze from Iona and studied the priest. He saw only warmth in the man's eyes, not the haughty coldness of the abbot and some of his friars. "If 'twere not so, his life would be forfeit, Father."

Father Monteith's eyes widened. Had the Viking just threatened Magnus? On Sinclair land? No, it could not be. None would dare so. The priest glanced sideways at the giant. Glam's grim visage hadn't changed. In fact, his features always had the same placid menace. The priest was confused. He sensed that Glam would kill without a qualm, but he did not fear him.

" 'Tis a fine gathering, wouldn't you say?"

Glam glanced at the huge assembly and nodded shortly.

"The good people smile and laugh as though at a festival," the priest went on gamely. "Our people and yours are eager to be part of a happy occasion."

Glam stared down at him. "Our princess means to outshoot your laird."

The priest smiled weakly. "But 'tis good fun, all in all."

He cleared his throat, forcing a wider smile. "Riding with the wolf at her side, the princess presents a glorious sight."

The truculent Viking said nothing. "She must have a brave, kind heart," Father Monteith added. "Not many would do more with Geordie McInally's tattered beast than run him through."

Glam nodded, his narrow gaze on the gray monster that trotted next to his mistress's horse. "I've offered to kill it for her," he said. "She'll have none of it. Her heart's too soft."

Father Monteith nodded, wondering what he could possibly say next. He longed to ask the Viking if he thought the nuptials would be soon, but dared not. 'Twould seem strange coming from the Sinclair priest. And he had yet to hear a single Viking mention the wedding. Perhaps they believed it would never happen. No, 'twould be best if he didn't mention it. He cast one last smile at Glam, then fixed his attention on his laird and the princess.

Magnus had his gaze on the princess and didn't notice until his stallion snorted and tried to balk that another had crossed his path. He frowned, then smiled crookedly at his comely assaulter. Elizabeth rode a white destrier given her by an indulgent father.

"Elizabeth," he greeted her. "Would you imperil yourself?"

Her tinkling laughter brought Iona's head around. Elizabeth caught the quick, tight glance and smiled winningly. "Milady of Icelandia, you must forgive old friends for their informal greetings. Magnus and I have been friends since my babyhood."

Iona nodded, then turned back around. Her gelding's gait quickened, and she soon put a distance between herself and Magnus.

He looked after her for a moment, annoyed that she'd not waited. Then he glanced back at Elizabeth, noting her mischievous smile. "You were always one not to let the dust lie, Elizabeth."

Her smile faded, and a look of pleading sadness filled her lovely eyes. "I feel abandoned, Magnus. I've not seen you these many days."

Caught between amusement and irritation, he edged his stallion closer. "And milady knows full well that I am betrothed and that it's proper for me to be seen in the company of my intended."

Elizabeth pouted. "And what of me, Magnus Sinclair? Am I to be thrown to the wolves?"

Magnus was anxious to get to Iona, who'd not looked his way since she rode ahead. "If you have patience 'twould serve you better."

"I tell you I have little, Magnus."

He shrugged. " 'Tis my best advice, milady." He turned his horse and cantered after Iona, scowling. Women could be a bother.

Iona rode to the center of the glen and dismounted. She removed her quiver from where she'd tied it to the saddle, trying not to hear the talk around her, forcing herself not to look back at Magnus in conversation with the beauteous Elizabeth. Fury, pain, and a fight to control her feelings had her quaking inside. For a moment she wondered if she should notch an arrow and let fly at the leader of the Sinclairs. Biting her lip, she forced herself to concentrate on checking her arrows. She'd win the day. She vowed it.

Sudden laughter startled her, and she gazed at the throng. She had not expected such a mass of people. Shakiness assailed her. It was a fool's bargain she'd struck. Did all these people know what was at stake? Surely Magnus hadn't told anyone. But why, then, was there such a gathering?

Magnus rode up behind her and dismounted from his giant black, who pranced and pawed the ground. Iona seemed unusually pensive. Was she having second thoughts? He had no intention of letting her back down, or of letting her win their contest, and he wanted plenty of witnesses to see that he won.

Would he always have to wager every point with his wife? he wondered, then smiled grimly. So be it. Even if by some ignoble fluke he didn't win this time, he had no intention of letting her get away, by herself, to Eynhallow. He'd wed her and take her there himself. Though what in hell she'd thought she'd do on that godforsaken isle he couldn't fathom. But either way, no matter what it took, she'd be his. It was his duty to care for and protect her; it was her duty to obey him and seek his counsel. That he wanted more from her he didn't dwell on. He had love enough from Elizabeth. He didn't need Iona's love.

Iona was so lost in her turbulent thoughts, she didn't notice Mavis standing by her side until the Scotswoman spoke.

"Milady, would you slake your thirst?"

Startled, Iona looked up, then forced a smile. "Thank you kindly, Mavis." She took the skin and drank the fresh cool water, redolent of mint and strawberry.

Mavis glanced around, then leaned toward Iona. "There are those of us who've wagered for your win, milady," she said shyly.

"Wagered?" Taken aback, Iona repeated the word more loudly than she intended. She saw Magnus standing nearby, looking at her curiously. When he walked over to join her, she whispered, "Did you know that there are wagers on us?"

Magnus did indeed know. Iona had befriended a great many Sinclairs, and he knew that more than one of them, including his warriors, had wagered on her success.

"It's the way of it," he said calmly, liking the way the blood tinted the satiny skin of her face. More and more she aroused him, more and more he wanted her with him, her bare skin touching his. "Scots wager on contests."

"So do Vikings," she said hotly. "But I had no idea this was to be a circus."

He shrugged. "Hardly that, milady. 'Tis but a diversion for the clan and—"

"And others as well, it would seem." She nodded at a passing woman who wore a blue and green tartan.

"Friends are always welcome on Sinclair land. It's the poachers and renegades we war against, milady, not those wishing for diversion."

His reproachful look was just a mask, Iona knew. Fury sliced through her. How dare he put on such a farce, insinuating that she would not want the people to have entertainments . . . and while he was sporting himself with his leman. There were plenty of servants in the castle who'd been happy to point out the special place Lady Asquith had in Sinclair's life.

Damn him. His words challenged her to withdraw. That she wouldn't do. "You seem to be such a kind, considerate leader," she said bitingly. "How is it your fame hasn't spread across the world, milord?"

" 'Tis a mystery to me, Iona," he said.

His very personal use of her name—for the first time— ran over her skin like silky water, making her actually shiver. She rounded on him angrily, then realized Mavis was still standing there, cheeks pink, eyes averted, a witness to their argument. "I am sure this will prove an interesting day," she said through clenched teeth.

"To be sure," he said, his deep, resonant voice still irritatingly mild. She was quite sure she'd heard amusement in his tone too, though his expression was bland.

"Then we'd better get on with it," she said loudly.

"Oh, we can take our time. There'll be latecomers, I'm sure." Magnus smiled benignly when he saw her eyes narrow, her fists clench. Anger trembled on her lips, but she bit it back and nodded tautly. Putting her off balance was such a delightful diversion. She was now looking forward to this contest with all the eagerness of someone facing the executioner's ax.

"So, milady," he went on, "what say you to the many who've wagered on you?"

"That I had not thought to find such wisdom among

the Scots," she said acerbically. Mavis turned to go, but
Iona took hold of her arm. "And will they be punished for
doing so?" She lifted her chin when those sky-blue eyes
darkened and Magnus scowled darkly.

She'd just insulted him and his leadership. All knew
that Scots, unlike the Northumbrians, Mercians, and Anglians, were free, able to make choices and speak out. And
his Sinclairs embodied that freedom. This haughty princess
deserved a thundering scold for implying anything else. He
opened his mouth to deliver that scold, yet said nothing.
He was loath to bring any darkness to those sea-green eyes.
"Scots think for themselves," he said by way of answer,
"and wager their own way."

She didn't answer, but reached for the skin of water
and took another long draft. "The taste of fruit and mint is
quite good, Mavis."

"Our clan flavors the water, milady, though we do have
sweet springs."

Iona was going to comment when she looked past Mavis and saw the woman's brother. Her eyes widened.
Dugald was suspended between two trees in a sling of sorts.
"Should he be here? He's still liable to drafts because of his
weakness due to his wounds." She frowned with irritation
and concern.

"Aye, milady, and so I've told him, but my brother is a
mulish sort." Mavis frowned. "If 'twere not for Spes and
Marta insisting that he stay put, he'd be back at our laird's
side, working with the men." Mavis shook her head.
"They're the only ones he'll listen to, milady . . . especially Marta."

"Your brother is a bothersome patient, Mavis?" Iona
asked, looking back at Dugald. Marta was there, glaring
down at her patient. Yet as Iona watched, Marta's expression softened and she bent down to tuck a tartan around
Dugald's shoulders.

Heaven help them! Iona thought. First Spes. Now
Marta. Glancing over to where several Scotsmen and a few
women gathered, she saw Kenneth—tallest among the

men—and Spes. They were gazing raptly at each other, seemingly unaware of anyone else.

"Yes, he is bothersome, milady," Mavis answered her. "Spes, Marta, and milord Kenneth are the only ones who can make him do as he's bid. 'Tis truly wondrous to see, milady."

"I'm sure it is," Iona murmured.

Mavis smiled widely. "Milady Spes has told us all many tales of a great warrior called Grettir, milady. Wondrous exciting they are. They are very like our great tales of bravery."

Iona was about to answer, when Magnus touched her elbow. He too had been studying the two couples. "I fear my chief lieutenant is taken with your cousin. Are all Viking women daughters of Lilith?" His fingers traced over her forearm, and he regretted the linen sleeve that covered her soft skin. Yet even that small caress could harden his body. Princess Asdis Iona had too much power. He wouldn't let her see that.

"None of us are daughters of Lilith," she said, averting her face.

"You dissemble, milady," he whispered, leaning over her and inhaling her scent. "You have the sweetness of wildflowers! Herbs! All the rich spices of Cathay are in you. You woo me greatly, like the witch Circe of Homer's tale."

"Nonsense." Iona's voice rose in consternation. She wanted to run, but her feet were rooted. Cowardice!

"Have you a cold, milady?" Mavis turned solicitously. "You sound frightful hoarse. Warm saltwater gargle is good, milady."

"Yes, do try that," Magnus whispered.

She felt Magnus's breath on her face and she turned to stone, though her heart beat hard enough to break through her chest. How dare he dally with Elizabeth and then try to seduce her?

"The sun is in a good position for shooting," she managed to say, glancing up at the sky.

He moved even closer. "You'll not win, Iona," he murmured in her ear. "Prepare for your wedding, and then my company when you journey to Eynhallow."

She turned from him, cold perspiration coating her body. "Where's the target?" She tried to walk away, but his fingers tightened around her forearm. The man was a warlock. How else could he wield such power over her?

He leaned down, standing behind her, and pointed, his arm touching her shoulder. "See? Down the glen, in the center of the croft." She smelled of mint and strawberry and he wanted to put his tongue in her mouth and taste more deeply of her and her wonderfully flavored mouth. Her hair had a spicy scent, reminding him of the hardy wildflowers and heather that grew among the rocks and along the cliffs. He wanted her, all of her, to taste, to take. And the fullness of his desire angered him. Was she a witch from Icelandia? No matter. She'd be his witch, but she'd be in his power, not the reverse.

"Y-yes, I can see it." Again she tried to move away, but he kept hold of her. "We should get started . . . get it over with . . . then leave."

Why didn't he release her? He was bewitching her. She felt faint, weak, longing to turn into his arms and let him take care of her.

The man was a devil! Let him keep the lush Elizabeth. She'd have her free access to Eyin Helga. Once there she'd soon forget him. Iona ignored the painful squeezing of her insides that told her Magnus Sinclair would be hard to forget.

Magnus knew she was desperate to get away from him, but he held her a moment longer. He loved her passion, the passion he'd first discerned in her that night on the strand. He'd grown certain since then that she was unaware of it, and wondered if her husband had been an unfeeling oaf. He knew from talking to wives that many men thought a woman's satisfaction was not necessary for a man's enjoyment. Magnus knew different, and so he'd teach his wife. But first he had to win this contest—and then he'd insist she set the wedding date.

He released her arm and smiled when she immediately

moved away from him. Head held high, her quiver over her shoulder, she strode into the middle of the glen.

When a great cheer went up, she faltered, her eyes widening. She gazed around her at all the people, as though she wasn't sure the recognition was for her. Smiling tentatively, she lifted her hand in acknowledgment. The cheer went on, then became deafening when Asdis Iona, princess of Icelandia, sank into a deep curtsy.

"Watch your back, Magnus," Kenneth said, walking up beside him. "She's won our people, I'm thinking."

"So she has." Magnus stared at her, then followed her, his long strides swiftly covering the grassy area.

Iona knew he was at her back when the cheers became unfettered roars of approval. Magnus Sinclair was highly esteemed by his clan and friends. When he took her hand and laid it on his arm, she didn't pull back, but neither did she look at him.

The walk down the center of the glen and across the croft seemed centuries long to Iona. She could feel the throb of Magnus's blood through his soft cotton shirt, could feel his warmth reaching out to ensnare her. At one point she felt like running to where they'd take their stance, but forced herself to maintain the dignified pace. She must never let him see the wild need growing ever stronger within her.

Two sets of eyes followed the pair, their hatred equal in strength, though well hidden. The Sinclairs must not know there were spies among them. That even as they anticipated the festival, others were plotting the downfall of the most powerful leader of the Highlands the most potent ally of Malcolm.

No, it wouldn't do for Magnus Sinclair to become even more powerful, as he would through an alliance with Princess Asdis Iona of Icelandia. If the Sinclair had the Vikings at his beck and call, none could gainsay him, not even Malcolm. That could not happen.

.   .   .

"We'll stand here, love," Magnus said to Iona as they reached the spot from where they would shoot. The endearment came easily to his lips, surprising him. He'd used no love names with any woman, but the Icelandic princess evoked one easily.

"I am not your love," she said tightly. "Have you no sense of decorum? What if someone heard you?"

He shrugged, masking his irritation. Where had she gotten her misbegotten ideas of decorum? And why in hell was she so fearful of her reputation? She was a princess of Icelandia, a widow in good standing, or if not, he'd never heard any different. "Today's a festival. Enjoy it."

She glared at him. "Is that an order, milord?"

"Must it be?" He almost smiled, liking it when her eyes turned the icy green of the North Sea. Then he wondered how many men had told her how lovely she was, how many had feasted on her as he planned to do and his amusement vanished.

They faced each other, taut, inflexible, neither noticing the man approaching them.

"Good morrow, milady," Old Terrill said smoothly. He ignored his laird's expression, clearly revealing his displeasure at being interrupted, and scanned the sky. "The heavens are most blue this day. And the bite of wind from the sea does not have as sharp teeth as its wont. The shoot should go well."

"Good day to you, Father," Iona said. An idea suddenly struck her, a plan for delaying the wedding. "Father," she went on quickly, "it was always a wish of my parents that the priests of Kirkwall attend me if I marry. I was wondering if 'twould be permissible for me to contact them. Or you could, if you deemed that more suitable." She knew that the church at Kirkwall was empty of all but a few friars. The Kirkwall priests would now be making their annual pilgrimage to Rome, which took months.

"Why, milady," Terrill said, " 'tis most gratifying that you request this of me. I'll send word at once."

Magnus studied Iona closely. He didn't like the eager light that sprang to her eye. There was trickery here. "No, Terrill," he said. "I will send word." He waved an arm and a man trotted to his side. Magnus turned away, whispering.

Iona tried not to show her jubilation. Weeks, mayhap months, could pass before they found the priests of Kirkwall as they walked from Bretagne to Rome. And she'd have time to persuade Magnus to let her embark for Eyin Helga while they waited. Once there, she could find excuse after excuse not to return. Yes, it was a fine plan. Elated, she turned to the priest, beaming.

"You seem in fine fettle, milady. May your bow be true," Terrill said impulsively.

Magnus finished instructing his clansman. As the man ran for his horse, Magnus looked at Terrill.

"So, old man, are you telling me that you too have wagered against me?" He stared down his nose at the elderly priest, aware that Iona had stiffened.

Red ran up Terrill's face, and he fidgeted, his gaze darting to the Icelandic princess.

She smiled. "Ignore Magnus Sinclair, Father. He but teases you."

Terrill was taken aback at her assessment, and shifted his gaze back to Magnus. Not even when he'd been a child, a most serious heir apparent to the Clan Sinclair, had Magnus ever deigned to tease. He could relax with his men at times, laugh, drink, and wrestle, and he could flirt, dally at court. But teasing and playing were unknown to him until a woman who could run the oars, battle with him at a convening of the court, and challenge him to a shoot came rampaging into his life. Aye, things were changing at the castle. The Sinclair was touched to his soul, and he didn't even know it.

Terrill smiled faintly. "Teasing, is he?"

"It's time," Magnus said shortly, then beckoned to an attendant.

"We're ready, Timon." He turned back to Iona. "Shall we begin, milady?"

"I'm ready," Iona said.

As was courtesy, Magnus would let his guest shoot first. He hid his surprise at the bow Glam brought to her. Magnus had assumed she would use the small hunting bow over her shoulder. The one handed to her, though made of the same fine hardwood, was much bigger. It was not as large or as strong as his own, but it was a worthy weapon, and every bit as well made.

They listened to the ritual instructions of the one Viking and the one clansman who'd serve as referees. Then they parted and took their assigned places.

When Iona fired her first shot, the sounds of the assembly rose in lengthy cries and sighs. She was a bit off center.

Magnus shot and was also off. Iona shot and came nearer the center. Magnus's next one was closer still.

Iona stepped up to the mark, fitted her toe into the dirt, and stared at the target for a long moment. She fitted her arrow to the bow, pulled back, and back, and back. Then, just as the strain began making her arms and hands quiver, she let fly.

Magnus knew he'd seen an excellent shot as the arrow arced into the air, its tail barely moving as it sped to the target. When the cheers rose to an earsplitting crescendo, he didn't need Timon's yellow flag, Iona's color, waved in the air to know it had hit dead center. When she turned to him with a toss of her head, her eyes shining with triumph, she was every bit a queen of Icelandia.

"My turn," he said quietly. "As I recall the terms, we can shoot once or in a sequence. 'Tis so?"

Iona's smile faded as she nodded. What was he thinking of? she wondered. He couldn't outshoot dead center, no matter how good he believed he was.

Magnus gestured to one of his warriors. A new quiver was brought with several arrows. Without looking at anyone, he went to the mark, dug in the toe of his elkskin boot, and studied the target. Then he aimed and shot, aimed and shot, aimed and shot, moving almost more quickly than the eye could follow, until the quiver was empty.

The glen was silent. Then a roar began, rising, building, filling the air.

Iona stared at the target, stunned and unbelieving. Her beautiful shot was encircled and stabbed by Magnus's arrows. A cry escaped her throat, one arm shooting out involuntarily as the arrow bent to the ground, then fell. "Foul!" she cried angrily. "Your arrows forced mine from the target." Her voice was lost in the booming huzzahs from the Sinclairs and the disappointed groans of Vikings and the Scots who'd wagered on her.

"So they did, milady," Magnus said, "but I shot fairly, and you know it. 'Twas not a foul, just good shooting."

His sardonic smile only exacerbated her temper. "If part of my arrow is in there, the shot will stand," she said furiously. When Timon waved the red flag, the color of Magnus's victory, she closed her eyes for a second. When she opened them, the roar of the crowd was deafening and Magnus was bending over her. He was laughing at her. She could see it in his eyes, though his features were composed into a solicitous inquiry.

"What now?" she asked hoarsely.

"Why, our short courtship, then our exchange of vows, Princess Asdis Iona of Icelandia." His lips brushed her cheek, and she stiffened like a pulled bow, the roaring in her ears louder than the shouts of the crowd.

∼ 8 ∼

The gods are on the side of the stronger.
—Tacitus

"Milady, will you not turn?" Marta pleaded with her princess. "We need to baste the garment for proper fitting, and your fidgeting might cause us to make an error." When Iona only shrugged, Marta smothered a sigh. "I fear your mind does not compel you to think of your nuptials."

"I've thought of nothing else," Iona said abruptly. Instantly regretting her tone, she turned to her friend and handmaiden and begged pardon. She'd been doing a great deal of that lately, snapping, then asking forgiveness. She'd never acted like such a ninny-hammer.

It was Magnus! He was like a whirlwind and a wall . . . if that could be. He was everywhere at once, checking on the nuptial arrangements, pushing things forward. He issued orders on every front, leaving nothing to chance. He'd even gained permission from the Kirkwall priests to allow Father Monteith to stand in. That hadn't pleased Iona, but she couldn't argue against it without sounding churlish. Whenever she made any suggestion anyway,

Magnus would reply in the negative and refuse to compromise.

She tried glaring at him when he interfered with the making of her gown, when he added something to the menu she'd already planned with the castle cooks. It did no good. He'd give her a breezy smile and go on his way. No argument she gave him for postponing the wedding—the short time of preparation, the need to get to know each other, her desire for her family in Icelandia to be there—slowed his forward motion. Magnus was determined and implacable. He'd smile, listen to her attentively, then plow ahead on his own course.

Iona had a smothering sense of helplessness. She was quite sure her jaw would never unclench again.

"Milady, please remove the garment," Marta said. "You are too distracted with your thoughts. I will work on it without you."

"Yes, yes, do that." Iona hurried to her mammoth armoire fashioned of bird's-eye maple. She slipped off the beautiful chemise and bliaut and reached for the more serviceable clothes she often wore when riding. Arranging these rides was one of the things Magnus had done that she heartily approved of. He'd assigned for her use a lovely-mannered mare and the congenial gelding she'd ridden to their archery contest.

After donning the linsey-woolsey hose banded in leather that kept her legs warm, she smiled at Marta and the serving women and hurried away. She was relieved to leave the room of bustling women.

Whistling Thor to her side, she left her airy quarters and rushed down the stairs. She avoided the great room, exiting through a side portal, then, almost at a run, made her way to the stables.

It never ceased to amaze her that Sinclair Castle was so large and well planned. Like most castles constructed to fight off enemies, it had two courtyards, an outer and an inner one, and turrets for watching and shooting. Within the outer wall the tradesmen, craftsmen, and vendors kept their shops and practiced their art, while within the inner wall lived the personal servers of the laird, his close family, and the guards. In that way, the castle was like many others. But Sinclair Castle was also large and roomy. In most castles Iona had seen, only the leader's sleeping quarters were commodious. Visitors and lesser folk had to fashion their own places. Not so in Sinclair Castle, where there were bedchambers for visitors and huge courtyards that could accommodate family and friends in case of attack.

Inside the castle, most of the ground floor was taken up by the great room. Below, the servants billeted and ate. On the lowest level were the dungeons, which were mostly used to store foodstuffs, wines, and ales. On the second and third floors of the castle were rooms for family and important guests. Iona could only marvel at the castle's many rooms and entrances.

A groomsman quickly saddled her mare, named Chookie, and led her out of the stall. "She's a bit fresh, milady, but there's no malice in her."

Iona patted the mare's nose. "She's from the desert stock. I've known others of her blood. Is Chookie then a Saracen name?"

The groomsman looked startled, then coughed back a chuckle. "It's a love name we give to children here in the Highlands, milady. Aye, it's a love name for a love of a mare." He stroked the animal's side, laughing when she sidled and playfully kicked out at him. He gave Iona a leg up into the soft leather saddle, then held the reins for a moment. "If you've a mind to leave Sinclair land, I'll escort you, milady."

Iona tried to smile past her sudden fury. Magnus again! Holding her in as he would a fractious horse. "I'm fine, thank you."

"Stay to the paths, milady. The ferrets don't have their holes there."

She nodded and, with Thor at her side, cantered away from the castle. On impulse she turned toward the cliff path. The mare delicately picked her way down the stony incline, but once on the strand Iona let her have her head.

They galloped along the slice of land under the cliff

until they reached a barrier of huge rocks. By then both she and the horse were out of breath. Thor was breathing evenly, his eyes alight from the run. When he growled suddenly, she looked up and saw a man approaching. Recognizing Einar, she hushed the wolf. "I trust you're not overdoing, my friend," she called to Einar.

"I'm perfectly well, milady," he said as he reached her. "I stretch my tight muscles by walking. And the sea lifts my spirits."

"Good. The sea is calmer than when we arrived."

Einar looked at the turbulent waters that crashed on the shore, the roiling surface a stark foaming white in contrast to the heavy green-gray depths. In all his years of sailing the Pentland Sea, he'd not seen it any different. Soon the summer solstice would be upon them and the breezes would soften, but the sea would keep its wintry cast.

He turned back to his princess. "You're troubled, milady."

She started, then shook her head and looked away. He clasped her horse's reins. "What is it?"

"I sometimes think I'll not get to Eyin Helga," Iona said, telling only half the truth. Not even to Einar, her most trusted and valued lieutenant and her friend, could she confess her shame and fear. No penance on earth could wipe away what her uncle had done to her. In the eyes of any husband, the sin would not be her uncle's assault, but her lack of purity. Anger at her uncle and shame that she carried the mark of his heinous deed visibly on her face and hidden in her body made her shake.

"You're trembling, milady. Please tell me what I can do. Do you fret because we are not at Eyin Helga?"

"Yes." And that was true. Yet she couldn't confess her deeper fear. Too soon she'd be marrying the laird of the Sinclairs and there'd be no fooling him. Nor would she explain herself to him before they were wed. As her husband, he had a right to know. Not otherwise. She would not bare her secret to a veritable stranger, and a Scot at that.

"We shall go to Eyin Helga today if that is your wish," Einar said grimly. No Scot would bar him from his ship if his princess commanded.

Iona shook her head. "Nay, that we cannot do. You're not well enough to command your ship just yet, my friend." Nor would she risk greater injury to any of her people . . . or to the Sinclairs . . . or to Magnus.

"I can do it," he said, his hands closing into fists. "Our men will help me."

"And how many Vikings and Scots would die if we try to leave before the marriage?" She shook her head again. "I can't risk another bloodbath. We've buried too many good people. I'll not start a war because of my arbitrary whims, Einar." She leaned down and patted his hand, which still held the mare's reins. "But you, dear friend, will soon be well enough to set sail for Icelandia. And that's where you must go. This uneasy, undeclared truce between us and the Scots could rip apart in an instant. Are you and Glam not stopping brangles all the time?"

Einar nodded slowly. " 'Tis true, but they are mere spats, milady. You must not fear for us. Our Vikings would die willingly for you."

"No, Einar. I want no more deaths."

He studied her for a long moment, then nodded. "I know you fear this marriage to the Scot."

Her eyes widened with surprise, then once again she looked away from him. Einar frowned in concern. Had Magnus Sinclair pushed for his conjugal rights, which were his under the terms of betrothal? Had he forced himself on the princess? Anger boiled through him. "Princess, tell me if the Scot has acted unseemly."

She turned back to him, shaking her head vigorously. "The Sinclair has been all that is proper."

Einar nodded once. "Then it is something else, Princess. I know it."

Iona studied him for a moment, then said, " 'Tis true, 'twas not my wish to marry."

She wished she could say more, but did not. She dismounted and stood at Einar's side, a feeling of foreboding filling her. God help her and her people if Einar ever read her mind. All of Icelandia would attack the Scots. It would be a slaughter. If she even mentioned what her uncle had done, nothing would hold back total war. That couldn't happen. She wouldn't let it.

Magnus watched from the cliff above. Neither Iona nor Einar had seen him, for they were too engrossed in each other. Anger swirled through him like the roiling sea. He could not hear their words, but he saw how Einar leaned protectively over Iona. Magnus ground his teeth. To spare his betrothed's feelings, he'd not tried to exercise his rights over her. But neither should she be alone with the Viking.

Raw pain had twisted in his guts when he'd rode along the cliff and spotted them below him. Since he'd won their contest a fortnight ago, she had avoided him at every turn whenever he'd tried to approach her. Now she walked her horse, unattended, with a man who was not her intended spouse. No matter that it was her captain, it was wrong!

Jealousy was a new and unwanted emotion for Magnus, and he couldn't help but react to its prod. He'd tell the Icelandic princess that he was to be her only male companion, unless she was properly attended by another woman, or mayhap by Glam.

The black stallion, sensing his master's unease, pranced and shook his head. Magnus held him with his knees, his eyes never leaving the twosome who strolled on the strand, their heads close together. He wanted to race straight down the sheer face of the cliff and confront them. She was the intended bride of Magnus Sinclair, not of that Viking, and he'd be damned before he let any Viking take what was his. Hauling back hard on the reins, he wheeled the stallion around and galloped away, dirt and pebbles rattling down the cliff in his wake.

Einar heard a sound and looked upward.
"What is it?" Iona asked.

He shook his head. "Nothing, 'twould seem. I thought I heard the neighing of a horse above us, but there's naught to be seen on the cliff top." But the sight of dust and the rolling of stones down the cliff face was not his imagination. Who had watched them?

Iona glanced up quickly, scanning the cliff. Was Magnus back? He'd gone to see about a ship that had sunk off the southern coast of his land. But he wouldn't be back this soon. Besides, if it had been Magnus he would've joined them. Still, it was getting late, and if Magnus had returned, it would be best he not catch her alone with her Viking captain.

"Perhaps I should get back," she said. "As the sun goes down, the wind freshens."

Einar stayed her with one hand on her arm. "Princess, your people love you. I love you. 'Twould be better that I wed you than have you become filled with fear and hate at being married to a Scot."

Iona couldn't stem the tears that filled her eyes. "No, my friend. The betrothal book has been signed, the names inscribed. Only a church order can change it, or . . ." Her voice trailed off.

"Or war. That's what you were going to say." Einar's expression was grim. "Then let it be war. We don't fear to die for you, milady."

She took his hands in hers. "Einar, my friend, say no more. My marriage will take place in three days. Let it end at that."

She easily mounted the mare and galloped off, not heeding Einar when he called after her. She spurred her mount up the steep, winding cliff path. At the top, sadness and weariness engulfed her. With her head down, she let the winded mare make its own way. When her reins were jerked back, she snapped her head up and stared at Magnus. "I thought you'd not be back this day."

He glared at her. "I could see that, Princess Asdis Iona of Icelandia." Jerking her reins, he led her at a fast canter back toward the castle.

She was about to question his harsh tone, but she had

to hang on tightly or fall. Finding her voice and temper at the same time, she tried to snatch control of her mount. "Wait! What are you doing? Sinclair, release my reins."

"Don't bellow, milady. The people are watching their future mistress and finding her wanting, I'm sure."

"Bellow? I don't do that. But your voice would split granite. What's the matter with you?" Using both hands on the reins and tugging with all her might barely made a showing against his superior strength.

All the Scots they passed watched open-mouthed as their laird, iron in his jaw and war in his eyes, led his beautiful intended at a perilous speed along the path to the castle. Many a person had to step back to avoid the clods of soil and stones flung their way.

Instead of taking her to the main entrance to the bailey, Magnus rode around to the rear of the castle overlooking the sea. The path was narrow and rock-strewn, and Iona briefly closed her eyes when her mare misstepped.

"Sweet Mary, are you intending to land us on the rocks or in the sea?" she muttered.

When she thought for sure they could travel no farther on the ever narrowing ledge, Magnus stopped and dismounted. He pushed back some bushes and opened a door.

"If you intend to put me in a dungeon," Iona said, her chin up, but her insides quavering, "I won't go. I don't like being shut away. 'Twould be better to throw me into the sea."

Her brave words penetrated Magnus's anger. He saw her trepidation, though she tried to mask it, and his ire dissipated. "If I imprison you, milady, it will be with me."

Relief flooded her at his gentler tone of voice. He slid an arm around her waist and lifted her down in one strong motion, and her heart thundered in her chest. Her hands barely grazed his shoulders, and she couldn't hold his gaze. "Where are we?"

"This is the laird's entrance. I rarely use it."

Iona pictured at least one woman he'd have carried back here, and red-hot anger filled her. "A most convenient way to bring your leman to your quarters, milord. I imagine the gate is well oiled, if any of the gossip about you is true."

The last touch of Magnus's irritation melted in the wake of her own temper. Strangely, it pleased him that she appeared to be angered about his other women—not, he added to himself with a burst of male independence, that it was any concern of hers. Most men of his station had both wife and mistress. Though he hadn't been with Elizabeth since the arrival of the Vikings, he wouldn't deny himself the pleasure of her bed once he was married. Actually, the only reason why he hadn't been with Elizabeth was because this damned princess had wreaked havoc with his life. If it weren't for her, he might've had many hours of enjoyment with his mistress. Was it no wonder he was hard at that very moment? Not since the Church had confirmed him had he been without a woman for so long. Iona and her horde were nothing but trouble.

He released the horses, instructing Perseus to return to the stables. He was certain the well-trained horse would. Then he turned to the door. "This way."

She didn't move. "I don't like dark places," she said again. Her voice was firm, but he saw the shadow in her eyes. Though the princess from Icelandia had fears, she didn't back down from them. But why did she have fears at all? Had she not been the beloved child and grandchild of powerful men who'd granted her every wish?

Perhaps her husband had mistreated her. Knowing her, Magnus guessed she would have chosen her own spouse. She may have chosen badly. But he was sure she wouldn't have let her husband have everything all his own way. She was much too spirited for that, and Magnus liked her spirit, her courage. Most women of his acquaintance didn't look him in the eye. Iona not only did that, she expected him to back down whenever they clashed.

"There'll be a lighted torch as we enter," he said. "It's taken care of twice each day."

"Wotan forbid that you stumble when you carry your leman through here," she said sharply. "No doubt it's no small burden. I've had ample time to see your heavy women."

Magnus smiled, amused by her tart words. He guessed she was embarrassed at having revealed a weakness and was trying to distract him.

"You call upon your pagan god, Princess. The Church would frown on such. As for heaviness, I've seen Viking women that could've tossed your great Grettir over their shoulder if they'd a mind to try."

Iona's lips twitched despite herself. "You're most ungentlemanly to cast aspersions on our good women." She looked up at him as they passed through the doorway into a tunnel. "You've read of our Grettir?"

"The giant of your ancient lore? I have. A most misunderstood man, I thought."

"How like you to comprehend another giant, milord Sinclair."

His laughter made her start as it echoed loudly in the tunnel, and her own smile faded as she looked ahead. As he had promised, a torch by the entrance lit the stone-walled passage. It was so narrow, Magnus would have to duck his head to one side to make his way through. She could walk straight up, but the sides were very close. It would be better to go singly. She took a deep breath. "Per-perhaps I should carry the cresset if I am to lead." The passage's darkness and narrowness was unnerving enough, and she started when a booming noise echoed around them.

"Nay, milady, I'll be at your side." He wanted her near, and slipped his arm around her waist. Predictably, she stiffened and tried to pull away. "We are betrothed, Iona," he reminded her. "It's permissible for me to touch you—or bed you, should we choose." Her body arched like a bow as she tried to put some space between them. "Something bothers you?" he asked. How she must've hated her husband's touch to react to his words in such a way.

"Nothing bothers me, milord. Perhaps we should hurry. That thunderous sound could presage a rock slide, could it not?"

"There's naught to fear, milady. Far below us is a cavern that the sea crashes into each day at high tide. When a storm sweeps from the north, the noise can be deafening." He grinned. "Many a thrashing I got for climbing up in there when I was a mere lad. It's another entrance to the dungeon, but far too dangerous for even the most intrepid warrior."

"And you were that, even as a lad," Iona said softly, picturing him as a boy attempting to climb about in the cavern with walls slicked by icy spray. His twisted smile had her chest squeezing in a most impossible way. How could such a villain as he look so endearing? God help her if she ever became fond of him. He had the capacity to wreak great destruction on her peace.

"I was walloped most regularly," he said.

She smiled. "I'm sure of that."

He leaned over her, the dancing beams from the torch lighting her face. "And how is it that you understand Gaelic so well, milady? Your mother?"

"Yes. She wanted nothing to do with her people, but she taught me the language." She glanced up at him. " 'Tis true that most Vikings understand your speech, though few of you comprehend ours." She heard his sudden intake of breath and asked, "Does that anger you? Then I must ask you how it is you speak Gaelic so well if you are truly Breton and Norman?"

Magnus was barely listening to her. Instead, his attention had become fixed on her mouth, its sensual shape, the fullness of her lower lip, its allure when she smiled. Her beauty beamed like the moon, but Magnus told himself her fascination for him was temporary. Once she was in his bed and he'd initiated her as Lady Sinclair, he'd quickly put her in a corner of his world and tend to his primary function as laird of the Sinclairs.

Realizing she was waiting for him to speak, he quickly recalled what she'd just said. "Aye," he answered, " 'tis true I spoke Breton and Norman, but my first speech came out Gaelic. My mother and father saw to that." He smiled. "And I do understand some of your speech, though I'm not fluent. Did you forget that Normandy was settled by your people?"

"We are kin to the Norsemen who settled there. We Vikings ne'er forget what's ours. That's why we sailed to Eyin Helga."

"And landed here."

"Yes."

He saw her shiver from the darkness, but was reluctant to move on. He enjoyed their conversation. Iona was unlike any female he'd known; her wit was sharper than most men's. At least she would never bore. Smiling to himself he drew her closer, pressing his face into the veil covering her head.

"I've picked up more words since your arrival," he murmured, recalling her muttered curses when they'd battled on the oars. "In fact, my vocabulary has become colorful." He whispered some of the words he'd heard her use that first day.

Iona stilled, her mind worrying over the hidden meaning of his drawled words. Nonsense! He couldn't mean she'd taught him any curses. She'd always acted with the utmost decorum with him, just as she'd been tutored. Except . . . She glanced up at him through her lashes. He was holding the torch away from them, and she could barely see in the gloom. His body was keeping her warm, but even more heat spread through her as she remembered their running on the oars. Glam had mentioned that she'd cursed like an oarsman as she'd done it. Wotan save her! Surely he didn't mean that.

"Release me, Scot. You take liberties." She felt small, helpless . . . and cosseted, hugged against his chest that way. He was so big! Damn his impertinence.

"Again, milady, we are betrothed. And that entails much of what you call liberties."

Wild with a trepidation she couldn't control, she tried once more to move back from him. His arm only tightened around her. That failing, she decided to direct his thoughts another way. And hers. Some of her fright came from knowing that she liked having him hold her. "Tell me how it was growing up here. Did you have a tutor for your letters? Did you grow to manhood here?"

Magnus looked down at her. The princess was well versed in battle maneuvers, and changing the enemy's focus was one strategem. And she couldn't have asked better questions to turn his mind away from her. "No," he answered slowly, uncertain how much to tell her. "I didn't come to manhood at Sinclair Castle. That was denied me." He hesitated. "Nor were my mother and father ever to see this land again. They died in Bretagne at the hands of assassins."

Iona felt his body tremble, saw his face twist in pain. Her hands moved up his arms as she tried to give comfort. "And you wanted to grow from child to man here."

He nodded. " 'Twas my right. Except for one paltry year, I spent no time here at all until we reclaimed my heritage a few years back. One foe after another denied me my true inheritance." He frowned, his hold tightening on her until she winced. He loosened his grip and pressed his mouth to her hair. "No, we weren't here very long in my childhood."

"Tell me about it." The agony in his voice had her own fears receding. What had given Magnus Sinclair so much pain?

"The tale is too long to tell all at once."

"Then tell me a bit at a time."

He laughed harshly. "You are a woman of persuasion, Asdis Iona of Icelandia." His mouth moved over her hair. "From the time I was a lad we were always warring it seemed. But it was the unknown enemies that were so fearsome."

"What do you mean?"

"My father had great wealth in land and friends, but along the way he'd gathered a host of foes. I can't recall a time of peace as a youngster. We were always battling someone. Most I knew. But there were unknown renegades and thieves who assaulted my father and mother and killed them. I have searched for them now for more than ten years, but to no avail. One day I'll find the marauders who took their lives. Mayhap then I'll have peace."

Iona's heart ached as she pictured the lad without father and mother, who knew he'd have to keep on fighting to keep his life, his name, and regain his land. "But you did conquer your foes?"

He nodded. "I've regained our land, sought out and destroyed many of the renegades who hounded us from our home. But I know that those who killed my parents still walk this land. I would sense it if they were dead. They're alive and threaten us yet. But they'll not win. Sinclairs inhabit this land, and we will stay. Or we'll die here."

Iona was so engrossed in his tale, she'd forgotten the closed-in tunnel until she bumped the wall. She gasped, and dread shivered through her. Why being in a cavern would make her think of her uncle, she couldn't fathom. But it was as though Skene had appeared in the tunnel and was stalking her. "Tell—tell me about your family."

Magnus felt her tremble again, this time with more than cold. Pulling her tight to him, he rubbed his hand up and down her back, holding the torch high so that he could study her face. "As I said, there's much to tell. And I want you to know it all, but it's too cold to linger here. You'd catch a chill." He felt her hesitation, and knew she wanted to hear something more. "My mother was a Dugald. It's from her that this land and castle come to the Sinclairs. Her ancestor built this castle from stone hewn from the cliffs. He was determined to hold his land against all comers. My mother was the last of his progeny. So when she married my father, who was a Scot through his mother, the Donnells of the West Highlands, she brought him her lands and monies, as is the custom. They determined that this land was of greater value to them and their descendants than what he held in Bretagne. My father changed his name from St. Clair to Sinclair and laid claim to this holding."

"Go on." As Magnus talked she became calmer. His voice soothed her, making the demons disappear.

"Some of the old families resented my father taking

over such a sizable portion of land, because they considered him a Breton. The trouble began almost from the day of their wedding."

"Marriage might be a poor bargain with you, Sinclair."

He heard the amusement in her voice and hugged her, surprised and pleased at her banter. "So it might. But I don't fear. If my enemies approach I can have you test them out on the oars, and wrest victory for the clan."

She chuckled, then touched his arm gently. "And you have a special nemesis?"

"I do." And the enemy was still out there. Why else would it appear in his nightmares?

She heard the pain and anger in his voice. "You cannot forget your parents' death."

"No," he said sharply.

She sighed, wanting to hug that young boy and protect him, even as she wanted to lean against the man and absorb his strength.

Magnus heard the sigh, and gave her a quick hug. "There's naught to fear, milady. I've sworn to keep you safe, you need not be afraid of the dark."

With that calm statement he ameliorated more of her fears than had been done over a decade, and she sagged against him. Barbarian he might be, but he was no Skene. She knew that.

The tunnel took a sharp turn. They walked on in silence for a minute, then Magnus stopped. He pushed his shoulder against a flattened portion of stone wall and it swung inward. He saw her start of surprise in the sudden light that bracketed them.

"It's a system of Egyptian wheels," he explained, "modeled after the ancient waterwheels. I had a canny grandfather who dabbled in the Egyptian way of doing things." He pointed to a place on the wall. "When this is pressed it moves the wheels, which in turn move others that activate the door. Let me show you." He took her hand, guiding it to the smooth stone, which was actually a small wheel. He showed her the proper motion several times, then said, "Now, you do it alone."

At first she couldn't. She either pushed at the wrong spot or with ill-timed pressure. After several attempts, and with Magnus's patient tutelage, she was at last able to activate the mechanism by herself.

She laughed out loud in triumph as though she'd conquered a small world, and Magnus laughed with her. "Come in, milady."

She stepped into the spacious room and looked around, smiling. A fire burned in a fireplace so large, Magnus could have walked into it without bending his head. "My, this room is spacious—" She froze, her gaze lighting on the monstrous bed. Her relief at being out of the dark place, and her peace of mind, fled. Blood freezing in her veins, she whirled to face him.

"You mean to rape me," she said.

∾ 9 ∾

What life is there, what delight, without golden Aphrodite?

—Mimnermus

Stunned, Magnus stared at her, speechless. Anger and another emotion, rose in him, a painful, nameless one, "Christ almighty, Iona—"

"Cursing will not mask the deed, sirrah. 'Tis plain to me what will be done." Nausea roiled inside her, and she was quite sure she would be sick when he touched her. It would serve the barbarian right.

"Sweet Jesus," Magnus muttered. Her body was shaking harder than her voice. It tore him to see it, even as he was infuriated that she should think that of him. They were betrothed. Rape couldn't happen between the betrothed. Uneasily he moved his shoulders, recalling more than one ribald story about screaming, crying women bedded by their intendeds and spouses. Magnus had pitied the laughing tellers of those tales. An eager woman was the only woman worth bedding. Now when he saw the fear in Iona's eyes, he felt . . . shame.

"I will never rape you," he said.

Still she did not move. Her face was a parchment hue, and looked as though it would crumple as easily as that writing material.

Magnus was unused to the protective emotion that cascaded through him, the urge to cradle her like a lost child. Their marriage was to be a political alliance, nothing more. Nonetheless, he winced when he saw how she steeled herself, as though she expected him to beat her. Even though her hands had curled into fists and she was prepared to defend herself, only a great will was keeping her on her feet. Her eyes were dilated in a blind, opaque way that underscored her blatant terror.

"Stop!" he bellowed, then regretted his outburst. She moved back from him, her eyes fluttering as though she didn't know whether to keep them open or close them. He realized she wasn't even aware she was wringing her hands, that her body swayed to some internal torrent of fear.

"I do not intend to rape you, Iona," he said softly. "Not now, not ever. But if 'tis your wish, we will wait until we're married before we share a bed."

That concession surprised him as much as it obviously did her. Relief washed over her face as he frowned. Ever since he'd seen her on the strand with Einar, he'd intended to take her and make her his that very day. Now that plan was like smoke. Damn! He reached out to her, but she flinched away, her lips moving as if in prayer.

"Do you hear me?" he yelled in frustration.

"The devil himself could hear you, Magnus Sinclair. You'll bring all the hounds of hell to your heels if you don't stop shouting."

"I'm not shouting," he said in a lower tone. "What in hell made you think I'd rape you?"

"It's the way of Scots," she muttered.

He reached out again and caught her under the arms, bringing her close to him. "We say the Vikings do that." Satisfaction filled him when she colored up in anger and wriggled in protest. He preferred that to her whey-faced terror. He would have preferred her dumping him in the freezing sea once more than to see her frozen in fear.

"Vikings don't do that," she exclaimed. "Only under extreme duress are they cruel."

"Hah!"

"Renegades might pillage and rape. We forage where we can, fight if we must. But we don't countenance renegades, Magnus Sinclair." Iona barely paid heed to her words. She was too giddy with relief. He wouldn't try to bed her now. She needn't disclose her secret just yet. Her people's safety could count on that! Like a lightning strike in her head, she knew what she must do. The day they were wed she'd insist on being taken to Eyin Helga. That way when she'd confess to him, he could simply leave her there and she need never face the outside world—or Magnus—again.

Magnus watched expressions of both satisfaction and sadness chase across her lovely face. "Now what do you see in that twisted head of yours, milady?"

"I don't choose to talk on it now. Aye, I don't even want to think on it anymore." She gazed around the room, avoiding looking at him.

"Don't you like my chamber?" he asked gruffly. He realized he wanted her to like it, not just agree to share it with him as was her duty.

He glanced around the cavernous room. It was in the top of the tower that faced the sea. Instead of a stone-and-wood ceiling as the other chambers had, a stone stairway on one wall curved up to a half floor of heavy planking that formed a balcony in the turret, overlooking the bedchamber. The lancets allowed plenty of light, and provided views of the sea and the only road leading up to the castle gates. He saw Iona frown at the lancets and smiled. "You like our glass bead hangings, milady?"

She nodded. "I've seen such in Egypt. But why don't they sway and crash together from the strong sea winds?"

"You've traveled far and wide, Princess."

She smiled shyly. "It was the wish of my grandfather and my parents that I do so. As daughter of the leaders of our people, I was to be prepared to take command. So I learned the varying tongues of our trading cities, and understand the language of trade, the lifeline of our people. Since I elected to leave, a quorum of wise men and women now lead Icelandia. But if there should be a threat, I would be empowered to lead."

Magnus was taken aback by her matter-of-fact statement of power. He knew few women who could command such power, and surely none who would be so casual about it. Iona was more than an exciting woman. She was a great force encased in a delightful body. He wanted her, badly . . .

Iona caught his narrowed look, and her body tingled from the heat in his gaze. "You were telling me about the glass curtains," she said, feeling the blood fill her face. How was he able to do that to her? And he enjoyed doing it!

"In Bretagne an alchemist friendly to our people experimented with the beads. He thought to find gold. Instead, he found that fire fused the beads and when put against the lancets allowed light to enter. I've used them in many of the openings, and once the castle is properly fortified, I will have the other chambers so covered." He moved closer to her, pointing over her shoulder. "You can see the iron hooks in the stone on each side of the lancets. The fused glass beads are fastened to them.

She nodded. "It's wondrous light in the room with such curtains."

"Aye, milady, 'tis true. And I needn't have as many flambeaux. 'Tis enough heat with the fire."

She glanced at the rather small grouping of burning logs and smiled. "I do not think to get overwarm in this chamber."

"You're cold." Magnus flinched with regret. He rarely felt the cold and liked his room chill, except when he bathed. He strode to the fireplace.

She followed him hastily and put a hand on his arm. "No, don't make it warmer. My skins keep me comfortable. I need no more heat."

"It will be warmer when you sleep here." It pleased him when she colored like a girl. He touched her cheek. "Shyness? Did not your husband rid you of that?"

"Husband?" she repeated hollowly. Magnus thought she'd been married! Lord, what a web of deceit she'd been caught in, with yet another item of the growing list of things that would have to be clarified on her wedding day. No, she couldn't dissemble with him about this. It was one thing not to tell him something, quite another to hide it deliberately when he faced her with it. Taking a deep breath, she stared up at him. "No one taught me about shyness . . . and I've had no husband." She glanced away, then back at him. He was gaping at her, obviously stunned. Had someone told him she'd been married? "What ails you?"

"You've never been married?" How could that be? he wondered. Could she be untouched? Nay! Not at her age. And not with such fire inside her. But he would know on their nuptial day. It had unsettled her enough to tell him what she did. He'd not discomfit her more by asking if she'd had lovers, though it tore at his insides to think that she'd had. "Shall we talk of this on our nuptial day?"

"It would be suitable," she answered, not able to meet his gaze.

He touched her arm lightly. "Then we'll say no more, now. But I would know more of you that day, as I will answer all your questions about me."

She nodded, then looked around the chamber again. Once more her gaze fell on the bed, and abruptly she whirled toward the door. "I must go."

"Not just yet," he said.

When she felt his hand at her waist, she jumped, but didn't flee. As if by magic, he was wooing the fear from her. "Was there something more you wished to say?"

She trembled when he turned her to face him. His hand at her waist massaged gently, while the other hand brushed back a strand of hair from her forehead.

"Your tresses are the color of the sun coming through the beads, my snow queen," he murmured, then bent his head and brushed his lips over hers.

"I'm a princess, not a queen," she said, the words barely escaping her throat.

"Iona, you'll be my queen, even as you're a princess of Icelandia." Desire was forged in him the moment he'd touched her. She'd gotten into his blood, moved him as none other ever had. He settled his mouth over hers again, liking the mint-rose essence of her, the honey sweetness of her lips. Tempting himself, he let his tongue touch her lips, trace the shape of them.

Iona pulled back, stunned at the hot wanting that coursed through her. Without thinking, she brought her hand up and cracked it across his cheek. Her hand stung, but he didn't move.

Silence crackled like fire between them. After a moment, Magnus gave a little bow.

"You have a good arm, Princess," he said dryly, trying to tamp his desires, which raged even at that light kiss. He'd never felt such heat, even at the moment of ecstasy with Elizabeth. And if he judged Iona's flushed cheeks and overbright eyes correctly, she'd been scorched too by their kiss. He saw her glance slide to his bed, and she shivered. If nothing else, her obvious trepidation about the mating act cooled his ardor.

"What is it about my bed you do not like, Iona?" he asked. The hangings were of heavy wool, and perhaps she'd prefer something else. "Would silk hangings from Cathay suit you better?"

"Frown not, Sinclair. I like the hangings. And the Egyptian beads covering the lancets. The refraction of the light is quite pleasing. I can see that the chimney draws well, too."

Seeing his look of amusement, Iona clamped her mouth shut. She was babbling like an Icelandic freshet! She didn't know what she liked or disliked at that moment. Her mind told her to run, but she couldn't move. He'd kissed her and she'd turned into a fool, plain and simple. That did not help her anxiety about the upcoming wedding night. Magnus was not like Skene . . . but might he hurt her as her uncle had?

Magnus's eyes narrowed on her. She seemed disturbed anew. "What have your people told you of me?" he asked abruptly, certain she'd been warned that he was an ogre, a despoiler of women. He knew the stories told by Viking and Scot of various enemy leaders. His name would be among them.

Startled, Iona stared at him. "Of you?" She blinked several times, casting around in her mind for something other than "accursed Scot." "Einar told me that you were a fierce warrior."

Relief washed over Magnus. "I am. And did he say anything else?" A deep urge to pummel the Viking twisted through him—until Iona smiled. He caught his breath at the dimple that flashed at the side of her mouth, at the hint of laughter in her eyes. An unlooked-for pleasure warmed his knotted innards. "So? There's more?"

"He said you were like all Scots, not to be trusted. I agreed with him." She laughed out loud.

He tried to cover his amusement with a frown, but failed. "You told him that, did you?"

She nodded, mirth bubbling out of her. The sound of her laughter sent his blood cascading through his veins. She was a truly sensuous woman, yet she knew it not. Her womanliness was so much a part of her, she didn't recognize it as such. There were no angles to Iona. She was all curves, swayings, undulations. And she intrigued him to the point that he often forgot all else when he was with her. He looked her up and down slowly, his gaze taking in the lifted chin, the feisty glint in her eye, the reckless cast to her inclined head, that porcelain skin. Nothing fashioned by man could equal its purity. He was eager for the day when all of her would be pressed to his body. "Are you challenging me on the oars again?"

"I might. And I could dump you again too."

He shook his head. "Once, but not again, milady. I've made mistakes in my time, but never the same one twice."

" 'Tis arrogant you are, Magnus Sinclair," she said spiritedly.

"Yes." He grinned. "I am."

Her demeanor changed suddenly, and she took a deep breath. "I still wish to go to Eyin Helga."

"I know." And she had more than one reason for choosing that isolated isle. He intended to know what was hidden inside Iona. No woman could be so complicated that he wouldn't know all of her in a short time. After that, his fascination with her would end. Why that thought was so unpleasing he didn't deign to question.

She began backing toward the door. " 'Tis past time to leave, as I've said. Marta and Spes will be worried."

"You're with your intended husband. No one will think ill of that." He followed her. "Tell me about Einar."

"Einar?" Surprised at his abrupt declaration, she stared up at him, then changed direction and strolled closer to the fire. "The Thorhallssons are an old and honored family. Einar was a thane who chose the sea life. He is one of Icelandia's most adept warriors and he soon became captain of all the warriors, and trade leader as well. My parents loved him as a son and looked on him as an Icelandic heir." She smiled. "Einar has the blood and the backing to be king if he should choose, but like me, he's happy with the quorum of administrators we have."

"And he is close to you?" Magnus asked.

Her smile broadened. "Oh yes. He's like an older brother. He taught me to shoot, and to handle an ax and sword. He always took care of me."

"I see." As if a burning faggot sat in his chest, Magnus had trouble breathing. She didn't love the captain of the Vikings, not like a spouse. "I'll give him permission to take his ship and his people and leave after we're wed."

Her mouth dropped in astonishment. "You will?"

"My word on it."

"Magnus!" Without thinking, she ran to him and threw her arms around him, trying to hug his mammoth frame. She couldn't encircle him, so she clung tightly. "Thank you, thank you. You won't regret it."

"I hope not," Magnus said dryly, his heart thudding against his breastbone. She'd not done such a thing before, and he couldn't say why it meant so much. But this first overt display of emotion toward him mitigated all the hedging and avoiding she'd done these past weeks.

Slowly his arms enclosed her. When she didn't stiffen, he lowered his face to her hair. "In three days we'll be wed." He'd said it to gauge her reaction and was disappointed when it came full force. Her body went rigid and she turned her face away.

"Yes," she said. She tried to draw back, but he wouldn't release her. "And then my people will go. And we'll sail to Eyin Helga."

" 'Tis most secretive you are with me, my betrothed. Am I not to know what you've hidden in your heart?"

Iona had to clear her throat three times before she could force the words out. "You'll know everything on Eyin Helga." When she pushed away again, he let her go. She whirled and strode across the room, tugged open the heavy oaken door, then let it thud closed behind her.

Magnus made no effort to stop her or go after her. "There's naught I'll not know about you, my princess," he murmured.

When he heard the door open again, he swung around eagerly. But a man entered, not a woman. "Oh, it's you."

Cormac laughed. "Just your uncle. Did you expect the fair Elizabeth?"

Magnus smiled, shaking his head. "It wouldn't do for her to come to me here. My intended has just departed." At his uncle's quick frown, he chuckled. "She's no witch, uncle. Our people would gladly tell you of her many kindnesses."

Cormac shrugged. " 'Tis so. In fact, she's also quite beauteous, despite her scar."

"When we are wed I will ask her not to cover her face. I find the mark most intriguing."

Cormac shook his head. "I'd be happier if your alliance was with another, not a Viking. I cannot help my forebodings. I fear for this, nephew."

Magnus clapped his relative on the back. "You've always worried too much."

"Aye." Cormac smiled. "It's not that many years we've been on this land."

"I understand your fears," Magnus said grimly. "But

none will gainsay us or take our land, Cormac. Not renegade . . . nor Viking. This is my vow."

"You still think of your parents and want vengeance. I too have suffered the sting of their loss. But I tell you, it's time to put your vengeance aside, Magnus . . . for the clan's sake. There's much to do to safeguard the family."

"I'll not shirk my duty, Cormac, but I'll not stop seeking the slayers of my mother and father. 'Tis my covenant."

Iona had walked outside to the bailey, fascinated as always by the hardworking Scots who plied their trades assiduously, as though each day were the last. She'd come to admire their hard work and had to revise her opinion that only Vikings knew how to get things done.

"You would be a trader, milady? Else why your interest in such menial tasks?"

Iona spun around at the softly spoken words. Elizabeth stood before her, beautifully attired as always. A small smile curved her lips, but Iona saw the spiteful gleam in her eyes. "Milady Asquith, is it not?"

"It is. I've but arrived with my father and our entourage for your nuptials. I felicitate you, milady, though I fear you'll find the lusty Sinclair not to your liking . . . at your age." Elizabeth smiled as Iona stiffened. "And I would say you are wise to wear your veil. Scots have an abhorrence of scars. They sometimes ascribe them to witches. I prithee they think naught of you." Elizabeth sketched a curtsy. "If you will excuse me, I'll find my chambers and rest before the evening meal."

Iona stood as though frozen to the ground, a killing anger throbbing through her. When she saw Elizabeth push a servant out of her path, she was hard put not to chase after the woman and smite her. Only the vision of what the ensuing cat fight could mean to the many observers stayed her. She'd have no one thinking she was jealous of Sinclair's leman.

She watched Elizabeth's curvaceous body until it was out of sight, then noted that some of the artisans had paused in their work to watch her. Smiling lamely at them, she hurried across the bailey to where she kept Thor. She'd feed the wolf and exercise him, and in doing so she'd forget Elizabeth of Asquith . . . perhaps.

The next afternoon a hunt was arranged, and as was the custom, all guests invited to the nuptials, friends, and relatives could participate.

Iona, mounted on her gelding and wearing the split Viking elkskin skirt that allowed her to ride astride, cantered over to a cluster of Vikings, returning their greetings and smiles.

"It's a good day for a hunt," Einar said to her as he tightened the girth on his saddle.

She eyed him critically. " 'Twould not do for you to strain your threads, old friend."

"I'm fine, Princess. I will hunt at your side."

"As will I," Magnus said, coming up on her other side.

Einar's eyebrows lifted slightly. "It is your right," he said.

Iona was pleased that the previous day's agitation had left Einar. Smiling, she turned to Magnus, and stared. His face was taut, red slashed his cheekbones, and his mouth was drawn in a straight line. She let her horse sidle closer to his. "What ails you, milord?"

"Naught." He reached down and took her reins. "Your captain can ride behind you, if he likes."

She gasped, tugging vainly on her reins as he led her away. "Release me, you fool!"

Kenneth rode up to Einar just as Magnus and Iona passed beyond earshot. "Did the princess just call Magnus a fool?" He glanced at Einar as the Viking swung into his saddle. "I'd not dare such."

Einar shook his head. "She's always dared too much."

Kenneth laughed. "For all our sakes, I hope she does not outshoot him this day."

"She'll try." Einar's laughter joined Kenneth's. "What a marriage it'll be."

"Like none other." Kenneth signaled to Dugald, who lifted his horn to call the dogs. "Boar have been sighted above the far croft."

"I'll wager I draw first blood, Scot."

"You're on, Viking."

Magnus had led Iona to where the dogs were being held, waiting for the call. She tried to draw him out, but he remained taciturn. Finally she concentrated on Thor, who seemed inclined to take on the hunting mastiffs. "No, Thor, you may not fight them," she said, snapping her fingers and bringing the wolf to her side.

Magnus watched her, though it had been his plan to ignore her. He'd been more than peeved to see her so relaxed with her Vikings, serene and yet obviously commanding respect. "I can't conceive that you could best Geordie McInally and his wolf," he said.

She turned to him, her smile hesitant. "Thor was easier to conquer than Geordie."

He laughed. "I'm sure of it."

The horn was blown twice. The handlers released the dogs, and in moments the hunters were in full gallop down the croft.

Iona had never seen the like of a Sinclair hunt. It was a frenzy, chaotic and dangerous, and did not slow for any barrier. The riders crisscrossed each other, scattered, reformed into a group, and then scattered again.

When they reached the level area, she looked around and saw there were a few Scots at her side. Magnus was a distance away, though, caught in a throng. She didn't dare try to reach him. Then the hunt turned, the dogs baying loudly, and a huge gaggle of hunters swinging in their wake. She had to gallop with them or risk being unseated, even though her Vikings and Magnus had gone westward. She slowed her gelding, allowing it to fall back and give her more room. As the hunt swept on, she reined her horse to a trot and looked around. Far to her left Thor was snuffling the ground near a copse of trees. She heard his low growls. Had the quarry fooled them all and doubled back? She spurred the gelding forward.

. . .

Magnus looked around for Iona and couldn't find her. His taste for the hunt vanished, and he turned Perseus away from the throng of hunters. Standing in his stirrups, he stared out over the hills, but saw no one. Then he caught sight of a movement in a thick stand of trees, as though someone had waved his arms. He pivoted Perseus and galloped back the way he'd come, then reined in when he was still a good distance from the woods. Innate caution had him approaching carefully.

"I have your blind side," a man said.

He glanced back and saw Einar riding on his left flank. He nodded and kneed his horse into a canter. When he entered the woods, he paused.

"Magnus Sinclair," a nasal voice called out, "I'd have words with ye."

Magnus whirled, sword in hand. "Show yourself, Geordie McInally. I recognize your skirling tones."

"Och, it's no com-pli-ment I'm needin' on me voice. 'Tis your wife who'll need tendin', I'm thinkin'." With no more than a slight bend in the bracken, the misshapen man appeared in front of Magnus.

Magnus whistled softly, surprised and amused. " 'Tis clean you are, McInally. Did thee fall in the sea?"

"Och, no. 'Twas thee rib who done it. Won me clean, fair, and square, she did."

Magnus laughed, then turned to Einar. "This is the man Iona bested."

Einar grinned, earning himself a scowl from the woodsman.

"I know thee Viking," McInally said. I knew them all, though they not see me."

His words reminded Magnus of what he'd said initially. "You spoke of the princess, McInally. What of her?"

"Aye, I did. And I tell you this, Sinclair. There are those who'd kill her. Her death is naught to me, but I been tested by few, and I'll not see her back stabbed."

Magnus leapt off his horse, as did Einar. "Who?"

McInally shook his head. "And wouldst I not have dispatched them myself had I known that." He spat at their feet. "Words I hear when I hide from men. Not always faces or voices do I know. But I ken the peril she faces. And you as well, Sinclair."

"Where did you hear this? When?" Einar snapped out the words, fury in every line of his body.

"In the glen and dark of night. I was sleeping in a tree as is my wont when the wolves prowl. I woke to their speech, catching not all of it. They melted away afore I could espy them. But I watch the princess, and her wolf watches too." McInally turned. "I will watch anon." The words were almost indistinguishable as he disappeared in the very center of the bracken.

"Shall I go after him?" Einar asked.

Magnus shook his head. He jumped onto Perseus and wheeled him sharply. "No. We find Iona. Now."

Einar was at his heels as they galloped over the croft.

Iona dismounted and crept near the copse and its ground cover of bracken. Thor's growls had grown louder, more menacing. She tried to gesture the beast to silence. He'd warn the boar before she was in position for shooting.

Suddenly the wolf whirled and charged at her, landing on her chest and throwing her to the ground. Her grunt of surprise almost drowned out the thud of an arrow striking a tree. Stunned, she lay where she was, trying to catch her breath as Thor turned and straddled her. He stared back at the copse, teeth bared, his warning growls filling the air.

Furious that some hunter was so inept as to almost hit her, Iona struggled to push Thor off her. Magnus's voice stopped her, though.

"Stay where you are, Iona," he ordered. "Don't move, Thor."

"Magnus?" Iona was confused, but when she eyed the arrow imbedded in the tree above her head, she trembled.

The shot was too close to have been an accident. "Good boy," she said huskily to Thor.

Magnus and Einar scouted the bracken, swords drawn, but found nothing. Magnus ran back to her, pushed the still growling wolf aside, and lifted her into his arms.

"I—I don't want you to think he attacked me," she said, clutching his arms. "And you mustn't punish him—"

"Einar and I saw the arrow. We would've been too late." He cuddled her close, his mouth at her cheek. "Your wolf will eat from my trencher if he chooses." He glanced up at Einar, who held the arrow. When the Viking shook his head, he swore mightily.

"You're angry with us?" Iona asked, still shaken.

"I'm not angry with you or your wolf, Iona." He lifted her, though he couldn't stem the shaking in his limbs. Someone had tried to kill his betrothed on Sinclair land. He'd find the culprits and hang them high. Not in all his days had he known such fear.

Iona was surprised when Magnus put her on his horse and climbed up behind her. "Surely we cannot hunt this way."

"We hunt no more this day. Einar, you will speak to Glam and Kenneth of this."

"I will."

She glanced at her captain, and winced at his ferocious look. "Nothing happened. Thor saved me."

Einar nodded.

"We saw," Magnus said, then set off at a canter, letting Einar bring her horse. More than once he tried to speak to her, but he couldn't get words past his tortured throat. His insides felt as though they'd been cut to ribbons with a claymore. Blood lust filled him. He wanted to kill whoever had tried to take her life. Under that wrenching fury was a fear he'd never known, an aching, pounding void that would never be filled if he lost her. Clutching her convulsively, he bent over her, shielding her from the wind.

"Magnus?"

"I'll take care of you," he vowed.

∾ 10 ∾

Bring water, bring wine, boy! Bring flowering garlands to me!
    Yes, bring them, so that I may try a bout with love.
                       —Anacreon

B y the day of the wedding the castle and its environs were filled with people. Tents of skin and woven cloth sprang up all around, many dyed in the intricate skeins of a family tartan. Reds, blues, greens, yellows, and black and white crisscrossed each other in the wondrous linsey-woolsey woven in the north country. The hillocks and crofts were soon so covered, it looked as though there'd be no room to graze the stoats and goats.

Some grumbled at the extra work, but most were gleeful at the festive air. Despite the added labor, there would be grand fetes and more food than most would see in a year. And all could eat. That was the rule of the clans. Peasant would dine with prince.

And there was profit to be made. Many a canny Scot put a renter's fee on tents, blankets, leather goods, and hunting gear. For days spear points had been hammered out by the blacksmiths and bows had been fashioned to be sold for the games. Everywhere men and lads whittled arrows, ax handles, spears. Bartering and selling were at a frenzy.

The Vikings, eager to compete in the games, found their own places to make their goods, which they considered far superior to anything the Scots could do. All the hammering, laughing, and shouting, mixed into a wild cacophony.

Inside, the castle had been turned upside down for boiling and scrubbing. It shone with cleanliness, and workers screamed if their area was put in disarray.

In the mammoth kitchen area behind the great room, meats and roots, put up to dry seasons back, were brought out to stew and simmer for hours. Fortunately, the smoke and cooking odors belched through the slits behind the oven walls and little of it entered the castle proper.

Dried fruits were fetched from dark cellars and left to soak in wines. Pastries were flattened on huge trencher boards, then filled with plump juicy fruits and fashioned into tarts. The tarts would be baked during the ceremony, then set upon the trencher boards, hot, succulent, and ready for the guests.

Iona directed the cleaning, baking, and housing of guests, helping every way she could. She even personally saw to the counting of linens for the guests. She knew full well that many a Scotswoman looked at her askance, but she needed to keep busy and simply ignored the questioning looks. On the day of the wedding, though, Marta and Spes refused to let her leave her room. She had nothing to do but wait until it was time to dress, and contemplate what that evening would bring.

"Did you know there'd be so many, milady?" Marta asked excitedly. "Even when our great king Harald came to visit we did not have more than this."

"Perhaps," Iona said absently. She was too busy trying to stem her rising panic to pay attention to the handmaiden.

"But, milady," Marta went on, "the king of Scotland is to come." And maybe even the leaders of Northumbria, or

Hibernia, or Mercia, or . . ." She faltered when Spes shook her head at her. "Pardon me, milady, I'll just get your dress. I've steamed it fresh and we've put the hot rocks on the creases." Throwing a worried look at Spes, she backed from the room.

"Marta is very excited about the nuptials, cousin," Spes said, not understanding Iona's obvious fear. Surely the Scot had been good to her. He'd brought her gifts, as was the custom—beautiful jewels, bolts of fine-loomed wool of every hue, and lengths of silks from Cathay. Yet Iona seemed unmoved by them, and had barely glanced at Spes when the gift that had come on this, the last of the days—a magnificent necklace of diamonds and emeralds. "Tell me what it is that burdens you, Iona, dearest cousin. I would help thee."

" 'Tis nothing," Iona said, not looking at her. "Truly, 'tis but bride nerves."

"I see." Spes didn't believe her cousin, but she also knew Iona could be very tight-lipped.

When Spes left, saying she'd help Marta bring the dress, Iona sagged against the bedpost. For long moments she allowed the worry, all her fears, to wash over her. Perhaps by letting them flow, they might diffuse, take another course, disappear. They didn't.

She heard her heavy door open, then the solid thud as it closed. Slippers swished across the floor. That sound told her it wasn't Marta or Spes. Pinning a smile on her face she turned, expecting some servants with her bath water. The smile fled, replaced by a look of surprise when she saw who it was. "Father Terrill! I didn't think I'd see you just yet." What did he want of her? She worried. She knew he was Magnus's closest confidant. Had the Sinclair a new directive for her? Her back stiffened as she braced herself. "How are you, Father?"

"I'm fine, my child. Though these still cool days chill my bones at times. I was hoping to see you for a moment, alone." He eyed her gently. "You are in a coil, milady. I see a pain hidden deeply in your eyes." When she opened her mouth to speak, he waved his hand placatingly. "I do not pry, milady. But I would have you know that I will listen if you ever have need to speak. Sometimes the painful buttresses caused by silence are removed by words." He paused. "Though I sense if you did talk of your agony, it would tear your being." He shook his head, tucking his hands in the sleeves of his tunic. "No wound should be so great, or should be allowed to fester. I would help you excise it if I could."

"Thank you," she said, trying to still the trembling of her lips. "You have been and are most kind to me, Father, but . . . 'tis naught to concern you. I will be able to come about, as the Vikings say." She swallowed. "But you will be at Father Monteith's side when we speak our vows?"

"If 'tis your wish, milady."

"It is." She liked this gentle man in his threadbare robe, his ascetic face like the images of the martyrs she'd seen in holy books. His slim body could've been described as emaciated, but there was an aura of strength about him, a goodness that went deep. And his eyes could see through the stout walls of Sinclair Castle. She cleared her throat. "I know you came from Bretagne and Normandy with Magnus's family, Father. Did Father Monteith come from there as well?"

Terrill smiled, understanding her ploy to distract him. Secrets were often painful. "Father Angus Monteith was with us for a while in Bretagne and Normandy. He'd come to plead for us to return to Scotland. But he was born in a region south of Athole, called Menteith. Many of his family were killed by the Mercians, and they fled north to this land. His mother was a St. Clair."

"You are wise in the ways of the families, Father. I would be honored to have you hear my vows."

"I cannot think the good abbot will applaud your choice." Terrill was relieved when he saw her smile with genuine amusement. Whatever goblin drove the princess had been put aside for a time.

"I doubt much would please the man." She quelled a grimace at the thought of the sour-faced leader of the friars, who would also be facing her at the altar.

"I've come to give you my blessing, milady." He lifted his hands.

"Thank you." Dropping to her knees, she bowed her head and listened to the Latin intoned above her. When the old priest switched to Icelandic, her head whipped up, and she smiled at him. "Thank you for that. I've missed the blessings in our language." She rose and gave him her hand.

He brushed his lips across it, then looked at her. "I would have you remember, milady, that Magnus too has secret pain." She nodded, again feeling sorrow for the young Magnus, who had lost his parents. "Mayhap," Terrill added, "you will comfort each other." He raised his hands in blessing again. "And I will ask God to send you children, and children of their children, so that your house will fill with all beneficence." When he saw a sudden sadness on her face, he smiled. "The runes do not see you as barren, milady."

As she stared speechless at him, he turned and glided from the room.

Iona continued gazing at the heavy plank door long after he'd pulled it shut behind him. Runes! The Vikings who clung to the old ways used them. It was blasphemy, but who would fault an old man's comfort? He did no harm. Besides, they could not tell the future. Nothing could do that. And she *was* too old for childbearing. She knew of no woman past the age of twenty-one who'd borne a child. "And nothing can change that, either," she murmured.

"What are you muttering, Iona?" Spes asked.

Iona started. She hadn't even noticed her cousin and Marta entering the room, carrying her dress.

"Nothing." Iona stared at the silk and woolen gown and felt queasy again. Naught that Father Terrill, or anyone else, could tell her would soothe away the fear.

Spes cleared her throat. "I heard the Sinclair ask you not to cover your face. Will you?"

"I don't know," she said.

. . .

In the great room, Magnus and Kenneth were discussing the final arrangements for the ceremony. It was to have been held in the hall, until so many guests arrived that it wouldn't be feasible. Slighting a family or a royal could precipitate a war. Though this had indeed happened at some weddings, Magnus had vowed that no ill will would mar his.

"I'll not allow the McLeods to stand near the MacDonnells," he told Kenneth. "The only bellicose actions will be in the field later when the men will joust at the games. See to it." He tossed the bits of tartan belonging to the many guests onto the table, spreading them out in a pattern, keeping those of hot blood apart.

"Aye, I will," Kenneth replied. "Tossing the caber and wrestling will cool their fevers. Glam has helped me arrange a place for the spear throwing. The Vikings favor that."

Magnus smiled wryly. "Don't let them beat us too handily. My bride doesn't need another hammer to hold over my head." He grinned when his brother laughed.

"Aye. The competition will be keen." Kenneth rubbed his chin thoughtfully. "Testing archery skills would bring a triumph of sorts, for our people are good at that."

Magnus stiffened at his brother's tone. "Have you heard aught of bad will toward the Vikings?"

Kenneth shook his head. "But I've had the feeling that some of the goodwill has faded, for both Scot and Viking alike. And for the life of me I can't find the reason for it."

"The Viking Einar is to be trusted, so says milady. Let him know of your fears."

Kenneth nodded, and his smile reappeared. "It'll be a rare taking to see these nuptials. All of Scotland comes, I'm thinking."

"Even milady's relatives from Iona?"

Kenneth shook his head. "No Skenes have been invited. It was the wish of the princess."

Magnus grimaced. "That will not set well with the king."

"Malcolm knows you for the most loyal and powerful laird in all of Scotland, Magnus. He'll not gainsay the lack of invitation to Skene." Kenneth hoped that was true. He had no intention of letting the Skenes on Sinclair land if the princess held them in abhorrence.

Magnus nodded as if he'd read his brother's mind. "All will go well," he vowed, and left for his chamber. It was time to dress.

As the bride and groom readied themselves inside, servants readied the bailey. A stand was constructed of stripped trees and anchored onto the highest section of ground. It would be the altar, and was large enough to hold a dozen people. The vows would be spoken there, and the mass celebrated. It would allow the hordes of people gathered to see the proceedings, though few would be able to hear.

In order to insure that his bride be warm enough, Magnus had ordered fire pots set on the perimeter of the stand. Their heat would penetrate to those on the stand, as well as to those who'd be on the inner circle below it. Other fire pots set around the bailey would take the chill off the onlookers.

Since the wedding was to be held only three hours after sunrise, the day had begun well before first light. By the time the sun rose, the castle was in a frenzy of chores. To the very point of the beginning of the ceremony, the whole area seethed with activity, with frantic attendants running hither and yon. The water clock dripped the minutes closer, closer, until at last it was the appointed time. The crowd of people took their assigned positions all around the bailey. A hush slowly fell over them as first the abbot and his entourage ascended the steps to the altar, and then Magnus, King Malcolm and his brother at his side, joined them. All heads turned as one to the incline leading to the main gate.

Only a minute passed before Iona walked out of the castle, Einar and Glam behind her. Magnus caught his breath at her beauty. She outshone the moon—and she wore no covering on her face! His heart squeezed inside his chest. He knew what it had cost her to reveal herself, and she had done it because he had asked.

As she crossed the inner courtyard to the gate, he knew there was nothing more glorious on earth or in heaven than his wife to be. Her hair, a silken moonglow nimbus, swung almost to the ground, covered only by a diaphanous silk the same white-gold color. Her bliaut was azure silk and flowed down her body in tiny pleats threaded with silver and gold. Her undergown was cream and silver, showing at her neck and wrists. Her ornamental corselet was of beaten silver and gold in a honeycomb pattern. Her coronet, as befitted her station, was of wrought gold studded with sapphires and diamonds.

She was a new moon in the sky, shining more beautifully than all others in the firmament. Magnus shook his head to clear it, but he could not tear his gaze from her. Her woven belt of silver and gold was wound once around her waist, then sat low on her hips. The ends swung back and forth across her body, beckoning him, titillating him. She could not know how beautiful she was. Otherwise she would not look so vulnerable, so innocent. When Kenneth sighed next to him, Magnus's fingers curled into fists. Damn! He was ready to strike his own brother for reacting to her beauty. She was a goddess, a Viking goddess come to test her wiles on him . . . and he welcomed the contest. Nay, he craved it.

" 'Tis a wonder she is, Magnus," Kenneth murmured.

"She makes a spectacle of herself in front of the people," the abbot said sourly.

Magnus turned and eyed the head of the friars, until the abbot looked down at the leather-bound parchment in his hands. "Beauty should not repel you, abbot," he said, an unmistakable warning in his soft voice. "Does not the Church teach that it goes hand in hand with goodness?"

"Aye," the abbot said, his eyes still downcast.

Nothing else was said as the bride made her way through the throng. More than one hand reached out to her. Magnus watched as she paused by both Scot and Viking and said something, clasping the hand of peasant and laird alike, time after time.

When she reached the wider area in front of the stand, she lifted her eyes to his. He saw a hint of a smile there, and a luminescent serenity. If he hadn't seen palpable signs of her agitation earlier, he could almost believe he looked on a happy bride.

He descended the rough-hewn steps before she could climb upward. Easily lifting her in his arms, he turned his back on the surprised Einar and Glam, who by law and custom should present the princess to him, and carried her upward himself. He heard the sighs, low huzzahs, and mutterings, but ignored them. At the top of the steps, he faced the throng and smiled with Iona still in his arms. A cheer went up.

"Magnus Sinclair," she muttered, "turn around and face the altar. You might offend the abbot and priests doing such a thing. And your king watches." She glanced toward the corner of the stand where Malcolm lounged in the chair of honor.

Magnus set her down in front of Old Terrill. "Malcolm would approve," he said.

They both bowed to the monarch, who inclined his head and smiled. But Iona had the distinct impression that Magnus didn't much care if he'd gained royal approval or not.

She faced Father Terrill again, but it was the abbot who cleared his throat and began an interminable series of prayers, with his friars, fanned out behind him, responding to his resounding Latin incantations.

She should've been used to the endless ritual. The priests at Kirkwall had the same reverence for long, drawn-out ceremonials, but somehow it had seemed friendlier in Icelandia. The abbot made it all sound somber and vaguely threatening.

She fought the strain in her knees, and her attention strayed constantly. To the king, to her Vikings, but mostly to Magnus. Deep within her churned the fatalistic surety that each word was carrying her closer and closer to her doom. What would Magnus do? As husband he had unlimited power over her, yet, oddly, she didn't fear his punishment. It was his disgust she dreaded.

Finally, he took her hand and they faced Father Monteith and Father Terrill. Iona listened carefully to the vows, blanching only when she repeated the one about obeying. When Magnus squeezed her hand, she looked up at him. The clod was grinning! She stumbled to the end.

Then began the mass. Halfway through, she began to feel light-headed. The abbot seemed determined to prolong the already lengthy ritual. She wondered if her trembling knees were visible through her gown.

Finally it was over. She looked up at her husband and immediately read his intent in his gleaming eyes. "Not in front of all these people—" she began, but he swung her off her feet and kissed her. She started to protest, but the fire he always ignited swept through her and she forgot all. She didn't even hear the roars of approval from the Scots, the lesser shouts of the Vikings. Magnus blinded and deafened, swallowed her whole.

At last he lifted his head. "Now you're my chatelaine."

"As you are my chatelain," she replied tartly. Before he could say more, she squirmed from his hold. Turning to the assemblage, she raised her arms.

The abbot gasped. " 'Tis not your place to speak, milady. That is your husband's prerogative."

She hesitated, then her gaze swept the crowd and she spoke, her words clarion clear. "I am Princess Asdis Iona of Icelandia, Lady Asdis Iona Sinclair, servant to her people, both Viking and Scot, and spouse to the mightiest lord in this land." She bowed her head as the people cheered.

Magnus lifted her hand and kissed it, then spoke too. "My wife honors me with her words. And I pledge my life to her, to her good, and the good of our peoples."

Her eyes widened in pleasure. He'd pledged fealty to the Vikings as well as the Scots, and the murmurs among the crowd testified that not all were as pleased as she. "Thank you," she whispered. She moved closer to him, meaning to take his arm to descend the steps. When her hand was taken by another, she started, then sank in a deep curtsy. "My liege," she murmured.

"And am I your liege, Princess Asdis Iona?" Malcolm smiled, but his shrewd eyes missed nothing.

"I will always defend my people and their king," she said, imitating his slightly saturnine tone.

When he laughed, Magnus grinned again. "My wife is a woman of honor."

"I see that." In an unusual move, Malcolm lifted her hand and kissed it. Since he was a king who generally decried ceremony, the gesture was noted, and murmurs rose and fell like a building wind. Then he waved his hand negligently. "Let the games begin."

Iona watched as Malcolm preceded them down the steps. He moved among the populace, talking, laughing. He spoke to Einar and the other Vikings, who almost smiled and bowed. "He's very personable, your king," she said to Magnus.

"Malcolm is at home in many places, from a peasant's hut to a castle. And he is a deadly opponent, for he knows games well and puts his all into the playing of them. He is participating in one at this moment. There're many reasons Malcolm would've attended our nuptials, milady . . . besides his prime one." He smiled at her questioning look. "He wants my pledge of support for any engagement to the south. There have been rumbles of trouble in Mercia, Anglia, and Northumbria. Malcolm wants a strong arm for attack . . . or retaliation."

She stiffened. "And could that be against Vikings too?"

"You lack trust, wife. I would not make war against your people—though I would defend my clan against attack."

She exhaled in relief. "There'll be none. Your king will be pleased with that."

He nodded. "Malcolm could always figure things well. He might be the shrewdest man on any throne this age."

Iona looked up at her husband, unexpectedly happy. Her fears were buried for a time as she and Magnus talked as friends, naturally, openly. She wouldn't dwell on the fact that it wouldn't always be thus, but would enjoy the moment. Though she'd always been included in political talk in Icelandia, she hadn't hoped for as much here. Yet Magnus spoke of his monarch and possible wars with her. That pleased her more than she would have thought.

"Your king will ask much of you," she said, "because he trusts you."

Magnus smiled down at her. "And some of what he asks he'll get." But he didn't want to think of Malcolm or any conflagrations that could await him and his clan. For today he wished to concentrate on his bride and their trip to Eynhallow.

As he escorted her down the steps and across the bailey, he savored the movement of her body bumping his. His blood heated to think of her naked and against him, mouth to mouth, breasts to chest, hip to hip, connected and loving. He wanted his wife with a fiery need that seemed unquenchable.

Leaning on her new husband's arm, Iona smiled. His arm was hard, like hammered iron. She couldn't help but wonder how other women saw him. No doubt they viewed him as highly desirable. Even now, when his marriage was not an hour old, she saw coquettish glances tossed his way. Saw some smile boldly when he looked at them—especially Elizabeth of Asquith. When Magnus nodded and smiled at her, Iona felt a connection throb between them. Did he feel so strongly toward the lovely Elizabeth? It was acceptable for a man to keep a leman though he be married. The thought of Magnus doing that sickened Iona, and she faltered.

Magnus stopped and leaned over her. "Tired?"

"No," she said, not looking at him. Would it take him long to forget the princess from Icelandia he'd married? A few days, perhaps. He could put her aside that very evening, banishing her from his lands.

Since the wedding had been in the early morning, the games would run until noon, when the feasting would begin. Shortly after the sun had risen high at midday, she and Magnus would embark for Eyin Helga. So soon, so soon.

Magnus frowned down at her, disgruntled at her obvious distraction. Her arm lay atop his, and he turned his hand to grip her fingers, bringing her closer to his side. He liked the feel of her. She constantly whetted his appetite with a desire to wrestle with her mind and her body. And he intended to do that. He'd discover all her secrets, especially why she saw fit to drift into another world when she was with him. It left a sour taste in his mouth to contemplate that she could be thinking of another man.

"Come," he said more sharply than he'd intended. "It's time for you to meet the families. Then we'll open the games." He wanted the schedule he'd set for the day adhered to closely. That way he and Iona could reach Eynhallow that day, and not on the morrow. His captain had told him the currents and winds would be favorable in the afternoon.

"And will you enter the lists?" she asked.

"No, Iona. And neither will you."

"I did not say I would," she said spiritedly.

He laughed. "I would spike your wheels if you tried, my princess. Many of the contenders today will have the blood lust in them, and want to battle to the death."

"And will you let them?"

"No, little one, I will not. That wouldn't be proper for our nuptial day." He paused to tip up her chin with one finger and kissed her quickly on the mouth.

"No, it would not," she said huskily as her heart flipped over from his caress. With an effort she pulled her gaze from his and noticed a man approaching them.

"Yonder comes your uncle." She tried to step away from him, but he gripped her hand and urged her forward.

He and Cormac greeted each other warmly, grasping forearms, then Magnus turned to Iona. "Wife, you already know my kinsman. And I hope you know he is a most important member of our family. He represents us not only at Malcolm's court, but at all others as well. And he served us well in Bretagne and Normandy." Hooking his arm around Iona's waist, he said to Cormac, "Now she is my wife, the lady Sinclair."

Cormac made a courtly bow to her. "I regret that because of my enforced absences from Sinclair Castle we have not gotten to know each other as well as we should, Lady Sinclair." He smiled charmingly. "I fully intend to change that."

She nodded and smiled in return, though in truth she felt awkward. Her last conversation with Cormac had been about stopping this marriage. "Please call me Iona. Family does not stand on ceremony."

"Aye, I will. And you must call me Cormac. You have a most beauteous name, milady." His gaze swept over her, and he shook his head. "And you are the color of the moon."

Magnus watched his wife redden, and felt a tightening in his throat. He, not other men, should be the one to compliment his wife.

"Thank you." Iona smiled at Magnus's uncle. He reminded her of courtiers she'd met in Genoa and Florence. His easy ways seemed a part of him. No rough-and-tumble Scot, this.

"Or you can call him uncle," Kenneth said, coming up behind them. "I've come to kiss the bride."

"Make it quick," Magnus said abruptly. "We must begin the games."

Kenneth laughed as Cormac grinned, and Iona stared at him in confusion. What had angered him? She accepted Kenneth's buss on the cheek, then offered the same cheek to Cormac. When she opened her mouth to speak further with the two men, Magnus whisked her up into his arms and strode toward the castle. Infuriated at his arrogance as well as embarrassed, she reprimanded him. "You are not to do this, Magnus Sinclair. Can you not see the stares we are evoking?"

"And why shouldn't they stare? You're a beautiful bride." He took a deep breath. "And I like you without your veil."

Astounded by his words, she could only gaze at him. "But perhaps I should walk."

"No." He was damned tired of all the men ogling her so openly. Had they no sense? After he broke a few heads they would better understand the proper way to treat Lady Sinclair.

At that moment Iona was glad he was carrying her. Her knees would've buckled beneath her otherwise. Had he just told her he found her beautiful? That her scar meant little to him?

"Tell me what you are thinking, wife," he said softly.

"My scar has not offended you or your people," she whispered.

"Why does that surprise you? Did you not know you were so lovely?"

She lowered her gaze, suddenly shy. "I thank you for the kind words, husband. I didn't think to hear such declarations from you."

Magnus frowned. "That can't displease you. I can see I shall have to get the blacksmith to hammer you a copper mirror."

" 'Tis not displeasure I feel, but surprise," she told him tartly.

"I see you have much to learn of me." He smiled, anticipation lighting his eyes. "And we will begin tonight."

Color flooded her face, and he laughed with delight. He would've continued the conversation, but the king had already preceded them to the field where the games were to be held and was waiting for them to commence them.

The pavilion that had been erected there provided shelter from the everlasting north wind, and they were served food and drink. Iona sat at Malcolm's right hand. Although Magnus's proper place was to the left of his sovereign, he chose to sit beside Iona. She glared at him for his lack of manners, but he only smiled, and the king laughed.

The games themselves were loud and bloody, but as Magnus had promised, there was no killing—although a few contenders had to be forcibly restrained.

Iona welcomed the distraction of the games, for Magnus's closeness kept her anxiety and anticipation running high. When he slid his hand to her waist, she stiffened. Slowly, he began to stroke her back, up to her neck and down again to her waist. She considered telling him to stop, but surreptitious glances at the king and the others on the pavilion showed her no one was watching. Besides, his hand warmed her, and those long strokes were strangely lulling, across her stiff shoulders and then down . . . lower . . . lower—

"Sinclair!" She nearly bolted from her chair, but remembered herself in time. Stunned, she glanced at the king. He was grinning! These Scots were a demented lot. They had no sense of decorum.

"You shock your bride, methinks, Magnus," Malcolm said.

"Nay, my liege, she's cold and welcomes my heat," Magnus drawled.

Malcolm nodded. "She comes from a land of hot springs. Mayhap you will need to find one on Sinclair land."

"She will have heat."

Magnus's words were like a covenant, spoken low but with a hard resonance.

Iona smiled wanly and reached for her goblet of wine. Her hand was shaking.

⪦ 11 ⪧

Eynhallow frank, Eynhallow free,
Eynhallow stands in the middle of the sea;
A roaring roost on every side—
Eynhallow stands in the middle of the tide.
　　　　　—From an old Orkney verse

The sea was a caldron of waves and breakers as they sailed north, always in sight of land but off and away from the shore currents that could grind a ship into the rocky strands of the islands they passed. Weaving through the strait was a navigator's nightmare, but the Viking ship moved steadily forward.

"That's St. Margaret's Hope that we passed some time back," Magnus told Iona. "Now we'll tack past Auskerry and between Shapinsay and Stronsay."

They stood together at the bow rail, Magnus with his back to the wind, sheltering his new wife. He knew she was surprised and pleased that he'd let Einar captain his own ship on this trip to Eynhallow, and he'd been glad to please her.

Iona nodded, only able to hear her husband because he'd pressed his mouth to her ear. Her heartbeats imitated the cadence of the wild northern waters. Though Einar and the captains of the two Scottish ships that escorted them had said they were delighted with the "good" weather, she couldn't help but wonder what bad weather would be like. Their ship was tossed like flotsam in the crosscurrents as they entered what Magnus called the sound, the body of roiling water that crashed between Rousay and Mainland. But Einar manned his ship well, guiding them easily through the rough seas.

"Land dead ahead!" the watch called. "Eyin Helga!"

"What would it take for them to call it by its right name?" Magnus asked, his mouth just touching her ear.

She shivered at that light touch. Magnus thought her cold, though, and immediately opened his skins and enfolded her inside them, against his body. She warmed almost to melting at once. The pounding in her blood wouldn't let her speak, even if she could be heard over the roaring of the water.

"Warmer?" Magnus asked.

She nodded, her gaze fixed on the just-visible island. Her heart raced. Eyin Helga! She'd arrived at last . . . but not alone. She had a husband. The wise women of Icelandia who had told her her destiny lay in the Orkneys had foretold nothing about that.

"Is Eynhallow as beautiful as you'd thought it would be?"

She nodded again. "I was here with my grandfather and father once before."

Sensing a change in her, Magnus leaned over her. The sight of tears on her cheeks startled him. "Tell me," he said brusquely.

She raised her eyes to his. "My destiny is here," she said.

"Then so is mine, Iona. Because you are mine."

Iona almost believed she'd misheard him, but from his grim look, the iron set of his jaw, she was sure she hadn't. She looked toward the island again, not sure how she should feel. Why had he said that? When he tightened his arms around her, she closed her eyes and tried to think of nothing. Her husband kept her warm. That was enough for now.

They anchored the ship and lowered the small, shallow, skin-lined boat that would carry them to the narrow strand. They had little time to make their landing because of the currents and tides. Only she, Magnus, Spes, Marta, and Glam would be staying, along with a few Scottish warriors to guard Magnus.

Iona turned to Einar, grasping his forearms as he bowed. "My friend."

"My princess. Always."

Einar's words carried to Magnus, who scowled.

Their supplies were loaded onto the boat and transported. More than once she thought the fragile-looking craft would capsize, but it didn't. It made two more trips before taking Spes, Marta, and Glam. She held her breath until she saw her friends on the beach under the sheer cliff.

"Glam did not need to accompany us, Iona," Magnus said, coming up behind her.

"He is my protector," she said simply. "By right of birth, he will be my guardian unto death."

"You now have a husband to guard you."

She smiled at his truculent tone, despite a stab of pain at his words. Soon he wouldn't want to protect her. "Yes, I do. But Glam's charge doesn't change. Only death can do that."

"He will not be in our house this night, milady. I assure you of that. There's room for your protector in one of the huts."

She shook her head. "That will be for Glam to decide. I don't tell him how to do his charge. He will decide where he sleeps, even if it is out of doors."

"Women are subject to their husbands, as are their retainers." Despite his chastising tone, Magnus was pleased at her familiar show of spirit.

"And husbands must cherish their wives . . . but in many cases that is a gnome's tale, is it not?" She smiled gently when he frowned. "Glam will be nearby. Do not seek to gainsay him. He will die for his duty, Sinclair."

"Are you never to call me Magnus, wife? You did so before our nuptials."

She faced him squarely. "Magnus." She touched his chin with one finger. "My spouse."

"That's right," he said huskily. He'd heard the quivering in her voice, as though she'd spoken a falsehood. Before she could step down from the Viking ship and into the arms of one of her men, waiting in the small boat, he swept her up into his embrace. Moving easily, his burden as nothing, he stepped down into the shallow craft, his balance so right that he barely caused it to sway.

She tried to wriggle free when he sat down and kept her on his lap. "Magnus, 'tis not seemly." The man was a barbarian and had no idea of decorum, but his heat seeped into her.

"You are my wife," he said, not adding that he couldn't bear to see another man, Viking or Scot, touch her. Though all had shown her the respect her new status demanded, the thought of some other man holding her had the bile rising in his throat.

Unable to argue with his explanation, Iona allowed herself to snuggle into his embrace, welcoming the protection from the biting wind.

They landed with a bump and a splash against the boulders strewing the strand. The men jumped out, not seeming to notice the cold water lapping up around their calves.

Magnus lifted Iona out and set her down on dry sand. She turned when she heard the unmistakable squeak of the oars being plied, then looked up at Magnus inquiringly.

"They need to bring on stores from our two Sinclair ships too." He gestured to the small Scottish ships.

She nodded. As Magnus cupped his hands around his mouth and began shouting instructions to his men, she took the chance to study him. Her husband was handsome, a bear of a man, but there was sleekness to him also. He fitted well into the rugged, forbidding environment of Eyin Helga, but she had the sure notion he would do as well in any court in any kingdom. His russet hair was threaded through with gold, thick and shining with health. He had no beard, but she knew it would be the same hue as the hair on his head. Bursting with confidence, he knew who he was, and he stood on the strand like the mighty Thor, able to roar down the elements to do his bidding. He was a fearsome man, who had wrested his demesne from all enemies, and who would keep it. He cut down resistance to his will with his mighty claymore, yet she didn't fear him.

He glanced down at her and smiled when he caught her scrutinizing him. "What goes on in that head of yours, my princess? Planning my demise?"

"How can you say that?" Mirth rose in her. "Have I not pledged to cherish you?"

"You have, milady. So you have." He looked back at the three ships. "Once all we'll need is on land and we're settled, the boats will leave."

Her hesitant nod had him frowning. Was she afraid to be alone with him?

"Come," he went on. "It's too windy for you to dawdle here. You'll catch the ague if you do." He turned her toward the narrow flight of steps carved into the side of the cliff. It would be slippery going, what with the wind tugging at them, but he'd keep her safe. "Remember to lean toward the wall. There are grips there if the wind strengthens. Fear not, I'll have my hand on you all the way."

"I do not fear, Magnus Sinclair. Have you forgotten I'm a Viking?"

"Nay, wife, but I'd hoped to spare your sensibilities by not mentioning it." When she swung around, glaring, he threw back his head and laughed. It pleased him like naught else to bait her. She so readily rose to it.

She shoved against his chest, then strode toward the cliff and started up the steps. She stepped incautiously, though, and slipped. She would've fallen, but Magnus was right behind her and steadied her.

"See," he said quietly. "Be careful, wife."

"I'm careful," she said breathily, wishing her voice didn't sound so strange when he was nigh. Magnus Sinclair was a devil of a Scot, and he would drive her mad with his ways. She was well into womanhood, past childbearing and worthy of his respect. It was foolish of her to feel so girlish. Yet what would it have been like to bear his child? Blood rushed through her, coloring her skin. She forced the impossible thought aside. "You must not treat me like a mere maid," she told him.

"Why?"

"My age demands more respect."

"Why do you make yourself an ancient, Iona? You're not."

She stopped and stared at him, hurt, humiliated. He must know her age, know she couldn't give him an heir.

Magnus was puzzled by the mistiness he saw in her eyes. She felt like a maid to him. He could easily span her waist with his hands. Her hips were wide enough to accommodate a babe, yet there was a slender girlishness to her that belied whatever years she chose to put on herself. Even her eyes had a childlike sparkle, and could widen with eagerness and curiosity. In so many ways she was the youngest woman he'd ever known. Her artlessness was engaging, and it annoyed him that she harped about her age.

"To me you are a maid," he said, and was taken aback when she whitened. She swung her head away from him as though he'd struck her. "What is it? Have you pain?"

"No," she said. But she was in agony as she faced the awful truth that she didn't want to be put aside by Magnus. She could live with humiliation, for no doubt he'd simply leave her here. But she didn't want him turning his back on her, and she was loath to wonder why. They'd jousted verbally about many things, and she'd grown fond of the encounters. She'd found he had great intellect and was more than willing to battle his wit with hers. She'd not expected that from any man but her father and grandfather. All other males treated her royally, or reckoned she had not a thought in her head. Magnus had made room for her in his life. She wanted to remain.

She hurried upward, and almost slipped again. When she felt his steadying hand at her back, she caught her breath, wanting to pull free, but making no sudden move on the treacherous steps. She couldn't cry. She was a princess of Icelandia and must accept her fate. Was it not foretold that she'd be here, on the holy island . . . alone?

When they reached the high field that ran right to the cliff edge, Iona stepped onto the crackling grass and paused. The ever-present wind whipped her scarves and cloak about her and rocked her body. The sky was slashed with slate and azure, as the sun tried to cut through the scudding clouds. If it hadn't been for the wind, the atmosphere would've been pleasing, almost soothing. She lifted her head to heaven, closed her eyes, and murmured an Icelandic prayer.

"Do you call upon Wotan, milady?" Magnus stepped up behind her, his hand loosely clasping her waist.

She glanced up at him, noticing how his eyes were the same color as the patches of blue above them. "Not this time, though I have."

"I think the abbot would deem you flirting with heresy."

"If you cared a fig what he thought, do you mean?"

He smiled. "Exactly."

She studied him for a moment, then turned and swept her arm in an arc, encompassing the wild, windswept island that seemed only good for sheep and the squawking terns overhead. "This is a homecoming of sorts for me. I was told that I would come here and find my destiny."

Magnus thought of Old Terrill and his reading of the runes, and how they'd foretold her coming to him. "And your other home is Sinclair Castle," he said. She turned to him, and he was pleased that she actually smiled. He touched her cheek, stroking one finger over it. "I like to see your whole face, Iona. And I do not think of this as a scar." He touched the intriguing mark. "It is a sign of beauty." He grinned when her mouth dropped open. "Does it surprise you that I would like it? Because I do, very much."

"It stuns me that you could be poetic," she blurted out, then turned fiery red at her indiscretion. When he threw back his head and laughed, she frowned at him. "You're most unseemly, Magnus Sinclair," she said primly, looking away so that he wouldn't see how she'd been warmed by his mirth.

He clasped her hand and tugged her around to face him again. "Now, don't tell me it isn't done, milady. This is Eynhallow. None come here but the terns and sheep, and they won't demand court manners."

"God save us if we act in an unconscionable manner," she retorted sharply.

He raised his eyes to heaven. "You're a sore trial to me, Iona, but I'll bear up."

She pretended to scowl. "Barbarian."

He watched her wonderful mouth twitch, fighting a smile. He pulled her hand through his arm, keeping her close. "I'm afraid we've picked a stormy kingdom, Princess. Let's get inside."

They had not far to walk on the high cliff. His mother's family, the Dugalds, had built a small fortress with a wall surrounding it. Long and rectangular, it was walled and roofed in stone, and mortared all over to keep out drafts. Five stone chimneys rose above the roof, one at each end, two in front, and one in back. Surrounding it were several crofter's huts, and Iona spied shaggy sheep grazing along with goats. They looked blankly at the intruders, then went back to nosing the grass for the sweetest stems and succulent roots.

"The herdsmen are Vikings," she said with surprise when a fleece-robed man swept off his leather conical hat and bowed to her. "I had not expected them to venture so close to your holding."

"Yes, they herd in the area. And they've been loyal to me," Magnus said dryly. The man who had bowed to Iona had been his tenant for years, but never had he made any servile gesture to Magnus. "I can see they knew of your coming, Princess."

Iona was coming to know Magnus Sinclair. He always used the most formal form of address when he was annoyed. She didn't know what had caused his ire at that moment, but she knew it was there. "Of course. Our ships

that bring them stores would've told them to expect me."
She waved to the man and called out to him in Icelandic.
Only a flash of his teeth answered her.

"And do they know you're Lady Sinclair now?" Magnus
asked.

She was about to answer when Spes and Marta called
to her from the house. She glanced at them, then back at
Magnus.

"Go about your duties, wife," he said.

"We'll talk again, Sinclair."

"Aye, we will."

She shivered at the soft promise in his voice, then hurried away from him toward the house.

For a moment as she was alone, she felt a damp, cold
foreboding, as though an enemy—a familiar one—lurked
nearby. But no. It couldn't be. Skene wouldn't come to
Eyin Helga.

She hurried into the house and followed the two
women down a dark corridor that bisected the domicile.
The back of the house was an afterthought, Iona was sure.
There was a large spacious room with a fireplace big
enough to roast an ox. On either side of it were short
corridors leading to an even larger area. The fireplace
opened to both rooms, so that cooking could be going on
on both sides. Large trencher boards were also set up in
each room, and shelves to hold the stores. Light came from
many torches stuck along the walls, and the huge logs in
the fireplace gave off a welcome heat.

"We have a house connected at the back," Spes said,
all at once shy with her cousin. "Marta and I will tend you,
then retire there, milady."

Iona swung around to look at her cousin and handmaiden. "You've both known me since we took our lessons
together. You are free Viking women, and will address me
as you always have."

Marta nodded and picked up a skin-wrapped bundle. "I
will put our things away, then I will tend to the feast for
Lord and Lady Sinclair."

"No, Marta. We ate our fill at the banquet—"

"And you must eat your first meal alone," Marta interrupted firmly, "so it will be a ritual one, milad— Iona. It is our way." She curtsied and left, taking another narrower corridor to the quarters at the back.

Spes tried to smile at her cousin. "I have not done my duty by you, Iona. Though I'm younger than you, I can only wish that I have knowledge to convey. I cannot tell thee what this night will be, for I do not know. But my heart aches for thee, knowing you chose it not." A tear coursed down her cheek. "I curse the day we landed on Scotland's shore."

"Shh, cousin. Say not such. Think of all the good things you've done on Sinclair land . . . and the people there who are dear to you." Iona smiled when her cousin reddened. "Do not agonize, I beg thee. I fear not." She was too numb to fear. She was prepared, but that didn't stop the bile from rising in her throat.

Iona was relieved that the next few hours were busy, as all the people and their goods were settled in the main house and the few vacant huts. Too soon, though, the evening meal was ready and she had to join Magnus— alone—in the great room.

"Marta has made us a meal," she said hesitantly, standing just inside the room.

Magnus nodded, watching her. She was skittish enough to bolt. Why was she twisting herself into such an agony? She was his wife now. "I will get the food."

Even as he said it, Marta and Spes glided into the room carrying trays. The aroma of roasting meat redolent with herbs filled the air. Along with the lamb there were root grasses and tubers that had been cooked with the meat.

Magnus was startled by the luscious repast. He looked up at the women. "You will have some as well. And you will teach our women to dress it so."

"Thank you, lord," Marta said, beaming rosily.

"Our food is in the back, lord," Spes added. She nodded to Iona, then backed from the room.

Iona couldn't do justice to the succulent fare, but Magnus ate almost all that was on the table.

Pushing aside his wooden goblet and trencher at last, he walked around the table and lifted her to her feet. "Our room is on the other side, wife."

"Yes," she said weakly.

When the heavy door closed behind her with a thud, she whirled around to face her husband. But he wasn't there! Spes was, a silk gown in her hands. He'd left her to the ministrations of her women.

Spes chattered to her as she helped her change and wash.

When she deemed Iona ready, she lit two more candles, kissed Iona's cheek, and left. Iona wanted to plead with her cousin not to leave her, but she couldn't find the words. Even if she had, pride wouldn't have let her voice them. She simply sat on a bench staring into the fire. When she heard Magnus enter, she rose to face him.

Magnus stared at her, clenching his teeth as he tried to force down the desire that raged through him. Her gown was of a creamy silk, and when she moved, it shimmered around her like moonbeams, outlining her wondrous form. He swallowed. "You look beautiful, wife."

"Magnus Sinclair, I would speak with you."

Though she whispered, he heard the urgency in her voice. A premonition of danger had him studying all corners of the room before he eyed her again. "Speak," he said calmly.

Iona took a deep breath and stared at his chin. She could not look into his eyes, or she'd lose her courage. "I do not come to you untouched."

Magnus struggled to keep his face expressionless, struggled to tamp down the anger. He did not want to hear of her lover. "You told me you haven't been wed, Iona." He forced himself to continue gazing at her. She looked to be cast in bronze. Her very stillness alarmed him as flickering light from the fireplace played over her features.

"Not until this day," she answered.

Fury fired in him again. He battled it down. "You've lain with a man who was not your spouse?" He'd kill the man, dismember him and leave him to the carrion birds.

Her fear made Iona reckless, and she lashed out at him. "And have you not lain with women who were not your wife?"

Magnus opened his mouth, closed it, opened it again. "Shrewishness does not become a princess of Icelandia."

"Promiscuity does not enhance the reputation of the Sinclair."

"But you have not answered my question. Have you lain with one who was not your husband?"

"No."

Magnus eyed her warily, wondering at the contradiction. But her nearly palpable fear told him she was not lying. "You talk in riddles, woman."

"You will hear me out?"

He nodded shortly.

"Many years ago when I was but ten summers, as I stalked small game on the isle of Stroma, my uncle stalked me."

She threaded her hands together as her mind forced her back to that terrifying time.

"I didn't like my uncle, but he was my mother's brother, so I tried to be courteous to him. That day, though, I feared the look on his face and tried to run." She swallowed, staring at a wall hanging. "He caught me . . . and he cut me with his dirk. But first, he put his hand up into me and deflowered me."

"Skene!" Magnus saw her body tremble, but didn't move. He dared not. His blood boiled through him in such a caldron, he feared it would burst through his skin.

Iona braced herself. Even though she wasn't looking at him, she knew what would be on his face. Enmity. Fury. And disgust. She feared that the most, and knew it would be there. Lifting her chin, she nodded. "Skene. Not even my mother knew of his evil, because at the time she treated me, my legs were covered with blood from the cuts on my thighs. I feared to tell her. I knew her grievous anger would cloud her good sense. My mother was quick to be riled. She would've enlisted my father and grandfather and embroiled us in a war. I couldn't do that. So . . . when she wiped the blood from my face and thighs, I told her naught of the injury within."

She stopped and drew in a shuddering breath. Magnus's own breathing was ragged, and a stream of curses poured from his mouth. He wasn't going to put her aside. He was going to kill her.

She sighed and shook her head. No need to go on. He wouldn't care to hear it, so she didn't tell him of the nightmares, of how she'd wake screaming in the night and her parents had been unable to comfort her. Still, it galled her that he would not see her as the frightened girl she'd been, but as the unclean spouse she'd become.

Long moments passed as Magnus tried to bring himself under control. Black rage had rendered him almost immobile, though his very skin and bones seemed to vibrate with fury. Not since his parents' death had he felt so impotent, and so consumed by blistering, blinding anger. And now it was worse. Someone had despoiled what belonged to him. By the code of the clan there must be vengeance. He wanted to kill, to wage bloody war against all who dwelt on the accursed isle of Iona. And he would pay back well the man who had dared to touch his Iona, Lady Sinclair.

Iona could stand his silence no longer and lifted her head to face him. "So," she said hoarsely. "It is your right to put me aside." *And your right to put me to the executioner's ax.* But she didn't say it. She couldn't.

Magnus felt such shock at her words, and such a deep admiration for her courage, that he just stared at her. He was jolted out of his contemplation when she smiled bleakly at him and turned away. He crossed the room to her and placed one hand on her shoulder.

She stiffened, bracing for a blow.

"What say you, Magnus Sinclair?" Her voice was so raw and rough, it hurt to speak. The end was nigh! God and Wotan would be merciful. They would let her die bravely.

∽ 12 ∽

Because of deep love one is courageous.
—Lao-tzu

Magnus saw the consternation on Iona's face, saw how she braced herself against the punishment she seemed to expect. He forced himself to keep his own expression mild, though fury burned through him. Damn! How long she'd carried her burden. When he got his hands on the son of a bitch . . . Mentally shaking himself out of the enjoyable conjurings of the many deaths he'd put Skene through, he smiled down at her.

"Do you wish to leave this chamber, Iona? If so, I will accompany you. I am your spouse."

His baffling words sent her spinning away from him. "Do you not comprehend me, Sinclair? I'm unclean . . . and—and past birthing. You have the right to put me aside. I can stay here with Spes and Marta as we'd planned—"

"They may stay, if that's your wish, but your husband will remain with you as well." He approached her again and touched her arm. "Tonight is our nuptial night, is it not?"

"Yes, but surely you don't . . . I mean, you may have an annulment. I told you of my plight, Sinclair, and—" The world whirled about her. Stars spun. She feared she would swoon for the first time in her life.

He grinned at her. "And now, by law, you may call me Magnus, just as I'll call you Iona."

"But . . . but you've been doing that right along."

He chuckled and brought her close to him. "So I have." When he leaned down so that their lips were almost touching, he felt her tremble. "And you can kiss me. 'Tis most seemly for a wife to do that."

Even as his lips touched hers, she was speaking. "Magnus, I fear you weren't listening. I told you that I'd be considered un—"

His mouth pressed tight onto hers, and his tongue parted her lips, thrusting inside in a rhythm that imitated the act he ached to perform. Breathing harshly, he lifted his head slightly. Only when his heart stopped slamming into his chest wall did he speak. "You must never use that term about yourself, Lady Sinclair. It would displease your husband very much."

Stunned, Iona could only watch his mouth descend again. Her knees threatened to give way, her body felt like soft tallow. "You're . . . to . . . call . . . me . . . Iona." She sighed, her eyes drooping shut as she sagged against him. She couldn't muster any more arguments. She'd worn herself out by telling him. She'd have to trust to God that all would be well. Mayhap she was a fool to believe his words, but she longed to do so, and would until he proved her wrong by heaving her from the cliffs of Eyin Helga into the sea.

Magnus stared at her for a moment, adoring her wonderful face with the skin finer than silk. Then he gave in to the urge to kiss that intriguing mark that curved down the left side of her face. When his mouth touched it, heat jolted through him, and he felt a wild joy. Hungry for her, he nibbled there, his breathing coming in shallow gasps as though he'd just run up a cliff. When she tried to back away, he tightened his grip, holding her close. "No, wife."

"Scar," she whispered.

"Beauty mark," he replied.

Not quite sure what was happening to her, Iona tried to balance her mind and body. But she had a strange sensation of disembodiment, as though her feet had left the floor and she floated. "Magnus . . . ?"

"Iona," he said softly. He sensed the rising passion in her and recognized her uncertain response to it. Nonetheless, she was enchanting. He could finally understand how Odysseus and his men had been ensnared by Circe. Iona wouldn't need a potion to work her magic. He had married an enchantress, yet she had no knowledge of her power over him.

He stared at her mouth, not able to tear his gaze away. He wanted to devour her with kisses, starting with that delectable mouth. He liked the fullness of her lips, especially the bottom one, and the way they quirked up at each corner, forming delightful indentations.

"Iona," he said again.

When her eyes fluttered open, he dropped his mouth to hers, sucking her upper lip while his tongue lapped at her bottom one. Then he kissed her cheek, seeking each pore, as his hands ran restlessly up and down her spine.

"This—this is not unpleasant," she stammered. "Though I'm not proficient in such."

"You soon will be," he vowed, loving her innocence. He was delighted that none had touched his wife in an intimate, loving way. He'd be her first, and she'd forget what her uncle had done. And after he had killed Skene, dismembered him, and thrown his body to the wolves, she'd think no more on her clansman's infamy.

His heart almost burst with pride for the woman who would share his bed for years to come. She'd been violated by a bastard and had held the painful secret in her heart rather than risk her people and family in war. She was truly a princess. She'd neither whined about it nor complained when she'd told him, only explained in short sentences what had occurred.

He hadn't realized his arms had tightened around her

until she wriggled to be free. He released her and she backed away. "What is it?" he asked.

"We are finished." She tried to smile. "Are we not?"

He stared blankly at her, then realization came and he smiled. She thought his kiss was a good-bye. And judging by her expression, she didn't know whether to be relieved or saddened. No doubt she feared the culmination. "No, milady, we've barely begun. I hope you've rested these past days." Satisfied, he watched her blush. No missish ways with his princess. She knew of what he spoke, though she'd had no taste of the beauty that could be between a man and woman.

He bent down and caught her behind the knees, swinging her up into his arms. Feeling her tremble, he shook his head. "Don't fret, Iona. There'll be joy, not pain, with me."

"How say thee? I can recall the pain and there is full measure of it." Unconsciously, she'd spoken in Icelandic. Magnus's smile told her he'd still understood. "You've begun to comprehend our Viking words."

"I have. It's fitting that a man should understand his spouse." No need to tell her that he'd pressed Einar and Glam for such tutelage, because it'd been like a nettle under his skin that his learned wife knew Gaelic so well and he only a smattering of Icelandic.

"Then I say to you again," she continued in Gaelic, "that I know of the pain, Magnus Sinclair."

Anger filled him once more. He'd scour the island of Iona until he found Skene. He stood still for a moment, reining in the anger, then carried her to the bed. "You'll have joy, Iona."

"But, Magnus, I cannot give you an heir."

"Kenneth is my heir." He laid her on the bed, then stretched out close to her. Excitement coursed through him at finally having her there. They would share such a night of passion.

"But you should think of the clan," she told him earnestly, turning on her side to face him and forgetting for a moment where they were.

"I have thought of the clan. And that's why we're

wed." He didn't mean it quite the way it sounded, and he saw her recoil. Sighing, he did something he rarely did. He explained. "I would've married you, Iona, even if I couldn't bear to bed you. But hear me out, woman. I want to bed you, and it has nothing to do with the clan or your Vikings. And I want you to want it as well." He chuckled at her stunned look. "I seem to have found the method of silencing you. I tell you that I think you're desirable, and you're struck dumb. Yes, 'tis a rare important find, I'm thinking, and 'twill serve me well down through the years." He reached out and swept the veil confining her hair from her head. The moon-gold hair spilled upon his pillow. As she lay still, caught in his gaze he grasped her ornate kirtle and lifted it up over her head. "I think you needs sit up, milady, so I might remove your gown."

As though realizing for the first time that she was in his bed, in his arms, and that he was undressing her, Iona scrambled backward. He caught her at the waist and lifted her to him, until their faces were almost touching. "How like thee this bed, Iona?" he asked in halting Icelandic.

"It will be good for sleeping?" His laughter made her smile, but she still couldn't quiet the nervous beating of her heart. She was to find her destiny at Eyin Helga. Was it Magnus?

"Mayhap it will be good for sleeping," he said. "Later." She would not sleep until he'd loved her from crown to foot and back again. He would make her burn as she did him.

He pressed his mouth to hers again, and it pleased him that she didn't pull back. Her hands actually touched his shoulders, although tentatively. He kissed her deeply, heavily, not holding back his heat. When he lifted his head, her eyes were closed, her breathing shallow and fast.

Moving quickly, he removed her silk nightgown, leaving her clothed in naught but the woolen stockings she'd kept on for warmth. He threw off his own clothes as though the splendid tartan and finely woven linen shirt were rags. Kissing her deeply again, he began unrolling her stockings. He couldn't help but caress her creamy skin along the way, and desire boiled through him.

When her eyes popped open at a particularly erotic caress, he smiled lazily. "It's fitting, Iona," he said. But behind her answering smile he saw panic. He kissed her again, giving passion and asking for it, as his hands eased over her backside. Her buttocks were sweet and smooth, and he was eager to taste them, taste all of her. His mouth opened over hers, and she parted her lips. Fire shot through him, and he began a slow, lazy exploration, his tongue sweeping into her mouth as his body hardened with want. She gasped with awareness, then shyly touched his tongue with hers. That caress sent shafts of desire slicing through him, and he groaned.

She pulled back from him. "Magnus? It's always like this?"

"No!" It had never been like this. But his explosive answer confused her, and her eyes were wide and questioning. He brought her back to his chest as gently as he could with his emotions rampaging through him. "Most never know this well-kept secret we share, Iona."

"Oh." The man needed to express himself better, Iona thought dazedly. Or mayhap not. His hands and mouth were eloquent enough. She couldn't stem the moan that tore from her throat. Then thought faded away and she became a leaf on the stormy sea, tossed and whipped and whirled.

Ceaselessly he caressed her body as he kissed her, his hands demanding and possessive. He could feel her quiver beneath him. Her heat was starting, and that sent the hot blood thundering through him. It gave him immense pleasure to know that his wife would be finding her own passion as she discovered his. But it shook him, too, that she could evoke such a torrent in him. His heart thudded out of rhythm when he felt her tongue slip inside his mouth. In her innocence she didn't know how close to the edge she drove him, and in her stubborn Viking way, she'd turned it all around, burning him up with her fever instead of allowing him to bring her to flame first.

He wrenched his mouth from hers. "You will have joy," he promised her again, then his lips moved down over her jaw, her neck. His tongue delved into her ear, and she cried out in surprise. That sound was more fuel to the raging fire she'd started in him. It stunned him that she could so arouse him, but he didn't stop his slow, wondrous voyage over her body. When he blew gently on her navel, she arched like a pulled bow. He chuckled and pressed his open mouth against her middle.

"Magnus? 'Tis seemly?" she asked weakly.

"Most seemly, my princess," he answered her hoarsely. His mouth traveled over her stomach, feeling it pull in reflexively as the sensations built in her. He had set a course for their loving, but his good intentions to slowly teach her passion through the hours of the night were eroding rapidly. He wanted her desperately and had to fight back his urges as he'd never done. He moved back up to her lovely satiny breasts. Pausing, breathing raggedly, he lifted his head to gaze into her eyes. Glazed and wild, they were as erotic as the rest of her.

"There'll be no walls betwixt us, Iona. In freeing you for love, wife, you'll have no need of your fears. Do you hear me?"

"Yes," she managed to say, her hands fluttering over him. He was driving her mad with an unnameable need. Her breath was like bird's wings in her throat. Words caught there. "Magnus . . ."

"It's fine, little one," he said, then lowered his mouth to her breast.

Iona called out to him, not even realizing she'd said his name, as he suckled on her. A hot tingling sparked in the backs of her legs, turning her joints to water and further enflaming that need she didn't understand. As Magnus's hands moved lower, she could feel the need like a blossom opening to the sun, wanting more and more light. Yet despite the passion consuming her, she feared the pain. Not all of Magnus's comforting words had eradicated it, and as his hands neared her womanhood, she became cool again, worried, withdrawing.

Magnus sensed the change immediately and pulled back. He nuzzled her neck and murmured, "Don't fret. I'll make it sweet for you."

He kissed her softly, then slid his body down hers until his mouth was close to the junction of her legs.

Even as she watched him, breathless, wondering what he would do, her fear filled her. Swallowing a scream, she braced herself, even as a part of her instinctively cried out for his heat.

Then his mouth touched her, and her hips lifted off the bed. Shock and pleasure raced through her in equal measure. "Magnus!" It must be wrong. But it was so beautiful!

"Shh, love. I'm loving you." Addicted already to the sweet taste of her, Magnus pushed farther into her, so that his mouth and tongue would erase for all time what her infamous uncle had done. Enraptured with what he was doing, he was soon so lost in the splendor of her, he didn't know where his body ended and hers began. His growls of pleasure matched her gasps of growing excitement.

When he felt her beginning tremors, the moist rushing, the quiverings, he pulled free and moved up her body, lifting her hips to receive him. He entered her slowly, easing past the shattered maidenhead that should have been his. Then he paused. "You're as pure as the driven snow, Iona, and I have your virginity."

"Magnus." Crying, happy, Iona reached up to embrace the man who was giving her a new world. The hard nub of want inside her still had her writhing with what she didn't understand. Even as it spread, she didn't know what it was, nor why her body pressed to his, why she clutched him to her. There'd been no pain and she was blossoming with fire. When he pulled back, she snatched at him convulsively, then released him sheepishly.

"We're done," she whispered.

"Not even begun, wife."

One hand at her nape, he kissed her as he thrust deeply into her, and he caught her gasp in his mouth. He reared back and she closed around him, trying to keep him. Then she gave in, surrendered to the rhythm, and allowed him to teach her the age-old dance.

"That's it," he murmured as her hips rose to meet his.

"Oh, Magnus. What is it?" The words burst from her.

"Life, Iona, life." Then he could speak no more as the wonder was upon them, and he caressed and loved his mate. His hand slipped between them to stroke her to fulfillment. He thrust again and again as she moaned and went with him, unable to help herself, embracing him as though she'd never let him go.

"More," she whispered.

He gave her more. And she gave it back to him.

Then they clung together, spiraling upward, needing each other with an elemental want that transcended all else. Ecstasy exploded within them, sending them into the firmament.

Magnus was the first to regain sense of the world. He rolled onto his back and pulled Iona across his chest. With some effort he managed to tug a plaid over them, then he held her, soothing her. "Iona, are you all right?" She nodded, and her thick hair slid over him like a silken cover. He laughed.

She lifted her head, though she hardly had the strength. "This is what men and women do night after night?" she asked dreamily, then yawned. "Oh. Excuse me. I didn't mean to be discourteous."

"You're not, wife," Magnus said, still chuckling. "And to answer your question, men and women get to do this every night if they're very, very fortunate." He looked into her eyes as she rested her chin on his chest. "I know you felt joy, Iona. I felt your passion." He watched the color rise, her gaze slide away from his.

"I did feel joy. And I didn't know it could be." At his upraised eyebrows, she tried to explain. "Well, I'm at such an age—"

"Iona, I've told you not to call yourself old. You are a beautiful, sensual woman. A bride." She blushed deeply again, and he realized how much his words had moved her.

"And we are going to do this every night, and in the morning, the afterno—"

"Magnus Sinclair, you're a—a profligate." She tried to be severe, but could not hide her smile. She'd never been so relaxed, so loose, as though her body still floated in the air.

"If I'm a profligate," he said, "I shall have to make you one too." He kissed her, his tongue touching hers and withdrawing.

She didn't like his cocksure smile that told her he knew she'd felt instant heat at his touch. "And I can return the favor." With a boldness born of new lovemaking, she ran her hands over him, watching his muscles flex where she touched. "I do that to you, don't I, Magnus Sinclair?"

"You do," he said, but stayed her hand when she dared to slide it lower. She wriggled free and grasped him, and he had to clench his teeth to keep back a moan.

Iona was mesmerized as his manhood hardened quickly beneath her touch. Heat quivered through her as she caressed him. She tried to smile at him, but her whole being was trembling with surprise and wonder. "It's not possible . . . I didn't think . . ."

He laughed as he began his own velvety search of her body. "Perhaps you have a magic, Iona."

Her own laughter surprised her. How could she laugh at such a serious time? How was it that Magnus did the same? What was between a man and woman was wondrous strange.

Flipping her over onto her back, Magnus looked down at her. "You should be resting, Iona. The hour grows late." And she would be raw and tender from their first lovemaking. He vowed never to hurt her, never to do anything that could call to mind her uncle's criminal assault upon her.

"I'm not sleepy," she said.

"Then is that an invitation I see in your sea-green eyes?"

"I do not tempt you, sir," she said snappishly, unnerved that he seemed able to see inside her. She wanted very much to know if she could fly among the stars again. It had been so wonderful, but she needn't show her eagerness to him. He was too full of himself already.

"Ah, but you do tempt me, sweet wife. You'd make Eve and Lilith exceedingly jealous with your wiles." He licked the softly perfumed skin of her neck.

She reared back, scowling at him, even as her heart beat like a tern's wing. "Magnus Sinclair, don't you think—"

"I think only that I want you at this moment, Iona. Do you desire the same?" He did not move until she nodded, then he laughed with triumph and hugged her. "You wanted to lie, Iona."

"I did," she admitted, rubbing one leg up and down his, liking the soft abrasion. "But I didn't want to deny myself . . ."

As her voice trailed away in confusion, he smiled. "Be assured, wife, that I will always accommodate you and seek to pleasure you."

"As I can pleasure you," she said quickly.

"Oh, yes, Iona. You do that." He moved away from her and swept the plaid back, wanting to let the firelight play over her satiny body.

She swiftly recovered herself. "Magnus, 'tis not—"

"Don't say it isn't seemly, Iona. I've told you that between us there can be no barriers, not even the darkness." He gazed down at her. "You're precious pearls all melted onto one flesh, Iona."

"I'm—I'm but a woman," she said, trying to cover herself with her fluttering hands. Was she not older than most of his women? How many had he had? All younger. More beautiful. She pushed at him.

He easily grasped both of her wrists in one hand and held them above her head. "You're an exciting woman, Iona, as eager for me as I am for you."

"You're . . . unseemly," she burst out, annoyed that he'd reminded her of her behavior. She'd had no intention of being so uninhibited.

He kissed her nose. "Your favorite word since we began

our lovemaking, but I tell you, it has no place between us. You vowed to be my own, milady."

With her hands still imprisoned, he looked his fill at her, adoring her full white breasts, the flare of her hips, her long, muscled legs. When he returned his gaze to her face, he saw that she'd been studying him as well.

"I like your body, wife."

"And—and you've a very healthy one, Magnus Sinclair," she said primly, then grinned when he laughed, throwing himself back on the bed and releasing her hands.

Emboldened by the heat coursing through her, and by the sensual man lying at her side, she rolled over until she lay half on top of him. She gazed into his questioning eyes, then leaned down and kissed him.

When she was satisfied she'd kissed his mouth long enough, she moved on to his forehead, his cheekbones, his eyelids with their fringe of thick brown lashes, his nose with the bump near the bridge, his firm jaw and chin.

Sliding down to his chest, she closed her eyes and let her hands see for her. His heart thundered under her touch in a cadence as wild as the pounding sea. Joy cascaded through her that she'd done that to him, that she had the power to shake him as he'd shaken her. She trailed her fingers around his flat nipples, tugging gently at the auburn hair there. Then, boldly, she kissed those nipples, sucking as he'd done, pulling, tugging, licking. His body bucked beneath her as his hands clutched her hips. Passion sprang full blown in both of them.

His skin was rough-smooth, the hairs on his chest caressing her soft skin as she slid farther down him. His aroused manhood pushed at her hand, and she circled it tentatively with her fingers.

"Touch me, darling." The hoarse plea was wrenched from him, his whole being poised for her magic.

She closed her shaking hand around his engorged manhood. When he groaned, a moan was pulled from her.

"Iona, you're a witch from Icelandia," he said, breath rasping from his lungs.

Feeling giddily happy, she smiled at him. "And this is seemly, milord?"

"Yes, milady, but only with me." He stroked a hand up and down her spine. "Don't let me interrupt you."

"No, I won't."

Her low laugh was like a caress that whipped over his skin, and desire rose in him like a tide. When she moved farther downward, her mouth gliding over his stomach, he stopped her. "No, milady." He rolled her onto her back. "That you cannot do, because then our wonderful sortie would be ended."

Iona smiled secretly, deciding to use that particular weapon later. "And did you like my ministrations, milord?"

He slid his hand between her silken thighs, then inside her. "Yes, milady," he said, his lips against hers, "I liked it well enough, indeed."

They kissed, open-mouthed, starving for each other, needing the heat and want, seeking it as if it were their only sustenance.

"You're so wet and warm, milady Sinclair," Magnus whispered. Then he caught her long unplaited hair in one fist, holding her still as he drove into her. When she cried out, his own gasps echoed her. In a powerful surge they were one. He spilled his seed into her waiting womb, their bodies shaking with passion's power.

After long minutes the sensations finally subsided. Magnus cuddled Iona close and gazed down at her, uneasily aware he could have hurt her with his ardor. But she was already asleep, a smile still on her lips. Sighing, he held her more securely and closed his eyes.

∽ 13 ∽

The Way of Heaven is to benefit others and not to injure.
—Lao-tzu

Iona opened her eyes and blinked at the unfamiliar surroundings, then realization came back like the sun blazing on ice. She'd become Magnus Sinclair's wife. She shivered with embarrassment when she recalled how wantonly she'd given herself to him, the hot, long, moist moments of the night, which hadn't ended until nearly dawn. He'd been wild with her . . . and there'd been no pain. Instead, there'd been a paradise she'd not dreamed there could be. She'd been lifted outside herself, and he with her. She'd cloven unto him and let him pour his seed into her.

Involuntarily her hand went to her middle, caressing there. A babe? Nay! 'Twould be a miracle. Such things didn't occur.

Stretching under the finely tanned skins and plaids, she welcomed their heat and that from the fireplace. Outside, the well-known winds of Eyin Helga howled a good morning. The high-ceilinged room was dark except for the light from the many tapers on the stone mantel. Eerie shadows danced on the ceiling, ebbing and flowing like a fantasy tide.

As sleep faded and awareness sharpened, she became more attuned to a murmuring sound of whispers and muted laughter. She turned her head, focusing on three women gathered near the fire. Witches? Pulling a plaid up to her chin, she stared at the women, who were fussing over a steaming copper tub placed near the fireplace.

"There's no need to whisper," she said. "I'm awake."

When they jumped back and remained immobile, she smiled. Then, seeing how they stared at her, the huge bed, the rumpled covers, she blushed and reached for the robe that was draped over the bedstead.

Alarmed, the three straightened and turned. One, who seemed the oldest of the trio, curtsied quickly and threaded her fingers together in front of her. "Milord told us not to disturb you just yet. He said that you needed your sleep after last night . . ." Recognizing her gaffe, the woman stared helplessly at Iona.

Iona wanted to pull the skins over her head and stay there for a year. Instead, she forced down her embarrassment and tried to smile encouragingly. "I thank you for the hot water for my bath, good ladies. I can carry on by myself."

The oldest woman shook her head. "The lord said we was to be your waiting women, milady. And so we must," she added doggedly, her face screwed into a martyr's acceptance.

The humor of it hit Iona. Her laugh curled around the room, startling her three handmaidens. "And what shall I call you three who've been consigned to the devil?"

Taken aback by her droll tone, the women gaped at her, then the first woman's mouth twitched with a faint smile. "We are sisters, milady. I'm Faith, Hope is the middle one, and Charity is the baby."

Since the "baby" was well into middle age, Iona's smile widened. "How do you do?"

"We're just fine, milady," the virtuous trio responded in unison. Faith took a deep breath and added, "We are Vikings, milady, loyal to Magnus Sinclair for he does not harm us. But he cannot own our hearts."

Iona nodded. "I thought you were Norse. My blessings to you," she said in formal Icelandic, then bowed to them as best she could.

The three immediately threw their heads toward the floor as though they'd bang them there. When they raised up, they were smiling, not broadly, but with a small show of teeth.

The formalities out of the way, Iona said, "Would you see to my clothes, please? I shall bathe myself. Though I don't suppose you have a hot spring on Eyin Helga, do you?"

The women blinked uncomprehendingly. Then Charity beamed and nodded, the tatting on her mobcap bobbing in her eagerness. "But yes, milady. I know of what you speak. Our father has told us of the wonders of such on Icelandia." She pointed out the lancet, although since it was swathed in skins, nothing could be seen without. "In the cave is such a pool, but 'tis never used. The demons wash their hair there, so we cannot go."

"Oh." Iona wasn't quite sure she'd heard aright, but since she intended to use the pool anyway, she didn't question. She'd have to listen carefully when these women spoke. Their heavy Gaelic crossed with Viking was difficult to comprehend. No matter. It would seem she finally had access to a hot spring, which she'd missed so much. Since arriving in the land of the Scots she'd not felt quite clean, though she bathed each day. This was a custom among most Icelandians. It didn't seem to be among the auslanders like the Scots, though, thank heavens, Magnus followed such a custom. The hot springs were so cleansing, so relaxing. She would find the cave on her own and use it. "Thank you, good women. You may leave me now. Just—"

A commotion at the door had all heads turning. Thump! The noise came again, and this time the door was flung open and Thor raced into the room.

"God save us, it's a demon!" Faith crossed herself and

huddled with her sisters. "Charity, you spoke of them and called one up among us."

"He's come from Sutherland to devour us!" Hope cried, bordering on hysteria.

"God save us," Charity shrieked.

"Thor! Come here." Iona sat up in bed, forgetting she wasn't clothed, and grabbed the wolf as he jumped onto the bed. "How did you get here? I worried so. I knew that Dugald and Mavis would feed you, but I feared you'd search for me and scare the good folks of Clan Sinclair."

None moved until a deep voice, resonating like the sunset bell, sounded in the room. "I couldn't hold him back anymore. He knew you were up here." Magnus watched Iona from the doorway, noting her bare arms and upper torso. She looked like a moon goddess holding one of the mighty guardians who sped across the heavens at her side. He glanced at the three women who were now staring at him. His almost imperceptible nod was enough to make them scamper around him and disappear.

"When did he come?" Iona asked, lifting her head and gazing happily at Magnus.

He saw the sheen of tears in her eyes and felt a pang. She'd been alone a great deal, not just all the years she'd been growing but during her stay at Sinclair Castle as well. And all that time she'd carried her burden, not just out of shame, but to protect her family and her countrymen. He understood that and admired it, but it wrenched him to think of her decision to cloister herself here on Eynhallow rather than to risk marriage because she could be considered unclean. What fools men were to judge women for men's flaws.

"Is Thor to sleep with us, then?" he asked, admiring her wonderful creamy breasts as she leaned around the wolf to look at him.

Iona tried to get the wolf off the bed, but all her best efforts were in vain. She laughed at his antics even as she tried to admonish him. "I'm that glad to see him, Magnus," she confessed.

"I see that. He came with us, but on another boat.

Glam kept him in an outbuilding overnight. Thor slipped away when Glam went in to feed him this morning, and he led your giant on a merry chase."

She laughed. "Yes, he would do that." Looking up at Magnus, she glimpsed the building fire of passion in his eyes. Suddenly remembering her state of undress, she scrambled for the plaid.

Thor looked bemused by her actions, but he was more than willing to join in the game. He tugged the plaid away from her again. She wrestled it away from him and clutched it to her front. Arms crossed over her breasts, she stared at Magnus.

"The water will get cool, milady," he said, entering the room and shutting the door.

" 'Tis true," she said, and waited for him to leave.

"Shall I help you?"

"No need," she said hurriedly. "The women told me that there's a hot spring on Eyin Helga," she blurted out. "That would be fine for me. Use the tub if you choose—"

"I've bathed," he said, then grinned as Thor, in a bid for Iona's attention, grabbed hold of the plaid again.

Tugging and pulling and whispering admonishments to the animal, Iona struggled to keep Thor from rendering her naked. He slowly and happily pulled the plaid away, though, and she couldn't fight the run of color up her face. Magnus propped himself against the doorjamb and watched closely as more and more of her unclothed body appeared.

"If—if you'll excuse me then," she stammered, "I'll get dressed and—"

Magnus whistled through his teeth.

The wolf paused in play and looked around. For long moments, man and animal stared at each other. Then Thor got down from the bed, looked once at Iona, and trotted across the room. Magnus opened the door and then shut it behind the creature.

Iona hurried to pull the plaid up to her chin, more than a little irked at how Magnus had wielded his power over her wolf. "Good of you to remove Thor," she lied primly. "Now, if you would be so good as to leave, I shall wash."

Magnus crossed the room in long purposeful strides, lifted her from the bed, and removed the plaid. Ignoring her sputters, he said, "Hot springs are good. We'll use the cave, milady, despite the demons—"

"You heard?" For a moment she forgot her agitation as she pictured him outside her door, waiting to enter.

"Aye." He wanted to keep holding her, to lay her back on the bed and repeat the wonder of the previous night, over and over again. But he knew that she could be chafed from her long initiation into the arts of love, and he resisted the temptation. "But since the tub is here now and the water hot, you'll bathe here this morning." He grinned. "And I'll help."

She stared at him. "Nay, Magnus. 'Tis un—"

He kissed her hard, his tongue delving into her mouth. When he lifted his head, he was pleased by her high color. "Don't say it, Iona. Between us there is nothing unseemly. I told you that."

"You're not arbiter of my behavior, Magnus Sinclair," she said. That look in his eye was indecent, she thought, and so she'd tell him when she could get enough air in her lungs to do it. Someone needed to chastise the arrogant leader of the barbarian Scots. His shoulders were as wide as the doors to his castle, and only Glam had greater breadth of chest. He held her as easily as he'd heft a cask of the abbey's heady brew that Scots drank as if it were goat's milk.

"Sinclair, release me."

"Nay, lady wife, I'm your handmaiden. In our land 'tis a husband's privilege if he choose." His gaze coursed over her body. "And I do."

"Hah! There's nothing subservient about you, Sinclair." Certainly not in that look that could melt the cliffs of Eyin Helga, or that seductive voice that could put ice to a boil. The shivers that assailed her had nothing to do with cold. The man knew it and still didn't release her. He was a barbarian.

"How you talk, Lady Sinclair," he said softly. Then, before she could protest, he lowered her into the steaming water.

Iona quickly slid down as far as she could. Resigning herself to washing in his presence, she reached for the soap. His hand was there first.

Smiling lazily, he rubbed the tallow soap, scented with some wild berry, against a soft washcloth. She eyed the cloth as though it were a viper, starting as he grasped her loose hair in one hand.

"Your hair is thicker and more satiny than any I've seen," he said, letting it drift through his fingers.

The will to push away from him melted in the heat of his touch, and she could only look up at him helplessly as he combed his fingers through her tresses. Then he twisted the heavy rope of hair around his hand, lifted it, and with his other hand began washing her neck and back.

"You needn't wash me," she said desperately, trying to keep her voice even.

"Shy? With your spouse? Shame on you, milady. 'Tis well the clans didn't know you were skittish. They'd have performed the bedding ceremony, to be sure, carrying you up the stairs of Sinclair Castle, then ringing round the bed, shouting ribaldry to bring you to the blush, and then demanding that I claim your maidenhead before them."

Magnus grimaced at his own words. He could've bitten through his tongue for saying that, for reminding her that her womanhood had been taken not by her husband, but cruelly by her knave of an uncle.

But Skene was only fleetingly in Iona's mind. The picture that formed was of the head of the Sinclair clan roaring at any and all who dared to enter his chamber on his wedding night. "You wouldn't have let them," she said. "I know you, Magnus Sinclair. You'd have had your men throw them off the parapet had they dared."

Relief coursed through him that she hadn't thought of the scoundrel Skene. "So I would. What was between us was too . . . fiery for an audience to share, milady." The run of blood up her face fascinated and warmed him. He touched the silken curve of her cheek, then his finger moved slowly downward to the delightful indentation between her beautiful breasts.

She gasped and slapped his hand away. "Milord, I insist you leave me to my ablutions."

Magnus laughed, wondering at his delight in her. She spat at him with gesture and word at every opportunity. She'd driven him mad since his first sighting of her. She'd broken his peace, turned his life upside down; had insulted him at every turn, privately and publicly, but he wanted no other. "I'm sorry, milady. That I cannot do. I cannot shirk my duty as your spouse."

"Laving me is your duty? Nonsense."

"No, milady. 'Tis tradition." He wasn't sure if it was or not, but he would begin one, if only to gaze on the delicious flesh of his Icelandic princess. He'd never seen such clear, creamy skin, and he intended to spend much of his days looking upon it.

Iona's body betrayed her by undulating in rhythm to his caresses. "There's no time for this," she said, gasping as he teased her womanhood under the water. "I would see the caves . . ." But her words melted away as he heated her with his touch.

"I too would see the demon lair, milady."

He whorled the cloth across her breasts, the feel of them a fiery impetus to his lust. He leaned down to kiss her mouth, his teeth nibbling on her lower lip.

"We did a might of this last night," she murmured, her eyes drooping shut. T'was her place to tell him nay, she thought. Surely married people didn't indulge the flesh at such a time. Not in the light of day!

Magnus stayed his hand as it hovered over her womanhood once more. "Are you sore, Iona?" he asked gently.

Her eyes snapped open, and she saw his concern. She couldn't tell him that she would welcome his hot invasion once more, could she? 'Twas better to push him away. But she couldn't. " 'Tis my duty to accede in my wifely duties," she said instead.

"I would have you want it as I do." He lifted her from

the tub and draped the plaid around her again. Looking down at her swathed in his tartan, he thought she'd never looked so enticing.

"You don't refuse me?"

"No," she whispered, her body swaying toward him.

Relief and delight swept through him as he picked her up and strode toward the bed. After laying her down, he slowly peeled back the tartan, as though in expectation of a great gift. She was still warm from the steamy tub, and she made him burn as each square of flesh was revealed. "I'll make you hot, Iona," he whispered.

"As I will do to you, husband," she answered, shaken by her own ardor and eagerness. He smiled, then turned away to disrobe. As he discarded his tartan and shirt, she saw in the light of day what had been hidden in the dark—a wide scar that started on his thigh and curled upward to his underarm. Startled, she gasped and sat straight up, reaching toward him.

He heard the sound and grimaced. Even though she was a healing woman, he knew she'd be disgusted by the scarred and puckered flesh across his body, the marks of many hard battles. When he felt her soft touch tracing the scar on his thigh, a groan was pulled from him, and he turned to her in surprise.

"How could they cut you so?" she murmured. "If only I or my wonderful mother could've treated you, you'd not be so marked." Her voice shook with the intensity of her emotion.

He sank down on the bed next to her. When she leaned toward him and gently kissed the jagged scar on his chest, he was sure his heart would burst. "And you would've kept me unmarked, Iona?" he asked hoarsely.

"Of a surety. These were not closed as they should've been, with proper threads and stitching." She looked up at him, her smile sorrowful. "I would've done better, Magnus."

Unable to resist the wonderful, unconscious invitation in her eyes, he gathered her to him. "You're a wondrous healer, Iona."

At the feel of his bare flesh against hers, a moan was torn from her. She fought the giddy sensations of heat that ripped through her. "Magnus."

"I'm here, milady. I want you."

" 'Tis not hard to have this wanting, is it?"

He chuckled. "No, 'tis not hard."

"And is it so with all the women you know?"

Her question startled him. What wife would question her husband about his lemans? Yet if he understood his spouse aright, that was what she wanted to know. "No," he said cautiously, realizing he was in dangerous territory. " 'Tis not all the same."

She studied him. "I'm glad there's a difference."

Touched by her simple declaration, he let his finger score down between her breasts.

Awareness swept through her and she turned a fiery red. It was more than the embarrassment at her nudity. It was Magnus and the way he'd made her feel. He was like the sun, demanding that she cast off her coverings and savor his heat, and she did so gladly. He was Adonis to her. His silky sinews, the muscular chest with its pelt of rough-soft chestnut hair, his long legs and thighs, and that wonderfully thrusting manhood that had brought her to the brink of madness. He was a devil, but instead of casting him out, she sought to embrace him, to follow him to his home in hell if need be.

His body was irresistible. To touch it was to be struck by lightning. And the burning didn't stop. To love him was to die, and she avidly sought that hot, sweet death. His body was warm, pulsating, hard and soft, muscled and smooth. And kissing it was the most exciting—

Unable to withstand her torturous caresses any longer, Magnus abruptly reared back from her. As she stared in surprise at him, he grinned wickedly, then pushed her down on the bed, rolling her over onto her stomach. She stiffened, but he crooned softly to her until she relaxed.

"What—what do you do?" she asked as his mouth moved up and down her body, making it tremble in rising want and need.

He responded by leaning down and letting his tongue trace her long spine. He carefully ministered to each rib along the way, as though he were marking his path on a map. "I'm loving you, Iona. 'Tis the Sinclair way of it."

"How like the Scots to have a manner of their own even in this," she said into the pillow, her body feathering with tiny bumps of excitement. When he stopped and was silent, she lifted up and looked over her shoulder. "Oh. So you see my flaw, do you? I've been marred so since birth."

He seemed fascinated by the red mark on her buttock, and she held her breath waiting for what he'd say. It was the bridal custom that she come to her groom unmarked by anything, and she was scarred in so many ways.

It was on the tip of Magnus's tongue to tell her she had no flaws, that he considered the mark an angel's touch, but he held back. The woman had power enough over him. Down through the years he'd been warned, by man, mystic, and monarch, against the power of others, against giving in to weakness. Lust for a woman was a weakness, and were not the Vikings age-old enemies?

"It's not something I'm proud of," she whispered, "but no one ever sees it."

The faint hurt in her voice made him lift his head and stare at her. Nay, there was no weakness in wanting this woman. And he had power over her too.

He smiled. "Are you daft, woman? You're marked by the goddesses themselves to be their own." He kissed the birthmark, then traced his finger over it. His wife was truly royal, but none, not even the king, would know of this. She was his, as was her mark, red and in the shape of a crown. Noticing how she bit her lips anxiously, he leaned up and kissed the back of her neck. "You have a crown on your wonderful backside, milady. And I would call it lovely."

" 'Tis but a birth scar," she said, her voice muffled as he pressed her face into the pillow. But her embarrassment faded as Magnus worked his wonder again. His hands and mouth explored her body, and she felt a wondrous joy.

Surely she'd be condemned for being so wanton, even with her husband.

Worse than that, she feared this sensual power he had over her. Could she trust him never to use it against her? Mayhap, but she promised herself that she would stay independent of him, that she alone would rule her actions. But even as she made the vow, all thought was blurring as his hand explored that most secret part of her.

She tried to stifle her cries of arousal, but he heard her. His own need at a fever pitch, he turned her over. She sprawled before him, love-filled, eager for the final joining. Her eyes entreated him as she whispered his name.

"Yes, my sweet, I'm with you." His voice was little more than a croak as he fought to control his body's fiery demands. He kissed her, taking her tongue into his mouth and giving her his, the rough cadence imitating his slow deliberate stroking of her body. His mouth followed his hands, lapping over her breasts, caressing her nipples until they puckered. Then his lips touched her stomach, felt it clench reflexively, paused at the sweet-scented triangle of curling hair, and lingered long on her thighs.

As he moved back to her womanhood, she sighed, anticipating the liquid wonder, the spiraling heat, the soft sweet explosion of her husband inside her.

Then he entered her with his tongue and she cried out at the gush of heat. The new rhythms were upon them and they moved together, thrusting faster, ever faster, wanting to give, wanting to take.

He felt her quake even as his own body tremored with the power that could no longer be contained. He moved up her quickly, taking her as she took him, crying out as she did.

∾ 14 ∾

Not unknown am I to the goddess Venus who mingles with her cares a sweet bitterness.

—Catullus

All moments ran together in a golden chain of want and giving. Iona didn't know when the wonder of the days turned into the heat of the nights. If there were times she felt guilty because of her covenant, she argued the cause of a just wife being subject to her husband. And yet in so many ways she was Magnus's equal. He never said that, but he treated her as such, and she flowered under his tender care. She was dizzy and girlish and she couldn't seem to help herself. He rarely left her side and often showed his affection openly, unashamedly. More than once she was shocked at his unfettered emotion. And he didn't seem to care who was watching when he kissed her!

Although she'd been loved and cherished by her family, and been very close to them all, they'd showed restraint with their affection, as the manners of the day prescribed. Her mother, father, and grandfather often kissed her, but in private, never in front of anyone.

Magnus, however, kissed in the morning, the evening, and all the day, and never cared who saw him do it.

"You have no shame," she told him breathlessly one afternoon as they were lying together in the heather after he'd chased her over the croft.

He grinned. "You have the right of it, Lady Sinclair. But why should I be ashamed of loving my woman?"

She ran her hand down his face, her finger pausing at a scar near the corner of his mouth. "And how did you get this?"

"Tossing the caber. I ran after the throw to see how close I'd come to another's mark. A splinter popped up and scored me." He leaned over her and kissed her between the breasts. "I like your mark better." He traced the scar on her face with his tongue. "It makes me hot, as hot as the one on your backside does."

"Magnus Sinclair!"

Laughing, he rolled her into his plaid and proceeded to remove her clothes, kissing the red crown on her buttock, then nibbling and nipping until he had her writhing. Then he turned her over and entered her fiercely, taking her passionate cries into his mouth.

The days were golden and the nights were roses of unusual color and vibrancy, black, purple, and deep, deep red. She whispered this to him one day as they lay under the makeshift tent he'd constructed near the cliff edge, so she could watch the birds and yet be protected.

"You have a witch's eye, wife," he said. "Only you could see roses at night. Night is black and dark."

"Night is velvet and soft, like a rose. Does the color matter? Any hue will do in the dark." She chuckled and pointed at a diving, screaming tern.

He smiled, watching the play of emotion on her face, the glint in her eyes. "You'd fly with them if you could."

"And so would you, husband."

"True. I like a challenge. But I never thought to have a wife who did." A wife who'd crossed a dangerous sea to begin a sanctuary for other women, he mused. A wife who'd had no reason to love men. Did she love him?

"What makes you frown, husband?"

"A wife who'd watch the birds and not pleasure her husband as she should." He couldn't tell her that he wanted her to say the words of love to him.

She gaped at him. "Pleasuring is all you've had, husband."

"Shame on you to mention it." He laughed out loud when she reddened, but before she could rail at him, he caught her in his arms, removed her clothes once more, and kissed the red crown that had begun to obsess him.

The days flew by. Neither Magnus nor Iona was in any hurry to return to Sinclair Castle, and they used any excuse to linger in their island idyll. It was a magic time when no troubles intruded, all anxiety was put off, and cares disappeared.

Many afternoons they'd don their Sinclair plaids and explore the island, enjoying its solitude, its wildness. Often, on a windswept moor, they'd stop to make love again, and each time they'd discover some new facet, a nuance that would make them laugh out loud from the joy of it.

"You're my siren," he told her one blustery afternoon as they watched the clouds billow above them. He'd known for days that he should return to Sinclair Castle, that there'd be important clan functions for him to handle. Since he'd first won the right to be on Sinclair land again, he'd been intuitive about his people and the land. When anything was amiss, he'd know it before it happened. Now, with Iona, his very passionate wife, who'd become an eager pupil in the arts of love, he'd been shoving all concerns aside, shunting the cares of lairdship away because he needed to spend more time with her. Oh, he knew that Kenneth or Cormac could handle most things, and that they would send a messenger if anything untoward occurred. Yet a holding the size of the Sinclairs' needed constant mastering and nurturing from its laird.

Still, loving his wife had become a wildly wonderful

obsession with him. Though it annoyed him that a mere woman could command so much of his attention, he was slowly coming to the conclusion that his wife was no "mere" anything. She had the heart and courage of a great warrior, yet she was a woman, all wonder and softness, and he desired her constantly.

"It's so wonderful here, Magnus," she said, pulling him from his thoughts. "So raw and awesome."

"It is, indeed." He twisted some of her hair around his hand as the wind tugged it free from beneath her plaid. He always protested when she braided it, and she'd taken to leaving it loose at times.

"And where on this isle of demons," he asked, "did you plan to start your sanctuary, milady?"

She smiled at him, surprised and pleased at his query. "I'll show you, if you like."

"All right."

He took her hand and let her lead him across the island. The gorse and heather waved in the wind in imitation of the sea, and the few stunted trees that dared to withstand the never-ending sea wind were bent almost double.

The rock-strewn soil was not easy to walk on, but Iona felt so much joy striding beside her husband, her hand clasped warmly in his, that she relished the journey.

They crossed a narrow declivity to a rough gorse- and bracken-filled croft. On its far side, near the ominous-looking sea, stood a building, older and smaller than Sinclair House, and not as welcoming. Though stoutly built, it was a dark and dreary place, notched into the cliff and exposed to the powerful wind.

"I would fix it up," Iona said hurriedly when she saw Magnus frown.

"Why not use Sinclair House?" The words were out before he knew he'd say them, but he didn't want to call them back, seeing her face light up like the sun. He'd have to be careful he didn't promise her too much. To see that look he'd give much of what he owned.

When she said nothing in response, though, he caught

her around the waist and pulled her tight to him. "Say something, wife."

She shook her head, tears welling in her eyes. "I truly don't know what to say."

He grinned down at her. "Ah, another weapon to keep you silent. I only need give you a parcel of land in the Orkneys."

She pinched his arm. "And would you give back Viking land to me?"

"Bold woman. This is Sinclair land, and I give you leave to use it freely." He tightened his hold and kissed her quickly.

"And you'd do this for us?" she asked, somber again. "For the women I'd bring here?" She lifted her hands to his face, cupping his cheeks.

"You're my wife," he said roughly, his blood thundering at her touch. "The house is yours to do with what you will."

"Oh, Magnus." She reached up on tiptoe and kissed him full on the mouth.

Stunned by the wonder of her kiss, since it was rare for her to initiate their caresses, he was immobile for a second, then he swept her up tight to him. "I tell you that I like it right well, Iona, when you do that, when you touch me first."

"Do you?" Both shy and excited, she couldn't stop touching him. He was so strong, so beautifully made.

"Yes."

"I like it too."

They headed back to Sinclair House, and Magnus kept his arm around her. He liked the feel of her body close to his, moving with him. "Tell me what you'll do first in your sanctuary."

Happily she sketched all the wonderful things she, Spes, and Marta had planned to start with, and what they hoped to achieve in later years. "And" she finished, "we'd teach the women and children to read and write."

"Read and write?" That was an innovation, he thought. Few of his clansmen could do so, and he was certain the

ratio would be much the same with the Vikings. "And will
you include Scotswomen in this plan?" As he asked it he
paused, his gaze on a patch of thorny bushes. He'd seen a
movement. He stared there for a long moment while his
wife enthusiastically told him her sanctuary was for all
women, Scot and Viking. There was no other strange
movement, yet he couldn't shake the feeling that eyes
watched them.

"Magnus? What is it?"

The anxiety in her voice had him dissembling. "A stray
sheep, I think. Now, you did say that Scotswomen would
come?"

She nodded. "Should they choose to do so."

"A year ago I'd have said it couldn't be done. But then
I hadn't met you."

"Now what do you think?"

"I think you can do anything you set your mind to,
Lady Sinclair." He swung her up in his arms, keeping himself between her and the clump of thorny bush. He'd have
some of his men check the area when he returned to Sinclair House.

"Why do you carry me?" she asked.

"Because I like to."

"Oh." She pushed her face into his neck, inhaling his
wonderful man smell that was like no other. Each day they
went to the cave of "demons" and bathed together in the
hot spring. More often than not they made love afterward.

"What are you thinking?" he whispered. He loved her
breath on his neck.

"I was thinking of the cave."

"Milady, you should not." He laughed and swung her
about, at the same time studying the area behind them. He
still couldn't shake the feeling that someone had been
there, watching his wife and him.

"And why is that, sirrah?" Iona asked. Despite his teasing tone and warm glance, she felt a tension emanating
from him. Why?

"Because I'll begin to think of your creamy pink body
in the hot water, your arms spread wide on the shelf of

rocks behind you, and the steam curling your tresses, my princess." He kissed her ardently. "Then I'll be rushing you back there, to disrobe you, follow you into the hot water, and let the steam meld us."

Her blood heated at his words, yet she had the distinct sense he was trying to distract her. "Magnus?"

"Yes." He tore his gaze from the rocky terrain around them and smiled at her.

"Something worries you. What?"

His eyes glinted with amusement touched with admiration. "You have a warrior's sense, my princess. But I'm glad you're womanly too."

Delight tickled through her, but he hadn't answered her. She wriggled out of his arms. "And?"

He sighed. "I thought someone crouched in the bushes back there. But there's no one," he added as her gaze immediately swept the area behind them. He grinned at her calmness. No tears or cries of fear. His lady was a worthy companion.

She looked back at him. "Is there danger for us?"

It jolted him that she viewed them as a couple. He hesitated, wanting to be open with her about his fears, but not wishing to agitate her. If he told her he had guards specifically for her—he'd assigned them the morning after their wedding, after she'd told him about her uncle—she might balk. He shook his head and told half the truth. "There are lookouts and guards all around us. We would know if there were enemies abroad."

"You say that, but you continue to scan the area."

He shrugged. "I've taken care of myself for a long time. Old habits die hard." And now he'd take care of her. If Skene ever dared to approach her, he'd die a thousand ways, and Magnus would disembowel the bastard while he still breathed. "Now come, wife. You know Spes and Marta like dinner at a certain time, and if we're late they may refuse to part with their persimmon-apple tarts."

She grinned. "As though you cared a fig what they thought." Her expression became pensive again. "I've noticed that Spes is quite taken with Kenneth."

"Only since first meeting," Magnus said dryly. "Kenneth is not immune to her—" At his wife's sharp look, he grinned. "Her persimmon-apple tart . . . and other charms."

"You are a boor, Magnus Sinclair," she said lovingly, leaning against him as they strolled on. Not even the coldest winds from the sea could touch her when Magnus sheltered her against him. "I do not know what her parents would say to such a match. No doubt her mother would cry bitter tears."

Magnus looked down at her, laughter lighting his eyes. "They'd probably be pleased she'd come up so far in the world."

"Wretch." She pummeled his chest, but then felt him stiffen. "What is it?"

"We speak of my brother and he appears."

Iona followed his gaze and saw Kenneth approach with two other men. One was Dugald. She frowned. Magnus had told her that either Kenneth or Dugald was to be at Sinclair Castle at all times . . . unless there was an emergency.

His arm around Iona's waist again, Magnus waited for Kenneth to reach him. "Well met, brother," he said.

Kenneth didn't have his usual wide grin. He nodded to both of them, then drew a deep breath. "I have a message from the king, Magnus. Once more he chafes at the slowness of banding the clans into a force. Some still angle away from the monarchy, his missive says, and he wants your strongest support for the cause of unification." Kenneth shook his head. "He fears Tostig and his powerful baron—"

"Urdric Kildeer," Magnus said softly, his hands flexing into fists. " 'Tis past time that the baron has made a push against us." He held out his hand, and Kenneth handed him the letter.

As Magnus read it, Kenneth turned to Iona.

"You are in great good looks, sister," he said gallantly, but his smile was strained.

"Thank you, Kenneth," she said softly, fighting against

the blood that stained her cheeks. It made her uncomfortable to stand in front of Magnus's brother and lieutenant. They would know what she and Magnus had been doing these many days. When she looked up at her husband, though, all uncertainty and shyness fled. His face seemed carved from marble, bearing a battle-ready hardness she'd not seen since their first meeting.

When she would've moved away, he caught her back to his side. "Stay with me," he said tautly, and looked at his brother again. "How goes it at Sinclair?"

"We're battle ready, as you would wish." A small smile touched his mouth. "You must be three men, I'll be bound. You make handling Sinclair look simple. I was half mad the first week."

Magnus nodded sharply. "Do you think Tostig will turn Kildeer loose?"

"The king does," Kenneth answered grimly.

"So do I."

"Malcolm will mount a countercampaign."

"So the Northumbrian baron challenges me again," Magnus said softly. When he felt a quivering at his side, he looked down at Iona. She was outwardly composed, every inch a queen. If he hadn't been clasping her to him, he wouldn't have known that she trembled. He smiled at her, one finger caressing her cheek. Then he turned back to Kenneth. "What say the other clans?"

"They know of the rumblings. MacDonnell, McLeod, and MacDougall sent an emissary, as did Hughes. They seek your guidance, and they stand with you. Even if all don't share your sentiments, they hide it now. Asquith too voices cautious support."

Magnus smiled tautly. It pleased him that Kenneth was learning to sift the loyalties, to qualify their strengths and weaknesses.

Iona bit her lip until she tasted blood. They couldn't have him. His scar-filled body had taken too many beatings. Let someone else lead. She wanted him at her side.

"Shh, milady. All's well," Magnus whispered to her, as though she'd spoken aloud.

She looked up at him and tried to smile. She was
Viking. She understood battle. She quailed only at the
thought of losing him, of not being able to die at his side.

At that moment she hated Dugald and Kenneth. The
urge to drag her husband back to the cave of demons, to
block the entrance with rocks and stay in there with him,
was so strong, she gasped at its power. At Magnus's sharp
glance she smiled slightly and looked politely at his
brother.

"I'll go," Magnus said. "But I'll test the ground first. I'll
not send the clan into it blindly. I'll take the first hundred
with Dugald. If we decide to battle at the king's side, I'll
send for the others. You keep a contingent at the castle,
Kenneth, and mind that you keep my wife under guard
here on Eynhallow. You'll check on her twice a week until
my return."

Seeing that Glam had joined them, Magnus nodded at
the Viking. "Yes, I know you'll guard my wife, but I want
more than one guard around her."

Iona's head snapped up. "Why? I have Thor and the
shepherds too."

"Because you're a Viking princess who's now Lady Sinclair. There's more than one who'd try to get at me
through you." His arm tightened around her.

"Be careful, Sinclair," she whispered teasingly. "Someone might think you care for your wife."

"No chance of that," he said huskily, then laughed
aloud when she poked him in the ribs. Recalling himself,
he shot sharp looks at Dugald and Kenneth. "You understand what you have to do?"

The two men nodded.

"Do not fear for me," Iona said. "Thor is my strong
protector, as is Glam." Despite her brave words, inside she
was crying and screaming. She didn't want him to fight
Tostig's army and the infamous Urdric Kildeer, baron of
Northumbria. Dark things were said of him. Even the Vikings knew of the dangerous baron, a man of devilishly
cruel reputation.

As though feeling her fear, Magnus kissed the top of her head.

Neither bride nor groom noted the shocked and amused looks cast their way. They had eyes only for each other.

"I have to ready my things," Magnus said gently.

"Yes, I'll help you," she said, turning with him toward the house.

"I shall miss our hot baths, milady," he added as they walked.

"Shh, some might hear you." She'd meant to sound annoyed, but even she could hear the pleading in her voice. Not all her royal training bastioned her against the pain of parting from her new spouse.

"I'll return soon," he promised her.

"See that you do," she told him sternly, swallowing her tears.

❧ 15 ❧

Thus parted the one from the other as the nail from the flesh.

—El Cid

Days flew like the terns, swooping fast, diving one after the other. Yet in the same span of time, the minutes clung to each other like barnacles to the underside of a Viking ship.

Iona threw herself into the work of the sanctuary, needing the arduous, demanding chores as she turned Sinclair House into a haven of caring and learning.

Ships arrived daily with supplies, and it became a daily diversion for her to watch the unloading from the cliffs. Precious scrolls, scribe's materials, and a few of the first arrivals from Icelandia came within days.

The house began to bustle with the comings and goings of visitors and those who'd come to stay. Soon the arrivals would spill over into neighboring buildings, and workers began readying them.

With each ship's arrival there was news either of Icelandia or of Sinclair Castle. Iona devoured every word about the battle waged with Northumbria. She received no personal missive from Magnus after the first week, but Kenneth assured her that was normal.

"And do you think all goes well?" she asked him after Magnus had been gone a fortnight.

Kenneth saw the concern behind her composure and hastened to reassure her, just as the shepherds and sailors were wont to do. He was touched by the way she'd captured the loyalty of the dour shepherds who inhabited the lonely isle. "Dermot tells me you cured his sheep and his sore knee," he said, changing the subject. "I don't know which was more important to him."

"Oh, the sheep, surely," she said, smiling.

He laughed. "They're in awe of you, Iona, and are most grateful for your skills."

"Not at first, though. Dermot insisted I do his injury before touching his sheep."

Kenneth grinned, then squeezed her shoulder. "Magnus is the canniest warrior in all of Scotland. That's why Malcolm wants him at his side. Fear not for him, Iona. He'll show up here one day soon, and surprise you."

But the days rolled into weeks. The moon waxed and waned once.

One morning a Sinclair ship docked and a messenger raced up the cliff to the house. Fear seized Iona so badly, she at first didn't comprehend his words.

". . . and so, milady," he finished, "there'll be no help for them if you'll not come and succor them."

Relief was the warm blood coursing again in her body, which had frozen with dread. "I will come at once," she said.

In a flurry of packing and arranging, the return trip to Sinclair Castle was arranged. Spes would accompany Iona, while Marta would stay on the island and run the sanctuary. As they set sail the next day on the morning tide, Iona couldn't help but compare this to her journey to the island. Her heart squeezed with pain, as it always did when she thought of Magnus, which was every hour.

The trip back through the straits was arduous and took

longer than her first trip to the island, because of adverse currents and rough seas.

It was near sundown when they reached the shore of Sinclair land. Tired as she was, Iona insisted on seeing her patients at once. "Putrid throats," the messenger had told her, adding that the malady afflicted man, woman, and child, and that some had already died.

When she saw the putrescence in the throats of the ill, Iona was horrified. "None must use the water directly from its source," she commanded. "We will boil the seawater to drink. Glam, check the water sources. Spes, have someone fetch some of that brew the friars make."

"The poison is strong, Iona," Spes said as she swabbed a child's throat with the alcohol.

"It is," she answered grimly. "We must work very fast."

All through the night the two women and their helpers labored over the sick of Sinclair Castle and its environs.

By dawn all the ailing had been ministered to, and the workers began with the first patient again, swabbing throats and mixing medicaments of paste and seawater.

Glam reported that one of the water sources was too close to a midden and had been despoiled by it. He'd walled it off.

Finally, two days hence, the crisis passed and the two exhausted women sought their cots while others took over the care.

Drained by the long days she'd spent setting up her sanctuary and then by the lack of sleep, Iona slept the sun around.

As she was rising on the fourth day to the news that the fevers had subsided and that there'd been no new deaths, a messenger galloped through the gates of Sinclair Castle. Iona descended the stairs in time to see Kenneth usher him into the great room.

"Well met, sister," Kenneth said. "There's a messenger from the king."

Her hand went to her throat. Surely Magnus would've included a message. He was supposed to be at the king's side. She rushed into the room, smiling with anticipation.

The messenger looked uneasily at Kenneth.

"Speak freely in front of my brother's wife," he said.

The man hesitated a moment longer, then relayed his message. The Sinclair lands were to be protected by Kenneth Sinclair as the heir to the holding, for the king had received word from Urdric Kildeer, baron of Northumbria, that Magnus Sinclair was dead.

"No!" Kenneth shouted.

Iona swayed on her feet, black dots flashing in front of her eyes, the stone floor tilting. She compressed her lips together to keep from screaming. "How?" The question was a strangled whisper. Magnus couldn't be dead. He was life, and all its light and force.

The messenger glanced at her stricken face, and his own features contorted in pity. "Milady, we searched for him. Those who saw him at the last say he was surrounded by other swordsmen." He swallowed heavily. "So, we only know he died fighting. 'Twould seem he fought bravely and slew many, and that he attempted to escape his attackers, but was unable." He bowed to her. "I, like the other warriors, regret giving you this pain, milady."

"Thank you," she said quietly, though her insides screamed in agony, burning and reeling with the pain she daren't put into words. "Please go to the kitchen and find sustenance. You will stay the night and journey back on the morrow." She spoke from rote, and the words echoed back to her as though someone else had spoken them.

The messenger bowed again and backed out of the room, his eyes filled with sadness.

Silence hung like a weighted tapestry between Kenneth and Iona. They could not look at each other, and at last Kenneth spoke.

"The word will've gone out to the clan that the laird is—"

"Kenneth, I do not believe my husband dead." He turned to her in amazement. "Do not say so in my presence," she added in a thin voice.

He swallowed hard and nodded jerkily in assent. "My mind too rejects such words, Iona." He inhaled shakily.

"But forsooth, I cannot allow you to have false hope. 'Twould wound you more, and I—"

"I'll not stop believing him alive." She swung away from him, striding across the stone floor. "I have my patients to see."

Kenneth watched her leave, knowing he should go after her, but too weak in the knees to move. Sagging against the mantel, he buried his face in his hands. Magnus!

The days passed slowly. The sea continued its pounding of the shore and the sun continued to rise each morning, though Iona prayed it would not. On the fourth day after the king's messenger had come, the clan gathered in the glen where she and Magnus had held their archery contest. Tartans covered the bracken and heather with their many hues as the abbot led the funeral mass.

"Milady, you must eat," Old Terrill said worriedly to Iona after they returned to the castle. "The service was long and tired you sorely."

She put a listless hand on his arm. "I'm fine, Father. So was the service." She moved toward the tables laden with food, greeting those who'd come from far and wide to pay their last respects to the laird, and making certain no platters were empty.

"She's torn apart," Kenneth said to Terrill, "but she doesn't stop her endless round of work. She will die too if she does not favor herself more."

Terrill nodded, shoving his hands farther into the sleeves of his tunic. "She wishes to sleep at night and not dream, so she labors long each day."

"And into the night," Kenneth added. "For the last three nights she was at the bedside of the lady MacDonnell, easing her whelping. She scarcely ate, and slept not at all till the babe was birthed. Then she went at once to Connery's hut and set their bairn's arm." He shook his head. "As laird I should command her to rest. Magnus would."

"I fear you must not interfere with the princess, Kenneth. 'Tis surcease from pain she seeks, and in her work she may find it."

Neither heard Cormac walk up behind them until the man spoke. "I too have seen the change in Asdis Iona. Could it be that the Viking loved our laird?"

Kenneth nodded. "I'm sure she loved him . . . and I think Magnus loved her." He frowned as Cormac arched his eyebrows. "You don't agree."

Cormac shrugged. "I don't consider love a principal part of connubial bliss. Dowry, devotion, respect, and common purpose to clan are the most important." He smiled. "I think they had that."

"True," Kenneth said.

"And what do you think of Elizabeth of Asquith, who grieves as much as does the Viking?" Cormac continued.

Kenneth shrugged. "She has not married another. She grieves for her aloneness."

" 'Twould not be a bad match for you, nephew. Her blood is sound, her family devoted to the clan."

Kenneth shook his head, and his gaze slid toward Spes.

"Ah, so that's how it is." Cormac slapped his shoulder.

"And do you not think that there could be love with Magnus and the princess?" Terrill asked Cormac, as though he hadn't heard the rest of the exchange. "I do."

Cormac smiled and shrugged. "I agree it could've been possible. Only I think Elizabeth was the love of Magnus's life. He only married the Viking to keep the clan from ruinous war."

Old Terrill screwed up his face, looking forlorn. "I see."

Kenneth scowled. "I agree Magnus was fond of Elizabeth—"

"More than fond," Cormac interrupted. "But what matter it now? The princess will soon return to her people since she carries not the Sinclair seed."

"How do you know that?" Kenneth asked. "It's not three full moons since their wedding. Perhaps Iona wouldn't know herself."

"None of the wise women predict it. I went at once to see them when news of the laird's death reached me."

Cormac shook his head. "He was a fool to marry a woman past birthing age."

" 'Twould seem so," Old Terrill murmured, wondering at how he could have read so wrong the runes that predicted an heir for Magnus.

Kenneth bridled at Cormac's words. "Past birthing age or no, Iona's a wonder. She has tended our ill and lame, and she's an eloquent advocate. She's settled many a small dispute with her wisdom."

"I applaud your loyalty and concur, nephew. But hadn't the princess some plan in mind when she ventured to Scotland's waters?"

"She has a sanctuary for women on Eynhallow," Kenneth admitted reluctantly.

"Then she will not be far from us."

Kenneth shrugged, gazing bleakly across the room at his sister-in-law.

"You are now laird to the clan," Cormac said. "You must tell her what she may do."

"Not now!" Kenneth said.

"Of course not. Let her stay as long as she chooses. But you must choose a wife soon, and 'twould be better to have but one Lady Sinclair in Sinclair Castle."

Kenneth nodded.

The day after the memorial service for Magnus, Iona left the castle to make her usual rounds of the nearby huts. She'd urged Spes to accompany Kenneth as he made courtesy calls on some of the other clans. Outriders and clansmen accompanied them, and they were not expected back until dinnertime.

Glam and some of the Scottish warriors had taken on the task of relocating the midden. Iona had more or less promised him she would stay at the castle, but her restlessness caused by too many thoughts of Magnus drove her out with her bag of herbs and medicaments.

"Come, Thor," she said to her wolf. "You and I are alone today. And it's peaceful on the far side of the glen."

After she saw to her last patient—the baby with the broken arm—Iona headed back toward the castle. She took her time, allowing Thor to scamper after ferrets while she gathered wild onions to make a potion for stomach ailments.

When she heard a crashing of branches in the small wood they were crossing through, she whistled to the wolf. He came bounding to her side. His hackles rose as he pushed in front of her and faced a thicket.

"What is it, Thor?" She dropped her canvas sling, its contents spilling onto the ground. Glancing around, she saw a wrist-thick piece of wood a little more than a cubit in length. She picked it up and balanced it in both hands in front of her. "Who goes there?" she called out in Gaelic, then in Icelandic.

She heard more crashing, then figures appeared from out of the trees. Her blood ran cold, and she regretted her impulse to leave the castle. Was Glam or anyone within earshot?

Facing her were three beasts, foaming at the mouth, teeth bared. Not of the wolf family, they were mighty mastiffs, dogs that were bred to battle wolves, or any other creatures, on command.

"Go back!" she ordered, her hand in Thor's ruff to keep him at her side. As strong as the wolf was, he couldn't possibly fight off three mammoth dogs. Red-eyed and battle ready, the three took stiff steps forward. "Back, I say."

She released Thor, who pressed in front of her, and hefted her staff in both hands. Keeping her weight on the balls of her feet, she shifted easily from one foot to the other. She knew she could be badly hurt by the beasts. She sensed them moving in for the attack and edged away from Thor, giving less of a target for the three predators.

When Thor stiffened and whipped his head around to look behind her, she whirled as well. Two more mastiffs stood behind her, growling low. Terror gripped her. She and Thor couldn't battle five mastiffs. Glancing around, she saw a thick grouping of oaks near the path. That would be the best place for a stand, for the trees would cover their backs. "Thor," she whispered. "Come." She moved backward a step at a time, her gaze never leaving the mammoth, red-eyed canines.

Just before they were set, the lead animal roared his challenge and lunged. Thor met him in the air, snarling and slashing with his razor-sharp teeth, bodies and heads colliding in a maddened strategy for best position for the kill.

Reading the situation correctly, Iona positioned herself for the flank attack against Thor. She rushed to meet two of them as they raced for Thor's soft underbelly, fixed single-mindedly on their target. Leaning down to avoid the flashing paws and teeth of the battling dogs and wolf, she swung her cudgel in dueling fashion, rapidly back and forth. Her surprise attack caught both dogs on their soft snouts, that most tender of canine flesh.

Then she tripped and fell. At once they wheeled to the attack.

"Aye, ya clumsy missus! Get to your feet or we're done, wolf or no." With that Geordie McInally threw himself at the closest mastiff, striking with his cudgel and then howling when the dog's sharp teeth grazed him.

Iona leapt to her feet, turning her back on the poacher to battle her own huge beast. She struck it just as Geordie hit his.

Both dogs flung themselves back, yowling in anger and pain. They were immobilized for a few precious seconds, but then the remaining two attacked from the other side, growling and snapping, drool whipping back along their muzzles and giving them a demonic cast.

Geordie took on the first two again, his growls as menacing as the mastiffs'.

Iona struggled to get her balance so she could give as much thrust as possible to her swinging weapon, but the battling Thor and his nemesis got in the way. Scrambling to a better position, she felt a ripping down her side as one of the dogs got her.

Her yell of anger and fear was drowned out by the bull roar of the Viking battle cry. "Glam!" she shouted in relief as she saw her protector wade into the melee, laying about him with his war club and bellowing his outrage. Two of the dogs turned on him, and he pulled out his sword to meet them.

Filled with hope that they would win this battle, Iona echoed the Viking battle cry and staunchly met another attack. Maddened by blood lust the dog threw itself at her mindlessly, snapping and growling and careless of its own life. She swung and connected with its shoulder, but the painful blow only further enraged it. It charged her again, and this time its claws raked down her front. As her bliaut tore, she swung once more, striking its tender side but overbalancing herself. As she tried to rise, the dog was on her, and she lifted her cudgel as protection. Then Glam was there, swinging at the animal with his club, brushing him off her as though the mammoth beast were no more than a flea.

She shouted her thanks and rolled to her feet to face the dog once more. On they fought, until she was out of breath and reeling from exertion and the shock of battle. At last she swung right. Her cudgel smote the dog's skull, and with a yelp of anguish, the beast fell. She tried to see through the sweat dripping into her eyes. Swaying, panting, she readied herself for the next attack, but it never came. As she watched, Glam delivered the coup de grace to one canine, Geordie to another. Then it was over. Five mastiff bodies lay on the ground. She sank down beside her wolf, who lay spread over the carcass of the leader.

Hands lifted her. "Milady? Are you all right?" Glam asked.

"Yes. And you, my friend?"

"Some small slashes only, milady."

"I'll see to them. But for now, we must take care of Thor. I'm sure he's badly hurt." She looked at Geordie. "I would succor you too. Don't go."

"I go, missus. I have my own ways of healing. And Geordie McInally gives your courage homage. I'm awa'." He disappeared through the gorse and bracken as though he'd never been.

"He fought well," Glam said.

"Look to Thor, my friend."

"I will, milady." But Glam froze in the act of turning away, gripping his club and sword once more.

Horses! Thundering over the ground like a herd of elk. Iona stumbled to her knees, gripping her cudgel.

Over a knoll and through the trees, a complement of warriors wearing the Sinclair plaid burst upon them, armed to the teeth, the Sinclair battle cry issuing from every throat. Atholl, Dugald's second in command, and now commander of the forces with Dugald at the king's side, led them.

Atholl swung off his horse before it had fully stopped. "Milady? God save us, are you wounded?" Gnashing his teeth, he studied her, then glanced around him. His lips curled back in a feral snarl. "Who did this to you? Who dared?" His angry curses were echoed by the other Sinclairs, who dismounted. "Curse them. These are trained dogs, not wild ones."

Iona's eyes widened in alarm. "What say you?"

Atholl scrutinized the bloodstained Glam and the staggering wolf, then said, "Milady, those that strike at you make war on Sinclairs."

"Aye!" The concerted bellow seemed to bend the trees to the ground with its force.

"I thank you," she said. "You will tell me all, Atholl, as we go. I would have a litter for Thor." Before she could say more, two of the men used their tartans to make a sling for the wolf, affixing it to their horses. Thor was too weak to protest this attack on his supremacy.

Steeds were provided for her and Glam, and as they made their slow, circuitous way along the path to the castle, word of the villainous attack spread. All of the Sinclairs in the area rushed to see her, until a mighty cavalcade was following her into the castle bailey.

Iona was stunned at the huzzahs, the rushing to kiss the hem of her garment, the affectionate handclasps and warm greetings.

"You are a lion, milady," Atholl said.

"You're a true Sinclair, Lady Iona," a man called out, and the rest cheered.

She tried to thank them but was too overwhelmed by their greetings, and too dizzy and weak from the battle.

Mavis appeared at her side. "I will wash your wounds at once, milady. Atholl said the dogs didn't have the wild disease, but we need'st have speed." Mavis caught her hand. "I've watched you many times, and you may tell me how to go on if you please, but hurry."

Iona nodded, knowing full well that if the animals had been crazed, they could only wait to see if she showed any fear of water, the most telling sign of the fatal illness. "Thank you. I will come at once."

Glam lifted her from the saddle and carried her into the castle. "Bring Thor," she ordered Atholl. "I'll not touch anything until Glam and my wolf are cleansed."

"Milady!" Mavis protested.

Kenneth, Spes, and the outriders rode into the bailey at that moment, and were confounded by the chaos that greeted them. Atholl told Kenneth what had happened, and Kenneth began bellowing orders. "Find who owned and trained the dogs. Don't rest until this is done. That they attacked Lady Sinclair means they attacked the clan. Find the foes."

Spes had already raced over to Iona, who was still instructing Mavis on how to care for Thor's wounds.

Tight-lipped, Spes put her hands on her hips and confronted her cousin. "You will listen to me, Asdis Iona. I will put women to helping the wolf and Mavis will see to Glam. But this very minute I will take care of you."

Iona smiled weakly. "My mother always said you had Viking spunk, Spes."

"And your mother would be horrified to see you now. Your skin is torn as well as your clothes. Your hair is even matted with blood." Tutting angrily to hide her concern, she urged Iona inside the castle and up the stairs. "How dare you go out without a proper guard. Your husband . . ." She faltered, tears springing to her eyes. "Forgive me, cousin. It was not my thought to hurt you by—"

"No matter," Iona interrupted. "I think of Magnus a great deal. He does not seem dead to me."

"But he is," Spes said. "I do not want you to live in false dreams. Your life is ahead of you, Iona. And you have Eyin Helga."

"Yes," Iona said faintly. She reeled, though not from the encounter with the dogs, but from a fresh onslaught of pain. Magnus!

Spes caught her around the waist. "How could you venture forth without proper escort? It's heartfelt foolishness."

"I know, I know." At the top of the staircase, she looked back down to the large entry hall. It was filled with people looking up at her. "I'm fine," she called, and waved.

Her smile faded as soon as she entered her bedchamber. "Bring the hot iron. I don't think the dogs were crazed, but my wounds need to be cauterized, as do Thor's and Glam's. At once."

"I'll see to it," Spes said, and turned to the serving women who'd followed them. "Go quickly and heat the irons. White-hot."

∽ 16 ∽

There is something beyond the grave; death does not end all, and the pale ghost escapes from the vanquished pyre.
                                                    —Sextus Propertius

"And I tell you something must be done," Kenneth said, smacking his fist into his palm. "She cannot continue like this." He strode up and down the great room, distress and anger marking his features, his footfalls resounding like drumbeats. "Nothing is as I wish it. No one has yet traced those mastiffs. Why should it be so hard? And now, Iona . . ."

"I know," Spes said, her voice trembling with her own fears for her cousin.

Glam, the only other person in the great hall, stood statue-still, only his dark green eyes moving as he watched Kenneth stomp up and down the great room. He knew of his mistress's pain and frowned on discussing such a thing with this Scot. But he hoped they might think of something that would distract the princess and give her her color again.

As though suddenly aware of the distress he was causing Spes, Kenneth paused, grimacing. He went to her, his arms outstretched, but, catching Glam's speculative glance, he pulled back. Instead of embracing her, he patted her clumsily on the shoulder. "Don't distress yourself, Spes. 'Tis not your doing that she grieves so."

Kenneth deeply cared for Spes and hoped to make her his bride when he was able to broach the subject to Einar upon his return to Sinclair shores. And he was fond of Magnus's widow too, and feared for her health. She kept up a strict regimen of work, never flagging, rarely resting. White-faced and determined, she always smiled whenever anyone was around. But if one caught her unawares, her pain was etched clearly on her face.

"But what can we do?" Spes asked.

He took her hands, squeezing them reassuringly. "I'll think of something." But what? He'd implored Iona many times to ease up on her heavy schedule, but she only smiled and kept on with what she was doing.

"The princess must work," Glam said baldly.

Spes rounded on him, fury in every line of her body. "Even if it is killing her, Glam? And it is. She doesn't sleep, rarely eats. All she does is minister to all who need her." She flung her arm in a wide sweep. "And that is everyone for ten thousand cubits in this godforsaken land." She covered her face with her hands, shaking her head. "Forgive me, Lord Kenneth. I didn't mean to malign your land."

Ignoring Glam this time, Kenneth embraced her. "Tell me what you want me to do, and I'll order her. Do you want to take her back to Icelandia?"

Stunned, Spes looked up at him, tears glinting on her face. "No . . . no, I don't want that."

Relieved, Kenneth hugged her again.

"She wouldn't go," Glam said. "Her work at Eyin Helga must continue."

Spes stared at him for a long moment. "Perhaps that is what we must do. We'll get her back to the Orkneys and her sanctuary. Mayhap she'll be happy there."

"She will still grieve," Glam said flatly.

"I know, I know," Spes said, irritation sharpening her

voice. "But it could be better there. She can remember their happy days, walk the ground they trod together, and do the work that God has set out for her. It's meet that she should do this, and in doing so, heal herself."

Kenneth took hold of Spes's arms. "I don't want to let you go," he said.

Deep red stained her face, and she glanced furtively at Glam. He looked back stolidly, making no move to exit. "I —I would stay with you, milord, but my place is with my lady." She tried to smile, but a sob interfered.

"I know," Kenneth said heavily.

"She will not return to Eyin Helga until she attends the McCloud birth," Glam said.

Happily, Spes looked up at Kenneth. " 'Tis true. She'll not leave when the lady McCloud is so anxious to have her at the birthing."

There was a clash of metal without, then the sound of the iron portal clanging open and shut. Cormac appeared at the top of the two steps leading into the great room. "What say you, laird? How goes the clan in my absence?"

Kenneth released Spes and strode over to his uncle, clasping arms with him in greeting. "Better for your return, Cormac. How goes the king?"

Cormac nodded coolly to Spes and Glam, then wandered over to the fireplace, raising his hands to the heat. "The war marches, though not as quickly as Malcolm wanted. The baron is a formidable foe."

Kenneth spat at the fire. "Tostig would be nothing without him."

Cormac looked around at the other two.

"I will join my mistress," Spes said hurriedly, recognizing that Cormac had something of import to tell Kenneth.

Glam stared at the two men, then he too thumped out of the room.

Cormac was silent for a moment, then said, "The giant likes me not, I feel."

Kenneth shrugged. "He treats all the same—except Iona."

"Mayhap you're right." Cormac frowned. "But we cannot be too careful, Kenneth."

Kenneth stared at his uncle. "You've heard something?"

"Yes. I have news." Cormac looked behind him to the archway leading from the great room. "And I know we have spies everywhere."

Kenneth bristled. "I trust Spes. And Glam is loyal to Iona, who's loyal to us."

"They're Vikings."

"Iona is a Sinclair now. And Spes is her cousin."

Cormac inhaled heavily. "And you would have her as your sweetling, I'm thinking."

"More than that. I wish to take her to wife."

His uncle winced and shook his head. "I'm fond of Spes, and of Iona, just as our people are. But I beg you, go slowly. I don't want to tell you how to handle the clan . . ."

Kenneth relaxed. "Why not? You often told Magnus."

Cormac nodded, his visage lightening. " 'Tis true. And he didn't always listen."

Both men laughed, then Kenneth strode over to the table to pour ale into a tankard. "I'm remiss in my duties. You must have a powerful thirst after your long ride." His smile widened. "But as usual you look as though you've just traveled across the courtyard."

Cormac quaffed the contents of the tankard and thrust it back at Kenneth for a refill. Watching his nephew speculatively, he absently kicked a giant flaming log, making sparks fly. "Malcolm wants us to commit more of the Sinclairs to the conflict."

"What?" Kenneth was alarmed. "That's not possible. Magnus made it very clear to Malcolm that only one hundred men would be committed to battle. Some of our best soldiers are with the king already." Kenneth poured ale for himself and drank quickly.

"True," Cormac said. "But the tide of battle has turned many times and Malcolm doesn't like the outlook. He wants more men."

"I like not to risk any more Sinclairs. It was Magnus's wish to hold the line." Kenneth banged his tankard down on the trencher board.

"The king demands fealty. You are his newest laird. The decision must be yours and yours alone."

"Aye." Kenneth began pacing. "What think you?"

"I agree with you. I don't like it. But I don't see how we can help it. Even Magnus wouldn't have held out against an open demand from his king. I will do my part to put Malcolm off as much as I can, but perhaps if you were to face him yourself, voice your objections, he would listen more closely."

Kenneth nodded. "I'll do that. I'm loath to risk the clan. Magnus and our people fought so hard to gain Sinclair land."

Cormac nodded. "And we must keep it."

The oubliette was so dark, dank, and dreary that it was night even when it was day. The only sounds were water dripping from the walls and the scurrying and squeaking of rats and other unseen residents of this, the lowest of all dungeons. Most inhabitants of such places rarely saw day ever again, remaining forgotten in the bowels of a castle.

Torches on the walls in the corridor above cast a pitiful, pallid pattern of light through the iron-latticed opening in the ceiling. That was the only way in and out of the cell, which was fashioned like a deep well. A little water and even less food were lowered to him by rope—when the jailers remembered.

The atmosphere was fetid and damp enough to make his skin pearl with moisture even as the walls did. The floor was slick with droppings, human and rodent. And the food was equal to the excrement. Thirst had driven him to the perilous exercise of collecting water from the walls. No doubt it was filled with foul humors that could sicken him, but Magnus was no longer fastidious about that. He was fighting for his life. He needed every bit of sustenance and cunning if he was going to survive. His eyes had sharpened in the darkness, and he had that advantage over his jailers. They only opened the ceiling grate once every two weeks, and there were always two of them: one to lower a torch with one hand and brandish a weapon with the other, the second to climb down a hemp ladder, also with a weapon, to check whether he'd died.

"Though why we bother, I don't know," one toothless jailer had confided to his companion the last time they'd checked on him. "He'll soon be dead. He'll be used as bargaining power, then slain."

" 'Twould be fine to know his name, I'm thinkin'," the other had replied.

" 'Tisn't for us to know. Sufficeth that he be a murdering Scot."

Then they'd left him. That had been almost a fortnight ago. Soon they'd come again, for there'd been activity in the castle above. He'd sensed it more than heard it, in his tomblike prison, and guessed that he'd be executed soon.

He'd expected torture, but that hadn't happened, other than being bound for almost an entire month after his imprisonment. Since the good baron excelled in torture, he must have special reasons for sparing him. If he was to save his life, he would have to act when his jailers came next. At least it would be better to die fighting than to be a victim of whatever the baron had planned. Perhaps he was devising some exquisite torture that would be his death. Magnus had no wish to be the main course at such a diabolic banquet.

So he prepared himself. There was no icy loch in which to douse himself, but he'd practiced leaping upward until he was able to grasp the grate more often than not.

Each time the guards had come, he'd feigned greater weakness and weariness. And it was only the two who came, without others to protect their backs. No doubt they'd come to think of him as docile, accepting of his fate, and might be careless.

They'd taken his weapons, of course, but they'd left him his torn and bloodied plaid. Woven cunningly in the edge was a small, well-hidden sheath, which held a short, thin dirk. With that, he had a chance.

He slept as much as he could, needing the rest. Besides, it let him forget about food. As used as he was to sporadic eating when in the field, the long months of incarceration had weakened even his strong frame. Four damn long months. What was Iona doing? They'd have told her he was dead. Did she grieve? Yes, for they'd shared a love. And he'd wanted more. First he would deal with this infamy, then he'd see to his wife.

Sighing, he wrapped himself in his tattered, smelly tartan and closed his eyes, standing against the wall. The rats would chew upon him more fiercely if he reclined. Tomorrow, the guards would be coming. He felt it. And he knew what he would do.

Sleep came quickly, and almost at once, the rats began their nibbling. They'd made a few sores on him, but he'd killed a score of them, so mostly they dined on the carcasses of their fallen comrades.

The rusty sound of the giant key turning in the lock above him brought him fully awake and alert. Whisking his plaid around one arm, he hid the small knife in his other palm, ready to throw it. He'd only have one chance.

"He'll not be ready for this," he heard one say. The man grunted as he heaved back the grate.

" 'Twill be fun for us," the second answered, "before the baron gets him."

"Is it true that he cuts their heart out alive and eats it even before they die?" The torchlight wove in agitation as he speaker shivered.

"Aye. My cousin is one of his torturers, and he says they're glad to die any way they can when the baron is through with them. If they are young boys, they do not die for many days. He uses them until their parts are torn and worn, Rufus says. A fearsome man, our baron."

The first one nodded as he leaned over the opening, lowering the torch into the cell. "And 'tis said—"

Those words were his last, as Magnus leapt into the air, grabbed the man's shoulder, and sliced his jugular. His body fell to the floor of the cell, landing with an ugly thud, the torch beside it.

"Ovus?" the second called. "Are you all right? I'll lower the ladder."

Magnus leapt again, grabbing the second man too and flinging him down. He twisted his body and landed on the man's neck, breaking it. He died silently, and the only sound was the hissing, spitting torch as it sputtered on the damp floor.

Quick as lightning, Magnus rescued the flickering torch. He waited for it to gain strength, then slipped his dirk and one of the guard's short swords into his belt. Holding the torch in one hand, he leapt upward once more, catching the edge of the floor with his free hand. He tossed the torch onto the floor, then heaved himself up out of the cell. He crouched by the opening for a long moment, listening. Satisfied no alarm had been given, he dropped his malodorous, vermin-riddled plaid atop the two bodies below. It wouldn't fool anyone for long, but it might be long enough. He replaced the grating as quietly as he could.

Taking deep breaths of the relatively clean air, he gazed around him. Every minute he could go undetected meant a greater chance of staying free and alive. Not all the baron's men would be as gullible as those two jailers, and there'd be hell to pay when his disappearance was discovered.

His dirk in his hand, he crept toward a set of stairs that wound up a wall to the next level and started to climb. While he was still hidden in the curve of stairs, he paused and gave a fair imitation of his captors conversing, in case of interested parties above.

Holding the torch in front of him so that his face was shadowed, he eased into the cavernous room at the top of the stairs. Not a soul seemed abroad, but Magnus didn't move.

Like most dungeons, this one was a rabbit warren of twisting corridors, damp stone floors and walls, and dank, sour smells. Magnus wrinkled his nose, catching a hint of fresh air. But several corridors led off this room. Which way to freedom?

Hearing voices, he stiffened. He tried to mark the direction, then stuck his torch in a wall sconce and slid sideways into the deep shadows.

"Where's Ovus and Anarchin?" The rough voice echoed in the chamber.

"In with the prisoner, I'll be bound. See the open door there. They won't have to bother with him much longer. The word is that the baron will be dealing with that one very soon." The man cursed. "Let's get out of here. I don't like this level. Come along and we'll check the west side, then get back up."

The voices faded, and Magnus moved swiftly, taking the torch once more and heading for the corridor the two had come from. Along the way he managed to lift another dirk from the wall armory. Neither it nor the short sword was of good quality, but they were better than nothing. On a far wall was a row of cloaks, and he plucked one off. The fabric was so rough that if the cloak hadn't been greasy and caked with dirt, it might've scratched his skin. But it would ward off the chill until he could find better, and the hood would hide his reddish hair.

Walking fast, but trying not to draw attention to himself, he climbed another staircase to another anteroom.

"Hey, you," a man called from across the room. "Have you come from Ovus's and Anarchin's sector? Is the prisoner ready to be shriven?"

Magnus laughed raucously. "He's quaking, I'll be bound."

"Aye."

Someone hailed the other man, who turned to answer. Magnus took off at a run, risking the echoing noise he made.

He climbed to another level, then another, and still no alarm sounded. As he walked along yet another corridor, still seeking an exit from the damnable dungeons, he guessed he'd finally reached ground level. The air was much fresher.

He rounded a corner. Suddenly, light hurt his eyes. He stood still, blinking several times until he could see properly. He was on the threshold of a large guard room, and there were armed men everywhere.

Cursing under his breath, he scanned the busy area. When he spied the armorer's wall, laden with weapons, he inhaled heavily. How to get there and get what he needed? He hefted one of his dirks, then his roving gaze fixed on a squire skittering from trencher board to trencher board. More than one of the burly men swiped at him. The boy was quick and managed to escape most of the cuffs. Then someone called out to the squire, asking him to fetch something. Putting down his heavy, unwieldy tray, the boy scurried to obey.

Magnus slouched down to half his size, so that he didn't tower over the others, then edged into the room. He crept to the large fireplace, watching everything but keeping his head turned away. He had to trust that he gave the appearance of a worker. Taking a precious moment to scan the room again, he then scooped up some cinders and rubbed them into his hair and on his face. Then he slid toward the trencher board and the abandoned tray, one hand grasping the dirk. Snatching up the tray, he lifted it face-high to cover as much of himself as possible. Still, bent almost double, he made his way across the room to the armorer's wall.

He placed the tray on the floor and was reaching for a sword and breastplate when the alarm came. As noise and clamor erupted behind him, he grasped a sword, then scrambled out of the way as the guards raced for their weapons. Face turned away, he tied on the sword, then managed to filch a chain mail shirt. He donned that and a helmet. He hadn't worn a helmet in years, and it felt cumbersome, bulky. But it helped hide his visage.

Acting as though he were following an order, he followed a group of men up a long passage. By his reckoning they should be heading to the inner courtyard. With luck he'd be near the postern gate, and he prayed it was well oiled. He'd only have one chance to get out. In minutes the castle would be swarming with the baron's men, and they'd look everywhere.

As he'd hoped, the passageway opened into the court-yard. The other men raced off, and Magnus held back, waiting until no one was nearby. It was barely dawn, with just enough light for him to scan the area. Relying on his knowledge of castles in Northumbria, he eased around to the left. There it was, the postern gate. Reaching for the ring, he pulled strongly. It was not well oiled. It resisted, then gave way, opening with a rusty sound. He looked behind him. Few were near him, and they were rushing to positions. Opening it, he slipped through and into the outer courtyard. Crouched down, he ran toward the back of the castle.

Guards were charging around the courtyard, paying lit-tle mind to him. When one did pause as though to ques-tion him, Magnus gestured toward the front of the castle. The other nodded and ran on. At least the throngs of shouting, running men provided a semblance of cover for him, he thought. They'd look to the horses first, then to any conveyance leaving the front gate.

Magnus was headed instead for the midden, in the back of the castle and far away from the noses of the baron, his family, and his guests. There, wagons would come to pick up the refuse and garbage and haul it away.

His luck was with him. A cart was being loaded now. He grimaced at the smell of the offal being shoveled onto its bed. Unhappily, it would be his safest sanctuary. God! Gritting his teeth, he shed his helmet and mail shirt and waited for his chance. It came when the shovelers finished and turned away, one waving the driver onward.

Taking a deep breath, Magnus sprinted for the cart. He dove forward, onto the cart and into the filthiest mess he'd ever encountered.

Holding his breath as long as he could, he drew up his legs, digging deeper into the horrid heap. Then, before he was forced to inhale, he made a small hole in the sewage and drew in air that was vaguely fresh. He fought the in-stinct to gag and peered out through the garbage to see the melee behind him as the baron's men searched for him.

Two soldiers stopped the driver and each drove their

swords once into the odiferous pile. They stepped back and, holding their noses, waved the driver on. He cackled at their revulsion.

The cart teetered around the side of the castle and toward the front. Just before it cleared the main gate, warning trumpets sounded. The tall ironbound doors to the castle clanked open, and several horsemen galloped out, spreading fanwise beyond the portcullis.

A man stepped out of the castle behind them and stood at the top of the steps. He was a large, barrel-chested man, clad in black with one gray streak in his thick ebony hair. His face was contorted with rage, and his booming voice had a rusty sound as he shouted to his subordinates. He stomped across the top step, brandishing his sword and cursing.

"Find him, blast your hides. Those men who let him escape will be roasted alive. Have you a desire to join them, let the prisoner remain unclaimed. Find him!"

The roar frightened ravens from the tower and they cawed their anger, swooping and diving, their satin-black coats glinting in the sun.

Magnus waited for the cart to be stopped and searched again, but none approached. Only glares followed the swillman and his swaying, stinking load.

As the cart tottered out through the front gate, Magnus stared at his old enemy. For years he'd been sure that the infamous baron of Northumbria had been a conspirator in his parents' death. Hatred swelled in him, blanking out all else, making even the offal that pressed around him lose its smell.

He hadn't seen Baron Urdric Kildeer, Tostig's most powerful warlord, in two years, but the man had changed little. His broad Northumbrian face had slashes of cruelty honed into its flat-boned features. His eyes were permanently narrowed, as though all the world were suspect. His detractors called him evil, his admirers called him the same. Magnus despised him, not with the cold detachment one reserves for a foe, but with a writhing, rippling, teeth-grinding contempt that burned through him at the very sight of the man.

As did most of the world, Magnus knew of the baron's vicious sexual appetites, his propensity for young boys and girls, and their sudden disappearances when he was through with them. His love of torture was well known too, particularly his devotion to the garrote that tied a man's feet to the noose at his throat, so that any movement whatsoever tightened it, choking off the air. It was immeasurably cruel, and almost always slowly, painfully fatal. His viciousness was not unusual, for torture was a common method of extracting information. But the baron excelled in weaving his black arts on children. It was said that he would dine while he watched the heinous death of some unfortunate. Other leaders were dangerous, lethal. Magnus understood that. But he despised Urdric because he preyed on the innocent.

As the wagon negotiated a turn off the drawbridge, the castle and its people receded. There were still shouts and the sound of running men, but none approached the wagon.

Magnus settled in for his grisly, odiferous ride.

Not Magnus nor those in Urdric's pay had noticed the horse vendor who'd paid more attention to the proceedings than he did to the hostler who was paying him gold for his two steeds. Since his hair had been dyed with cinders, and his face blackened as well, none took him for a Viking.

When the hostler turned around to tell the vendor he'd take more of his fine steeds, the seller had disappeared. The hostler shrugged. He'd certainly gotten the best of the bargain, so he had no quarrel. Perhaps the vendor would come again.

The Viking ran like the wind to the horse he had tied in the thick wood, not far from the baron's castle. Bent over the steed's neck he kicked it into a gallop, heading for the sea a few leagues down the road.

More than an hour later, he heard the familiar and

comforting sound of a tern screech. The signal had been given by a Viking lookout.

Seemingly careless of his neck and that of his steed, the horseman let the animal plummet down the almost sheer face of the cliff to the strand below. With great strength, the animal managed to keep his footing.

A Viking ship danced in deep waters off the shore, the half-moon bay protecting it from the buffeting winds and waves of the great North Sea. They'd ventured far south in their quest, and now, with booty loading them down, they only waited for one last man and his barter from the horses he'd stolen from a vassal of Baron Kildeer.

A small boat was sent to fetch the man. When he boarded the ship, he walked straight to its captain.

Einar answered the man's salute, curious about his obvious, breathless excitement. "Well?"

"I bring news, Lord Einar. Of Magnus Sinclair."

Magnus rode the noxious cart until it reached its destination. He really didn't care where it was, as long as it was out of sight of the castle.

By the time the cart slowed, his smelling abilities were all but dead and his entire body was coated with slime. He was so intent on gaining his freedom and returning to Sinclair land, though, he scarcely noticed little else. When the cart stopped, more sickening swill spilled over his face, and he held his breath, bracing himself. He didn't want to kill the driver, but he had every intention of doing so if there was the least sign of alarm. But there was only silence. He waited, ears straining. It worried him that the man didn't dump his load at once. Could he have been spotted?

The sun beat down and the load began to steam. Finally, certain the driver was gone, he eased out of his smelly confinement. In front of him was a mountain of sludge filling a pit. That's what he would be dumped into when the cart was upended. No! Enough.

Pushing one shoulder free, he wriggled his body down so that his feet slid off the open end of the cart. He paused for a moment, scrutinizing the area. There were no visitors to the smelly midden. He wrenched his body back and forth so that he tipped the cart downward. Much of the load slid off the end with him, covering him again. He stilled when the nag pulling the cart stamped its hooves, but still no one appeared.

After an eternity he moved again, slithering on his belly across the ground to the far side of the cart, then toward a straggly copse of trees. When he gained their thin cover, he scanned his surroundings once more and sniffed a familiar acrid scent. A tannery! No wonder they had a midden right there. None that worked around raw skins all day would notice the gagging smells.

And water! There had to be that. A tanner needed water and fire.

Crouched down, he studied the lay of the land. Not too far to his left was a decrepit hovel, sod-roofed and stone-walled, its rough-hewn door fractured and askew. A bench sat in front of it, and lying across the bench was a pair of worker's trousers and a shirt, the material thin and faded, but still serviceable. Apparently they'd been scrubbed and hung to dry. They would do for garb.

Off to his right he spotted the pond, scummy, brackish-looking, and patched with a thin layer of ice. Numbing cold. But he'd swum in the North Sea on the coldest days. It would be worth it to cleanse himself of the stench.

What made him want to laugh for joy was the sight of a wooden bowl of lye soap sitting on the bench in front of the ramshackle hut. The tanners probably used it to clean the skins. The abrasive soap would scrub the last bit of flesh from a skin, and, with God's will, it would clean the filth off him.

He crept to the bench, lifted the soap, then back-tracked to the pond. Entering the water quietly, he slowly submerged himself several times, each time moving away from where he'd been. Then he fetched the soap and laved his body, slowly and completely, scouring his head and every orifice. He submerged, surfaced, and washed again. He did it over and over, until he felt clean, until he couldn't see a tinge of the fetid brown ooze that had imbedded itself into his being. His body was red, raw, and clean. He paid no heed to the tick marks and the bites of other creatures that had inhabited the oubliette with him.

Returning to the hut, he dried himself with a tanner's apron, then donned the worker's trousers and shirt. They too smelled of lye. It was a welcome odor.

After pulling on a too-small stocking cap to hide his hair, he turned to leave. He was eager to be on his way, to put distance between himself and Kildeer. He would head north for Malcolm's court. It would take days, but it was a shorter journey than to his own Sinclair land. Hearing voices, though, he melted back into the straggly copse of trees, dropping to the ground.

"I tell you," a man said clearly as he neared the hut, "I heard Kildeer's warriors talking at the tavern. It would seem the good Tostig will have a pact with the bastard Malcolm. The bastard Scot has invited his leaders to meet with good Tostig and the baron and others. And the women will come as a sign of peace." He cackled. "I 'eard them speak of the Viking queen who married a dog of a Scot. It is said she might be there."

Magnus clenched his teeth to stay still. Were they speaking of Iona? But why would she go to Malcolm's court? No.

The second tanner belched mightily. "Is she a beauty?"

"Some have seen 'er. 'Er hair is the color of first frost, so they said, with skin the hue of goat's milk."

" 'Tis a farce. None but a witch could have such."

"So she is, they say. She brought Scots back from the dead with her black powers. The devil's handmaiden, I've no doubt."

"The baron would want such a one. His tastes are many, and he dances with the devil. He might lay siege to Malcolm in his own castle and claim the Moon Witch."

When the men laughed, Magnus choked back his rage. Iona! It couldn't be. He'd left her safe on Eynhallow. But the description. Could it be any other?

"Aye," the first man said in a hushed tone, "no man'll want 'er after the baron has his way."

"Mayhap the baron will finish her when he's through. It'd be a mercy."

Magnus ground his teeth, swearing at God and all the Fates who seemed to give comfort to his enemy. With all his heart he wished Kildeer to the River Styx in a leaky boat, so that he burned and drowned. But not for him the forgetfulness of death, but vivid memory in everlasting damnation.

But Iona! Curse her if she were at Malcolm's court. What'd possessed her to put herself in harm's way? The thought of any other man, especially Baron Kildeer, getting his hands on his wife made his blood run cold.

His fear for her, combined with a lack of sustenance, the anguish of months of imprisonment, and the tanners' words, fired his imagination into near delirium. Had any touched her? Would she let them? Had the heat he recalled, the beautiful burning passion that had sustained him all this time, been false? No, it had been real, and for him alone. To force such intense affection would be base indeed. But had she done it?

Watching the two tanners, Magnus squelched the longing to strangle them, to choke off their air until their life's blood burst through their straining veins. Their words had driven him mad.

The bigger of the two held several pairs of deerskin boots aloft. His dirt-encrusted hands covered with swaddling, he carefully brushed each boot against the grain and then back again until the rich fur glinted in the noonday sun. "Aye," he said with satisfaction, "these'll be fine specimens for the baron's men to ponder. We'll get a pretty pence for them."

"Careful not to gouge a piece of the skin," the more wizened man said. " 'Twould be death by garrot." He shivered, glancing around anxiously.

The other man nodded and set the boots on the rickety bench. "Let's go fetch the other things," he said, and they

turned to leave. But the bigger man paused, squinting over
his shoulder at the bench. "Was not the lye soap out 'ere?"

The smaller one turned around and shrugged. "Mayhap
it's elsewhere."

"Fool. And so 'twould be." He cuffed his friend on the
shoulder, but said no more of the soap as they walked away.

The voices had barely faded when Magnus left the protection of the copse. Blood lust still throbbing through
him, he snatched the largest pair of boots and slipped them
on. They were snug, but would do. Still cautious, he made
his way to a glen not far from the winding road the cart
had traveled. It would be better for him not to travel the
roadways.

After he'd gone a fair distance, he glanced around him.
The glen was still, no birds or creatures stirring in fright.
He was alone. He started off toward the north at a slow run
that would eat up the miles, but not tire him. Off the
road, the way was rougher, filled with rocks, bracken, and
thicket, but at least he had cover if anyone approached. He
had to get out of Northumbria. His life was not worth a
pence. By now the baron would have a bounty on his head,
dead or alive, and he'd no wish to grant anyone his head.

So he pushed himself ever northward to the Scottish
border, fury, frustration, and uncertainty warring within
him. He had no thought of discomfort as unused muscles
strained and ached, as the icy blasts of the December wind
swirled around him.

Dusk fell, and he found cover and slept. Traveling at
night over strange land could bring injury or worse. 'Twas
better to risk traveling in the light.

Day dawned and he headed north again, his back to
the weak winter sun.

At the end of a sennight, he was gaunt from sparse
meals, and his clothes had begun to tatter from getting
caught on nettles and burrs. Sleety mists enveloped him,
but he paid no heed. He had crossed the bleak Northumbrian moors and was in Scotland again. His mind was fixed
on Malcolm's court and what he'd face there. His feverish

brain had begun to picture Iona with his enemies, feasting with them, laughing with them. Jealousy scourged him, though he'd not admit its presence. But if Iona had betrayed him and their vows, he'd lock her away in the dungeon of Sinclair Castle.

～ 17 ～

We live, not as we wish, but as we can.
—Menander

Iona sat on the mare Magnus had given her and gazed down at the sea from the cliff high above it. Though the winter solstice had passed, the day was mild, the sun beating down like a blessing. But even if a gale had been wailing, Iona would have been there, watching Einar's ship and two others maneuver their way into the harbor of Sinclair waters.

She was baffled that he was there, when he should have been in safe harbor, snug against the winter seas, but she was glad he had come, for whatever reason. She hadn't realized how much she'd missed Einar and the other Vikings, especially since Magnus's disappearance four months earlier. Pride filled her at the way the ships tacked in smartly. Then the sails were lowered and the powerful arms of the rowers brought them closer to the strand.

Iona's mare, as though sensing her excitement, pranced and snorted atop the cliff. Behind her, the Sinclair warriors who always guarded her back watched with interest.

"They be your Vikings, milady," a man called Keown

…aid to her. He was a cousin to Dugald and had become her friend.

She nodded, noting the man's smile. A few months ago Keown would've run for his weapons and sounded the alarm at such a sight on the North Sea. Would that Magnus could see how his people and the Vikings worked side by side. A familiar grief stabbed at her, making her smile falter.

Magnus's face had not faded in her mind. She could see him clearly. When she looked down on the strand she was reminded of the day they'd met. It seemed eons ago when he'd faced her after she'd defeated him on the oars. She missed him sorely, and resisted all her brother-in-law's and Spes's importunings that she return to Eyin Helga and remain there. The three short visits she'd made to the island had been anguish enough. And then she'd stayed within the grounds of the house. It would've torn her heart out to walk the crofts, to watch the terns, to visit the hot spring . . alone.

Keown's voice jolted her from her sad thoughts. " 'Twill give you much joy to see your kith and kin, milady."

"Aye," she answered. "I have not seen them for many moons past." She frowned. "And I had not expected to see them until the spring. But I'm sure naught is amiss." She smiled to cover the wrenching sadness that filled her. She'd have been married a year come late spring, but would have no celebration with her spouse. He was gone from her, and yet he lived in her being. He'd taught her about love, and she couldn't forget that.

"I'm eager myself to see Einar again," Keown said, grinning. "I have some new wrestling holds he'll not be able to break." He looked up at her steadily. "Though I'm sure the Sinclair could've done it."

Iona knew whom he meant. Not even after four months as laird had Kenneth ever been called the Sinclair. Only Magnus had earned the honorable sobriquet.

If it sometimes tore her heart that most Sinclairs, unlike Keown, went to great lengths to avoid discussing her beloved Magnus with her, she was well aware they sought to spare her feelings. She was grateful for their kindness, but it was not the Viking way to forget the dead. Many a Viking would rail at the heavens, call back the spirit, and enjoin it to stay a part of their lives.

Seeing the ships were nearly ready to anchor, Iona took her leave of Keown and let her horse pick its way down the narrow cliff path to the strand. She knew Keown and the others would keep an eye on her from above.

When she reached the edge of the water, she dismounted. She was eager to talk to her people. Einar would have news of Icelandia, and perhaps would have brought more women for the sanctuary. She sighed. She should join Marta there, but she was loath to return. Putting the painful thought aside, she called over the water, "Ho, Einar! Warriors of Icelandia. Ho!"

"Ho! Princess of Icelandia." The bellows from the Viking throats tore through the sounds of crashing surf, scattering terns and skuas into squalling, flapping protest.

"Landing in the sunshine is a good omen, milady."

Iona turned and smiled at Glam. She hadn't heard him approach, but she'd known he'd not be far.

"It will be good to speak Icelandic," he added, making her smile widen. How he hated the Gaelic, and for all he tried, he hadn't become more than passable in its usage. "Be happy this day, milady."

"I will." If only she'd been younger, she thought, she might've carried Magnus's child. She pressed her hand against her middle and sighed. Her monthly had come only a week after Magnus had left Eyin Helga, and her disappointment had been keen. 'Twould have been wondrous if there had been a child.

The boats were anchored and the oars were shipped, standing like lean oaken soldiers saluting the sun. As one, with Viking flourish, the men left the ships. Splashing through the water onto the strand, they didn't pause. They ran up to Iona and dropped to one knee to pay her homage. Hands over their hearts, they looked up to gain her beneficence. In slow, singsongy cadence, they murmured the formal Icelandic greeting.

"Greetings and hail, warriors of Icelandia," she answered. "Vikings, be proud." She swept one hand wide to include all. She called each one by name and inquired as to his health and that of his family. Iona didn't move until each from the three ships came ashore and was given the ceremonial greeting.

When the ritual was completed, Iona looked around, puzzled. If the men had followed custom, they should now be running up the cliff path to find jugs of frothy ale. But none left the loose semicircle they'd formed around her. The men were restless, shifting about, talking in whispers . . waiting.

As captain of all the ships, Einar was last on the strand. The men tensed as he approached her. He bent down before her, catching her hand and bringing it to his forehead. "Asdis Iona, princess of Icelandia, I greet you, and bring your warriors safely home to you."

"I thank you for this, friend Einar. You've done your duty well." She eyed him curiously. "But why are you here and not on course for Icelandia? Full winter is nearly on us."

Einar hesitated. " 'Tis true, my princess."

"What's amiss? You're taut as a drawn bow, good friend."

"I am, my princess." He took her arm and urged her to walk, not toward the cliff path but along the sand.

"And the men know the reason for your discomfiture," he said softly. Heavy dread dragged at her. More bad news. There was small consolation in knowing that she could receive no greater blow than when she'd heard of Magnus's death. "Tell me."

Einar inhaled deeply. "You need me not to tell you that our people would die before disclosing information we wish to clothe in darkness."

The formal Icelandic chilled her blood. "I know that," she said, forcing the impatience from her voice. Einar wouldn't be hurried.

"As is our custom when we enter hostile territory or a

land we are not familiar with, we send out runners. This time it was Thorbjorn."

"A most trusted and worthy scout, agile of mind and fleet of foot," Iona murmured as she was expected to do.

"A warrior, son of a warrior . . . and truthful."

She stiffened at the hesitation. She knew from Einar's words that she should brace herself for his news. "Go on," she said tightly.

"He stole some horses and took them to sell at a castle owned by a warrior lord of King Tostig, Baron Urdric of Kildeer by name. Speaking the language, he exchanged gossip with the hostler as he bargained with him, and he gleaned some news. While they were talking, there was a commotion. When they asked what was amiss, a guard told them that the devil Scot had somehow escaped from the oubliette, which was passing strange since no one had ever done so.

Thorbjorn was told that had the prisoner not been such a giant ogre, he couldn't have overcome his guards . . . and that he must be recaptured since it'd been assumed by all his clan that he was dead. The baron himself led the search, for the prisoner was to have been tortured and executed that very day.

Iona faced him, and Einar saw how her eyes had glazed over, how her hands shook. "Milady—"

"Do you say to me it's Magnus?"

Her hoarse voice was almost unrecognizable. "We talked long on this, milady, the men and I. Thorbjorn was questioned by the boatmen and by me. We asked many questions. We stayed in the area many days. The prisoner wasn't found. The baron was livid. The two jailers that had been killed by the prisoner were burned to cinders. Others were put to the torture. Some were flayed alive. This much fury would not have arisen over an ordinary man."

"You do think it's Magnus," Iona said. Not dead! Not dead! Her mind and soul screamed with delight, incredulity, fear. Fresh pain mixed with hope. "Tell me."

"We think it is," Einar said, knowing he could be condemning her to new agonies. "We will return and hunt down the prisoner, so you'll know."

"I'll go to him."

Einar hesitated. "I know I can't dissuade you from your course. Wotan knows I tried when you would come to Orkney. But now you must hear me out. There could be trouble, Princess. Let us think on it and talk."

She nodded slowly. "We'll talk . . . and plan. And then we'll go. In three days' time. No more. We must hurry. Magnus must be saved."

Einar nodded in agreement, accepting that she fully believed the fugitive to be her spouse.

"I hated lying to Kenneth and Spes," Iona said to Einar, pulling her hood up over her head as the Viking ship tacked to the south. As agreed, they had left the Sinclair land three days after Einar's arrival, leaving Spes and Marta behind. Glam, of course, accompanied Iona. "But Kenneth wouldn't let me travel to court with Cormac and him as I asked. My brother-in-law fears for me too much." She shook her head, frowning. "Many will be at the court to attend these talks of peace. Mayhap Malcolm will finally get the clans to band together. Do you credit it, Einar? I, for one, hadn't expected a pact of peace between Tostig and Malcolm so soon."

"None did," Einar said, scanning the sky. It worried him too to take the princess to Malcolm's court. "Though Kenneth knows not our news, I agree with him. Many of Magnus's enemies are at Malcolm's court, and there could be danger for you there. As the widow of the Sinclair you command envious power and respect, my princess."

"Fear not, Einar. Nothing will keep me from this course."

"I trust not this peace pact."

" 'Tis wisdom to question it. Yet I can't argue against it, since it works for us. It was an unforeseen aid for us when the king's messenger arrived yesterday, demanding Kenneth's presence at the court. With Kenneth gone this

morning, he could not stop me from leaving with you."
She grimaced. "Although I will not enjoy facing him when
he sees me at court."

He nodded. "I know you wanted to tell him what
Thorbjorn heard, but since we know not what we face nor
who our enemies could be, 'twouldn't be wise to enlighten
even Kenneth of Sinclair as to our schemes."

"What think you of my husband's people, Einar?" She
looked at the dark sky, wishing the storm clouds would part
and let the sun warm them some. With God's blessing, the
frigid winds might be blown away and replaced by early
warming.

Einar shrugged. "Months ago I would've told you that
they were traitors, thieves, and assassins." His face cracked
in a smile. "Now I find them to be traitors, thieves, and
assassins . . . but not all. They are like our Vikings. Good
and bad."

She laughed. "I'm not sure my mother would not be
vexed with our findings, friend Einar. But in truth I agree
with you. There are good and bad among them. And many
I could call friend."

He nodded. "I trusted your husband."

"So did I," she whispered. "And I believe he lives."

"If so, we'll find him. One of our ships precedes us and
will scout the area." He smiled when his princess chuckled.

"As always, you're ahead of me, my friend." She patted
his arm, trying to force thoughts of Magnus to the back of
her mind. If she dwelt on him, her energies would be dissipated, her perceptions dulled. She was going into battle,
the battle of her life, in order to find her husband. And
though her weapons would be simpering words, fluttering
eyelashes, and coy smiles, she would glean information
about him. And then . . .

Einar inclined his head, noting her pained distraction.
"I would always do my duty by you, Princess, as would all
our people."

She nodded. "I know that. Your fidelity has never given
me a moment's pause. But we have enemies, Einar. So does
Magnus. We must make all speed to find him." Again she

gazed at the silvery clouds that whipped around them like the angry sea. *Magnus! Magnus, where are you? You must be alive. I will not suffer so again. Why do you not seek me, Magnus?*

The journey by ship down the eastern coast of Scotland to Malcolm's castle was only three days. Not a long journey, as Viking sea voyages went, but the roiling winter seas tossed both ships off course more than once, and the bitter winds caused sore discomfort.

Often the sea would slap and grasp the ships, rocking them, trying to suck them to her depths. At the worst times, Einar would command his princess to go under cover and would scramble into the rigging himself to save the sails as the North Sea buffeted them.

On a clear, cold morning, the last day of December, with the watery winter sun glinting down on them, they steered close to the rocky coast where Malcolm kept court. As they raised the Sinclair guidon along with the Viking crest, a longboat put out to greet them. This was both a courtesy and a caution. No one of any stature could land without this singular greeting, giving protection to the landowner and formal courtesy to the arrival.

The lieutenant who greeted them, wearing Malcolm's tartan and crown upon his shoulders, studied the visitors, then bowed deeply to Iona. "Well met, Lady Sinclair, princess of Icelandia. Your messenger has brought us the glad tidings of your imminent arrival. I greet you in the name of his royal person, Malcolm of Scotland. Your presence is eagerly awaited by our king, and he bids you a thousand welcomes and all beneficence for you and your fellow travelers. He wishes you at his court with all speed."

The formal grace of the courtesy words couched the command, masked the urgency. Iona, tutored in court manners, heard the overt and covert messages clearly.

"We are honored by the king's request," she replied, "and make all speed to accede to it."

The lieutenant smiled and waved his boat back to shore. It would be for the Vikings to land their princess, as was customary. The lieutenant didn't like Vikings on his strand, but the king's command had been quite clear. Lady Sinclair was to be treated like the royal she was. But it had been a shock for him to see the woman some called the Moon Goddess. 'Struth, she was a beauty.

The two Viking vessels shipped oars and slipped quietly toward the strand.

Einar leaned down to Iona as they prepared to debark. "It's my plan to accompany you with twenty of my best warriors, Princess. The rest of the crews will split to protect the ships. Thorbjorn and our third ship will be nearing Northumbria now, and he'll be sending information by runners. We'll soon know more."

He helped her down into the waiting boat and said no more until they reached the strand, where another group of Malcolm's people waited to greet her.

"We must use all caution, milady," Einar whispered.

"I know," she whispered back. "Northumbrians will be here to discuss the peace pact." Her smile was hard. "I have learned to listen in their language."

Einar nodded once. "And the court is the place to use your ears, milady. You might not always see me, but I'll be at your back, as Glam is. We will know the right of it soon enough."

"Thank you, my friend." She eyed the approaching entourage as Glam moved to her left side. Einar stayed on her right. "I do believe we are getting royal treatment, my friends. The contingent is in high numbers, and Magnus's colors are upon the guidon next to the king's."

"Take care, milady," Einar said. "Mayhap we step into the bear's den." With that he offered his arm, and they moved forward to meet the entourage.

≈ 18 ≈

Deeper and more profound, the door of all subtleties!
—Lao-tzu

Iona was fatigued in mind and body. Even her face hurt from smiling. She sat on the raised dais, dining at the king's side, but she felt no elation, no enjoyment. All manner of humanity was stuffed into the great room, like goose down in a quilt, and spilled out into the anterooms. There was never any quiet at Malcolm's court, and though he seemed to find this atmosphere most amenable, Iona felt as though her brain had swelled from the noise, that her eyes and ears were bulging with the force of laughter, chatter, and music. Sweat, food, and spilled wine made a noxious aroma that assaulted her. The boiled beef and root vegetables heaved uncomfortably in her innards. She longed for the privacy of her suite. If only Einar were still at the castle, but he'd gone days earlier, following a rumor about Magnus. He'd hunt it down, and perhaps at last find the laird of the Sinclairs. There'd been so many disappointments. Mayhap this time . . .

Iona had learned little with all her court cavorting, and her hope to find Magnus alive and well was flagging. She clung desperately to the first news that Thorbjorn had brought.

It had been nearly a fortnight since her arrival, and no word. Her heart was as frozen as a wintry pond. She existed only on hope, a hope that was dimming, dulling.

"And what say you of the fete, Princess Asdis Iona?" Malcolm asked.

"The jugglers are magnificent. From Cremona, I've no doubt." She focused on her surroundings. The king was too sharp not to notice anything amiss. She'd have to be more careful.

"So they are. You've traveled, milady," Malcolm said, smiling. "I'm most impressed at your accomplishments."

"As I am with yours, my liege."

The king's hearty laugh was abruptly cut off. "Ah, here comes our new ally, Baron Kildeer. I think he fancies you, my dear. He would dance with you."

"I'm flattered," Iona lied. If the king's hard eyes were any criterion, he didn't fancy the Northumbrian any more than she did. She rose to her feet when the barrel-chested noble made his request to dance with her.

"Take care of our princess, Lord Kildeer." Malcolm was smiling, but there was iron in his voice.

Kildeer bowed, then led Iona down from the dais onto the stone floor, already crowded with dancers.

Iona was thankful that the quick step, bend, and sway of the formal court dance allowed her to remain well away from her partner. She'd been close enough to him at other times. It was as though his eyes were live snakes that sought to twine around her.

She'd actually been physically ill after the first time she'd been in his company, shortly after her arrival. When they danced, his hand stayed upon her a shade too long for courtesy. More than once he'd had the audacity to interfere when others would've danced with her. She'd noted, however, that though the baron was disliked by many, few challenged his power. She struggled to mask it, but she deeply resented his overt machinations to lay claim upon her. Now she tried to ignore the nausea his presence evoked and concentrate on the intricate court dance.

A man watched from the corner of the great room, his face shadowed by the stone buttress that curved up to the ceiling. Magnus had been in Malcolm's court for many days, his bearded face and deliberately stooped carriage adequate disguise. He sought his betrayers, those who'd maneuvered him away from his men in battle so he could be captured by Kildeer.

His heart beat in his throat as he watched Iona dance with Kildeer. The Northumbrian had paid marked attention to his wife during her stay, daytime and evening. More than once he'd seen him riding beside her to the hunt, she looking like a goddess astride a white steed. Now his most grievous foe was in front of him, dancing with his wife. He hated Iona at that moment, even as reason asserted that she couldn't have refused the baron his dance.

Magnus looked away from the pair, studying the throng as he'd been doing for four days. Soon he'd be recognized, or he'd show himself, but he needed the time to study the court. Kildeer had imprisoned him, but who had helped him?

He'd stayed totally hidden for a week after his arrival at Malcolm's castle. He'd hovered near the kitchens and the stables, listening to the gossip, finding out who was in residence. When he'd heard Tostig and Malcolm had actually signed a peace pact, he could've choked on his ire. But he'd tamped it down, biding his time.

That night he'd contacted his loyal childhood friend Dowell Mackenzie, who was ever at court. Landed and wealthy, he preferred the court life to the country, but he was a renowned warrior, and Magnus knew he could trust him. He'd learned much from Mackenzie about why Malcolm and Tostig had agreed to talk peace, and Mackenzie had loaned him clothes too.

"Ah'm built along your lines, Sinclair," the Highlander had said, "but that shirt pulls some across your chest." He laughed, then sobered. "If you've come to fight a war with Kildeer, I'll watch your back. But Malcolm will like it little."

"I know that. And battling at Malcolm's court will solve nothing. I need to know how Kildeer managed my capture, for I know it was he."

Mackenzie frowned. "Think you one of the clans that fought beside you spawned a traitor?"

"Aye. It could be. I've made enemies." And he'd been betrayed. It still angered him that he'd been overpowered, taken by a foe. He blamed his own laxness, his blindness to the perfidy of someone close to him. But he would find the traitor and kill him.

Magnus thought of that conversation as he adjusted the Mackenzie tartan over his shoulders. He would have to see about getting his own tartan. Cormac was at court, as was Kenneth, but he'd not apprised them of his presence yet. He was not yet ready.

He looked at the dance floor once more. *Don't think about your wife with your enemy,* he told himself. Still, his insides squeezed in fury whenever the Northumbrian touched her hand or her waist. He hated seeing her with the man. And had she forgotten him?

What equally infuriated him was seeing her decked out in her finery. In their time together he'd never seen the magnificent gowns and jewels that adorned her here. Nor had the gems come from Sinclair coffers. She looked every inch a royal, born to the purple. Her bliaut glittered with precious stones, as did her hair and hands. She was the most ravishing of all the beauties at Malcolm's court.

As Magnus continued to watch, Kenneth crossed the floor almost in front of him, heading grimly toward the dancers. Apparently, he felt Kildeer's attentions to Iona were too familiar, and he grabbed Kildeer roughly by the shoulder.

Magnus was too far away, and the din of conversation, music, and laughter was too loud for him to hear the obviously angry exchange of words. He did see Kildeer's hand drop to his side where his dirk hung, and, instinctively,

Magnus moved. He strode swiftly through the throng, and as he was recognized, murmurs followed him. "The Sinclair," people whispered, and by the time he reached his brother's side, all eyes were on him. Magnus looked only at Kildeer.

"Stay your blade, Baron, else I'll be forced to spill your blood on the floor. 'Twouldst make it too slippery for the dancers, I vow."

He didn't take his eyes from the baron as he heard Kenneth gasp and Iona sob his name. She staggered, and though he longed to go to her, he didn't. He knew better than to show any vulnerability to such a deadly foe.

The music faltered as many of the guests turned to watch the angry tableau in the center of the room. Among excited murmurs, some reached for their weapons. When Malcolm stood, though, all were silent and still.

"I want this murderer arrested!" Kildeer shouted into the sudden quiet. "I'll have his head!"

"I want silence," Malcolm said as angry voices rose among the crowd. The king's men moved through the throng, wordlessly enforcing his command until there was not a whisper. The king smiled at Magnus. "I see you're not a ghost."

Magnus bowed tersely to him. "No, I'm not. But I would've been—"

"I want the assassin executed!" Kildeer interrupted. "He killed two of my men in my own demesne. Does the king deny me the right of satisfaction? Deny me his head?"

Malcolm eyed the Northumbrian, then nodded to Magnus. "Answer his charge."

"I escaped his damnable dungeon," Magnus said simply. "In doing so, two guards were killed."

He felt Iona's shock like a touch from her hand, but still he didn't acknowledge her or glance her way. He kept his gaze on Kildeer, except when he responded to Malcolm. Courtesy to the royal demanded eye contact.

"You needed help to draw your net about me, Kildeer," he said to the baron. "I'll know who your Judas was soon enough."

He didn't blink an eye when Kildeer drew his sword. Such good luck had not been his in many a moon. Crossing swords with the Black Baron would give him great satisfaction. Drawing his life's blood would be just recompense.

He was reaching for his own sword, though Malcolm shouted at them to cease, when Iona turned swiftly and kicked the baron behind the knee. He staggered, and she bore down on his sword arm.

"Stay!" she cried. " 'Wouldst you have an imbroglio in the court when a peace pact has just been agreed? 'Tis unseemly." She gripped with all her might, even as she felt the baron's muscles bulge to free himself. The baron was in the best of form, well fed, well trained, battle ready. Magnus was not.

Her last words jarred Magnus, spinning him back to Eynhallow and their golden days together. Had others shared her magic since then—been heated and spun to the stars with her wondrous passion? The wild imaginings he'd suffered during his torturous journey to Malcolm's castle rose up in him again. She'd never said she loved him. What would stop her from taking her comfort with another man when she believed him dead? But damn her. He'd kill her if she'd cuckolded him.

He eyed her for a moment when she glanced his way, her message of entreaty clear. He was not to force a fight. Nodding once, he stepped back.

Kildeer's face contorted with his effort to control his own blood lust. "I'll not disturb the fete. But I'll make charges through my king." He glanced at the Scottish royal. "Tostig is returning to this court anon."

" 'Tis your right," Malcolm said. "And Tostig will be welcomed to the peacemaking as he was before." Though his voice was mild, his eyes glittered. "You're safe in this court, Baron Kildeer. And you'll have the hearing you wish in front of your king, and me, and others. What say you, Magnus Sinclair?"

"I welcome a chance to tell the truth of it."

"So be it. There'll be a convening as soon as we can

gather those who'll sit in judgment besides Tostig and myself. Who will speak for you, Baron Kildeer?"

Magnus braced himself when the baron almost smiled. Whatever his plan, it boded ill for Magnus or any of his clan. When Kildeer's gaze touched on Iona, Magnus's blood turned to ice.

"I'll have Scola, the scribe of Northumbria," he said, "and Erwic Skene, one of your own, from the island of Iona." He did smile now, as Iona's lips parted in a rough exhalation, and she stepped back. He bowed to her. "It should not surprise you that I'd choose your able kinsman, milady. He is a man of many talents and has become friend to me. It would seem that reading of the law is a family trait."

"As you say, good sir," Iona said, her words formal and distant. The baron's eyes had a cruel cast that made her shiver. When she felt a hand at her back, she knew it was Magnus. Stiffening her spine and lifting her chin, she turned to the king. "By your leave and my husband's, I will speak before the court on his behalf."

Gasps broke through the protocol of silence. Many a mouth dropped, many a head shook.

Malcolm's eyes narrowed. He raised one hand, and there was silence. Only Kildeer smiled.

"I've spoken before the Althing," Iona went on, "and stated proceedings, not just for nobles but for the people as well. I'm qualified."

Magnus nodded shortly. "I would wish it so."

The king nodded as well. "Let it be set down that Magnus Sinclair has given his consent, and that the baron of Northumbria has named his advocates. Since both have seen fit to have a convening and have given such consent, I'll not withhold mine." His smile was like a strike of fire across his face. "Magnus, you did not tell me your wife was so endowed." He glanced at Iona. "And thou art a healer as well," he added in Icelandic.

She bowed.

"'Tis true she's wondrous able," Magnus said, "and touched by the gods."

Iona heard the ragged edge of cynicism in his tone, and eyed him warily, wondering at the changes in him. He was a stranger with a beard, harder, thinner, with eyes opaque . . . killing. His thin smile was colder than the ice floes around Icelandia, and his face was implacable, inscrutable.

Unaware of his wife's scrutiny, Magnus eyed Kildeer. The baron knew about Iona being an advocate. No doubt Skene had told him. But did he also know what her uncle had done to her? Was this convening contrived not just to destroy him, but to attack his wife too, with the grievous deed that'd been done to her in childhood?

"The fete will continue," Malcolm declared, nodding to the musicians. "Sinclair, you wear another's tartan. How is this? You must join me at the trencher and tell me all."

"Aye, I will." He took hold of Iona's elbow and started toward Malcolm.

Kildeer stopped him, stepping in front to confront the king. Though there was deference in his manner, there was harsh purpose in his voice. "I do not think my cause will be served by having Sinclair disclose facts to you that I would consider false, majesty."

Magnus bristled, his hands curling into fists. When he felt a touch on his sleeve, he looked down at Iona.

"It is well for you to say nothing until we've convened," she said.

Kildeer laughed harshly. "Listen to your helpmate, Magnus Sinclair. It could tether the black humors of your soul."

Magnus fought to keep all expression from his face. " 'Tis true that only the fool brays like an ass. Trust you to reaffirm such in front of the court, Kildeer."

"Enow!" Malcolm thundered, stepping down from the dais. He unhooked Iona from her husband and led her away. "This court brangling would destroy the ears," he muttered. "And the pact of peace."

"As you say, your grace," Iona said absently, glancing over her shoulder at her husband.

"Sinclair, you'll die," Kildeer said through his teeth.

"One of us will." Magnus stared at his enemy. Was he

the unknown giant of evil that had haunted his dreams since the death of his parents? Anger twisting his guts, he asked, "Have you been to Normandy and Bretagne, Kildeer?" The baron's eyes widened. With surprise? Or fear?

"I have . . . but not for many years," he answered as though weighing his words. "Why ask you?"

"I'd wondered if we might have met there," he said cryptically, and turned away to speak to his brother. Fury burned through him as he contemplated the dastardly murder of his parents. Kildeer had ten years on him. And though masked, the leader of the attack that had taken his parents' lives had been a big man, along the lines of Kildeer. He could be the one. He'd die for a thousand reasons now, but mostly he'd die for trying to frighten Iona. He longed to go to her, but stayed a moment to greet Kenneth. The two men clasped arms.

"We believed—" Kenneth began, but cut himself off when his voice broke.

Magnus shook his head. "Not now, brother. We will speak later, in private." He glanced around the hall. "Where is our uncle?"

Kenneth shrugged. "I do not know, but I would guess he is dining in private. There is a woman . . ."

"I understand," Magnus said, a grin flashing across his face. "And speaking of women . . ."

"Yes. Go to your wife, Magnus. We will talk later."

Magnus turned and strode eagerly toward the dais. His steps slowed, however, when he saw that Malcolm was bending over Iona, smiling at her. Not even the king had the right to touch his wife! The simmering ire that had heated in him since he'd first woken in the oubliette boiled anew. Was the king one of her coterie? Or were her affections claimed by an enemy?

He stepped onto the dais, taking his place not beside his monarch, as was his right, but next to his wife. He stared down the courtier who dared to frown up at him from that seat. "Move."

The courtier moved.

Malcolm chuckled. "Your court manners need some polish, Magnus."

"I'll work on it," he muttered.

The monarch laughed again, then turned to speak to those on his left.

Magnus sank onto the trencher bench. A servant filled his goblet with ale. He quaffed it in two swallows, then held the goblet out for more.

Watching him, Iona gave way to the anger that had been born out of her shock at seeing him and his cool ignoring of her on the dance floor. "What kept you?" she asked tartly.

He whirled toward her. "I was talking to the baron . . . my late jailer."

"Then you were there," she whispered, tears filling her eyes as anger fled.

He frowned. "Meaning?" he asked.

She lowered her voice. "Thorbjorn stole some horses from one of the baron's vassals—"

"Good."

"Listen. While he was selling them to the hostler, there was a great commotion at the castle. Some said a Scot had escaped. None knew his name. But some had seen him and described him as a bear of a man." Iona gazed out at the crowd, inclining her head and smiling at those who watched her and Magnus. "Einar reported it to me, and we set sail for Malcolm's court three days later. We came here to find you."

"Did you?" He couldn't keep the vitriol from his voice. "I thought you'd come to dance and cavort, Princess of Icelandia."

Her anger rose again at his sardonic tone. "How good of you to realize that I'd need distraction in my life."

She turned away, and Magnus scowled at her. Why the hell was she so irritated? Had she languished in a prison these many months? No, she'd been feted and fawned over at court. She'd smiled and simpered her way into the good graces of every oily courtier there, he'd be bound.

At that moment Elizabeth, who'd married a MacDou-

all after Magnus had been declared dead, approached. Her
hands were outstretched and tears glimmered in her eyes.
Magnus gave his former leman a broader smile than he'd
intended. "Well met, Elizabeth."

"Milord, your presence brings joy." She bowed deeply
to him, then sent a curt nod Iona's way.

"And now I see why *you're* at court," Iona said bitingly,
low enough for only Magnus to hear.

"Your acerbic ways do you no credit, milady, nor does
talking from the corner of your mouth."

When she would've risen, he clamped down on her
arm. "No need to give the maggots at court flesh to feed
upon," he told his wife, then turned back to Elizabeth, still
standing before him. Since she was below the dais, her full
breasts almost rested on the table, her décolletage revealing and enticing. Her bliaut was of a sheerness to titil-
late the imagination and invite flirtation. "Thank you for
our concern, Elizabeth."

"All of Scotland weeps in gratitude for your safety, milord." She sighed, her eyes charmingly misted with moisture.

"Not all," Iona whispered.

"My wife and I thank you, good Elizabeth." Magnus
ignored his wife. "And we hope to welcome you to our
home when we return there." He barely winced when Iona
kicked him under the trencher board.

"I was bereft when they said you'd died," Elizabeth
went on.

"I did notice that," Iona said sweetly. "Was it not
Cuthbert of Mercia who consoled you?"

Magnus would've laughed at his wife's canny hit if it
wouldn't have been a breach of etiquette. She was spitting
like an angry kitten. He'd not seen that side of her, and it
tickled him.

Elizabeth glared at Iona, then curtsied to Magnus.
"Mayhap I will see you anon, milord."

"Mayhap." He moved his leg instinctively and just
missed receiving another good kick from his spouse.

When Elizabeth glided away, a heavy silence lay between Magnus and Iona.

"If you'd but release my arm," she said finally, "I would leave."

" 'Tis rare a woman keeps her teeth long when she locks them together as you're doing, wife."

He glanced at her. She was bewitching, more beautiful than she'd been on Eynhallow. Those sweet memories had sustained him when he'd been in the oubliette. She was glaring at him now. That should've annoyed him, but instead it reminded him of her fire in bed. A sudden lust rose up in him, and he abruptly stood.

He bowed to Malcolm. "I would leave your presence and take my wife to her quarters. Believing for such a long time that I was dead and then seeing me again so suddenly has overset her." Iona kicked him again as he lifted her to her feet. "She's had a shock."

Malcolm nodded. "You've chosen well, Magnus Sinclair. Your wife is a rare beauty."

"I agree."

"And methinks your lady hides her shock quite well, Sinclair, but . . ." He waved his hand. "You have permission to leave us. I would seek my bedchamber too had I been parted from my bride such a time." He smiled. "There's no need to color up, milady. 'Tis natural."

Iona bowed, not responding.

Magnus took her arm, laying it atop his, and they strolled across the huge hall toward the stairs. Smiles and bows followed them, though more than one wary eye watched them. Iona bid good night to many, but Magnus merely nodded, saying nothing.

They exited the hall and started up the stone stairs that led to the guest chambers.

"You'll not share my bed," Iona whispered fiercely.

"Iona, you are my wife. 'Twould be *unseemly* dare we sleep apart."

"Don't throw my words back at me." She scampered away as his hand flitted over her waist and backside. When she glanced at him, though, remorse touched her. He was thinner. He'd suffered. Was he well? "I could brew you a posset."

"Not tonight." His hand feathered over her hip. "I recall your bottom as being the fairest in Scotland, milady."

"Beast!" He'd all but fawned over Elizabeth!

"Husband." He loved the look of her.

"Don't think to share my quarters."

"I must."

"It's my duty to succor you have you need of it. You don't. You thrust your leman in my face—"

"I couldn't knock her away from the trencher board."

"You—you ogled her, sirrah."

He was not displeased by her obvious jealousy. It went a long way to laying his suspicions to rest. She was not cold toward him, and for that he could stand her ire, her glares.

She stalked past Glam, who stood guard before her door. Glam glanced at Magnus, nodded shortly, then stared into space again.

Magnus followed his wife into her bedchamber, closing the thick door behind him.

Once in the stone-walled room, its heavy tapestries swaying slightly from the strong breeze coming off the North Sea, she faced him. "You're the larger, you take the bed. I shall rest in front—"

"We'll both take the bed. If you don't choose to honor me as your husband, so be it."

His silky tones had her stiffening. "I'm not the one who was in such a fury in the hall below, sending out sparks of hatred that burned anyone within touch. I'll not—"

"I was unreasonable." He had to smile when her jaw dropped. "And I'm normally a reasonable man."

"Hah! You? Why, I—"

Before she could blister him further, he returned to the door, opened it, and spoke to Glam.

"What did you say to Glam?" she asked suspiciously when he returned.

"I wanted water for a bath."

"Oh."

She never took her eyes off him as he strolled around

the room, seeming to have forgotten her presence. He whistled tunelessly, and she shook her head. What a fool he was to do that. The ancients in Icelandia could've told him he was beckoning demons.

Within minutes attendants began arriving with copper kettles of steaming water. They dragged a heavy metal tub in with them and set it in front of the fireplace.

After they left, Magnus stripped down, got into the tub, and began washing.

Iona readied herself to give him a bone-splitting sermon on his gall in not contacting her on his escape, his high-handedness, his insulting assumptions, but his body distracted her. He was quite beautiful, but what or who had marked him so? Bruises, blisters, bites, slashes crisscrossed his form from head to toe. Anger at the cause of those wounds surged through her with a flaming, vengeful heat. She went to her cupboard and brought out a fistful of healing herbs, then marched to his tub and dropped them into the water.

They frothed and bubbled, and fragrances steamed on the water. He looked up at her. "Thank you." When she nodded sharply, his smile widened. He sank down to his neck, wincing, and grinding his teeth in discomfort even while he muttered his pleasure. When he doused his head and would've begun scrubbing it, other hands were there. Iona massaged his scalp, soaping gently and touching, testing with her healer's hands. He held his breath.

"Where is the hell you inhabited, Sinclair?" Her fingers skated over his skin, pausing at the lacerations and bites. "I would know who did this, Magnus Sinclair."

Her outraged whisper had him grasping her hands and squeezing gently. "Don't. It's over."

"Your torso is marked from top to bottom. Some have festered. Your scalp is full of bites and healed-over sores. Rats?" Her voice shook.

He nodded, putting his head back and looking up at her. "Don't fret, my healer, I'm better than I ever was."

She caught her breath at his words, comprehending his double meaning. "Barbarian," she whispered.

He laughed. Her caring radiated through him. He wanted it. Her look of pain warmed him as nothing had since he'd been dropped in the oubliette. He'd missed her so much. She'd been his tie to sanity in that black hole.

"And you're so thin," she whispered, "and more scarred . . ." She choked.

"No matter." He cupped her hands in his, swinging her around so that she stood beside him. "All goes well with you, Lady Sinclair?"

The firm grip of his hands had her body heating. "All is well. Sinclair holdings are productive. Monies come in from the farms—"

He laughed and clasped her hands tighter when she would've pulled back. "Nay, milady, stay. My mirth is directed at your practical mind, not at your cherishing. From the way Sinclair lands and holdings are set out, and with the trusted men who oversee them, I was sure your report would be positive. My father had years to plan how his and my mother's birthright would be handled. It was a good plan."

When his look darkened abruptly, she leaned over him. "You have a black side, Magnus Sinclair. Methinks I was not the only one with a secret."

He hesitated, then nodded. "I dream of a giant, an incarnation of evil. I know in my soul it's a man—though Old Terrill thinks it could be a woman. The dreams began after my parents were killed by masked and unknown intruders, who tried to kill me and my brother as well. Mayhap one day I'll comprehend the dream and know who the slayers were."

How strange, Iona mused, her heart going out to him, that Magnus had shared her horror, though in a different way. She'd known his parents had been foully murdered, but she hadn't known he'd been there, that he'd seen it. They'd both been scarred so young, seeing their once safe worlds destroyed. " 'Tis anguish to suffer alone."

"Aye." He kissed her hands.

"All is well with both our peoples," she whispered, not

able to stop her hand from lifting to smooth the wet hair from his forehead.

"I asked about you."

"I'm . . . I'm fine." It had been easier when she'd viewed him as a patient. As a man Magnus was too powerful, too enthralling. From the moment they'd met he'd plumbed her soul and brought out of her emotions and passion she'd not thought possible. She hated the vulnerability; she didn't hate the man. "I'm fine," she repeated. "The work goes well on Eyin Helga—"

Magnus suddenly surged to his feet, splashing the stone floor with water. As soothing as the bath was, he couldn't stand to sit still for so long.

"Now I feel clean," he said. "When we get back to Sinclair, I'm going to douse myself in the sea. What say we have some mulled wine before we retire?" Before she could answer, he went to the door, stark naked, opened it, and whispered instructions.

So instead of lying in front of the fireplace wrapped in skins to sleep, Iona sat upon those with her husband, drank the hot spicy wine, and listened to him describe his imprisonment.

"You hide much from me, Magnus," she said when he finished, "so I know it was far more terrible than you convey."

He smiled at her, but his eyes were hard and cold. He would not rest until he'd unwound the riddle of how he'd been trapped and caught.

"It was bad," he said, "but now we have a different battle to wage and win. And you must defend me, wife. How will you do it?"

"With the law. And we will win." She paused. "But my uncle . . ."

"The fool," Magnus said. He quaffed his wine. "His death will be slow."

"I don't think he would surmise that I—I would tell . . ."

Magnus reached for her, lifting her from the rug and onto his lap. "Whether he realizes I know or not changes not the outcome. He hurt you. Don't think of the swine. His life is forfeit." He kissed her forehead, loving the scent of her. Roses. Where did she find them? " 'Tis passing strange that it will be several new moon till we celebrate the first year from our nuptial day, milady. If truth were told, that time seems eons ago."

"Yes." Her eyes were closed as she savored the feel of his strong body. She'd almost forgotten his heat, his comfort.

He lifted her and carried her to the bed, then lay down beside her. "Would you deny me, Iona?" He didn't need to ask that question. 'Twas his right to take her. They both knew that. But he couldn't, wouldn't. They both knew that too. Their passion always had been sweet, giving. He'd not give it the tart sting of taking.

She reached for him, her arms winding around his neck. "I'm your spouse, Magnus Sinclair."

"I do not forget that." He kissed her lips, not able to stem the hardening of his body, the thudding of his heart. He made slow sweet love to the woman who'd haunted his dreams. If a trace of suspicion lingered deep in his mind, it didn't dampen his ardor. Their passion let him bury it in her scented loveliness.

Iona gave herself to the man who'd stayed alive in her mind, whose face had been in front of her hourly, though she'd thought him lost to her. She gave all of herself without any doubt, any hesitation. She loved him.

[...]

19

*But the attitude of reverence and love seldom exists
without some admixture of fear.*

—Confucius

The convening was on a sunny day, five days after
Magnus had showed himself upon the dance floor. It would
be in the great hall, and by dawn the inner and outer
courtyards were crammed with guests, oglers, and onlookers. Peasants, serfs, and artisans joined the titled throng
until they spilled out onto the nearby croft. The words of
the convening would be shouted to them by strategically
placed speakers who had great, thundering voices.

Iona changed her toilette twice, for twice she dampened her raiment with the hot moistness from her quivering body. The second time she dragged her clothes off and
searched out new ones, her husband entered their chamber
and jerked his head at the handmaidens.

"I need them," she said breathlessly.

"No. I'll dress you. But first I'll swab your body with
cooling essence, and we'll talk."

"No time." Iona didn't even try to tell him how badly
she needed to compose herself for this important and aus-

tere day. This was a solemn occasion, one that would be put down by the scribes and preserved on precious scrolls.

Magnus took a soft lint and began to pat her body. "Ordinarily this would lead to other more delightful moments—"

"You jest at such a time!"

"I do not jest."

"How can you grin on such a day? You're daft, Sinclair."

"Only for you, Iona." He kissed her bare shoulder and sighed. "Best not do that. Your skin bewitches me. I would taste it always."

Her nervousness forgotten, Iona tried to scowl at him, but he insisted on kissing her. She reared her head back. "As your advocate, sirrah, I must insist you put on a serious mien. We convene as the sun rises high."

Magnus smiled with satisfaction. Her scolding had given her color. There was no more pallid hue to her countenance. She looked ready, pugnacious and feisty, the way he loved her to be. Love? That was a strange word to jump into his mind. After all, she was but a wife . . . his life . . . his dreams. No!

"What causes you to frown, husband? Have you doubts, or has your bravado deserted you?"

"I trust you and worry not." He watched as she turned from him to dress, a frown marring her own face. She thought of her uncle. The bastard would die for haunting her so.

When she was satisfied with her appearance, she turned to him. "I am ready."

He offered his arm. "You will tear their heads off down there."

"I intend to win," she said quietly. "Shall we go?"

The convening began when Malcolm, Tostig, and those chosen as overseers of the convening took their seats. Malcolm nodded and the roll was called by the crier.

"Oye! Oye! Come round all who would hear and com-

prehend. And so it will go forth in the reign of our good
and beloved sovereign, Malcolm of Scotland. And by the
laws of the land and of God, good Tostig of Northumbria
will also preside beside our sovereign. Oye! Oye!" The crier
nodded to the king, who gestured to Kildeer's advocates to
rise and make their case.

"I speak for us, my liege," Erwic Skene said. He stepped
forward, glancing sideways at his niece.

Magnus saw how she stiffened and threaded her hands
together. But even as he contemplated the thousand ways
he'd make Skene suffer, his attention was caught by one of
the judges. The abbot from Sinclair land! He sat straighter
in his chair, studying the man whose livelihood he provided by heavily endowing the abbey. The abbot didn't
like him, and the feeling was mutual. But was there betrayal here? Or merely coincidence?

He looked over the throng of spectators until he fixed
on Glam and Einar. He let his gaze return to the abbot,
then focused on them again. Neither Viking changed expression by a flicker of a lash, yet when Magnus looked
again, their gazes were on the abbot. He couldn't even
explain to himself why he'd given the signal to them and
not to Kenneth, who stood not far from them. But he
trusted their instincts. They would find out about the abbot.

"Begin," the king told Skene.

"First, we protest the illegality of the presence of a
woman advocating before this convening. Since we've
adopted many of the Roman laws for our own, we must
adhere to them. Namely, I call to the court's attention
Iniquum est Ingenuis Persona esse Liberam Rerum Surarum.
That is, the law on inheritance. I most forcibly stipulate
that this woman has commandeered land belonging to
Thorfinn, deceased king of Icelandia, as her own. Not only
is this against our laws, this land is in contention with our
own claims, that is, Scotland's, including properties of
mine on Iona. She is a false claimant and in defiance of the
law. An outlaw cannot speak before the convening. Ergo,

my client is the victor since he is the only one in legal contention."

Skene fell silent, and the crowd murmured behind him. The king pondered long, not looking at the other members of the convening board and ignoring the growing clamor in front of him.

"I move against such an arbitrary judgment," he said at last. "Princess Asdis Iona is a royal in her own right. She takes lands deeded to her from Icelandia, where it's legal for her to do so. And since in her own land she's a bona fide advocate, we can accord her no less at this convening. Proceed."

Fury limned Skene's face for a moment, then it smoothed and he bowed to Malcolm. "We concede your wisdom, my liege. As such we will go forth and prove our case against one Magnus Sinclair, damning him forever in front of this gathering." Skene paused and looked around at the huge throng, his face somber, his eyes aglitter. "We will show that Magnus Sinclair did willfully enter the castle of Urdric Kildeer, baron of Northumbria, and lay about him in a warlike manner, killing four men of Northumbria before he was imprisoned—"

"I protest, my liege," Iona interjected, jumping to her feet. "The number of dead in question was two. How has it been able to jump to four?"

Skene answered. "My lord Kildeer had not realized that two others had been slain as well. A runner brought this information only yesterday."

"Proceed." Malcolm waved his hand and sank back in his chair.

Iona quickly turned to the scribe who'd been aiding her and asked him to seek out that runner and learn what he could. The man raced off.

"The baron," Skene went on, "had no intention of doing aught but bringing Magnus Sinclair's murderous actions to the attention of King Tostig and yourself. This would've been done had not the barbarous Sinclair performed yet more mayhem in the castle. When righteous

men sought to apprehend him, he invoked his mentor Lu
cifer—"

Great sighs and gasps rose among the crowd.

Iona stood again. "I protest. Erwic Skene did not see
Lucifer, nor did anyone else. I move that such be scratched
from the scrolls, and I petition this convening to instruct
that the advocate not give himself more than human
power to discern the inhabitants of the netherworld." She
sat down, back straight, her expression tranquil.

Malcolm nodded. "No more of that, lest in calling
upon the devil, you invite him amongst us."

Some laughed, but many frowned, crossing themselves.

"Very well," Skene said. "I'll say no more on that. For
now."

He went on, building his case step by step, a fabric of
half-truths, smooth lies, and distortions that colored and
damaged. When he finally resumed his seat, a host of faces
eyed Magnus with distrust.

Iona walked forward to speak. She looked around
calmly and waited until all whispering and rustling had
stilled.

"Justice will be served," she began, "when those who've
betrayed the cause of truth and right are punished. And, in
accordance with the laws of Scotland and of Northumbria
we shall activate the Lex Transgressio Maiestate to punish
the offenders."

There was a thunderous cacophony of nays and yeas.
Even Magnus straightened on his stool, staring at his wife.

Treason! Everyone knew the translation of that Latin
law, which would only be activated when someone com
mitted serious crimes of betrayal against his leader or his
country. But who was a traitor?

Iona waited until the hubbub died, glad that Malcolm
hadn't intervened for quiet. She had their attention now.
"Magnus Sinclair is charged with the murder of several
'righteous men' on Kildeer's land. The baron wants redress.
Am I correct?" She looked right into her uncle's eyes, star
ing until he nodded. "How ironic. It's no coincidence that
the four men who died directly after Magnus Sinclair's es

cape were guardians of the deepest dungeon in that castle
. . . the oubliette . . . the death chamber . . . the hole
from which only the dead can be raised." She struck out
her arm, pointing to her husband. "He freed himself, bitten
by rats and other vermin, weakened by little food and water, he freed himself by overpowering his two guards and
killing them. The other two men, according to witnesses I
shall call at the proper time"—her helpful scribe had done
admirable detective work during Skene's hour-long speech
—"were disemboweled by Baron Kildeer himself because
the prisoner had escaped. We take no credit for these heinous crimes, nor do we duck the issue of killing to be free.
One is infamous butchery, the other is just."

Sighs, gasps, and muttered imprecations greeted her ti-
rade until Malcolm hammered the trencher board in front
of him for silence. Iona knew she was being far more blunt
than was customary, for advocates would normally dance
around the real issue, stalling and prolonging. Urgency
kept her on the point, on the attack.

Magnus was enthralled by his wife's performance as she
presented his case. Once she'd attained the floor, she kept
it. She all but scoffed at Skene's attempt to take it back
from her with his blustering objections. Iona commanded
the audience's attention, and she got it.

"Does a man not have the right to protect his life when
it's threatened?" she asked. "Must he submit to butchery
rather than defend himself? Is it honorable, decent, or
moral to give away one's life without taking all manner of
risk to preserve it?"

The onlookers muttered answers. Yes. No. No.

"And so, honorable assemblage, you accept as truth
that a man must guard his person, even if it means taking
the lives of those who threatened it?"

It was unorthodox to question the huge group of spectators of a convening, but not illegal. When a resounding,
thunderous yes echoed in from the outside, Iona kept her
countenance impassive. She'd not been at court for this
long without knowing that the visiting Northumbrians
were not well thought of and that the baron was consid-

ered cruel and barbaric. She played on that as though she strummed a lyre, and the music wooed the majority to her side.

The king could've censured her, but didn't. Iona spread her arms like wings and quoted Roman law in strong, sure words, first in Gaelic, then in a smattering of Northumbrian, and finally in Icelandic.

The criers repeated her words, stumbling over the unfamiliar ones but plowing on to the end. Cries and huzzahs rose from the courtyards. The Icelandic princess had won the masses to her side.

Iona paused, turning left and right to encompass all her audience within the great hall. "Must a man sell his soul to the devil by giving others permission to take his life?"

"No!" roared the crowd, bringing the king's tankard down on the trencher board.

Iona turned away from the crowd after it quieted. She stared at the conveners one by one, her gaze lingering on the abbot, then resting finally on the king. "We will show that Magnus Sinclair, honorable lord of Scotland, warrior for his king and his people, savior of his family from those who would've ravaged it, has fought once more against the elements of darkness that would threaten him, his country, his king." She bowed, then walked regally back to her seat next to Magnus.

All were silent. Had the Viking princess just coupled Baron Kildeer with the devil?

Skene leapt to his feet, his face mottled, his rage barely contained. "I insist that we—"

"You insist?" Malcolm said. "This is a convening, Erwic Skene of Iona. You may request." He eyed the royal from Northumbria. "What say you, Tostig?"

"You may request," Tostig muttered, his mouth barely moving. Not once had he looked toward his chief warrior Baron Urdric Kildeer. But a message seemed to thunder through the air from royal to lieutenant. The royal was not pleased.

Skene saw his faux pas and ground his teeth. He'd been put on the defensive. He bowed stiffly to the court, then turned to his opponent. His mouth contorted in a smile as though he too had a message to send.

Magnus caught the look and started to rise, fists clenched. He'd kill the slimy bastard in front of the whole court. Iona gently pushed him back onto his stool. "You'll not always stay me, my sweetling," he muttered.

She felt his fury toward Skene as though he'd sent fire catapulting across the great hall. "I'll not always want to, Sinclair."

Skene looked back at the monarchs. " 'Twill be as you say, my liege. And I bow to the wisdom of Tostig as well. And to him, as well as to the king of Scotland, I must stress the need for the court to consider—Iniquum est Ingenuis—"

Iona stayed seated, but said, "My liege, this issue has already been settled."

Malcolm nodded. "It has. We reject your request."

Skene begged, pleaded, and cajoled, but Malcolm would not consider his reasoning for disqualifying Iona. Backing down, though barely masking his chagrin, Skene called his witnesses. One by one they testified that Magnus had most certainly slain many Northumbrians, not in honorable battle but sneakily, garroting them, stabbing them, ambushing them, simply because he was a bloodthirsty barbarian. To cap the day, Skene used a most colorful and macabre ploy, within the laws governing convenings, but scarcely used in the modern times of Malcolm. He produced for the edification of the convening the heads of the so-called victims.

"These are binding as evidence of the veracity of the witnesses, oh illustrious convening," he shouted.

The great hall was in an uproar. More than one rushed from the convening, his mouth covered. Some laughed nervously while others voiced disgust.

Iona herself had all she could do not to lose her morning meal.

After he'd finished with his array of evidence and witnesses, Skene stayed standing, his head swiveling. He smiled as though his assessment of the situation pleased him. Then he waved away the men who carried his grisly evidence, and took his seat again.

"Stay," Iona said, standing. "And continue to hold the heads up for all to see, if you please," she continued, impervious to the gasps and sounds of distaste. " 'Tis not my desire to offend the assemblage. But 'twould be most remiss of me if I did not examine the evidence on my client's behalf." Smiling, she inclined her head to the conveners, who nodded as one. Then she walked toward the ghoulish evidence that was held high. "Do any know these . . . persons?" She pointed to the four heads.

A few men raised their hands, and she gestured them forward. Their names were given and they swore an oath of truth.

"I thank you." She turned to Skene's many witnesses. "And did you know these men?" They all nodded aye. "And were they Northumbrians?" Yes again. "Which of you are Northumbrians?" When all said that they were, she nodded. "Let the scribes set it down as such." She glanced around the room, smiling, then looked at the witnesses and those who claimed to have known the murdered men. "And who of you Northumbrians are in the pay of Baron Kildeer?"

As though they looked upon their own demise, the men turned a putty color and froze. They saw clearly the yawning pit that the princess of Icelandia had led them to.

Iona coughed delicately. "I must remind you that you've sworn an oath, and I promise you the protection of the great Malcolm and Tostig for your truth. This is an honorable and just convening. No witness can be turned upon for giving true testament." She eyed the two royals. Both nodded, and she smiled even more sweetly at the witnesses. "You may answer in safety. If any would gainsay you or be punitive toward you, whether master or peer, that person shall forfeit his life. Now, witnesses tried and true, you will answer my question. Who among you are in the pay of Baron Kildeer?"

When all the witnesses nodded reluctantly, raised their right hands, and whispered they were, a roar of murmurs rose into the rafters of the great room. The shouts of the criers outside echoed in the sudden silence that followed the tumult.

Iona wrapped the silence around her like a cloak and waited until she was sure everyone watched her. "It saddens me to say this, but I fear we cannot accept the veracity of such witnesses. By their very blood and fealty they cannot give the objective truth, which is the only acceptable truth in such a convening. I call upon the members of the convening to note that such evidenciary material and such witnesses must be suspect. Ergo, they must be struck down in the manner of just law." She walked closer to the hideous evidence. "I cannot see the mark of Magnus Sinclair upon these heads, nor can I see the truth upon the lips of those who'd incarcerate him in violation of decency."

She threw wide her hands. "Magnus Sinclair fought for freedom, and in doing so took the lives of two imprisoners. We admit to that. Nay, we are proud of that. Magnus Sinclair did not submit to torture or the terrible fear of the oubliette. He chose to live, and did so. He's no criminal. 'Struth, he's a hero—"

Cheers interrupted her.

"—and I ask this convening to find for Magnus Sinclair in the interests of justice."

"I object!" Skene leapt to his feet.

Shouts and boos split the air. Malcolm banged his goblet until it was dented.

"Sinclair must pay," Skene shouted, "for his perfidy for invading a friendly land and striking down its citizens."

"At the time of Lord Sinclair's imprisonment," Iona countered, "Scotland and Northumbria were warring. The opposition knows this. Everyone here knows that."

She pointed at Magnus, making the mistake of looking at him. The glint of admiration in his eyes startled her, and for a moment she almost faltered. Damn Sinclair and his power over her.

"Honorable convening," she went on, "I beg you look at the truth. That Magnus Sinclair had the stamina to stay alive, fight his way out of an oubliette, and make it to this court is only testament to his greatness as a man, and as leader of Scotland's greatest clan. 'Twould be unjust to do less than pay him the homage he deserves." She bowed to Magnus, then to the assemblage, then to the conveners.

The spectators cheered and applauded, calling out Iona's name. Malcolm quickly hushed them.

"This convening is adjourned," he said, "as to such time as it will take to come to an agreement and a judgment." He banged his dented goblet, then he, Tostig, and the others filed from the great room.

Excitement rippled through the assemblage as everyone settled down to wait. Some left to relieve themselves or to partake of food, but each always left someone behind to save his place.

The Alexandrian water clock that had been trundled into the great room dribbled the passage of time.

Many shivered in the inner and outer courtyards, for the pot fires didn't fight off the chill wind from the North Sea. None left for home and his own hearth fire, though.

The sun dropped into the western sky, staining the clouds red. The cold wind rose as dusk succeeded the day.

The nobles had servants running hither and yon to bring ale and bread, while outside sweetmeats were hawked along with mulled ale.

Darkness fell.

"Eat something," Magnus commanded a white-faced Iona. They had adjourned to their chambers immediately after Malcolm and the others left. "You've won, wife."

He was so damned proud of her, he could've choked with it. He'd been at more convenings than he could count, and had witnessed long-winded, stumbling, loud, soft, able, not so able advocates. Never had he heard a stronger, more sure advocate than his wife. He had not known she was so wise, so canny, so certain of her power. He was almost annoyed that she'd given him another reason to love her.

"Don't say we've won," she said. "Not yet." She sipped

water, not ale, and refused the goat curd pie and venison pastries.

Magnus took her in his arms, loving the feel, the scent of her. "You'll soon be too meatless for me to hold, Iona."

Distracted, she laughed huskily. "Then what will you do?"

"Feed you up, of course." He smiled and then kissed her. "This court interferes with far more pleasurable work, methinks." Feeling her tremble and seeing tears spike her lashes, he kissed her again.

"Magnus, I—"

Kenneth ran into the room, his face flushed. "Come, they've returned to the great hall. At last." He glanced at Iona's pale face and her white-knuckled grip on her husband's arm, and his face softened. "You've done exceedingly well, little sister. I'll be bound Magnus will be back on his land before the moon changes. And I'll be glad to have him back, handling all the business that has made my head ache."

Iona did not look reassured. Magnus hugged her close, then took her hand and led her from their chambers.

When the kings and conveners returned, they were greeted by an excited uproar, then quiet. Those who coughed were glared at, those who shuffled were shushed. Not a word must be missed.

Malcolm banged the trencher board and cleared his throat. "King Tostig and I, and those of the convening, find that though Magnus Sinclair was imprisoned in a Northumbrian castle, he was not known to Baron Kildeer, and had been incarcerated as a renegade because he'd been taken when he was out of his senses. So"—Malcolm gazed at Magnus—"it's the judgment of the convening that there can be no censure directed at the Northumbrian baron, Urdric Kildeer."

The crowd answered with curses and cheers.

Iona reeled and whitened, and Magnus put his arm

around her, supporting her. "Fear not, milady," he whispered.

Malcolm took a deep breath, looked around the assemblage, then back at Magnus. "It is also felt by King Tostig, myself, and the convening that though Magnus Sinclair killed men on Northumbrian land, he struggled to save his own life as an imprisoned warrior should, thereby absolving himself of any guilt in the death of those who stood in his way."

Roars of approval drowned out Malcolm's last words.

Iona gripped her husband's hand, blood flowing back into her pallid cheeks. Magnus lifted her hand and kissed the palm lingeringly, letting the curious see how he honored his spouse.

Malcolm waited for silence. "Therefore, in the interests of justice, the convening has decided that the two antagonists shall be called blameless and the matter settled now and forever."

Amid more cheering, there were groans and angry mutters. It had not been settled in the minds of all.

Iona's delight was all-encompassing. She looked up, laughing, but her mirth died at her husband's serious mien. "Rejoice, Magnus, it's over. We'll go back to Sinclairland. None can hurt us now."

She shook his arm, trying to bring his attention back to her. He was stern, rock-jawed, his eyes like hammered iron as he stared at Kildeer, who stared back at him. "Magnus?"

It wasn't over, not as long as either of them lived. Magnus had become convinced that Kildeer was the figure that filled his dreams. The man who had killed his mother and father.

With great effort he looked down at his wife, and his hard expression cracked in a small smile. "You're a wondrous advocate, Iona, princess of Icelandia, Lady Sinclair. We will do well together, I vow. We return to Sinclair on the morrow."

.   .   .

With all the conferring needed to be done with the king and with Cormac, who'd been traveling for the king and arrived too late for the convening, it was three weeks before they took the Viking ship northward.

Iona was distracted during the journey. She'd missed her monthlies, though she'd not been ill, except for the sea gripe that had taken her when she'd boarded the craft. It was unheard of for her to be ill on a ship. Magnus had commented again on her loss of weight, saying she was pale. Then he'd smiled strangely and caught her close to him.

It couldn't be, she thought as she lay among warm skins in the stern of the vessel. It couldn't be a babe . . . could it?

With good winds and friendly currents they made the trip quickly, not blown off course once. When they landed on the Sinclair strand, though, there was no one to greet them.

"I like it not," Einar said bluntly.

"Nor I," Magnus said, staring up the twisting path to Sinclair Castle. "Something's amiss."

Alert and watchful, Vikings and Scots made their way upward. They waited until all were gathered at the top before moving on, battle ready, toward the castle.

"Wait," Iona said as they neared the outer wall. "All is well. There is Spes." She waved to her cousin, who was all alone and walking slowly toward her. Freeing herself from Magnus, she ran forward, ignoring his shouted warning.

"Spes! We're home. Magnus is with me." She flew over the ground, arms outstretched. "All is well. And I have much to tell you."

Someone grabbed her around the throat from behind, yanking her to a stop. She struggled to get her short sword into play. She was being throttled. As the blood pounded through her ears, she heard Magnus roar his anger and thought she saw him racing toward her.

Then the world around her erupted as hordes of Northumbrians and renegades engaged the angry Scots and Vikings. Magnus couldn't get to her.

"Now you will finally die, Asdis Iona, Viking slut." The hissing voice was frighteningly familiar. Skene! "And not all my father's pleadings will save you."

Fury and cunning replaced her shock and confusion, and she went limp. His hold tightened for a moment, then lessened. The second it did, she slipped her hand into her bliaut, found the blade she always carried, and sliced it down into her uncle's leg. He squealed with rage and pain, loosening his grip even more. She dropped to the ground and tried to roll free, but he was quicker than she expected. His strong arms encircled her once more, one around her throat again, and he lifted her.

Skene laughed harshly. "You're no match for—"

The Viking battle roar stopped Skene. It'd never been louder or more infuriated. More than one battler, Scot and Northumbrian alike, stopped warring to stare as Glam strode forward, beating his chest. Filled with blood lust, he eyed his quarry and bellowed his challenge.

∾ 20 ∾

He harms himself who does harm to another, and the evil plan is most harmful to the planner.

—Hesiod

Time stood still for all warriors, Viking, Scot, and Northumbrian. All had heard the Viking giant's booming challenge, letting all know that only he would engage Skene of Iona.

The battle slowly fell away as one after another the warriors lowered their weapons, curious to see the outcome of the duel between the Viking and the Ionan.

Magnus's own gaze was fixed on Iona. Cold fear twisted his soul even as anger at Skene consumed him. She showed no fright. She even tried to smile at him, but he knew her serenity was a mask. She was fair sickened by the memories of what her uncle had done to her as a child. Now the swine had a headlock on her, was hurting her. Magnus forced the anger that engorged his throat back down into his blood. He couldn't afford to make a misstep by letting fury guide his movements. Nothing would keep him from saving her, but for now Glam had taken charge.

Einar had stayed at Magnus's side and scanned the area.

"Warrior after warrior sheathes his weapon. 'Tis nothing like I've ever seen in countless battles."

"Most unnatural," Magnus agreed tightly.

Einar followed his gaze. "He'll not kill her with Glam on him. She's his shield. Fret not, Sinclair."

"The bastard's hurting her."

Einar smiled blackly. "Our princess can withstand. She's Viking."

"She's my wife," Magnus said through his teeth. "I'll tear his heart out for this."

Glam banged his chest again and shouted to the sky. "Wotan wants your black soul to feed to the carrion dog." He dropped his sword and approached Skene weaponless. "You're a cur who deserves no warrior death, and none you'll get. Despoiler of innocents, destroyer of children, I will tear your head from your shoulders."

"Kill him! Kill him! Skenes to me!" Skene yowled, angry and fearful. "Strike down the Viking dog!"

When some put bows to shoulder, Sinclairs brandished their own weapons. Impasse!

"None will kill me before I tear out the heart of this despoiler of children," Glam roared. "It is my sacred vow. Stay back!"

"Kill him," Skene screamed. "Fools, he's nothing but a man. Slay him!"

Magnus made a silent command, and all the Sinclairs responded, readjusting their positions. Some of the Vikings comprehended the ploy and moved also. They made a phalanx, forming a screen between Glam, Skene, Iona, and the attacking force. Every other man faced outward. All sights were covered.

"Sinclair!" Skene called. "Call off the Viking dog, or I break her neck."

"No, Magnus!" Iona cried. "Don't— Aagh!"

Magnus stood motionless, though his insides churned with fear. A single move from Skene would snap her neck. "Wait, Glam!" he shouted to the Viking. " 'Tis my right."

Glam eyed him for a long moment, then swung his gaze back to Iona and Skene. " 'Tis true, according to law."

"He holds my wife," Magnus added, praying Glam understood.

Glam nodded. "Good Queen Margaret is before you, but she would comprehend your claim." Flexing his giant arms, he deliberately swung his body in a wide turn away from his adversary.

Iona stayed still. She'd read the message that had flown between Glam and Magnus. If Skene were wise he wouldn't—

Skene loosened his hold to better grip his sword for throwing.

At the same moment, Iona sagged forward as though she'd fainted. Her weight dragged at him, throwing him off balance. As he scrambled to readjust, Magnus and Glam were charging toward him.

Skene reared back, fighting to hold on to both his sword and Iona. He realized his mistake even as Magnus wrenched Iona from his grasp. He turned to meet the Viking, sword up.

With a sweep of his mighty forearm, Glam sent the sword flying through the air. He grabbed the Ionan around his middle and lifted the cursing man high into the air. The snap and crack of bone was louder than the crashing sea below as Glam broke Skene's back. Turning, he heaved outward, and the still screaming Skene whirled through the air off the cliff edge. The terns screeching drowned out the sounds of his body being crushed on the rocks below.

Glam turned to face Magnus. " 'Tis done as 'twas writ in the heart of good Queen Margaret. Now you may kill me, as is your right, Sinclair."

Magnus shook his head, hugging his wife. "No Sinclair will ever harm this man." His clarion declaration was greeted with resounding ayes.

In the silence that followed, foe looked upon foe. Men moved warily. As was the custom in warfare, there could be surcease from battle when men regrouped. But the warring must continue until both sides decided to withdraw or there was a decided victor.

Magnus released Iona. "Go to the castle and wait for

me." He pressed his hand to her middle. "Take every care, wife." Then he raised his sword, looking toward the Northumbrians. "The battle is joined!"

Iona backed toward the castle as Scots and Vikings engaged the intruders. What had Magnus meant? Could he have guessed she might be pregnant? No. He'd never think she could conceive. Where was he? Her heart turned to ice when she spotted him in the thick of the fray. He was engaging two Northumbrians . . . and Urdric Kildeer was moving up behind him!

Reaching for her sword, she ran toward him, shouting at the same time. "Magnus! Your back."

Startled, the baron looked her way, but Magnus only managed a quick glance over his shoulder.

"Stay back, Iona," he roared, dispatching one adversary.

Iona paused only long enough to loop her bliaut up between her legs and hook it around her belt. Then she confronted the baron.

"You'd have been wise to heed him, milady." Kildeer brandished his sword and moved toward her, sure he'd dispatch her swiftly.

Iona parried, dancing away from him and chuckling when he looked astounded. In the second he was off guard, she swept in and pinked his cheek before darting back out of the way. When he ground his teeth and lashed out, she stopped smiling and settled to her task. The baron meant to kill her. She was going to do everything she could to prevent that.

Magnus was sweating, not from exertion but from fear. She was behind him. So was Kildeer. Two able swordsmen were in front of him. Damn Iona. She was nothing but trouble. Lunging, he ran one of his foes through, then turned grimly to the other. Slashing fast and furiously, he settled him quickly.

"Baron!" he shouted. "Turn to me."

Kildeer did in one sweeping slash, sending Iona backward to stumble and fall, unhurt but out of it.

She scrambled back, giving her husband the room he needed to maneuver.

"To the death, Sinclair. And I'll take your lands and your wife. I'll use her well before I give her to my men. She'll intrigue me . . . for a while." He smiled.

Magnus smiled back, understanding the ploy of inciting a foe to anger. Still, he couldn't prevent his thick flood of fury at the baron's words. "Nay, Kildeer. I fear she'll be busy with her duties as Lady Sinclair. But mayhap she'll spare a prayer for your black soul."

Kildeer lunged with his sword, slicing across Magnus's middle with the dirk in his left hand.

Magnus fell back, narrowly missing a lethal cut.

As before, the other warriors sheathed their weapons, watching the two overlords battle across the high ground above the sea, and then down the hill from Sinclair Castle. There was no sound except for the clash of steel against steel, and of the North Sea crashing on the rocks and strand.

"Methinks this will settle the war," Einar said, coming up behind Iona.

She made no reply. When Kildeer struck downward and caught Magnus's arm, she was cut. The dirk sliced across his chest and parted his tunic, and she gasped. Magnus!

Back and forth they fought, near the edge, away from it, down through the middle of the warriors and back.

Sweat darkened the tunics of both battlers. They suffered cuts and slashes, and both bled, but neither gave way.

Her gaze fixed upon her husband, Iona prayed. *Mother of God, protect Magnus. He's my husband, and he's been sorely hurt by his confinement. He's not nourished for battle, as is his opponent. He's a strong man, but even he's been weakened. Help him.*

The sun began to fall, but the duel didn't wane. Neither did it wax furious. Each adversary knew he was in for a long struggle, and they tried to pace themselves and find any advantage. The smallest weakening in defense must be seized upon.

Magnus could feel the strain. He knew that the time in the oubliette had lessened his stamina. But determination fueled by a deep dark anger gave him the strength to go on. Kildeer was a superb swordsman, strong as an ox, and cold-blooded as an asp. Warring was a joy to the man, not just something he did when ordered by his king. Battling and killing were food to him. Magnus feinted and nearly caught a fatal cut.

Kildeer smiled, and Magnus knew he'd seen a weakness in his strokes. Soon he'd go after it. Magnus would have to be ready.

He gambled, giving the baron the opening he sought by swinging his arm wide.

Faster than a sea snake, Kildeer moved in, slicing a deadly blow.

Magnus sidestepped, almost too late, and twisted, bringing his sword up. Kildeer's strong thrust carried him past Magnus, and Magnus's blade went right through his middle, impaling him.

Northumbrians shouted, cursing, but a lieutenant threw down a piece of white cloth. The two armies gauged each other, then, as though a silent signal had been given, weapons were lowered. Northumbrian men, at a nod from Magnus, went forward to lift the baron onto their shields.

Iona ran to her husband, her arm going around his middle.

"Do not strain yourself, milady. I can stand." He put a hand on her head, unable to stop its trembling.

"I know." She could've cried. He bled from so many slashes. The swellings on his face and chest were red, but would soon turn bluish.

Einar supported him on the other side while Kenneth eased Iona away.

"To our quarters," she said shakily. "He needs tending."

She began to follow the entourage of warriors, but a hand on her arm stayed her. Glam, close behind her, growled his displeasure at the foreigner who touched her. Iona too frowned at the man, who wore the Skene colors. "What say you? Hurry. I must succor my husband."

"I mean you no harm, milady. I am Targill of Iona. I carried the banner of Erwic Skene, but my leader is Enslo Skene, your grandfather. It was his intention that his son not hurt you in any way. I was ordered to intervene if such occurred." He smiled tiredly. "And I would've, but you'd champions enough." He lowered his voice. "Your grandfather longs to see you, Princess, and he begs that there be no ill will between you."

"Even after the death of his son?"

"His order to me was to protect you from his son. What say you, milady? Milord is aging."

Iona stared at the man for a long moment. "I too would like an end to the hatred. Tell my grandfather he's welcome on Sinclair land, and on Eyin Helga."

Targill bowed low. "I'll take my men away and the message will be given. I take it upon myself to tell you that you will hear from your grandfather very soon, milady."

Iona nodded and turned toward the castle, forgetting the man already. "Come, Glam. We must see to our lord."

The enemy was retreating under the watchful eyes of Dugald and a hundred Scots and Vikings. When the Northumbrians lifted Kildeer, though, Dugald shouted for them to stop.

"That's Sinclair steel. We'll have it." With a mighty jerk he pulled Magnus's sword from Kildeer's body. "Take your leader and go. There's no more war on this land today." He picked up the white cloth of surrender and wiped the blood from his laird's weapon.

∽ 21 ∽

Let your light so shine before men, that they may see your good works, and glorify your Father which is in heaven.
—Matthew 5:16

For two days and two nights Magnus fevered. Iona sponged and washed him innumerable times, used medicaments and herbs on the sores, bruises, and slashes, and never left his side.

Kenneth, Spes, Einar, Old Terrill, and Marta, who'd returned from Eyin Helga, all tried to make her sleep. She found them a nuisance.

"But, milady," Marta said, "you're with child." She smiled proudly for a moment before frowning with concern.

"Yes, and I've never felt better. Don't fret."

"Milord will be angry if you sicken, Iona."

"So he will," she whispered, touching his strong face. It wasn't quite as pallid as it had been.

"Is it not a miracle that you'll give birth?" Marta whispered.

Iona smiled tiredly. "Truly it is. Leave me, Marta. I would stay with my husband."

They were in the tower bedchamber, where he'd been taken after his battle with Kildeer. He'd walked almost the entire distance, his knees not buckling until they'd reached the top staircase. Warriors had caught him up then, ignoring his growled protests.

When he'd been placed on the bed, he'd sunk into a fitful slumber for several turns on the sandglass. That was when Iona had gone over him thoroughly to see if he'd need leeching—he didn't—or if any bones were broken—they weren't. His fever was caused by a number of things, the many blows from the battle plus the cruel incarceration, which had sapped even his strong constitution.

When he'd first woken in the grip of fever, he hadn't recognized anyone around him. She'd been fearful one of his wounds had putrefied, but not so. Rest was the most important medicine he needed, which would allow the heated black humors in his blood to cool.

She slept in the tower room with him, on a cot, so that she could hear every sound. For a respite she sometimes climbed the spiral stair to the turret balcony. She could look down on him and be comforted by that.

She was about to ready herself for bed when he shifted in his sleep. She bent over him, and was startled when his eyes shot open. "The men at court ogled you in your fine raiment, Iona," he said angrily, staring straight at her.

Though she was quite certain he wasn't really aware of her, that the fever spoke for him, she was taken aback.

"How many touched your delectable body, wife?"

"Do not spew the offal in your mind at me, husband," she retorted angrily, then was irritated at herself when Magnus eyed her blankly. He was out of his head, she reminded herself. Nevertheless, he'd spoken his thoughts. Damn the man. How dare he impugn her honor! Tonight she'd sleep on the balcony. Otherwise she might end up hitting a patient for the first time.

She turned away even as he spouted more of his innuendos. Stalking across the tower room, she climbed the spiral stairs to the platform. She sank down against the

railing to watch the patterns of moonlight shining through
the glass beads. She was too nerved up to sleep.

That fool, she thought, then silently spouted every vili-
fying term she could think of, castigating her spouse.
Somehow it soothed her. Little by little she unwound, the
tense anger leaving her. Her head fell, her eyes drooped,
and she dozed.

Waking with a start, she looked around her. Her
mother had woken her, shouting danger. That couldn't be.
Her mother was dead. Iona shook her head, telling herself
she'd been dreaming.

Then she heard a noise. A scraping. She blinked her
eyes, staring down into the room below. Yes, the hidden
door to the tunnel had opened quietly. All was blackness
except for the torch high on the wall. Two figures, caped
and hooded, glided toward the bed. She opened her mouth
to call out, then froze. The figures moved stealthily, crossing the room to the door that led to the hallway outside
Magnus's bedchamber. They put the bar over the door.

Turning, the two wraiths approached the bed, pulling
swords out from beneath their cloaks. Horrified, Iona
looked down on the assassins. They seemed to be in no
hurry, and why not? None would've seen them enter from
the tunnel. None knew of their presence. And they no
doubt assumed she lay beside her husband.

Forgetting caution, she yelled at the top of her lungs.
"Magnus! Magnus! To arms. Vikings to me!" Then she
flung herself down the spiral stairs. Her short sword was at
the bottom. She grabbed it and whirled toward the caped
duo, who turned to engage her.

Someone pounded on the barred door. Voices shouted.
Then Magnus was out of his bed, naked and reeling, but
his sword in hand. He saw her at once, then homed in on
the other two.

"Death!" he bellowed, and charged forward, staggering
but not halting.

In the hall beyond, the bull roar of the Vikings mixed
with the battle cry of the Sinclairs. The door to the tower
room boomed and rattled as the warriors strove for entry.

Iona tried to maneuver her sword for striking, but each time her adversary moved out of range. Ire sustained her, a fury at those who dared to attack her husband in his bedchamber. Her enemy was clever and fast, though. More than once she had to roll away from a down slash of her foe's sword. She was desperate to dispatch the assassin so she could open the door and others could fight Magnus's fight for him. He was too weak for jousting.

As she dueled with the assassin, they came near the one torch that lit the room. Light flickered over the assassin's face, and Iona almost dropped her sword. "Elizabeth!"

"Damn you! You should be dead." Elizabeth lunged with dirk and sword.

Iona fought back, her skill coming to the fore as she retreated. From the corner of her eye she saw Magnus still battling the other. Concern for him distracted her, and she realized her mistake as Elizabeth closed with her. Their swords locked, and Elizabeth raised her dirk to strike. Iona twisted away, but she felt a burning sting down one arm. Slipping, she lost her footing and threw herself as far out of the way as she could.

From somewhere came the rending, tearing sound of wood splintering. Iona paid it no heed as she fought for her life. Pointing her sword upward, she tried to protect herself. She was stunned when Elizabeth's triumphant smile turned to a scream. Then she saw that Glam had the woman in a viselike hold, imprisoning her in his huge arms and swinging her off her feet.

"Thank you, friend." Iona wasted no time on the screaming, writhing woman, but rose to her feet quickly, looking to where Magnus struggled with the second assassin.

Others, armed and ready, had rushed through the doorway, but they stopped, watching the death struggle.

Iona wanted to call out to her husband, but didn't. He needed all his concentration. He feinted, then thrust his weapon with all his strength into his opponent's middle.

The black wraith crumpled, and the hood fell from his head.

"Cormac!" Kenneth shouted.

Cormac sagged to the floor, coughing and glaring around him as he clutched his arms to his wound. "Yes, damn you, yes. Cormac Sinclair, rightful head of the clan." His bellow weakened him, and he slid to his side. "I'll not finish the night. 'Tis just as well." He eyed Magnus, laughing harshly. "I almost killed you. It would've been the coup that gave me the clan. It was rightfully mine."

Iona raced to Magnus, holding him up. "Did you know?"

He nodded slowly. "I suspected when I was in the oubliette." He put his arm around her. "Then when Glam and Einar found out that the abbot was a confidant of my uncle, I began to put things together." He smiled down at her tiredly. "I saw you fighting Elizabeth. You did well, but you could've harmed yourself and the babe."

"No. We're both fine." She fought back tears. Wars! Would there never be peace?

"It's over now, wife. Our life is beginning again."

They looked down at the supine Cormac, who was breathing raggedly.

"You'll not succor him, wife," Magnus said harshly. "*You're* the one in my dreams. *You* killed them. Why?"

Cormac coughed, a trickle of blood at the corner of his mouth. "You're a fool, like your father. I . . . was . . . the only one . . . suited to lead . . . so I set about taking my rightful place." He gasped. "I'm Sinclair. You're too weak to lead."

"You killed my mother and father and tried to kill me that night."

Cormac grimaced. "You have the devil's own luck, Magnus. You were too much like your father. I knew I had to kill you. 'Twas Kenneth I could've manipulated. After a time I would've seen to it that he followed you to the grave. It would've all been mine, as was foretold to me." Pain twisted his features. "You fools never knew. I . . . was careful . . . bided my time. Had to move when you married the Icelandic bitch. She might've conceived, though there was not much chance." His gaze shifted to Iona. "The dogs . . . they should have killed you."

Magnus's hands clenched in rage, but his voice was calm when he said, "Our firstborn comes to us in the autumn, Cormac."

"Damn you to perdition, Magnus. How . . . the hell . . . did you get out of the oubliette? No . . . one . . . ever has. Kildeer . . . swore to me." Blood gushed from his mouth. His head fell to one side.

"Burn his body and bury the ashes in the bog," Magnus ordered. "He will not be shriven."

"All these years," Kenneth whispered. He gestured to some warriors to remove the body. "Is it over now?"

"What of me?" Elizabeth cried. "Magnus, my family is old, and loyal to Sinclairs. I didn't know Cormac's plan. I didn't . . ." Her words died when he pointed to her.

"Banishment," he said roughly, pulling his wife to his side. "All clans loyal to me will shun this woman. Banishment for the abbot. All clans loyal to me will shun the churchman."

"No! No!" Elizabeth screamed. "Where will I go?"

There was no answer as Glam hauled her from the room.

"The nightmare is ended for all time," Old Terrill said softly. He gazed at Magnus and Iona. "I saw the white light with the green center, the light that would save Magnus. It was you, Asdis Iona of Icelandia. You've earned your world. Take care of it . . . and the child." He glided quietly from the room.

Iona didn't bother trying to urge Magnus back to his bed. She ordered hot water, lint, and battens to bind his fresh wounds.

He pulled her to him, examining the cut on her arm. "Spes, you'll tend this first."

Spes nodded. "I will, milord."

"And will you marry my brother?"

She blushed a fiery red when Kenneth laughed, then she nodded. "I will, milord."

"Good. First tend my wife, and tell me the bairn is safe."

Iona frowned at her husband. "I thought to keep it a secret for a time."

"Nay, you couldn't. I know your form full well. Soon the news will travel throughout the land, and you shall have the best to attend you."

She glared at him when some of the warriors lingering in the chamber chuckled. Every Sinclair would know by morning that an heir to the Sinclair was expected.

With Spes and Marta fussing and fretting, Iona and Magnus were soon tended. Clanswomen quickly straightened their chamber, then all were gone and they were alone.

Magnus hugged her to him, swinging her up into his arms.

"Stay! Your wounds. Have a care." She clutched his shoulders.

"They don't pain me." He stared down at her. "My one lasting anguish would be in losing you. I'd be strapped to the rack for all time. I almost did lose you. Damn Elizabeth."

She put her hand over his mouth. "Forget her. She's gone from our lives."

He saw her pensive look as she caressed his lips with her fingers. "What is it?"

"How strange it is that I thought at the convening that the traitor was Skene, who'd sold himself to Kildeer. But the real traitor was Cormac. I never guessed."

"It was not something I wanted to accept," Magnus said, kissing her fingers.

"Magnus, today one of my grandfather's men told me that he wanted to see me. I invited him to Sinclair Castle."

"Good. I was hoping you would. Enslo Skene is an honorable man, not like his son."

He put her down on the freshly made bed with its layers of Sinclair tartan to stave off the chill nights. "I think Elizabeth counted on my interest waning, not waxing. But not even I knew how much I would come to love you." When he saw the tears spring to her eyes, he smiled. "Being with child makes you emotional, my sweet Viking." He laughed when she nodded shyly, then pulled down her chemise to kiss her breasts.

Sighing, she clutched his head. "I can't believe we'll have a child. Weren't you surprised?"

"No. I knew you would have a child, sweetheart. And our passion will give us more."

"Oh, Magnus, don't get your hopes—"

He kissed her protest away, coming down on top of her, but braced carefully on his elbows.

"I won't break," she said, "and neither will the babe." She was wild to touch him herself, so she wasn't gentle when she hauled him down on top of her. "I'm furious at you for being away from me, for scaring me for all those months. I command that you don't do it again."

Commanding a Sinclair! Magnus thought. Not even Malcolm dared. But he only chuckled and then loved his wife, kissing her body from crown to foot, acceding to all her demands. Love swamped them like a storm on the North Sea and they went with it, willingly, giving, giving, giving the tempest of love to each other.

↶ EPILOGUE ↷

Love conquers all things.
—Virgil

Castle Sinclair was in an uproar. The laird had bellowed for one full arc of the sun because his wife was slow to birth. No amount of pleading from Spes or Marta kept him from the birthing room. And the more his wife thrashed in the throes of labor, the worse Magnus became.

Afterward, he knelt at her bedside, warily eyeing the tiny babes that lay at her breasts. Two of them! "They're too small," he told his wife hoarsely.

"Marta says they're very healthy. A boy and a girl. Surely a miracle."

"You always overdo things, Asdis Iona, princess of Icelandia. You're not to frighten me that way again. I demand it."

"I accede to your demands, husband," she said softly, liking the light feeling of her body and quite determined to have more baby Sinclairs. "I love you."

"You're my life, Iona, my Viking beauty." He pressed his mouth to the scar on her face, the part of her he loved most. "You will never leave me, my sweetling. I won't allow it."

"I shall always be with you, beloved," she murmured sleepily. "For you are my destiny."

All scars in soul and body disappeared from the Sinclair land that day. Only sweetness and beauty of the soul remained, and there was joy and feasting throughout the clan.

ABOUT THE AUTHOR

HELEN MITTERMEYER is the author of over forty books written under her own name and the pseudonyms Hayton Monteith, Danielle Paul, and Ann Christy. Her work has also appeared in such magazines as *Skiing*, *Redbook*, and *Prevention*. Helen writes at a ferocious pace (sometimes three books at the same time) but still finds time to serve her community through a multitude of social service organizations—the Girl Scouts, the Special Olympics, and charities for the homeless and the blind. The mother of four grown children, Helen lives in Rochester, New York, with her husband, Whity.